Praise for P. J.

BATH HAUS

"A hit among some of the hottest thriller writers working today."
—*Parade*

"A nightmarish white-knuckler about the tenuous relationship between stability and control." —*O, The Oprah Magazine*

"A white-knuckle ride to the dark side of love and infidelity. . . . A smart, steamy thriller laced with heady questions about control and shame." —*The New York Times Book Review*

"A wildly entertaining thriller with twists and tension to spare."
—*Entertainment Weekly*

"The tension builds to unbearably claustrophobic levels. To say more would rob readers of the 'no, he didn't' suspense that makes *Bath Haus* an unexpectedly twisted, heart-pounding cat-versus-mouse thriller." —*Los Angeles Times*

"Suspenseful, sensual and exceedingly clever, this thriller is the literary equivalent of sipping a glass of white wine while listening to your neighbors have a lovers' spat . . . before one of them picks up a knife. Vernon has an electric style that leaps off the page."
—*The Washington Post*

"[An] adrenaline-spiked pulse-pounder." —*The New York Times*

"*Gone Girl* with gays and Grindr. Come on, with a pitch like that, how can you *not* be intrigued? . . . [*Bath Haus*] absolutely delivered." —Jezebel

P. J. Vernon

BATH HAUS

P. J. Vernon was born in South Carolina. His first book, *When You Find Me*, was published in 2018. He lives in Calgary with his partner and two wily dogs.

pjvernonbooks.com

ALSO BY P. J. VERNON

When You Find Me

BATH HAUS

[A THRILLER]

P. J. Vernon

ANCHOR BOOKS
A DIVISION OF PENGUIN RANDOM HOUSE LLC
NEW YORK

FIRST ANCHOR BOOKS EDITION, MAY 2022

Copyright © 2021 by Philip Vernon

The Library of Congress has cataloged the Doubleday edition as follows:
Names: Vernon, P. J., author.
Title: Bath haus : a thriller / P. J. Vernon.
Description: First edition. | New York : Doubleday, 2021.
Identifiers: LCCN 2020051998 (print) | LCCN 2020051999 (ebook)
Subjects: LCSH: Gay men—Fiction. | Spouses—Fiction. | GSAFD: Suspense fiction.
Classification: LCC PS3622.E753 B38 2021 (print) | LCC PS3622.E753 (ebook) | DDC 813/.6—dc23
LC record available at https://lccn.loc.gov/2020051998
LC ebook record available at https://lccn.loc.gov/2020051999

Anchor Books Trade Paperback ISBN: 978-0-593-31131-8
eBook ISBN: 978-0-385-54674-4

Book design by Maggie Hinders

anchorbooks.com

Printed in the United States of America
10 9 8 7 6 5 4 3 2 1

For Barry

Asphyxia (n)

A lack of oxygen and excess of carbon dioxide in the body that results in unconsciousness and, within four to six minutes, death.

Clinical asphyxia is divided into five stages:

I. Surprise Respiration

When danger is recognized,
a deep and forceful inhalation occurs.

1

OLIVER

This is a fucking mistake.

My heart beats against the back of my sternum like it might knock itself still.

I kill the ignition and Nathan's SUV sinks into silence. My wedding band slides right off, joining spare console change. Nathan and I aren't married, but he insists we wear rings.

The iPhone buzzing in my pocket is a miniature washing machine. Nathan's calling. I wait it out, don't move. A simple phone call that I treat like a kidney stone. Excruciating and it needs to pass. He leaves a voicemail.

"Oliver. Dinner's wrapped up, headed back to the hotel now. Give me a call if you can. Wondering what you're doing. Did you remember Tilly's heartworm medication? Don't forget. It's important. Call me. Love you."

Mental note: return Nathan's call within the hour. Thirty minutes is his typical limit. If he doesn't hear back within half an hour, we fight. But he's out of town, and I can stretch it to an hour. He can't fight me from Manhattan, and it sounds like he's been drinking anyway.

Cars jam the parking lot, bumper to bumper, nose to nose. Hidden from uninvited curiosity by a blanket of thick tree cover. No rhyme or reason or pattern ties one vehicle to another. A rust-scorched Pontiac sits beside a sleek black Mercedes. The polish on the Benz captures light from a lone streetlamp, painting itself in electric-blue waves. Countless more juxtapositions abound. Cross sections of the city. Not a single thing in common among their owners.

Except one: the desire to have sex with other men. Anonymously.

Breath fights me on the way out, clawing my windpipe like something feral. Oddly, my heartbeat slows and for a moment, I worry perhaps it has stopped altogether. One sneaker in front of the other, I make for a lone door—windowless, heavy. The building is unmarked save for the name I'd found online days earlier:

Haus.

I tug the handle, and the door creaks open on one, two, five sets of metal hinges.

Low lighting, obviously. And a smell, pervasive, that soaks everything. I can almost wring it from the air. Cheap sterility. A pungent odor that's at once recognizable. The purple bottle. Lavender, I think, and adjacent to Pine-Sol on every supermarket shelf.

"Hey." A man greets me from behind a glassed-in desk. Not unlike a bank teller. "You a member?"

No, I say—only not aloud. A cough, then: "No."

"You need to be one." He pushes a clipboard through an opening and I note the thickness of his fingers. He's large, but his sweatshirt still hangs loose. His features are drawn to the center of his face, needlessly crowding it.

"How much?" I ask, certain I've spoken out loud.

"Forty bucks. For the year. And I need your ID."

Not bad, and an ID makes sense. No minors allowed. Here, a birthday is the difference between no strings attached and the sex registry. I slide him my driver's license: Oliver Park. Twenty-six years old. Washington, DC. Organ donor.

A flare of blue Xerox light crosses his face. The abrupt flicker leaves behind a wake of blackness as my eyes readjust. For a fleeting moment, Nathan materializes in the dark and my pulse spikes. But seeing things in the dark is normal. Things that aren't there. My thoughts return to the copy machine. Proof of my visit crowds the tip of my tongue with questions, and I tug my bottom lip.

He reads my mind: "For our records. We never share it, but we need to know our patrons. Legal shit." A pause. "You signed?"

I nod and trade his clipboard—cash attached—for my license.

"If you're gonna drink, you gotta leave a card."

"You can do that here?"

"Only in the bar. Two-beer max. One if you want liquor." I'm quiet for a beat, and he taps his finger. "Look, don't sweat the charge. If you forget to cash out, it'll say *dry cleaning*."

"Yeah. Okay." Regret from walking in sober—fear of whiskey dick or something stupid like that—vanishes as I slip him my credit card. Dry cleaning's not the best cover because Nathan handles ours. But I'll pay with cash after.

"Perfect." He stoops beneath his desk, and for a few long seconds, I'm alone again. When he stands, he holds a cream-colored towel, folded into a neat square. Atop it: a single-use packet of lube, two condoms—fruit flavored—and a brass key on a rubber cord.

"Nine zero three." He grins, and his narrow eyes crease. The corners of his mouth nearly touch his beady irises like a feline's. "Have fun."

"Thanks."

When I've lingered too long, he gestures to the door on my left. I'm suddenly a bit like Alice. I've just met the Cheshire Cat, and Jefferson Airplane drums over which pills do what in my head.

Through door number 2, rows of lockers wait. I'm eager to leave the solvent reek of cleaners behind, but it only thickens. I'm also not alone, and my heart hiccups. Men stand and sit and linger in stages of undress, manspreading on changing benches, tiny towels intentionally parted.

None of them are particularly attractive—or if they are, the darkness is a mask—but that's not the point, is it? What's important is that I've left my life behind. I've abandoned its norms and its mores for Haus. Where we all play half-hidden in shadow and nakedness and thirsty eyes aren't transgressive.

Haus caters to consequence-free expression, and I'm going to give in. An odd decision only in that I'd sworn I'd already made it. Somewhere between a heart-thumping Google query and cranking Nathan's car, but apparently I hadn't. Until now.

I locate the nine hundred row, find 903, and slip my key in.

What would Nathan say if he could see this? Of course, he can't. And he won't ever know. His conference keynote is long over. He's left NYU Langone Medical Center for his hotel. The Millennium Hilton according to his e-confirmation. Awake or not, he'll expect a call back soon. The longer his voicemail grows stale, the more he'll needle later. His statement, *I love you,* will assume different punctuation. *I love you?*

I pull my T-shirt off, and gooseflesh crawls up my bare back.

Nathan's thumbing through news on his phone. Or if not, he's fast asleep. Glasses on the nightstand next to iced water. No, water's not quite right; Nathan sleeps beside a hotel tumbler. It would've held bourbon but it won't by now. And it won't have been his first. One hour, timestamped, and I'll call him from his own car in the parking lot.

My chest tightens. I draw in breath, slip khaki to my ankles, and step out from my shorts.

I'm in black briefs now. Briefs and sneakers—no socks. Nothing else. An older man, pear-shaped and lumpy, stares in obvious ways. He consumes both my flesh that's exposed and my flesh that isn't. When our eyes meet, he doesn't look away and I'm embarrassed for him. Then I remember where we are.

An undeniable pleasure blooms. This man lusts for me and being objectified is an intoxicating little feeling I've missed terribly.

I toy with removing my underwear but opt to keep covered. At least a little bit. *Don't get ahead of yourself.* I wrap the towel around my waist and hang the key from my wrist. I don't need Nathan's medical degree to know to keep my sneakers on. No amount of lavender solvent justifies bare feet on this tile.

The leering man's no longer there. He's likely vanished down a black corridor, hazy from steam, and I follow suit.

Down the rabbit hole and into a space that feels dark enough for developing photographs. Hot jungle air. Low red light touches everything but corners where shadows of men grind and thrust and bob. Moaning. Hushed words, frightening and thrilling.

"Yeah . . ."

"Don't . . ."

"Yes . . ."

"Take . . ."

I pad down another humid hall. Stifling, door-lined, and each door is numbered. The inevitable looms on either side of me, like a sharp knuckle about to knock. A sign behind the Cheshire Cat had detailed room rates and these rent by what? The hour? The minute? The hall spills into a kind of gallery where projectors paint the walls in flickering vintage porn. Grainy cowboys smoking cigarettes and cock. No volume, but you wouldn't need it—the space teems.

My palms are wet and itchy. Am I really prepared to do what I've come here for? What I only just decided I would do? I've come this far, and this is *very* far.

I find what appears to be a lounge, and drink relief like cool water. A casual refuge. Barflies. Sultry Britney belts "Toxic" on a TV over the counter, and I could be in any gay bar now. I'll take a seat here and regroup.

Breathe, Oliver.

"Vodka tonic?" I ask a shirtless bartender in jeans so low it's a shame he's off-limits.

Black light sets his teeth aflame in fluorescence when he bares them. "Locker number?"

"Nine oh three."

He winks and slides a glass of well liquor my way. The drink has bite, and a thrumming pulse hurls alcohol through my blood-brain barrier. I'm done in two swallows.

"What are you looking for?"

The voice comes from behind, but its owner sidesteps and claims the next stool over. The accent takes me by surprise. Scandinavian maybe.

He's in a towel too. Rubber flip-flops. He moves with intention, and his shoulder muscles tense and relax. A tightness in my gut says I'm buying whatever the hell this stranger plans to pitch. He's muscular and svelte at the same time. Taller than me, but most men are.

His eyebrows lift and he smiles before repeating himself: "What are you looking for?"

Blond bangs frame deep eyes. Ocean deep, actually, and Alexander Skarsgård here just might drown me. I clear my throat. "I'm not sure yet."

It's the truth, which means I'm off-balance. In situations like this, the truth is what we offer when we don't have anything better.

He draws closer, and I flinch. A second, knowing grin, and he reaches into my glass for ice with long fingers. He places a wet cube between full lips, where it starts to melt, before slipping it inside his mouth.

When it cracks between his teeth, my resolve—what little there is—

does precisely the same. Our eyes meet, and I resist the urge to look away. Something taunting says he wouldn't let me. His ocean-deep eyes would chase mine. Pin them down, pin *me* down.

Tiny hairs on my face and chest stiffen with static charge. His hand finds my thigh, travels beneath my towel. Fingers run the hem of my briefs.

"I'm Kristian." He whispers unfettered possibility into my ear: "I have a room."

I nod, and he stops just shy of my crotch. Dopamine—and whatever the fuck else makes a body high—rafts through my veins. I'm intoxicated and trailing him down a hall.

Everything is about the present. Nathan doesn't exist here. Nor does the home we've made together. This is Wonderland, and Wonderland only exists in the now. There is only *now*. The door shuts behind us in a room couched in darkness. My heart pounds, and Kristian says he can feel my pulse in every part of me.

Electricity snaps, arcs from me to him. We kiss.

The towels are gone. As are my briefs. He spins me to face a sweating wall, my palms flush against it. Steam from saunas and showers and whirlpools pipes in through unseen vents. Dampness crowds the air, pools in body crevasses.

We slip against each other, but he holds me firm. His mouth on the back of my neck.

I turn long enough to say: "Condom."

"I have," he answers, and I swallow the softball in my throat. My thoughts barely keep pace with my heartbeat. I'm doing this. No more thinking about it. The bridge is crossed and every moment after this will exist in the light of a new truth.

I've pulled a trigger. I've cheated on Nathan, and like a gun, I can never un-fire.

He brings my wrists together behind my back. I expect he's fumbling with the condom or the lube or both.

Only he isn't.

Instead, his free palm pushes its way between my shoulder blades. I turn, and his grip on my wrists tightens. His fingers reach my neck, and my heart catches fire. I'm vulnerable for a moment, but soon his hand will run through my hair, gripping it for what's to come.

That doesn't happen either. His fist stays on my neck.

I'm vulnerable still, and something isn't right. The knot of excitement shoots from my groin to my chest. It constricts my ribs in tandem with Kristian's hands. I only now appreciate the length of this man's fingers as they find their way around my neck.

Another line is crossed. I jolt, start to spin.

"No you don't!" Like a spring trap, he catches my arms and twists them behind my spine. My body stiffens. This is wrong. Everything is wrong. Adrenaline pumps like jet fuel, and my insides swell with heat.

One hand firm on my neck, he threads the other through my back and elbows. Pinning me with his forearm and chest, his fists clamp my throat like a vise. And like a vise, they squeeze.

My arms contort. I struggle, and he pulls tighter.

Spasming, I gasp for air that isn't there.

Eye spots bloom and grow and float, and my consciousness snaps into a single thought. It takes longer to resolve because my brain's suddenly oxygen starved.

This man with the ocean-deep eyes. *He's killing me.*

2

NATHAN

When do you call time of death on a marriage?

I suppose sometimes spouses do something wrong—something cardinal—and it's as obvious as calling clinical TOD.

My marriage was over the moment my husband's fist connected with my jaw. Or the instant my card was declined, because why invest in mutual funds when slots hold higher payoffs?

Oliver and I, however, were less a violent plunge and more like subtle slippage. An exsanguination so slow, ignoring it comes far too easy. Determined to numb one more bad hour, we didn't realize we'd numbed our way through one more bad day. One more bad year, numbed. How many do we have left?

"You've reached Oliver Park." The second call he's sent to voicemail. *My marriage was over the moment my husband fucked a man who wasn't me.* "Leave your name and number and I'll get back—" I hang up just as Mother returns her own phone to her clutch. She sits opposite me, face sharp like a peregrine falcon in the flickering of the table's tea light. Her layered bob, perennially blond and meticulously effortless.

"But you're not *actually* married," she says as I spin white gold round and round my ring finger. Turns out meeting her at my hotel for a nightcap and confessing my marital stagnation were both regrettable choices. "No certificate, no children, no mortgage. You've literally nothing to lose."

"That's not helpful, Mother." I shouldn't have to see her every time I'm in the city. It's a habit begging to be broken and never more loudly than in this exact moment.

"It's the truth," she says, shrugging as my second bourbon finds white linen. "You know what really isn't helpful, Nathan?"

Her eyes flit to my drink—double, neat. I turn the tumbler. "It's been a long—"

"That's two, and it's your last. You're starting to slur." With practiced elegance, she sips the dry martini she's been nursing. Before I can argue, she's carrying on: "I don't like what he's doing to you. And I've tried, Nathan. Father and I both. We've tried to build trust."

Trust. Interesting word choice. More so because Mother always selects hers with surgical precision.

"What has Oliver ever done to warrant suspicion?" Hypocrisy sours the words as they leave my lips. "And don't say money."

"You can't deny the considerable disparity between—"

"We've been over this," I scoff. "Cars, cards, accounts. He asked me *not* to put his name on anything. It felt unearned. Life insurance was a fight. That sound like someone looking for a payday?"

She hesitates, prosecutes her tired case from a fresh angle: "Oliver requires too much coddling. You're neglecting your own health, and I don't appreciate—"

"Coddling?"

A waiter loops by, and she waves him off before I can send for another drink. "You know what I mean."

I don't, but between this liquor and the cabernet courtesy of conference catering, my brain's unspooling. Revealing uncomfortable truths I'd rather not explore with Dr. Kathy Klein—retired shrink turned community pillar of the Upper East Side. I switch subjects: "Had a fucked-up nightmare the other day."

She flinches at the language, but the battle-ax in Alexander McQueen chooses her, well, battles carefully. "What did you dream?"

She can't shake the compulsion to kick over logs in her own son's skull. I exploit this when it suits me. Another swallow of triple malt, and the tenseness in my shoulders starts to melt, the knots that riddle my back, unwinding.

"I pulled a scorpion out of my mouth."

"Jesus, Nathan." Mother's voice catches, and I won't tell her how the black thing, slick like gunmetal, had clung for dear life as I extracted it from my throat. That its writhing pincers had buried into my tissue like a tumor. "That's—"

"Fucked up. Like I said."

"How did it happen?"

"I was in a hospital bed, surrounded by you and Father and—"

"Oliver?"

"Yeah, he was there." Mother stiffens her spine because sharing even a nightmare with Oliver irks her. "I told you all something was wrong. Something was inside me that wasn't supposed to be there."

"We didn't believe you?"

"No. The internist said I was fine. Delusional, of course."

"The *internist*?" she ribs. "You didn't pull rank as a surgeon?"

"I don't know if I was one in the dream. Besides, when Oliver and you and Father weren't looking, she'd break into this wicked smile. She knew I was telling the truth." Another burning gulp down the hatch. "And finally, when the writhing was too much, I screamed. I reached in and screamed through my own hand in my own mouth."

"Any idea what this might mean?"

"I worry about myself. My emotional well-being. I'm jaundiced."

"And what of the scorpion?"

"Isn't that more your wheelhouse?"

"Humor me."

I puff my cheeks. "Something toxic inside me? Maybe malignant? It's called *cancer* because tumors latch like a crab. A scorpion's not so different."

"Anxiety causes dreams like that," she says with earned-ish confidence. "Night terrors. No cancer. Your nerves cultivate harmful narratives in your subconscious. Dreams of untrustworthy people—"

"Liars. That doctor. She was a malicious liar."

"At the very least, talk to him." She returns to Oliver as if to say *speaking of liars*. "Tell him what you're feeling."

"I'm not ready yet. I'm not in a headspace for confrontation."

What makes you think there'll be one? I imagine her asking. Instead: "You can't rely on his intuiting of your emotions."

"Why not? I intuit his. I speak his body language. What he's feeling and when he's feeling it, and there's just this inevitability. This tension—"

"He's ungrateful, and it creates tension."

"He's not ungrateful. He just"—her stare strengthens to a low-burn glower—"he needs direction."

She arches a finely sculpted brow. "And you're the right person to provide it?"

"I don't know." The words coil uncomfortably in the pit of my stomach. I don't like confessing to not knowing. I'd rather go down with a sinking ship—drowning passengers and all—than admit I'd steered into the maw of an iceberg. But that's not what bothers me about my answer. It's the honesty.

Mother obliges: "You're not. Furthest thing from it. Just because you're older doesn't mean you owe him some sort of tutelage. And you'll get hurt if you keep trying."

Older stings when it lands, but perhaps she's correct about that last bit. After all, how many relationships subsist in these gray areas? The ambivalence-soaked air of relationship purgatory is stifling, bordering on painful—

"Your father and I brought on a new CFO for the Klein Family Foundation." A conversational departure, but I can instantly tell I won't like it. "Dartmouth. Good Connecticut breeding. Man named Stuart. A *contemporary* of yours and if he wasn't gay, your father might have to keep an eye on me."

My neck flushes. "Seriously?"

Faux surprise falls over her like a stage curtain. "What?"

"You're pitching new boyfriends while I'm asking for advice on saving my marriage?"

"Relationship." She overenunciates. "You're not—"

"We're in a bad spot, but aren't those what define love? The *downs*, how you manage and endure them because who the hell has trouble with the *ups*? This, right now"—I splay my fingers on the table—"is the shit nobody talks about because it's hard."

"Nathan—"

"But we're stubborn. Both of us. I'll do the work. We will both do the work."

"You've always been loyal; you've always kept your word like we've taught you. Loyal and tenacious." Pinching her glass by the stem, she gives a little ground. The only question is why? "Tell me, though. What makes you so confident he'll keep his?"

"Because I know him." I run my tongue across the top of my teeth and worry they've turned serrated. "I know what he's capable of when he tries."

"So do I." She beckons a waiter with a black AmEx, but her eyes bore with unsettling urgency. "And that's what scares me."

3

OLIVER

Kristian's grip leaves no room for error.

Nathan's home in two days. Tilly can make it two days with no food, no water. I pray a toilet seat's been left up but can't recall.

The fire in my chest erupts as something buckles in my throat. My face fevers, and my cheekbones might pop out and fall to the floor.

Hands and arms, legs and torso, I shake. Tremble with fear and muscles tensing unnaturally. A dollop of saliva gathers on my bottom lip and drops to my sneaker. Kristian's feet are behind mine. His toes whiten as he leverages his weight against the floor tiles. Onto me.

There's no one to turn to. No one can help. Even if there were, I can't reach out. I'm in a hidden nook within a hidden world where anonymity's the whole point. Anonymity breeds apathy. When you're anonymous, no one cares to save you.

It won't be long now. A minute at most. His lips are on my ear, warm breath breezing inside my head. It's invasive, mocking. His hard dick presses the dimpled small of my back.

In Haus, I was vulnerable before his fist ever found my throat. Why didn't I appreciate this?

Behind my spine, my finger brushes the brass key hung from my wrist. The coldness of its jagged teeth is a finger snap for focus. Fight or flight. Survival.

I stretch my hand. My vision tunnels as I will my fingers to lengthen and Kristian kisses the inside of my ear.

We sweat profusely. From our pits and groins and backs. Drops run down our arms, our legs. Strike the dank floor in enormous, slow-motion splashes. Moist chemistry collects and mixes between us. We were slippery from the start, but now we're lubricated and I have a shot. A lifetime of experiences, and I'm reduced to one possession: this single shot.

I gather my dwindling strength, whatever pulsing life remains. I drop one shoulder and twist down like a threaded screw. Wet skin dissolves friction. I tear the key from my wrist, plunge it into his cheek, and drag through flesh.

His ocean-deep eyes widen. Maybe he screams. Blood, inky black in the low light. Kristian holds his blood-dripping face with both hands. And I'm sprinting down the hall.

· ·

Clutching my throat, I finally gasp air. Other men know something's wrong. Someone taps my shoulder, and I jerk away. Whatever he says is muted. I'm still underwater.

I bolt past the porn projections, run through crowds and down snaking hallways. A million years of evolution scream that Kristian's closing in.

Haus becomes a sprawling labyrinth, sinister in purpose. The red light of the darkroom just before the lockers—it glows ahead. *Almost there, Oliver!*

I'm naked, and shame grips me like Adam and his original sin. I snatch a towel from a hamper pile and cover myself. It's stiff in places, a foul and repulsive cloth like cardboard. Chest heaving, I burst through the door to the entry space.

"You okay, man?" The Cheshire Cat knots his brow. His concern urgent.

"The locker." My hoarse voice quakes. "Nine oh three. Open it."

What does he think? That I've been injured? I'm still clutching my throat. No, not injured. Fucking assaulted!

He springs from his seat, and I follow close into the locker room. He's saying something as he fumbles with a master key. He might want to know if I need a doctor. I'm sure he's asking what happened, but it's all muffled. His mouth, filled with marbles. My ears start to ring. My eyes dart from man to man. None of them are Kristian, but it's only a matter of time until one is.

My shorts are on. Then my shirt. My wallet and phone, in my pocket. I lose more time, and I'm dashing through the parking lot.

Scrambling into Nathan's SUV, I slam the lock. I punch the ignition button with a shaky fist as my eyes go teary and burn.

Through the leafy thicket, a parade of highway headlights strobe. A reminder that the world I've come from still exists. That had I grown cold, a lifeless mass on the floor of Kristian's rented room, this world would persist without me.

I can't hold back, and sob.

A fist thuds against the window. Inches from my head, and I scream.

Kristian's hand slides, painting a streak of cherry syrup down glass. For a white-hot instant, our eyes meet, and I floor the gas. Backing up, headlights wash out his face, but it's him.

Kristian vanishes into blackness as my tires squeal onto the street.

• •

The front motion lights flame alive. Back in cloistered Georgetown, and I'm doused in shameful yellow light before our townhome. The towering brick facade, Georgian-style, tall shutters; the whole place regards me with judgment.

Kicking off my sneakers, I stumble into the foyer. My keys and phone thrown atop the round entryway table. They strike the bone china vase, and Nathan's fresh bouquet of pink tulips shudders.

The curving staircase to the second and third stories whirls by. I pass Nathan's library with its floor-to-ceiling bookshelves and ivory fireplace. Its French doors are always shut, but they're paned with elegant glass. His parents, Victor and Kathy, scowl from their portrait on the mantel there. Painted eyes that pull bile up my throat.

4

Parlor doors swing in their pockets as I stagger into the drawing room. All Nathan's things—*our* things—sit as I'd left them. Warm, earthy tones. Midcentury modern. Scandi. Accent antiques.

As I flip on a table lamp, Tilly's nails click against mahogany floors. Nathan's blond cocker spaniel has roused from her crate upstairs in the master and comes down the steps. I make for the bar cart and slam back a gulp of tepid gin. Sour acid climbs my throat like a rain-swollen gutter. I choke back a second shot and drop the bottle on the coffee table so hard its glass top might break.

My legs buckle and I collapse into the sofa, bury my face in my hands. I rock back and forth, crying. Tilly rounds the corner, barking like a home invasion is unfolding in Nathan's absence. Her sharp yaps send me to my feet. A force, invisible and powerful, compels me to move. I pace the drawing room, circle the dining room table and its tall spray of orchids three, four times. I punch the kitchen counter and race upstairs.

Twisting the faucet of the en suite claw-foot, I step in as piping-hot water reaches the showerhead. Clothes cling to my skin because I haven't undressed.

I claw at my shirt and shorts, nails digging deep. I tear and peel and strip as though skinning myself. My clothes are a sopping heap on the tub floor when I grab Nathan's Head & Shoulders by mistake. I pour it over my scalp and knead.

Deeper and harder because I want Kristian's breath out of my skull. The damp breath he exhaled into my ear. His long fingers on my wrists. His palm crawling my shoulder blades on its way to my throat.

Tiny droplets gather and bloom into swirling clouds of steam. Worms writhe beneath my skin, and I tear the top off Nathan's shampoo. The plastic cap snaps in two. I turn it over my shoulders and chest.

Scrub. Knead. Repeat.

Heat splotches my skin, and when the hot water's gone, I step out. The hanging towel is a jarring reminder of where I've just fled. A bathhouse. I dry off with a robe instead.

I stand in my bedroom, our bedroom. This is my life. The room I woke up in this morning. And the morning before. And the morning before that. Nothing's changed.

Nothing has changed, I repeat to myself. And I'm starting to believe it. This place and the place I escaped can't coexist. They're too different, our home and Haus. It's like wrapping my head around the sarin-soaked rubble of Syria and a tennis court in Connecticut.

Did I dream it? Am I still dreaming? Yes, I'm imagining a memory from only moments earlier that never really happened. There's no evidence of it transpiring. None of Kristian. None of what he did. What he *attempted* to do. My rational self knows this is a lie. That brutal, truthful part taunts, knowing I need only look at my reflection and see my throbbing throat displayed as deep bruises. Kristian's grip tattooed on my skin, glove-shaped and horrifying. I silence this part of me.

Nathan has trouble sleeping, and he keeps a bottle of Ambien tucked in his nightstand. Ambien is different. The TV ads make that point loud and clear: *Ambien, the non-narcotic nighttime sleep-aid.* I swallow two with spit and collapse, still in the robe I toweled off with.

The double sedative burns off adrenaline. Thoughts grow muted, muddy. A bizarre euphoria blossoms. A body high just before the tremendous, inescapable weight of sleepiness. Tilly licks sweat from my shins. She's not allowed on the bed. I tell her to get off but realize that, again, I only think I've done so. As she curls against my chest, my vision tunnels, and I drift, lost to the watery static of the still-running shower.

•   •

I wake in my own bed, beneath my own sheets. They're airy and light like a fresh morning. Sunlight tumbles from our bedroom's long bay window, broken in even bands by plantation shutters.

The rays vanish and reappear with passing clouds. A coarse fabric chafes my thighs. Towel-like because I'm in a bathrobe.

My peace fractures into a million shards. Needle sharp and hazardous.

I bolt upright. Tilly jumps to the floor. My eyes bulge in my sockets, and the horrors from last night break through like rushing water. Splintering my mind's frail dam, taking everything with it. An unstoppable force.

My heart seizes when I hear it: the shower's running.

Across from our bed, the bathroom door's ajar. Just enough to catch water spilling over the edge of the tub.

I throw back the sheets and leap to the bathroom. My feet splash into a pool of water. My clothes from last night: I left them in the tub. They blocked the drain.

I shut the faucet off. The spillover drain gurgles—working overtime. I fling a cabinet open and pull towel after towel after towel onto the floor. They instantly become waterlogged. Saturated, and when there's none left, I dart to the linen closet down the hall, and gather more in my arms.

"Goddammit!" I scream as a thought strikes like a hammer to my face: Nathan's home tomorrow.

The bath empties, spitting water in a final, draining swirl. My clothes only partly blocked the drain, and less water pours from the showerhead than from the faucet. Still, there's going to be damage. Significant damage to Nathan's dream home. Our century-old dream home.

Shit. Shit. Shit. What's below this bathroom? A stairwell in the kitchen leading to an unfinished cellar. I turn to leave, to check the stairwell ceiling, but something catches my eye. I grind to a dead stop. My reflection in the baroque vanity mirror.

My feet press cold water from scattered towels as I draw closer. My gaze is pulled to itself like a magnet.

I run a finger down my throat in a diagonal trace. Over my stubbled Adam's apple. Dull purples. Dark blues in places. Greens, muted and sour.

Undeniable proof. Evidence beyond all doubt. Not for the first time in my life, the bruises on my throat gather into the unmistakable shape of human fingers.

5

I rap my knuckles on the kitchen's marble counter. In the stairwell, water's gathered in the space between the first and second stories and soaked into the plaster.

A list of priorities materializes. First, the water damage. Yesterday was Saturday, today is Sunday, tomorrow Nathan returns from New York.

This isn't spilled cabernet on a cushion. This is serious. Our contractor, Darryl—I can tell him it's an emergency, which of course it very much is. I'll pay whatever it takes to get him here on a Sunday. But the fact of the matter is, we'll need new plastering. We'll need the moisture dried. Hardly a one-day job with zero advance notice.

No, I can't hide my recklessness from Nathan. But I can invent an explanation that departs wildly from the truth. Which brings me to priority number two: my throat.

A parade of solutions—half-baked and foolish—marches by. Cosmetics are the most obvious. A foundation to match my skin. Then there's clothing. Turtlenecks. I don't own a single turtleneck, and it's mid-June in DC.

A terrifying reality sinks its teeth in. Nathan will see the flooded bathroom. He'll see my bruises. No rational way to conceal either. This means contingencies, dramatic by their very nature. And dramatic means emotion—that won't be a problem for me. I already teeter on the edge of sanity.

It also means action. Ramifications. Consequences.

I was mugged. I was mugged and must commit myself to the idea here and now.

Jumped on my night run. It happens all the time in this city, and my taking up running was Nathan's idea, anyway. If I'm lucky, he'll conclude we don't need to file a police report. To do so would be an exercise in futility because I don't recall details. The assailant was masked. See? The assailant. I can't even gender my attacker.

Nathan must be convinced medical attention is unnecessary, and if it was, he's a trauma surgeon at Walter Reed hospital, for fuck's sake. Simple assault and a stolen wallet pale in comparison to his combat casualties. Mental note: lose my wallet, report my cards as stolen.

After I hang up with our contractor, my chest unscrews a thread or two. My thrumming heartbeat settles.

"Water damage in the master bath? I can stop by midafternoon," Darryl had said on the other end. "Between two and three. Give it a look-over."

"Thank you, thank you, thank you," I replied with disproportional gratitude.

Things are moving. I'm beginning the complicated process of tying up loose threads. Maybe, just maybe, Nathan won't find any to pick.

I'm engaged in a cover-up too. One that consumes all attention and keeps me from reliving, rethinking the events of last night. I've compartmentalized. I've locked them in a dark corner of my mind. My stomach turns when the thought of confronting them bubbles up like noxious swamp water.

Keep moving. Keep thinking.

A fierce longing strikes. I want Nathan home. Not this second, obviously, but soon. I want to talk to him, and see him, and touch his stubbled jaw. I want to know with certainty that he doesn't know, and I want to forget. When he's standing here, the present will crowd out any other realities. When our chests press together, there'll be no space for last night to exist.

Something chimes. My iPhone, abandoned on the entry table.

It's Nathan, and I regret my wish.

"Oliver." He sounds clipped and tired. Hungover maybe, probably.

"Hey." I ooze cheer as if masking the state of things at home. The state of my life in his absence. "Sorry I didn't call you back. I fell asleep early. How's New York?" I brace for Nathan's answer, pray he'll skirt the unreturned call.

Unexpectedly, he does. "Got a closed-door working group all day today. Resuscitation fluid strategies. Whole blood versus blood products versus saline. That sort of thing."

He says *that sort of thing* as if bells will sound in my brain. I try to pay attention to his work, but I don't have the wherewithal to keep up. I'm insecure about this, so I never complain or ask for an explanation. "I'm sorry."

"Had a late drink with Mother, which was not a good idea. Predictably."

"Really sorry on that front."

"It is what it is. And also, not your fault."

"Then you're home tomorrow?" I want him to say his working group may spill into Monday. I will him to tell me this. Or maybe the airline's texted. His flight's delayed. A mechanical issue or lack of an allocated aircraft.

"I am. Mid-morning flight. Ten fifteen."

Fuck. "Guess you couldn't get one sooner." I overcompensate. "I'll make dinner. Something special. Whatever you want."

He breathes static into the receiver. "Anything. Not chicken. They've fed us chicken all week. Even the breakfast sausage is fucking chicken."

I laugh and worry it comes off forced. Which, of course, it is.

"I'll call tonight?" he asks. "FaceTime?"

"Sure." I answer too soon. My third mistake. The bathtub was my second. The bathhouse, my first. He's asked two questions, and I've provided a blanket *yes* to both. FaceTime. As in, we'll converse via video call. As in, my throat will be in frame.

"Perfect. Talk then. Love you."

I start to whisper "I love you too," but he's already hung up. I'm happy I don't have to say the words. It's not that they're untrue. They very much are, despite our problems. It's that my own duplicity sours them. Saying those words aloud to Nathan on *this* morning curdles my stomach like months-old milk.

I need room, a breather. As much as I don't want to, I need to process things. To determine what they mean to me and for me. Perhaps not last night, but everything since.

The kitchen junk drawer holds a tiny screwdriver, nestled among rubber bands and thumbtacks and Tilly's heartworm chewables. Tool in hand, I make for the hallway just before the dining room. The powder room door stands to my right, but I turn left. Between the closets on the opposite wall sits a duct vent. The grate is original to the home. Iron painted white. A swirling floral cage that I unscrew and sit gently on the hardwood.

Reaching in, elbow-deep, my fingers find the paper carton.

•   •

Our backyard is narrow. Landscaped and urban, and I sit on one of two stone benches in a back corner of lilac and magnolia. The tall homes of neighbors lean over into the space. They can see me smoking from upstairs windows. Nathan doesn't like smoking. Nathan hates the idea that I used to smoke. This would make him livid.

I pull a long drag, and my Marlboro glows cherry orange. Smoke sweeps my lungs, and my mind sharpens. Ashing into a coffee mug, I begin to feel sorry for myself.

I'm the one covering up. I'm the one concealing and masking and taking pains to set things right. But I'm the victim. The victim of an attempted murder.

My stomach twists like a wet rag, wringing damp fear from itself.

Murder. A man who entered my life in a chance moment tried to end it just as fast. His motive, inconsequential. Sociopathy, perhaps. But it's not *only* that he tried to choke me, to squeeze the life from me. We were intimate. We were intimate when I decided he'd fuck me. We were intimate when our bodies, wet with the salt of our sweat, the adrenaline of our arousal, pressed together.

The intimacy of sex mirrors the intimacy of murder. At least murder that requires one to use one's hands. To breathe into his ear. The French call orgasm "the little death."

Is this what they had in mind?

•   •

"We'll start early this week. Finish up by Friday," Darryl says as I lead him to the front door. He's old. Ill-fitting jeans and a purple-and-orange Clemson cap. A fatherly type who instills a spoonful of calm, and I wonder if dads do that for their sons. I wouldn't know.

He's worked with us from the beginning. With the house even longer—before Nathan claimed the property, it belonged to the Klein Family Foundation. An asset of Victor and Kathy's philanthropic trust, whatever the hell that means. "I'll come by Tuesday."

"You can't start now? Maybe get it done by Monday?"

"Home's historic." Darryl lifts an eyebrow. "Even the baseboards are works of art. You're kidding, right?"

No, but I laugh. "Thought I'd ask."

Tuesday. It'll take until Friday to finish, which means Nathan's initial impression of what's happened will be as I arrange it. I must make this impression digestible. Take as much edge off the shock as possible.

"This is about a thirty-five-hundred-dollar job," Darryl says, sucking air between yellowed teeth. "That gonna work for you boys?"

"Sure. Absolutely." The price tag is painful, but what choice do I have? My hand covers my throat. I'm unsure if he notices or finds the gesture odd. "Thanks so much again," I add as the door closes behind him.

Thirty-five hundred dollars. Shit. It's not that we don't have the money. We have it. Nathan's a surgeon. It's that *I* don't have the money. I'm not a doctor. On the contrary, I don't have a college degree.

I dropped out way back in Indiana before my path ever crossed Nathan's. I make excuses for it anytime the opportunity presents itself.

"I wanted to travel," I lied to Tom, one of Nathan's friends. Tom Vogt is a senatorial staffer on Capitol Hill. I'm painfully aware I'm not anything like either of them. "I wanted to learn lessons college can't teach."

I condescend. As though I were the beneficiary of some elusive enlightenment the conventionally educated can't relate to. The follow-up question is nearly always the same. "Where have you traveled?"

I've left the United States a grand total of one time to backpack through southern Europe. Spain mostly. On the hunt for an overhyped Eurotrashy drug carnival in Mallorca that disappointed. But I stretch this single experience as far as I can. I turn phrases to create the impression of multiple trips. Tasteful trips.

"Madrid, of course. Train to Lisbon. But Barcelona's always been my favorite. Barceloneta Beach. Catalonian flags on every balcony, all fluttering together."

"Catalonia," Tom had parroted. "Romantic. Go with anyone?"

Hector. "No."

Tom smiled indulgently and tried to catch Nathan's eye. Nathan whose eager ears had sharpened for my answer. It's stupid. I'm stupid, but dwelling on this won't help. I move on to my arrangements.

When it comes to lying, there's a golden rule: tell as much truth as you can. The truth is, after all, the easiest to remember. It's the most consistent with inarguable fact. There are two inarguable facts in my situation. My bruised throat and our flooded bathroom. A traumatic event, the catalyst of both.

Only this last part needs to change. I was not at Haus. I was not the victim of attempted homicide. I was mugged on my run. My reaction to this new reality remains the same. I'm distraught, panicked, and afraid.

Jumped from behind, tackled to the ground. I fought back, my hair and body gathering dirt. My attacker choked me. I acquiesced before it went further by giving up my wallet. At home, I showered while reeling fresh from trauma. The truth takes over at this point.

The clothes I wore to Haus aren't for running. The T-shirt's fine, but khaki shorts not so much. So I wash them and return them to my drawer. I swipe a pair of jogging shorts across garden gravel before soaking them in the sink.

I ball them up with my tee and underwear and toss them in the hamper. I make sure they're the only items there before cleaning the driver-side window of Nathan's tuxedo Range Rover. A black, clotted handprint baked by the heat. Windex turns it bright red again, and the paper towel looks soaked with something fresh.

Next, my stolen wallet. A narrow alley cuts behind our place. The city collects garbage and recycling each Monday morning—the day Nathan returns. Wallet in hand, I walk the length of the alley to the end of our block. A pair of garbage and recycling containers sit to one side. They serve a mid-rise apartment building and brim with eclectic refuse.

I hesitate. My cards are all replaceable, and new ones are already on the way from the bank. Ditto my driver's license. A significant hassle, but replaceable nonetheless. None of these things give me pause.

It's the photo that stops me. The smiling woman with a Peter Pan haircut minus the youthful sheen. My mom, Deborah Park.

She's dead, and it's the only photo I have. When she passed, I'd scoured the blue Cracker Jack box of a house we lived in for more. Even a picture with Dad in it could be cropped with scissors. But after searching the Facebook albums of far-flung kin, I concluded this was it. This is all there is.

Commit, I tell myself. *You were mugged. Commit.*

But I can't. I slip the picture in my pocket and hurl the wallet into the dumpster.

The tips of my ears burn. I'm the victim here, yet I'm making tough calls. Excruciating choices. Guess there's no such thing as a one-hit trauma, and I scream.

"You all right, son?" A reply from nowhere, and I jolt. Behind the containers, a binner raises his worn head—a hard-up man collecting bottles for cash. Sun has leathered his face. His silver hair, knotted. His clothes more ill fitting than Darryl's.

"I'm okay." I give a shaky nod, and he returns my gesture just as nervously.

Has he already gone through these, or is he only getting started? Has he seen what I've tossed? If anything, his abrupt presence is a sharp reminder that there are so many ways for me to fuck this up. So little is in my control.

I ball my hand into a tight fist—knuckles white—and punch brick on my way in through our back door.

The pain is instant and hot. Skin peels from my knuckles, and blood fills the space torn tissue leaves. This is okay. A good thing for my story.

Maybe I fought back.

6

breathe deep. *Commit.*

The word has played on a loop in my mind all afternoon and into the evening. Sinking deep into the sofa, I've skipped the frantic search for ways to hide my throat while FaceTiming Nathan. Instead, I adjust the lighting in the drawing room to capture it.

I hold a trembling phone in front of my face. My palms are soaked to the bone, and instinct screams to mask my anxiety. But on this call, emotion is okay. Emotion helps.

I scroll to *Nat.*

A high-pitched ringing squeals. My face resolves in the feedback window up top. As small as it is, my bruising is plain. No way to miss it on his end. I brace for the plunge and the weightlessness to follow.

"Hey."

Nathan's face materializes from blackness like it did inside Haus. He appears fatigued. His sandy-brown hair is tousled; the loosened knot of a baby-blue tie sits at the frame's bottom. Worry and suspicion mark his eyes, and his brow knots. "What's on your neck?"

I massage my throat.

"Oliver, is that . . . are those *bruises*?"

"Yeah." My eyes dampen. "Yes."

"What the hell happened?" Nathan's voice climbs an octave. It does the same when he becomes accusatory, though this is not his intention now.

I'm on the brink of pushing an enormous bomb out an airplane's bay doors.

"I was robbed." There. I've said it. The bomb detonates with a concussive blast. I'm no longer in control of the damage it does. Nature and chance will determine what its fires burn and consume and destroy.

"Oh my god." Nathan brings a hand to his mouth. His words, his actions hold sympathy. I'm relieved because I'm a victim. I've done nothing wrong. The world is chaotic, and I've been struck by the evil that stalks it. "Jesus Christ! He hurt you?"

A second nod. "I went for a run last night, around ten." I maintain truth's timeline. My golden rule for lying. "On the way home, somebody jumped—"

Nathan interrupts: "Somebody? One person? Or more?"

His analytical mind, clinical and often cold, turns. I almost see his neurons synapsing, hear the pop and crackle as they fire. He won't make this easy, and I don't resent him for it. I'd do the same were our roles reversed.

"One person," I answer before qualifying. "I think one person." Nathan won't make this easy, but I can still muddy the waters at every bend. Every chance I get, I'm determined to obfuscate. To confuse and daze both of us.

"And he choked you?" Nathan decides my attacker's male.

"He straddled me. On the sidewalk. He choked me, but when I threw my hands up, he stopped. I told him my wallet was in my back pocket. Said I had cash and cards, so he took it and bolted."

"He didn't speak, did he? To you? Did you hear his voice?"

"No." I get ahead of Nathan's line of questioning. "He wore a gray ski mask. I didn't see any features. No identifiable marks. Nothing. Long sleeves, long pants, sweats." I'm providing too many details. The color of the mask. The make of his pants. My voice stutters. The swelling sadness is very real. I'm reacting to actual events. They depart from my words in meaning, but they hurt as deeply.

"Oh my god," Nathan repeats. "Shit. I'm so glad you're okay." He exhales as he says this, and he is glad. He's thinking of all the ways this could've turned out. I could've died. He's thinking he could've lost me—that upon his return to DC, he'd be identifying my body atop the sterile steel of an autopsy table. Instead, I'll greet him, happily, from the curb at arrivals.

"Oliver, you need to see a doctor. Did you call the cops yet?"

"No."

He raises an eyebrow. "No, you don't want to see a doctor, or no, you haven't phoned the police?" Nathan's parenting me now. He's ten years my senior, for one. And it's in his nature. It serves him well in the operating room, but I resent it.

"I didn't report it. There's nothing to say to police. I can't even give a description. I've called the bank. The cards are all canceled." How much cash did I carry last night? I started with eighty dollars. Four twenties. The membership for Haus set me back forty, but I need to account for the entire amount withdrawn from the ATM. "Eighty bucks was taken. I know it's not pocket change, but it's not enough to warrant—"

"You could be seriously injured, Oliver. You need to be examined. And you need—"

"I need you home," I say. "What I need is to not be alone."

"I'm back soon." He softens his tone. "It's going to be okay. Everything's gonna be okay."

I permit myself to believe him, ignoring the fact that I've lied. His conclusion that *everything's gonna be okay* rests on a foundation of untruth, and therefore, he cannot know this.

"Someone should come by. I'll have Tom over to—"

"No," I cut him off. "No, please. I don't want company. I'll be fine until you're back."

An uneasy silence settles between us.

"There's something else," I add. "Our bathroom. When I got home, I just wanted a shower. I needed to wash off from the pavement. I was upset and not thinking and I undressed in the tub. My clothes blocked the drain. I left it running. It flooded a bit."

I brace again, body rigid as though this were a second bomb equal to my first in magnitude. From Nathan's perspective, they couldn't possibly be equated. A tiny voice needles: *Or could they?*

"That's fine." He smiles, and I rush to say I've already phoned Darryl, had him to the house, but Nathan interrupts. "It's okay. We'll fix it. Things are things. You're okay and that's what matters."

You're okay. Another conclusion drawn from lies. I'm the furthest thing from it. The raw self-awareness burns.

"Speaking of things," Nathan starts, half his smile vanishing. "Funny, huh?"

"What?"

"Your phone," he says, but I don't follow at first. "He didn't take your phone."

My heart rate spikes. My phone. Fuck. Another mistake. I bottle my reaction, but my face has already changed. My jawline, tensed and betraying.

"Just thought he would've taken it."

"It happened fast. I don't know he had time to think. When he got the wallet, it was over for him. These guys are opportunists." I make this last observation with a hint of authority. The fact is, I should know. We're both aware I've stolen before. Before Nathan. When the man in my life was named Hector.

Nathan agrees. He tells me he loves me, and he couldn't be happier I'm safe. He calls me a survivor, even. He has no idea how much so, but I must say the words now. They still taste like hot vinegar. "I love you too."

"I'll see you in the morning." A quick grin and the call's over. My screen, black.

I fall back onto a plush cushion. Our coffered ceiling, the object of my blank gaze. I exhale and knead my sternum as though digging inside myself to massage my heart. But there's no denying it: I'm relieved. A sudden weight vanishes. I've accomplished no small feat, speaking to Nathan just now.

My phone. It's not the implausibility of an attacker not taking it, it's the oversight. The fact that I didn't think of it beforehand. I'm capable of glaring mistakes, and what else haven't I considered?

MeetLockr. I need to delete the app.

Last night at Haus was an escalation, the culmination of many building moments. Boundaries broken, lines scuttled, thresholds crossed. I'd started weeks ago, growing more brazen, thirstier with each passing day.

Nathan was on call at the hospital. Friday night, and the house was all mine. I ambled down to the cellar and plucked a cobwebbed bottle of red. A pinot noir ironically labeled "Mephistopheles." If Nathan blunts the edge of his days with four pours of smooth bourbon, no reason I couldn't indulge. He's the one separating flesh by scalpel, not me. There's a world of difference between my reception desk and his OR.

Besides, wine's not trouble for me. Though I worry about Nathan occasionally, and more so recently, alcohol's never been *my* problem.

Halfway through the bottle—Phil Collins's "Another Day in Paradise" on the record player, laptop open on the dining room table—I simply looked. No harm in that, I told myself. The hundred-billionth human to ever say such a thing.

I logged on to *Casual Encounters. M4M*. Men for men.

Next, I scrolled through them. Read them. *NSA;* no strings attached. Permitted my mind to devour sentences and posted photos. A menagerie of butterflies teemed in my stomach. My breathing, heavy.

Masc Jock Seeks Power Bottom. Clean. DDF.

Masc meaning masculine. An alpha-male type. Not discernably gay. *Power bottom:* a receiving partner able to take control. *DDF:* drug- and disease-free. No STIs. No meth or Molly.

Smooth Bottom Twink for PnP. Hung white guys to the front of the line. Must be cut.

PnP: party and play. Nearly the opposite of DDF. I've never met this guy, but I already know him. I've encountered countless iterations of him in the past. He's a twink, meaning hairless and young. A gay wide-eyed deer or lamb, though judging by his post, the image of innocence is deceptive. He's a bottom, as he indicated. Casually racist. A size queen with strict specifications.

Pig Hosting at Airport Marriott. Bare Only. Dump Load and Leave.
Self-explanatory.

JPEGs accompanied most of the posts. Hard dicks. Backsides. Boys bent over. Rarely faces, and I never engaged anyone. Never replied. In the beginning, it was enough to simply look. I'd masturbate and promptly shut my computer. My interest, significantly waned.

Thumbing through my phone now, I find the next rung in my escalation. A gay hookup app. MeetLockr. It allows a single profile pic, and GPS tracking shares the physical distance between two users. A surrogate measure of the ease with which sex between them is possible. Unlike the Casual Encounters site, I had conversations here.

I downloaded a separate app to hide it from Nathan, who knows all my passwords and frequently uses my phone when his is charging or out of reach. The app disguised a folder with the icon of something innocuous—a calculator. The idea came from a *New York Times* piece on teens hiding sexts from Mom the same way. Open the PIN-protected "calculator" and there's MeetLockr.

Hidden apps within hidden folders or not, I must delete it. All of it. And not just to cover my tracks should Nathan grow suspicious, but for my own sanity. I've endured terror, panic, guilt, sadness. Kristian's long fingers in my tumbler, ice cracking between his sharp teeth. But stringing all these feelings together in a single, sinewy thread? Shame.

I've already cleared my browser history, but now I'll delete both this app and the one that conceals it.

I open the false calculator, hover over MeetLockr, hesitate.

I need only to press my thumb and swipe all this bullshit into oblivion. To excise it from my life like a malignancy. But I don't. The cogs in my brain turn. Steam gathers in vats inside my mind. Pressure builds, begs for release. Maybe even on its hands and knees.

One look. I'll have one look; I'll masturbate and forget everything during those precious few seconds when I'm done. A last go before it's over. Done with forever.

MeetLockr takes longer than usual to load, and my cheeks flush. My right hand trembles. I slip it beneath the elastic waist of my sweats. Feet on the coffee table, I spread my legs. Inside my underwear, I take hold of myself and tug.

My left hand scrolls through my message in-box, searching. Smearing my screen with sweat. Countless exchanges with countless men, none of whom I've met or seen in real life—I think. I search for a meaty thread. One where we'd talked at length. Exchanged dick pics. Admitted to long-buried fantasies only anonymity can surface. Fetishes that persist deep beneath the psyche like fungus in damp soil.

I open one such exchange and carefully search each pic the man sent. I'm getting closer. Edging toward orgasm.

A noise springs from my phone, and I jolt. A startling that almost makes me cum. The chime's familiar. It has spurred exhilaration many times in recent days. A new message.

I open it. The account displays *!* instead of an alphanumeric username. The avatar is a headless torso. Trim and muscular. The picture ends at the man's neck. Adonis's, fresh from a visit to the Gay Guillotine. A blue text bubble appears.

Hi.

Impulse sends my thumbs typing, but I stop myself from answering. This isn't why I'm here. That feeling, the shame, this is over. Whatever *this* was. Whatever's wrong with my life, with Nathan specifically, it no longer justifies this.

I'm about to delete this message—and all the others. My erection has vanished along with any swollen desire. Another bubble appears. The bouncing ellipsis of a forthcoming reply.

It's a photo.

A knowing smile. Ice-blue eyes as deep as the angry slash in his cheek.

Hi Oliver.

II. Dyspnea

Breath is held involuntarily, blood pressure spikes,
and pupils dilate.

7

NATHAN

When I close my eyes, Oliver's throat is all I see. The violent bruises circling his neck like a garrote. He could've died. He says some son-of-a-bitch tweaker stole his wallet, but what he meant was some son-of-a-bitch tweaker nearly stole him from me. Irrevocably.

I'd hung up, half stumbled from my room, and beelined for the bar where Mother had rendered unsolicited judgment barely twenty-four hours ago. In this new light, her "advice" seemed even crueler, and I was palpably angry. Two double bourbons smoothed the edges but, given my present task, they may have been overkill.

Oliver lived. Oliver is fine. The only fallout is hard lessons, learned hard.

From the back of Lecture Hall E, I both scroll through my slide deck and quadruple-guess the stiff drinks. Colleagues trickle in for the day's final talk. The presentation—"Tough Choices in Trauma"—is mine, and fuck if I can concentrate. It's a case study with a laughable title, but I've added thorough notes to each and every slide. These bullets are even more important because I've taken creative liberties with small details.

Not lies. Omissions. Mostly.

You've only got to read them, Nathan. No one expects anything performative. Get through it. Get home. Get Oliver's injuries examined by someone besides Oliver.

"Dr. Klein, hello." A mousy young woman in an NYU blazer taps my shoulder. Second year at best, no makeup, eye bags so large an airline would make her check them. "I've got iced water already onstage."

Neat bourbon would be grand.

"Did you bring a flash drive?"

And why would Oliver not go straight to an ER? Or the police station?

"A what? Sorry. What did you say?"

"A flash drive?" She gestures to an AV setup at the front, and I wonder how keen this mouse's nose is when it comes to alcohol. "To load your presentation?"

"Yes, I did. Here." I shut my laptop and fish through the bespoke bag by my feet.

"Thank you, sir." She hesitates when I surrender the drive. Perhaps she's caught a note of liquor after all. And *sir*? How old does she think I am?

"Is there something else?"

"Uh," she stutters. "It's three till. Shouldn't you take the podium?"

I check my watch for no good reason and make for the stage. *Just get through it,* I repeat over and over and over. It's a room full of trauma surgeons. All a particular breed of distilled narcissist. Of the general US population, sociopathy occurs at an estimated frequency of 1 percent. Among incarcerated males? Twenty-five. And in this particular room at this particular time?

You don't want to know.

I could strip naked and slur the whole goddamn thing—slides in Comic Sans—and not a single, self-involved claimant of the esteemed title of Fellow, American College of Surgeons, would raise an eyebrow. Not while quietly memorizing their own presentation notes. Or choosing cherry-red paint for the BMW they're ordering online like Door-Dash. Or perusing Tinder or Grindr or Bumble or MeetLockr for that last, tepid hotel fuck before flying home to wives with saline breasts or husbands with spray-tanned obliques.

"All set?" Needy Mouse has followed me to the front. Breathing down my own neck while Oliver's finger-shaped bruises flicker behind my eyelids.

"I am."

"How about warnings? I can signal when you're running out of time—"

"Fifteen minutes." I smile, and before she can ask another goddamn question: "For Q and A. And then five to wrap up."

"Sure thing, Dr. Klein." She scampers off as the lights draw low on a full house of white coats. Deep breath in. *Forget Oliver. You can forget Oliver. One hour, and that's it.* I adjust the skinny mic, and here we go.

"Good evening. I'm Dr. Nathan Klein. Combat Casualty Care. Walter Reed hospital." Cue obligatory conference joke: "I'm today's last talk, so I'll keep it short. I just ask that you do the same. Keep pontificating to a minimum."

Obligatory laughter and electric-blue light beams from a one-story screen to my right.

"This is an early career case study from my residency in South Bend, Indiana. OR management—the nuances, the communication, the order—it's all on-the-job training, and this was mine." I strike the space bar too hard, and a ten-foot photo of mangled human materializes onscreen. A black bar across his eyes for privacy. Though I recall them having rolled so far back into his skull, the censorship is a formality at best.

"Caucasian male. Twenty-two years old. Rural Indiana kid." It occurs to me I could also be describing Oliver and my voice breaks. "Polytrauma stemming from an agricultural accident."

I move to the next slide, but what if things hadn't stopped where Oliver said? What if he'd been killed and a decade later some Dr. Jackass paints a black bar over his shredded face?

"Injuries included—"

"What was the accident?" A man interrupts, his face masked by hot projector bulbs.

"I said agricultural."

"No shit. It's Indiana." *Man* was generous. *Asshole* is more accurate. "But what specifically? Combine? Farm structure collapse?"

"Tractor overturn," I snap, and hope he reads it for irritation. "By far the most common rural trauma beyond vehicular. Hemothorax, spleen laceration, left femur fracture, and, this is important"—I take a sip of water and hope no one notices my tremor—"a severed thumb."

A breeze of chuckles from the featureless crowd.

"During resuscitation, the thumb arrived onsite. Patient's friend dropped it off in a cooler full of ice. Bagged between cans of Busch Light."

More snickering and the low hum of useless AC. I tug my wet collar.

"Good thing, right? Thumb's in the trauma bay and seemingly still viable."

Spotty murmurings in the affirmative.

"I secured his airway, diagnosed the spleen laceration by ultrasound, and determined the femur wasn't a time-sensitive priority."

"Not so much the thumb, huh?" That same, smug asshole from seconds earlier. Does he think this is a conversation?

"Correct. Necrosis is an irreversible bitch."

I cringe the instant *bitch* leaves my lips. Between Oliver, the panic, the bourbon, and the asshole, it just came out. The light laughter it earns is decidedly disapproving and my heart thrums.

"We transferred him to the OR for an emergency splenectomy, but the thumb's presence had already broken our rhythm. Disrupted my team's focus, and suddenly I've got surgical techs preoccupied with preserving it. Metabolic derangements, hypotension—we're seconds from a dead kid, and a severed digit steals the show."

I've finally got the room. Nothing like beer and amputated thumbs to hold attention.

"Now I've got a real problem and very little time to solve it." I toggle the mouse. "And . . ."

Oliver's face peers back from the darkened audience. Bruised throat. Dead eyes. I blink, and something unfortunate happens: while scrolling, I somehow close the window entirely. The whole damn window. Gone.

This is a problem, and my cheeks flush. I can't regurgitate this case off the cuff because, again, I've altered the ending. Oliver was nearly choked to death, and now my notes have vanished. And maybe I'm more than tipsy. And I've burned a solid minute squinting in silence while my pulse pounds in both ears.

"And?" A woman. Seated somewhere in the front.

"And . . ." I wipe my brow. "And so . . ."

Click. Click. Tap. Scroll. Click. Nothing!

"Just give me a quick second." Where the hell is Needy Mouse when she's *needed*? "Having some technical difficulties here."

"Dr. Klein," Mouse whispers. She crouches in the aisle just below. "We're okay. Everything's working."

"No, it's not." My mouth is ashtray dry. Desiccated and I'm lisping. "I can't pull up my notes."

"Dr. Klein—"

"It's not working." I reach for my water and knock it over. It strikes the carpet with a mic-aided boom and rolls. "Jesus!"

"So, what did you do?" Asshole again.

Breathe, Nathan. Regain control. Oliver—

"With the thumb?" Another man. My bumbling's registering. My talk's coming apart. It's as fragrant as a pinhead of blood in a vast ocean. And this crowd is nothing but tiger shark through and through.

"I directed my team, the nurses . . ." Christ, where the fuck did my notes go!? I'm clicking through browsers, rapid-fire opening and closing whatever files my cursor finds. Where the hell—

"Sir?" Mouse asks. "Are you okay?"

I'm not a fucking *sir*. I'm about to scream at her, to bolt and book a flight and get home to my husband who's been almost killed when, just like that, my presentation is back. My notes reappear. All of them. Diligently crafted. Ordered and bulleted and waiting to be ticked through.

Oh. Okay. You're back, Nathan. Back online.

I draw breath, offer the crowd a wide smile. "Sorry about the water, folks." Then a wrist flick and a white lie: "Procedure for carpal tunnel four weeks ago. A surgery from doing too many surgeries."

It engenders sympathy and explains my shakiness and they laugh.

"As I was saying, in a case like this, you've got to make hard calls." The room settles back into silence. "Tough choices, and it was evident the kid's life and the kid's reattached thumb were mutually exclusive outcomes."

My confidence growls like an engine with fresh gasoline, and I proceed to instruct the crowd on the criticality of rhythm. A narrative about the power of succinctness in the face of insurmountable pressure. How fierce patient advocacy often looks cruel. How I had just seconds and very few words to spare, and deftly used both. Brevity to demonstrate gravity.

The message was received. The thumb was abandoned. The patient was saved.

And my presentation, mercifully finished.

Needy Mouse signals a warning for questions, and the subject matter naturally lends itself to softballs. I bat them away, one after another. Anecdotes of similar experiences from the audience drain more time, and my lungs finally expand.

The last barrier to returning home to my husband behind me.

My creative liberties had blended seamlessly with fact. Regardless of my *actual* course of action, the outcome was the same: I made the call, and the kid's alive today. Tossing back beers on a tractor in some cornfield. Nine fingers, but a beating heart. Because that's what I do. That's what I'm good at. I fix things.

Shouldn't we keep it on ice? a surgical tech had asked, referring to the thumb but neglecting the massively hemorrhaging spleen on the OR table. *Maybe perfuse it?*

Heparinized saline, another resident suggested, suddenly blind to the thumb's profoundly hypotensive owner. *Flush with heparinized saline.*

But the choice was mine. The patient was crashing, the room was fixated on an inconsequential digit, and sometimes fixing big things means breaking tiny things. Rendering them moot because the stakes are far too high. *Dr. Klein, we can reattach—*

Tiny things like a young man's thumb.

Dr. Klein? Oh my god, did you just—

The one I'd deliberately dropped to the floor and crushed with my shoe.

8

OLIVER

Kristian's found me. He knows my name. He knows who I am.

Despite the sudden cold, my cheeks swell and grow warm to the touch. I've broken out in a fever. Panic wraps my arms and legs, my fingers and toes, in invisible needle pricks.

I no longer sit on the sofa, having sprung to my feet the instant my name appeared. As I pace half circles around the room, my eyes dart to my phone. Over and over and over again. It's fallen between two couch cushions where it came to rest when I threw it. Like it was a rattlesnake. If I'd held it a moment longer, I would have been bitten. Milky venom seeping inside my body from hypodermic fangs.

Think, I tell myself. *Think!*

But thinking is the very last thing I want to do. I don't want to know how, or when, or where. Least of all, why.

I hyperventilate, cover my face with both hands. I'm standing before the powder room sink. I gulp cold water straight from the brass faucet. Note the dark bruises that clasp my throat. I drink again, repeating the process start to finish. Finally—when the explosion of energy from seeing Kristian's face in the raw light of day wanes—I begin to unpack things.

It's not Kristian. Yes, it is. The photograph, crystal clear. Blond, cheek-length bangs. Dark brows. Ice-blue eyes like a sled dog.

He doesn't really know who I am. Yes, he does. He called me Oliver.

He doesn't want anything from me. He must. Why else message me? He pointed his sharp chin to the right in the photo, making prominent the laceration in his cheek from my locker key. The taut stitches pulling his flesh back together.

How did he find me? He told me his name, and I didn't share mine. But it doesn't matter. The reception desk at Haus scanned my driver's license. With the commotion I incited, I drew the front man away from his desk and files. Leaving copies unattended for opportunistic eyes.

What are you looking for? He speaks to me again, his voice accented and soaked with false promise. Entrapment. His palms work their way from my back to my throat. My wrists are bound. His breath crawls inside my ear, whistling within my skull. I'm choking. A frantic search for air.

For the second time today, I scream.

• •

My Uber pulls to the curb a block away from the police station. I'd been in no state to drive or to touch shoulders with strangers on the Metro. The thought of asking the driver, "Take me to the police," made me cringe. I gave him a cross street instead.

During the ride here, I second-guessed myself. If I talked to the cops, if I told them the truth, what happened last night, I'd initiate a chain of events entirely out of my control.

But *control* is what spurred this decision to come forward. Nathan can't find out about Haus or Kristian. Nathan can't discover what happened, but I *can* continue to exploit his absence. A rapidly closing window at that. I can initiate an investigation of some kind.

Hands in my pockets, I take the sidewalk with faux confidence.

I'll disclose everything to the police in Nathan's absence. It's drastic, but I'm dealing with a killer. Kristian is a killer and his brazenness suggests he has much less to lose than I do. Or that he holds better cards. Or both.

It took all of me—and two shots of Dutch courage—to respond to that *Hi Oliver*. I snapped screengrabs of the exchange, which included his face, and flipped them right back his way with a simple text:

911.

He never replied, but I'm making good on my threat. I'm going to do this because Kristian tried to kill me and now he's stalking me.

The station emerges ahead. A brick two-story painted a not-so-calming canary yellow. Surveillance cameras perched along the roofline stoke unease in my gut. I swallow hard and pray this works. That the threat of a police investigation dissuades him from ever contacting me again. That Nathan and I can carry on with our blissfully banal lives like we've always done.

Before I fucked up.

• •

Truth be told, this isn't the first police station I've been inside.

I walk through spinning doors, sign my name at reception, step through a metal detector, and gather my things on the far side. Then I wait.

Some minutes later, a uniformed officer collects me. "This way, please," he beckons as I trace his steps. His tone is short. He's had a long shift. He takes me to a room with a table and two chairs. No windows. A metal filing cabinet. Not exactly a peeling-paint interrogation room from *Law & Order,* but certainly nothing warm either. Somewhere in between. Burnt coffee and printer ink thread the air.

When the door unlatches and swings back open, I flinch. A smiling woman walks in, and I'm instantly relieved. Be they gay, straight, bi, or none of the above, I prefer my doctors and my bosses and my friends and, apparently, my cops to be women. I'm far more at ease with women, more comfortable talking to women about how I have sex with men.

"I'm Detective-Sergeant Rachel Henning," she says. Plainclothes: jeans and a light, fitted button-down. Sleeves rolled up, skinny arms, and a clunky man's watch wraps her wrist. We shake hands.

"Oliver."

"Pleasure to meet you, Oliver." She takes the opposite seat. A folder under her arm finds its place on the tabletop.

She speaks with an accent that's vaguely familiar. Midwestern, maybe. Michigan's Upper Peninsula? I ask her where she's from, hoping to forge a personal connection with the woman who's about to learn my deepest, darkest secret. The most recent one, anyway.

"Born and raised in Alberta." She runs a hand through neck-length hair. "I understand you'd like to file a criminal complaint?"

"Yes."

"You've come to the right place." It's intended as a joke. I do laugh, anxiously, and I'm sure this is the point. An icebreaker she's likely used in dozens of conversations like this one. In this very room. "I'll get to the forms in a bit. The paperwork stuff. But first"—she leans back, her jawline relaxed—"I'd like you to just talk. Tell me what's going on."

I lick dry lips. My leg bounces beneath the table, tapping out Morse code on bad linoleum. Deep breath in, then: "I was assaulted."

Detective Henning says nothing. Her steely eyes scan my neck.

"Someone tried to kill me." The detective leans forward. She's used to people lying to her. She can likely detect physical tells if only for the sheer number of lies she's been fed on the job. She won't find any here. She can scour my face for them—I hope she does—and she'll come up empty-handed. She'll appreciate the seriousness of my predicament.

"I did something I shouldn't have." I rub my throat. "Last night. I visited an establishment."

"An establishment?" Detective Henning needs details.

"A bathhouse. You know, like, a gay one." I pause to make certain she's following me. When she asks which, I plow ahead.

"Haus. I met a man there." My bouncing knee gathers speed. My teeth chatter. "He said his name was Kristian. We started to hook up. We kissed. Went into a room, a private one I guess he rented. We were going to have sex . . ." I close my eyes, swallow, stay my knee with a fist. "He tried to strangle me. To death. Before he could . . . finish . . . I cut his face with a locker key."

"Where specifically on his face?"

"His cheek. The right one. Then I ran out as fast as I could." I pull my phone from my pocket. My screengrabs will dispel any doubts she has. Kristian's face. The taunting.

Her eyes narrow as she scrolls. "You're positive you didn't introduce yourself? Exchange phone numbers? Perhaps you don't recall? Had you been drinking?"

"I'm certain." I don't answer her last question. It's irrelevant. I had a single drink at Haus. The Dutch courage I downed before replying to Kristian is another matter. Can she smell it on my breath? On my skin?

The silence between Detective Henning and me is thick, stiflingly heavy. She's digesting what I've said. "You said you were *going* to have sex?"

"I wasn't raped." The abrupt proclamation feels foolish. I'm not even sure that's what she meant, but a lifetime portraying masculinity—what I'd been conditioned to believe was masculinity—compelled me to clarify. "Not raped. There was no penetration. He choked me before."

"But the expectation was that sex would occur?"

"Yes."

"Was there any conversation regarding the activities you both planned to engage in?" Detective Henning asks. "A reason for this man, Kristian, to assume he had permission to choke you?"

"No." And *permission*? Would she ask a straight man that question? Like gays are all kink all the time? *Fifty Shades of Grey* is nothing compared to bread-and-butter gay sex. "Absolutely not."

She eyes my throat, my bruises. "Have you received medical attention?"

"No."

"Your injuries might need—"

"My partner is a medical doctor." An impulsive attempt to direct the conversation away from my injuries and back to Kristian. It's also very informative.

"I see." She pauses, retools. "Where's your partner?"

"Out of town. A conference in New York."

"His attendance at this conference is verifiable?"

"I don't see why it wouldn't be."

"Huh," she says, hard stop. Her brow peaks like she's seen all this before, heard this story already. A rerun and she's curious whether Nathan did this to me. She's wondering if I've come up with an elaborate cover for the bruises on my neck. But she must see I'm not lying. And what would be the point if I was? Why come here to report a fantastical crime that my partner perpetrated? A desperate plea for help?

"Do you need me to verify—"

"I'll take care of that." She clicks her pen and slides a legal pad my way. "Just note the location here."

"Sure." I pull my shoulders back, scrawl *NYU Langone Medical Center* shakily. That she can verify so much with so little is unsurprising—yet still jarring. "And I'd appreciate discretion. Given, you know, the circumstances."

Detective Henning hesitates, then: "Every effort will be made to be discreet, but investigations necessarily probe where we might not be comfortable."

Her words tighten my stomach, but before I can protest, she cuts me off. "I'm not going to get into the specifics of attempted homicide, but I can tell you this much. You've been assaulted."

Of course I've been assaulted!

"It's evident from the markings on your neck that the intention was to cause significant harm to your person. Given the intimate context, where on your body, it looks like aggravated assault." Her gaze finally departs my throat.

"Aggravated?"

"Much more serious than simple assault. Significantly so." She takes back her legal pad and I shiver. "A couple of last q's before I leave you with the paperwork. Drug use?"

"What?"

"Do you use drugs recreationally?"

"No." The sweat pearling on my brow, the trembling and chattering and rubbery concentration; there's not a lot of daylight between symptoms of both withdrawal and recounting that time you were strangled in a gay sex sauna.

"How about sexual partners? How many?"

"Are you for real?"

"Are you?" Her question strikes like a bat to the skull, and the blow leaves me reeling. "You said Nathan's your partner. Not your husband?"

"Yeah." I wipe my forehead.

"How about that, then?"

"What?" I follow her eyes to the wedding band on my finger. "We just, we like to wear them. Like an engagement ring or something, I guess."

Another uneasy stretch of silence.

"I want to be clear with you, Oliver." The edge in her tone dulls. "What you're describing here is serious and very concerning to me. I want you to know I'm fully appreciative of the situation. Of the physical and emotional harm you've experienced."

Despite her incredulity, this last bit loosens the knot in my chest. Maybe this is it. This might do exactly what was intended. Kristian will be confronted. My threat may have already scared him off, but Detective Henning will be the death knell for his game. Whatever the hell that game actually is. I'm even a bit proud. I stood up. Refused to be scared—at least, visibly scared to him.

"You've done very well providing us this photo," Detective Henning says. "Bathhouses are required by law to keep registers of patrons. I'll let you know what turns up."

I exhale. "Thank you."

She opens the folder to a pile of waiting forms. Humiliating and invasive queries thirsty for wet ink. "I want to emphasize something else. Your well-being. You're a victim, Oliver. I can put you in touch with services. People you can talk to. Counselors. Would you like contacts?"

"Yes." Though I won't be speaking with anyone on any list. Victim services are completely outside the scope of my mission here.

As I put pen to paper, she pushes her card across the table. "You can call me. Anytime. If you recall details, want updates, anything." The smile she wore when she first walked in reappears, suggesting our time is over. "And I may contact you. If we locate your attacker."

"Sure." I wince as crime TV flickers through my mind. Perps in line-ups. Victim IDs. "Of course, whatever needs to happen."

"Thanks, Oliver."

If she calls, when she calls, I'll figure it out. Nathan works in twelve- to fifteen-hour stretches. There'll be plenty of ways to cross that bridge when it comes.

She abandons me to complete my paperwork. The forms. The details. The timeline. A description of Kristian—I'm careful to note the accent and its perceived origin. My own medical history, with a heavy focus on all things tawdry.

When I've finished, another officer returns me to Detective Henning.

"Perfect." She tucks the folder under her arm and we walk up front together. On the way, I order an Uber and grow guiltily confident. Detective Rachel Henning seems to *maybe* get it. The entirety of my situation, that is. There's nothing special about it. Just another person caught in the wrong place at the wrong time. I put myself there, which I take responsibility for, but knowledge of that fact must stay out of my relationship.

Just before reception, she stops and turns my way.

"Please have your throat looked at," she says. "If not by your partner, then somebody."

• •

The Uber peels off into darkness, and I find an unwelcome guest waiting at the house. Tom. Fucking Tom Vogt.

I search vehicles on both sides of the dimly lit street, making sure my eyes aren't lying. His Audi convertible sits across from our place—top down. Goddammit. I told Nathan *no*. I told him I didn't want company. Why didn't he listen? Even if he didn't believe me, why couldn't he just respect my wishes?

Nathan is such a fucking parent. I pause, noting how quickly I've returned to square one. From covering up to longing to resentment over the course of a single day. The guilt makes me even angrier.

"Oliver!" Tom strides my way. He waves both hands wildly like a Gucci'd-up circus chimpanzee. A smarmy, lanky, smug kind of corporate gay.

"Tom." I half-ass a smile. "How are you?"

He embraces me too tight and our chests press. When he pulls back, worry lengthens his face. "Oh my god, Oliver. Nathan called me. He told me *everything*. I can't believe it." Tom wears his usual handmade blazer atop his usual pressed button-down and tailored slacks. He must've driven straight from work, tapered crocodile shoes clacking on city sidewalk.

I hope he didn't see what car I got out of—

"You just Uber home?"

"Yeah." Heat crawls up my back. "Had to run a quick—"

"Were you at the ER?"

"—errand." What's with the rapid-fire questions? Is this a wellness check or has Tom been tasked with something else? "The ER is overkill for this."

"You're not a doctor, Oliver."

"It's not a big deal." Masking my irritation isn't so easy. Even if Nathan called him, Tom has my number. Tom didn't have to be a surprise. Something unsettling says he wanted to be just that.

"Oliver, my god. Not a big deal? You were mugged. And . . ." He leans in. I shut my eyes tight. "Your throat. Jesus. Does it hurt?"

"I'm fine. I mean, it's okay. It did hurt, but it doesn't now." He follows me up the front steps. This won't be effortless; he won't conclude his presence is unnecessary at best. I fumble with my house key. Tom hangs back a few feet, waiting to be invited in like a vampire.

"Want, like, a drink or something?"

"Please, and I hope you'll have one too." He plucks his phone from an unseen jacket pocket. "You've sure as hell earned one."

Earned one? I'm being rewarded for surviving with both his company and a cocktail?

I unlock the front door. Tom's eyes are on his screen, ballerina thumbs pirouetting over slick glass. Part of me is grateful his attention is elsewhere. Another slice resents him even more for it. Some friend of Nathan's. I've been assaulted, and he can't be bothered to keep his phone out of sight while he dutifully checks in.

But Tom's important. A Senate staffer. Duty never stops calling, I guess.

I'm in the foyer when he taps my shoulder. "You missed this."

"What?" I spin, and he pinches an envelope between two fingers like a cigarette. Pastel stationery that might accompany any corner-store card.

He shrugs. "Must've fallen from the slot."

Right, I haven't checked the mailbox since Nathan flew out Wednesday.

"Thanks." I take the envelope along with the rest of the mail—bills and a Williams Sonoma catalog for the Williams Sonoma dream house it was delivered to—and set the whole stack on the entryway table. Square envelope on top.

"What can I get you?" I gesture to the drawing room's bar cart.

"Scotch if you've got it. Just a finger or two," he says.

As I pour two drinks, I track Tom in the corner of my eye. Salt-and-pepper hair artfully disheveled. Fingers racing across his phone at light speed. He loosens a top button and meanders into the library, stopping beneath the decades-old portrait of Nathan's parents. Kathy's grimace cranks a burner in my lizard brain. Hot as the Fourth of July we flew to New York for me to meet her.

The sweltering stroll down East Sixty-second Street to the Kleins' co-op had brought my greatest nightmare to breathing, beating life:

they were *that rich.* By the time we passed Park Avenue, the heat and the panic had me gasping. Even the doorman gave a pity nod when we walked into icy air and carpeting so plush I nearly sank to my ankles. Kathy didn't open her own front door but stood waiting in the foyer, crossbow cocked and ready.

"This must be *Olivier,*" she greeted.

"Great to meet you, Kathy." I reached for a handshake that never happened. "It's actually Oliver."

"He's very handsome, Nathan." The dual precedents of mispronouncing my name and speaking of me in the third person were set. We followed her wake of rosewater perfume deeper into a gilded WASP nest, and she turned to say, "If he'd like to smoke, he can use the terrace off the dining room."

Nathan shot me a look. "Oliver doesn't smoke."

"Curious." Kathy's jaw tensed and for the first and last time, we made eye contact. "Thought I smelled cigarettes. In any case, if he changes his mind, he knows just where to go."

I'd bit hard into my lip and finished her thought: *hell.*

"At least it's not hanging over your bed," Tom says, catching me staring at the painting. He wanders back into the drawing room, still banging away at his phone.

"Is that work?" I ask, offering a tumbler.

"No." He pushes his tongue against the inside of his cheek. "Meet-Lockr. There's a Republican conference at the Kennedy Center. I'm up to my balls in midwestern closet cases. Literally."

"Here." I thrust his drink at him harder than intended and nearly spill it. Something about the way he says *midwestern.* He doesn't seem to notice. Or maybe he doesn't mind—he's nearly finished the pour when I take a seat in an opposite high-back.

"Speaking of work," Tom says, "you called off, right? Tomorrow? You shouldn't be going in after everything. Take a breather. Nathan'll be home. Enjoy the day." He draws out his last few words. Second-guessing his flippant attitude?

Work. Shit. With everything that's happened, I forgot about it. In this singular and very narrow case, Tom is right. I shouldn't go in tomorrow.

He's also inadvertently created an opening, and I seize it. "I can't call off. It's actually a big day, and I should be asleep already." This is a lie, and Tom's dark eyes narrow suspiciously. He might not believe me, but it doesn't matter. Social protocol takes over. Even vampires must take their leave.

"You're right. Maybe it's best to go in. Keep from dwelling." Tom stands, his empty glass on the coffee table. No coaster. I notice only because Nathan would have had a seizure.

"You've checked in." I laugh. "You can report back that I'm okay. Tell Nathan I love him, and I'll see him soon." Tom smiles nervously as though my joke makes him uncomfortable. This gives me a spoonful of pleasure. The first I've had today, in fact. We hug once more—too close again, and his hand brushes my hip bone. Only for a flash, but long enough to register. Tom's a master of ambiguous body contact, and locking the dead bolt behind him is beyond satisfying.

He's not even to his car, and I've opened my laptop. I need to email my boss, Dr. Kimberly Martin. A med school colleague of Nathan's. I'm the receptionist at her private practice. Answer phones. Schedule appointments. Take the occasional patient blood pressure when the technician's hands are full.

I don't mind the job. Kimberly's cynical humor is a reprieve from Nathan's moral absolutism, and she's the closest thing to a real friend I have in this city. Even if she is Nathan's first. It's that I simply don't have a choice *but* to work there. Nathan got me the job. It's difficult to land employment of any kind because of that tiny checkbox on every application. A housekeeping detail that torpedoes my chances like the fucking *Lusitania*. Every. Single. Time.

Have you ever been convicted of a crime other than a minor traffic violation?

Gmail takes its sweet time to load, and I write an email to Kimberly, explaining the situation—the robbery—and that I won't be in tomorrow. I'll keep her posted. When I shut my laptop, my thoughts catch on my most pressing concern: Nathan's home tomorrow.

I scroll my phone for the screengrab until Kristian's ice eyes stare back. My hackles rise, and I tap the screen.

Are you sure you want to delete this photo from your device?

Yes. But it could still be useful, and I'm being paranoid, given to emotional spirals.

If I'm not careful, I'll avalanche.

9

I circle arrivals at Reagan National for the fourth time.

Inching along with my hazards flashing, but security keeps waving me off. LOADING AND UNLOADING ONLY, the sign they point to. Waiting in the cell phone lot was an option, but I can't stomach sitting in a silent car. Claustrophobic and coffin-like.

No, I must keep moving, keep doing. I'm already a wreck. Another of Nathan's sleeping pills couldn't stop me from waking at three thirty in the morning. Intestines twisting. Liquid shits. I fixated on the ceiling as if in some kind of vegetative state. Like the victim of a highly venomous snakebite. Conscious paralysis on a ventilator while the body clears the toxins. I couldn't do or concentrate on anything else. I only stared—unmoving, for hours.

When I turn beneath the arrivals overhang again, Nathan's curbside. Roller suitcase, fashionable jeans, and an NYU sweatshirt. A slice of color from the lemon oxford underneath. It's overwhelmingly hot. A damp and stifling June day in Washington, but Nathan's bad circulation keeps him cold on planes.

He waves, collects his bag. I swallow, unlock the doors, and pop the trunk.

It shuts, and he startles me by my window.

"I'll drive," he says after opening the door.

When we switch places, he hugs me, tight but hesitantly. The sort of cautious embrace one gives the fragile. Someone you fear you might break. We kiss briefly. Remnants of cologne and jet fuel and starched linen cling to his neck.

"I didn't want you picking me up in the first place."

"There's no point in a cab when I'm home from work—"

"I'm on expenses," he interrupts. "Your well-being is all that matters right now. Priority number one."

The same security guard chases us off. Nathan shifts gears, and we pull away from the pickup zone. Silence unspools while he buckles up and finds his way into a far lane.

I'm awash in opposing feelings. Happy and relieved to see him, to smell him, to hear his voice. I'm also wrapped in suffocating guilt, as if Kristian's hands were still around my neck. The bruises Nathan has yet to comment on.

I stifle my unease as best I can. I can't smother it entirely—if I could, then I'd have done so—but I can lock it away. At some point, I'll have to deal. After I've dealt with Nathan. The house, the bathroom, everything else first. "Nice flight?"

"A little turbulent," Nathan answers. He's older than me, more attractive, lean and distinguished. At least, I've always thought so. He's one of those rare men who age well. Sandy-brown hair and an aquiline nose. An early streak of silver above each ear.

He's very fit too. More substantive than me, but he's got the natural frame for it. I've got the frame of a scarecrow. A scarecrow from Tyre, Indiana.

His hand finds my thigh. The touch of his fingers makes me flinch, and I hope he doesn't notice. Or that he chalks it up to rough road.

"I've got groceries in the back seat," I say happily. "Stopped by the store on the way. Dinner tonight, remember?" *You're okay,* I tell myself. I'm unwinding. The content of my conversation is returning to baseline. Domesticity. Dinner. Nothing beyond an impending glass of wine.

The turn signal chimes as Nathan merges onto the highway. Eyes fixed on the road ahead, he asks, "Think they'll be okay back there for a bit longer? The groceries, I mean?"

"Duck needs to defrost. Why?"

"We need to make a stop on the way home."

"Sure." My agreement is a natural response. Like breathing or the beating of my heart. Nathan's always needing to make a stop on the way home. To cross one more errand off his list. Tie up some hanging chore. His type A personality works in list form.

I don't think much of it until the cross streets start ticking by like a time bomb. A countdown to the street I'd given an Uber driver last night. I've only just begun to wrap my thoughts around the possibility when we pull into the parking lot.

What am I going to do? What the fuck am I going to do!?

Screws in my chest tighten, clamping my lungs within a squeezing set of ribs. Like a pair of balloons in the careless hands of a child, and they might burst any moment.

Nathan looks my way and opens the driver-side door. We're at the police station. The same one I'd left just last night. Nathan's going to make me report being assaulted.

For the second time.

• •

That same burnt coffee reek.

An aroma gone so stale, it's a stench. Nathan and I sit at the exact same table in the exact room from before.

What had been friendly territory has gone full-blown hostile and my guts churn. If Detective Rachel Henning walks through that door, she'll turn from ally to enemy in Nathan's presence.

Will it even be her? Detective work is shift work, at least according to TV. Same as Nathan's trauma calls. Detective Henning and Nathan both catch cases randomly—whatever a dangerous world sends hurtling their way.

I count back the hours since she asked whether Nathan's conference trip was verifiable. How long is a shift? When did Detective Henning's start? There's no way for me to answer these questions. Of course, she'll figure it out when she sees the paperwork. The victim's name, a duplicate. The crime, a different thing entirely.

As long as she's not here now, I can explain it away later by phone.

Nathan holds my hand under the table. His touch is both tight and ice-cold. My instinct is to snatch myself away. We're in public. I've never been comfortable with PDA no matter the kind. We're different that way. Nathan's from New York. As in, the City. He's never experienced life as a gay man in rural Indiana. Affection driven underground. Taboo. An invitation for contempt and violence.

Hector and I would leave an empty seat between us in the movie theater. Order takeout for dinner; eat in our apartment, where affection was liberated.

Tension pent up. Transgressive. No doubt the misplaced undercurrent of wrongdoing made sex explosive and primal. Great sex and violent arguments. Hector's hands around my throat in both instances.

No doubt it also played a role in what we got mixed up in. First him. Then me. The constant hunt for an outlet. For sexual energy, then for other things.

Nathan is nothing like him, and I couldn't be more grateful. Hector and I weren't sustainable. We were a cigarette. A smoldering stimulant. A filthy habit.

Perhaps Nathan and I aren't sustainable either. But he's well adjusted, confident, and secure. This self-assuredness has rubbed off, as was the intention when I agreed to move here. If we're unsustainable, we're less like a cigarette and more like the sun. A seemingly endless supply of energy to draw from. An expiration date that's more of a technicality than a reality.

I smile at Nathan through a bit bottom lip.

"Don't be nervous," he instructs. "You're a victim."

I want to scream that I've heard that before. In this fucking room—

The door opens, Detective Henning walks in, and the blood drops to my feet. Same jeans. Same light button-down. My knuckles whiten around Nathan's.

"Hello." She shakes Nathan's hand, then mine. "Detective Rachel Henning."

I leap into the conversation before she can even sit down. "I'm Oliver Park. This is my partner, Nathan Klein."

Nathan shifts in his seat. Is he taken aback by my sudden gregariousness or merely getting comfortable?

"Nice to meet you both," Detective Henning says, and my stomach flutters. Is she . . . is she still an ally? Is she going to play along with my stupid game?

Her same sharp eyes meet mine and linger there.

"I've brought paperwork to file a criminal complaint," she begins, before leaning back in her chair, fists clasped atop her lap. "But first, I'd like you to simply tell me what's going on."

It takes every fiber of my being, every muscle, every strand of sinew holding me together, to remain still in my chair. Detective Henning plans to let me get away with this charade.

•   •   •

Nathan and I exit the police station. Assault and robbery, reported. Filed away. Or, rather, paper clipped to the folder already bearing my name. My fingers and thumbs are ink stained from giving prints. Detective Henning hadn't asked for prints yesterday, but she did this afternoon.

"That wasn't so bad, was it?" Nathan says as he opens the car door for me. "It's like the detective said: the probability of catching your attacker is unknowable. Unless you don't report. Then it's zero."

His lecturing might've been bothersome in the past, but it rolls off my back now. Surprise elation leaves no room for resentment. The more distance Nathan puts between us and the police, the further I process my discussion with Detective Henning. The second, lie-riddled one.

She'd dutifully listened to my cover story. I dutifully filled out a fresh set of forms. She said she'd be in touch. This time, I expect a call from her sooner rather than later. To demand the explanation she didn't ask for in front of Nathan. To parse the differences between my reports.

She also asked to see a timestamped receipt verifying Nathan had been out of town until noon today. Domestic incidents must account for a significant volume of her caseload. Nathan had plenty of receipts on his phone, but he seemed put off by the request.

We turn onto our street, though we still have many blocks to go. Something else Detective Henning said sticks out. Something I hadn't considered. She'd been referring to the fake mugging.

"These things are rarely a one-off," she said, taking a question from Nathan. "They typically fit within a larger pattern, which is why it's critical to report, no matter the chances of recovering whatever's been stolen. Every reported incident is another opportunity to discern a pattern."

Nathan had nudged me beneath the table, no doubt vindicated. She might've been speaking of muggings or robberies, but she could just as easily have meant my attack. The same logic applies to my lies and my truth.

A larger pattern. There wasn't anything special about me specifically. Pure happenstance, chance, that my path crossed Kristian's within Haus's darkness. Half-naked on a barstool in a stew of sex, I was an opportunity for a lurking predator. Someone who'd been stalking the tall grass all along. Patient and hungry.

It could've been someone else, which means it could've happened before. Maybe even since. The knot in my throat goes down like a sandbag as that horrifying realization sinks in. And if I hadn't escaped? If I hadn't slashed his face with a key?

No other wounds or scars or bruises marked his exposed body. The small room was dark, but my lust-driven eyes searched him from head to toe—taking in every detail. Down to his neatly trimmed pubic hair and uncut dick. One of two things is true: either I'd been his first or there are others. Guys whose fingers hadn't found a weapon with which to fight back. Where are they? Or, rather, where are their bodies?

An invisible centipede scales my spine. What would they look like by now?

As the car brakes, I come up for air. Breathing in the relative safety of my home—my and Nathan's home—but still wondering why the hell Detective Henning covered for me.

10

Legs cramped from economy plus, I park in front of our house. Cut the engine, cut the lights. A three-story townhome, four-sided brick. A Georgian dollhouse with black, functional shutters—I'd been so particular about the shutters actually closing over the windows. When I took possession from my family's foundation, it was the first thing to change. I didn't want anything ornamental adorning our forever house.

Because that's what it was.

Roots with Oliver made sense. The very same roots Mother would have me sever. She doesn't appreciate how deep they run, how inextricably they bind me to him and him to me. A thick knot of pulsating emotional vasculature. Cutting them risks killing both of us.

I collect my roller from the trunk and follow Oliver through the front door. The heavy aperture behind which the manifestation of my life plan unfolds with deliberate predictability. A routine I suspect Oliver finds stifling at best. And at worst?

Tepid. Boring. Banal. Everything he resents is everything keeping him safe. On the straight and narrow.

"Want a drink?" he asks from the drawing room as I drop my things off in the kitchen. "Glass of wine or something?"

"Please." I hesitate, dehydrated from the flight, and last night's liquor's still jackhammering my temples from within. "You know what? Don't bother. I don't need the calories. Maybe tea?"

But he's already appeared in the doorway with an unopened merlot. Beneath a five-o'clock shadow that's much closer to midnight, Oliver dimples his cheeks. "Sure?"

He doesn't typically push booze on me, but maybe I can afford a few alcoholic carbs after all. "One glass."

"You got it." The sound of the cork slipping from a fresh bottle is more satisfying than I'd care to admit. Though being honest with myself—if not everyone else—has never been a challenge. He tips the bottle and slides a glass of oaky red my way.

I take a swallow. "What did you get up to while I was gone?"

"I got mugged." He smiles as if it's a joke, though his tone's the furthest thing from comical. The fingerprint bruises on his neck look more menacing each time I see them.

"Anything else?"

"Not much." He plucks a second wineglass from the cabinet. He's never been a drinker, thank god, but he's given himself quite a pour. Probably—and justifiably—nerves. "Just, uh, the usual stuff. Trashy books, trashy TV, shit like that."

"Oh?" He has too much time on his hands home alone, and now look what's happened. "Nothing else?"

"Tom came over. But you knew that already."

"And running."

"Huh?"

"You were out for a night jog." I spin my glass on the counter by the stem. "When the . . . when it happened."

"Yeah. I was."

"Go for more than one while I was away?"

He turns his back to me, plugs the bottle with a decorative stopper. "No. Just that once."

It's not so unusual that he'd say he'd gone only once. It's how he waited until he was no longer facing me before answering. I wasn't lying to Mother; I speak his body language.

A sudden question occurs. "Isn't it heavy?"

"What?"

"Running with your wallet?"

He spins my way, slaps the dish towel over his shoulder, and drains a final bloodred gulp of a glass he's finished in what, two swallows?

"I hold on to it in my hand."

"Uh-huh," I say. A marked pause as we lock eyes. Uncomfortably, so I pivot: "What shows did you watch?"

"Nothing memorable." He shrugs. He could be avoiding specifics because he's hiding something. Or perhaps he avoids them because he's apathetic. Fleshing out details takes energy. More than I'm worth. Deep roots can still be mildewed by apathy.

He widens his eyes as if struck by a sudden thought. "I left a duck recipe on the printer upstairs. I should start food prep."

As he vanishes down the hall, I call out, "I'm gonna change. Clothes smell like airplane."

A muted reply: "Sure, Nat."

I start to leave my wine on the counter but opt to bring it with me. Taking the curved staircase one slow step at a time, I run through our experience at the police station with Detective Henning. Something about the conversation didn't sit right. Asking for verification of my travels, taking my fingerprints as if *I were* the one who put hands on my husband.

Boyfriend, Mother's disembodied voice whispers. *You're not* actually *married. And he's not* actually *your husband.*

I shut the door to our bedroom. Footfalls on the vaulted ceiling suggest Oliver's in the third-floor study like he said. I'm not naïve or stupid or willfully ignorant when it comes to the consequences of apathy. It's happened to Mother too many times to count. Her pain is a big part of why I fixate on fidelity. Whatever understanding or unspoken agreement she may have had—or still has—with Father didn't ease decades of emotional estrangement. For everything Kathy Klein isn't, the woman's ability to endure heartbreak is, well, heartbreaking.

Unzipping my bag on the duvet, I reason through an imaginary affair of Oliver's.

None of the typical symptoms are present. No incessant phone calls, only to turn into hang-ups when answered. No sudden preoccupation with appearances on his part; he runs for other reasons entirely.

He's attractive. No denying that. Strung out, fresh from outpatient detox, and he still stole my breath. Brown hair that bleaches in summer. Jaw square as any all-American boy-next-door's. Skinny, sure, but I've got a type. He's got an ass any bottom would kill for and a smile that sinks teeth into you. No one would call him sophisticated, but he's nothing if not intelligent. Extraordinarily so, and surely some man would see what I'd seen years ago. Fall hard, same as me. Decide to say *fuck it if he's taken* and go for it.

I drain the wine, pull on a cotton tee, and rummage through my bags for moisturizer. Plane air is brutal on the skin, and mine isn't youthful like Oliver's. Speaking of.

Deep breath, and I slip his phone from my back pocket.

He left it on the kitchen counter. It's low on battery and his charger's in the bedroom. Maybe I've done him a favor by bringing it up here. I run my fingers over polished glass—chipped because Oliver doesn't take care of his things—and tap the screen.

Anyone whose mind had traveled where mine had would peek at a lover's abandoned phone. Make themselves feel better—or worse. I unlock it with the same pin for everything else. Scroll his calendar, where literally zero events are scheduled. His texts, but they're all from me with an occasional back-and-forth with Kimberly—my friend, his boss. The phone call with me. The FaceTime with me. The call with Darryl about the flooded bathroom I've yet to appraise.

Back on his home screen, I swipe for a very particular app. A calculator, and when it opens to reveal nothing, the back of my skull tingles.

This is a surprise.

Oliver deleted MeetLockr.

11

OLIVER

"Tilly has no water," Nathan calls from downstairs. Not even home an hour and I've already disappointed him.

"Sorry, babe," I shout. Our third-floor office is a nook. A tiny space where the sharp roofline angles the ceiling down in awkward places and directions. Six-foot-one Nathan has to stoop, so he's rarely up here. I come here to hide.

We have a desktop computer, an older model, on a heavy desk. I cleared the browser history on my laptop, deleted MeetLockr from my phone, but I'm unsure if my tracks have been covered up here or not.

It's possible I used Nathan's aversion to the third story as an excuse to leave it for later. But now there is no later. Everything must be removed.

"Oliver?" he calls as I press *delete permanently* after ticking every available box. Cookies. Autofill forms and passwords. Search engine terms.

"Coming!"

Back in the kitchen, Tilly's water bowl is already full. Refilled by Nathan. But I could've sworn I'd done just that. In fact, I have the distinct memory of doing so this morning. I plunge a finger into the water. It's not cold, not fresh.

Why would Nathan say something like that? Why would he accuse me of being irresponsible just for the sake of doing so?

Is he punishing me?

Of course he doesn't know. He can't know. Dragging me to the police station is testament to that. *Police.* My heartbeat leaps with my thoughts; I made a false report. I doubled down. So why did Detective Henning play along? Why didn't she call me out?

I'm being paranoid again. Over Tilly's water dish for fuck's sake. Besides, my memory might be mistaken. I can hardly blame it, given all the lying, all the narratives I've bought into enough to deliver earnestly to Nathan. To Detective Henning. To myself.

What else might I have misremembered?

Nonsense. I palm my face. Tap water comes out ice-cold, but Nathan might've run it hot by mistake before turning it back. The result, a luke-warm bowl.

Get a hold of yourself. Deep breath in. Deep breath out. *You're being ridiculous. Paranoid and ridiculous.*

On the topic of paranoia: my phone sits by the KitchenAid mixer. Carelessly left behind when I remembered the upstairs computer. But that's the nice thing about excising secrets. You can leave devices for eager eyes because there's no longer anything to find.

Nathan reenters the kitchen. "Bathroom's something else," he says, tossing our mail stack onto the counter. "We're not showering in there for a while. Did Darryl mention an estimate?"

"Three thousand," I say, but my voice catches, and it comes out garbled.

Nathan knots his brow.

I clear my throat. "Thirty-five hundred dollars."

"Jesus," he says. Avoiding Nathan's eyes, I carry the grocery bags to the sink. I fill one side with water to defrost the duck and change the subject. "What do you think about currant-and-cinnamon glaze? For the bird tonight?"

"A bit Christmas, no?" Nathan sorts through our mail, dividing it into stacks to recycle and stacks to open. "Is there something more summer you can do?"

"But this is the recipe I printed—"

"Evening's supposed to be cool. Maybe we can have it on the patio? Like orange duck or something?"

"Sure." The still half-frozen bird strikes stainless with a bubbly thud. "I'll find one for orange duck."

"Wonder what this is?" Nathan asks. I turn to find him holding a yellow envelope. The one Tom collected from our front steps as he followed me into the house last night. I'd forgotten all about it.

A thought strikes like a bolt of electricity. Crackling static panic.

The envelope has no addresses. No sender. No receiver. Which means the mailman didn't bring it. Someone would've had to drop it off personally. A *personal* message.

I clench my hands into tight fists. Kristian knows my name and he knows my address. If he looked at my license, he saw it.

Nathan tucks his index finger beneath the sealed paper lip and tears.

My heart drums like a turbine engine. This is it. This is game over. I'm a fool. Foolish for thinking I could keep it from Nathan. Foolish for not predicting what Kristian might do next. What he might do with details gleaned from my ID.

I bite my tongue, taste the warm tin of blood.

Nathan unfolds a slip of stationery. Light from the window over his shoulder shines through cream paper, revealing pen ink. It's handwritten.

My knees start to buckle, so I lock them. I steady myself on the kitchen counter.

"Oliver," Nathan starts, words wrapped in anguish. "Oliver, why?"

His eyes meet mine. I say nothing. My thoughts grind to a halt, incapable of producing speech even if I did have words.

Nathan squints in disbelief. "Smoking?"

What? He tosses the note on the counter, and I snatch it up. I scan line by line, struggling to consume the message quicker than my brain can unpack it. Key words jump out. *Summer. Cigarettes. Considerate.*

It's not from Kristian. I exhale. Sweat from my thumb smudges the salutation, but it reads, *Dear Neighbor*. A note from next door. It's summer, and they leave their windows open to cool off. They ask that we be considerate before lighting up in the back. Secondhand smoke drifts inside their home.

Returning the note to the counter, I catch heat from Nathan's glare.

"Why were you smoking?" He almost glowers. "You quit. You promised me. You agreed that it's filthy and disgusting."

"I'm sorry." I try to bottle explosive relief. "I'm really sorry. I have quit. I bought a pack yesterday. Between the mugging and the bathtub, I needed something. I felt stupid after, and I've already tossed them."

Nathan tapers his eyes, but he's buying it. Unhappily. "You promised—"

"They're gone. Taken out with the garbage."

He opens his mouth but stops short of a rebuttal. This isn't a battle he'll win. My excuse, though untrue, is a good one.

"One cigarette." I try to laugh, to joke. "It could've been worse." Nathan will know that's the truth. He'll know to be grateful that after such a harrowing experience, I've only given in to a cigarette.

"I'm going to do my travel expenses." He abandons me in the kitchen, but I remain still. Frozen by relief and terror in equal measure. A false alarm, sure, but how much luck do I have left? How much more can I afford to squander?

Kristian knows my address if he knows my name. His behavior might be part of a larger pattern. A pattern of spinning sticky webs in the dank corners of bathhouses. Long needle-like legs walking silk tightropes, creeping toward paralyzed prey. Wrapping spindly fingers around their necks. Mouth parts moving and chewing like spinning blades.

That's the thing with spiderwebs. Spiderwebs and patterns. They grow. They expand to fill whatever space they occupy.

Kristian messaged me. He reached out through sex and steam and walls painted in porn. Through the anonymity of Haus and out into sobering daylight. He followed me. And he's expanded.

Hi Oliver.

12

Down the hall, Nathan spits mouthwash into a guest-bathroom sink. I sit on the edge of the bed, listening to the sounds of his nightly ritual. Buzzing electric toothbrush. Flushing toilet. Lathering soap.

This is the routine I chose. This is all I wanted. Normalcy. An escape from the dangerous direction my life had veered. *Nathan's promise*. How Nathan saved me.

The lights turn off, and he pads into our room. Cheeks bright pink from liquor.

"Pepper spray," he says, keychain mace dangling from his finger. "Keep it on you when you run, okay?"

"Sure." He tucks it in my nightstand. It's not in any sealed packaging. When did he have time to buy me pepper spray? "Thanks."

"I kept it in my work bag." He winks, seeming to read my mind. "For late shifts, but I'd rather you have it."

He slips from silk pajama bottoms and casts them on the leather Eames lounger in the corner—a name I know only because Nathan's taught me what good chairs are. His shirt comes off next, tossed just the same. He stands in tight-fitting underwear and glasses.

Thin wire frames I found charming, effortlessly sexy, when I first saw them. Not so much because I have a fetish for guys in glasses, but what it meant when he wore them with me. It meant intimacy. No contacts. No meticulously coifed hair. Just glasses and zero styling gel. Nathan, natural, without the mask. He kisses me and climbs into bed.

"Christ. What a day," he says. We're both on our backs beneath cool sheets. Our eyes fixed to the slow-turning blades of the ceiling fan. "I nearly fucked up my talk."

"I doubt it was as bad as you—"

"The assault, it threw me for a loop. I couldn't concentrate and I closed out my notes midway through. Stumbled. Stuttered. The whole thing almost came apart."

"You're not a politician, Nat. You're not Tom. No one expects a crisp—"

"*I* expect it." He draws in a deep breath. "One mugging and you've got bruises, we're down a bathroom, and I nearly lost respect from colleagues. Whatever fucker did this doesn't appreciate or care how much damage he caused. And for what? Eighty bucks?"

"I'm sorry." What else can I say? He's right about everything. Except the mugger.

His hand finds mine beneath the blankets. He hooks my pinky with his, and soft lips travel my neck. "Don't be sorry. This isn't your fault."

Only it is, and for a moment, I consider reciprocating. Then he kisses my ear.

Fragrant with mint and bourbon, his breath whistles past the tiny hairs inside. A breeze that diverts blood flow to my chest and sours my stomach. A fight-or-flight response. I turn to mask my revulsion. "I'm sorry, I'm really tired, and I'm still—"

"It's fine," he whispers, his breath mercifully drifting into the space between us instead of my ear, like Kristian's. "It's just I've been away for nearly a week, so . . . is this okay?"

I know what he's asking, and I nod. He begins to masturbate under the sheets with his left hand. His right wanders beneath the elastic hem of my briefs. He fondles me as he jerks himself off.

He hopes I'll stir and stiffen, but it won't happen. I've got nothing for him but guilt.

I'm amused by what this might look like to an outsider, someone expecting a relationship between two men to be saturated in sex. Straight men saying gays have it good because it's all sex all the time. Whenever they want it. However they want it. Just males and their wanton biology.

Nathan and I did have good sex a handful of times. Never what I would call great, but I try not to compare. It isn't fair, and it isn't helpful. But Hector and me—that was great sex. You can't miss something you've never had, and the inverse is also true. You can't lie to yourself when you know you've had better.

Nathan pulls his hand from my underwear and rolls out of bed to wash up. When he returns, he opens his drawer and sleeping pills rattle.

"Did you take some of these?"

"Huh?"

"My Ambien?"

How does he know? He can't count in the dark, and no way he senses the vacuum left from three missing pills. But it doesn't matter how. Only that he does.

"I couldn't sleep after."

"Be careful." The bottle shakes as he pops one. "It's a slippery slope. You know that from your meetings."

"I know." I shorten my tone, hoping to punctuate the topic. I fail.

"Might be a good idea to head back to NA. Maybe just a meeting or two until this blows over and we get back to normal?"

Get back to normal. Now, there's an idea. I want that more than anything. Normal is what saved me, got me out of the need for Narcotics Anonymous in the first place.

Nathan doesn't wait for an answer. "A place to talk things out."

"I'm okay, Nat. I promise."

"The cigarette too—"

"It's not the same thing. You know that." My cheeks fever. "Don't pretend otherwise."

"All right." He sighs and turns his back to mine. "Good night, babe."

"Night." I shut my eyes, but sleep is an impossibility.

· · ·

In the morning, the Metro escalator descends with a certain inevitability. Down a vaulted, coffered tunnel to the station below. My commute is a lengthy trip on the Red Line from the District to Kimberly's office in Silver Spring, Maryland.

"Don't forget to leave a key for Darryl in the mailbox," Nathan had said before departing in pale-green scrubs. I'd caught a glimpse of myself in the foyer mirror. The bruises ringing my throat seem to have grown worse, but it was hard to tell. And even if they did fade, does it matter? They're either there or they aren't. How much or to what extent is irrelevant.

I skipped running this morning for Nathan's benefit. If I was mugged, I should have a traumatic response, right? The truth is, I've never needed to run more. Runner's high combats the itch for other, less healthy ones—and now my *legitimate* traumatic anxiety has no outlet. It simply builds like a pressure cooker.

I crouch close to the side of the escalator, but people still push past me. Bumping my left arm. Brushing my shoulder with theirs. My eyes are dry. I don't need a mirror to know they're bloodshot and bagged.

I'm in no hurry. If I'm late, my ordeal over the weekend is an ideal excuse. Still, I can't shake that niggling sensation. Eyes on me, frosting the back of my neck. I feel I'm being watched in the eerie way people do. My pulse thumps in my ears. A guilty conscience. Has to be.

A train hisses up, sending feral pages of *The Washington Post* snapping through the air. The doors open. I find a niche and take hold of the steel bar. Departing the station, we all lurch backward then forward in synchrony.

I start to play an episode of *This American Life* but find a missed call instead.

"Hi, Oliver. Detective Henning." Her voicemail ramps up my heartbeat. It keeps pace with the hurtling train. "Call me back as soon as possible. I have a few questions for you. This is my cell. Talk soon."

I hang up and scour passenger after passenger, every face in the crowded car. I'd managed to compartmentalize, to push thoughts of Kristian out of my mind for most of the morning. A return to routine made pretending easier.

Detective Henning's message put a stop to that.

I spin and crane my neck left and right. None of these faces are Kristian's. There'd be no mistaking it. Even if I forgot the details, even if I could lose sight of those ocean-deep eyes, or his sharp brows, or swept blond hair, there'd be the wound. The laceration on his cheek from the key that saved my life. He cupped his cheek with both hands. Blood between long fingers like wet black paint.

No, Kristian's not here. I can stop thinking otherwise. Sure, he knows my name, he might know where I live, but I haven't heard from him since I replied on MeetLockr. Since I threatened him with a police report, and then took the extra, monumental step of making good on it. And now—bouncing up and down with the train—I search for him where he isn't. Where he can't be.

Of course Detective Henning wants to talk. She's parsing two reports. I am either a victim desperate to keep the lid on an indiscretion, or a manipulative narcissist drawing cops into his drama. For her, the truth must lie somewhere between the two. But what about for me?

The train brakes. Metal screeches. The doors retract.

Another thought springs from a place of optimism. Maybe Detective Henning's already put a stop to it. Perhaps she's checked the records Haus keeps. Matched a photo ID to Kristian's face. She needs me to view a lineup. *That* I can do.

I breathe deeply. Fear is making him a bigger monster than he is. Somehow, he found me on MeetLockr. His avatar was faceless, and mine was too for obvious reasons. But I messaged a lot of guys. Sent them face pics once I'd seen theirs. Had I engaged with Kristian before? Every second of distance between now and then corrodes my memory. One already working overtime to forget.

Sometimes swapping photos escalated in explicitness, sometimes not. The point is, there were many of them. I wouldn't necessarily have remembered Kristian's face. He was intoxicating within the damp exoticism of a bathhouse, but those eyes might not come through the same in pixels. Still, he might've recalled me. There must be significant overlap between MeetLockr and Haus's clientele.

I've almost convinced myself I'm safe. The detective's job is likely already finished, and I'm simply needed to tie up loose ends.

Almost.

Because I can't stop scanning the crowd. Each station bringing fresh faces to scour. None are familiar, none are threats, but it doesn't seem to matter.

Because I can't shake that feeling. That goddamn feeling. The one that tells me I'm not safe. No, doesn't tell, screams. Bulging veins and blue-faced hollering. I'm not safe because I'm being watched. In my pocket, I loop the keychain of Nathan's pepper spray around my pinky.

And I know who's watching me.

13

I'm relieved Kimberly's not in yet. I have time to get situated at reception, to breathe. To prepare for the onslaught of questions about my fake mugging. To call Detective Henning.

Still half an hour until the patient door opens. FIRST CHOICE INTERNAL MEDICINE. DR. KIMBERLY MARTIN, MD stenciled on frosted glass.

We're on the fifth floor of a mid-rise comprised entirely of doctors' offices. And we're the only interior suite, meaning zero windows. I'm unsure if Kimberly likes it this way, a distraction-free space for delivering care. Or if she simply made the mistake of having ovaries on a floor with no fewer than twelve sets of hetero testicles. Swinging to and fro in shriveled scrotums beneath Saint Laurent slacks. Hoarding all the windows for their own private practices.

Okay, Oliver. You can do this.

I sit down at my reception desk, grab the phone, and dial out. On my iPhone, I scroll through my call log for the detective's cell. She answers on the first ring.

"Detective Henning? It's Oliver Park."

"Oliver, hello." She sounds winded. "Give me a sec. I've got a tray of coffees in my hand."

"Sure." A rustling on her end.

"Okay," she starts. "We need to talk."

I coil the phone cord around my index finger and brace. I expected this. She may have gone along with my game at the station with Nathan beside me, but now she can be real. And in my experience, real's never nice.

"I need to be candid with you," she says. "There are consequences for what you've done."

"I'm sorry," I tell her, and I mean it. "I didn't have a choice; Nathan made the decision to report what I told him."

"Again," she corrects. "To report again."

"Look, I can go through my statement, my real statement—"

"*Real* statement? You see how problematic this is, right?"

The tips of my ears burn. She must know which one is which. The report given when I sat before her as a desperate puddle of a person. Not the one I recited while Nathan's shoulder touched mine, our hands held.

"I—"

"You need to understand what a false report means. I've now got to disclose that you came forward twice. With two versions. Vastly different accounts."

"Disclose?"

"In the event we find your attacker, the district attorney's office will require everything I have, and you've given way too much."

"But one's—"

"You lied. Both statements cannot be true. If we charge your attacker, we have a duty to hand over all evidence to the defense, including your false report." A brief pause. "In the meantime, my job is to follow up on your allegations."

Allegations? With each passing second, Detective Henning pivots more adversarial. She wasn't letting me *get away* with anything. Permitting me to lie to both Nathan and herself? An investigative no-brainer, and why didn't I see it?

She goes on: "If I verify what's happened, then my next job is to collect evidence and construct a case." *I didn't see it because I don't see anything, ever.* "Cases are built on credibility. Mine and yours, understand?"

"I do." *But am I credible? Even to myself?*

"Which brings me to my other point."

I hold my breath. Anticipating her next words. Willing them to be something along the lines of *we've found him!*

"I have a second significant problem," Detective Henning says.

The words slice like a knife, hope spilling onto bad office carpet. "What's happened?"

"We've approached the bathhouse with your story. There's no match to your attacker's first name or the screengrab you provided."

I open my mouth to speak, to counter her, but pause. There's no point. She's telling me the facts, and nothing will change them. I let myself into Haus. I let myself into Kristian's room. Then I let Detective Henning into my life. Now that she's here, what's stopping her from destroying everything? Tearing down lie after lie. Veneer after veneer, each tissue-paper thin.

Instead, I ask for details.

She obliges: "It's possible this man used a fake ID. There are hundreds of reasons to, as you can imagine. I'm working on a subpoena for Haus's records. So far, they're being cooperative. They want to keep their name out of the media, but they won't hand over something like that without a court order."

"Makes sense." The damage such a list might do? Wandering and winding down dark, wet hallways, the bodies of men against one another. Getting off. How many have wives? Name recognition in this city, of all places? Outing diplomatic staffers from some nations sends them flying home to floggings and nooses.

"But I need to be certain of something else." She reads my silence for bated breath. "When I visited Haus, the receptionist wouldn't share the list per the owners. But he did welcome inquiries. I asked about Kristian. Showed your photo. Came up empty." She hesitates. "I also asked about you."

We've gone from *knowing what's true* to *allegations* to *asking about you* jarringly fast.

"They couldn't find any record of you."

"But I was there." My voice trips. "I know I've given two reports, but I can't be any clearer. My first one is correct. The second one's a stupid cover I gave Nathan. I never intended for anyone but him to hear it. It's only because he's so goddamned insistent and stubborn that—"

"Oliver." She sharpens her tone. No-nonsense. A box cutter. "There's zero record of your visit to Haus."

Her words—what she's trying to tell me—finally sink in. No record, but I was there. The surreal darkness, a cocktail of danger and possibility that was so damn exhilarating. That smell. That biting scent of lavender cleaning solution soaking everything. The Cheshire Cat's lips curving into a wide grin. The blue flash as he made a copy of my license.

"Is either of your reports true?" Detective Henning asks.

"Of course they're true."

"They're? As in both?"

"No. I misspoke. The first is true. I was at Haus!"

The blackness the flare left behind was the canvas against which Nathan's face painted itself. The fear when I saw his eyes in that instant had reverberated in my bones. As hard as I tried to convince myself otherwise, it was all too real. I was inside Haus.

"There has to be a record." Panic squeezes my voice into a whisper. "The front desk, he made a copy. I saw him scan my ID."

Detective Henning exhales. "You sure you've given me the correct establishment? Are you certain it was Haus and not some other place? There are several in the city and—"

"No," I interrupt. "It's Haus. There could be a thousand bathhouses in the same neighborhood, and it'd still be Haus. That's where it happened. That's where Kristian tried to kill me. I googled it earlier that day. Haus was the one I chose. The address I plugged into my phone. I can even show you . . ." I stop speaking. Everything besides the screenshot—which she's already seen—is gone. My browser history. My MeetLockr app. My recent searches in Google Maps. I can't show Detective Henning. I can't show her it was Haus and nowhere else.

"Okay," she relents. "Let's say it is Haus. That you're positive, and you were there. The fact remains they were unable to produce documentation."

"Unable or unwilling?"

"At this point, either means the same thing."

Another thought crawls through my mind like a spider. I told myself on the Metro that Kristian didn't have time to memorize my address. Not with a bleeding face and all the ruckus.

"You need to go back. You need to go back to Haus. Nine zero three. That was my locker number. And the room, I don't remember which one, but I hurt Kristian. Badly. I sliced his cheek." My voice escalates. "There must be blood. Even if they've scrubbed the whole place, no way they cleaned it all. They can't have. There could be a bloody fingerprint. Or DNA, there's always—"

"We're looking at everything," she says before I unravel into a full-blown rant. "Is there any reason to believe the record of your visit wouldn't be there? I've got to follow up on this. Two different reports from the same victim? Doesn't look good, Oliver. If I can't even place you there—"

"He's taken it," I whisper.

"What?"

"He's taken it. The copy of my ID. He stole it. I know one was made. The front desk made it. The guy, he even assured me it'd never be shared."

Time to steal the copy. Kristian had plenty of that.

"The receptionist doesn't recognize you. He was working the front door that night and says he never saw you." The statement slices me open like a scalpel. "He admits it was dark but doesn't recall the incident you described. He doesn't remember helping anyone open a locker. Or seeing anybody run out in a panic."

"He has to." Disbelief grips my throat as tightly as Kristian had. I bite back tears. "He has to remember."

Silence on her end. The sound of everything coming apart. I'm telling the truth, but if anything, it's making me look like a liar.

"Court order's working its way through the pipeline," Detective Henning says. "It's possible the establishment is obfuscating. Nothing shutters a place quite like violence, but places like Haus? A fire there will burn itself out at no public expense. So they might do anything to avoid it."

Like Haus? Would she prefer to see this fire burn itself out? What happens to me then?

"But if what you say is true, if Kristian's got that copy, then we need to react appropriately. If he has your address, your photo, your license number, then you are vulnerable to stalking."

I'm *vulnerable to stalking*. Meaning I've drawn a dangerous man onto streets where the privileged make their homes. The Haus fire has leapt so suddenly into leafy Georgetown that the public's at risk. Well, the segments of the public that matter most. Is this why she cares?

"We're doing what we can. Surveillance cams, canvassing. But Haus was built for privacy, as I'm sure you appreciate."

So much so, it feels like I've swallowed sandpaper.

"All things considered—considered and *true*," she qualifies, "we're dealing with a dangerous person. I'd like a marked car outside your place until we get more information. Remember what I said? About patterns?"

"They repeat," I say. They wouldn't be patterns if they didn't. "Do you think there are more? Guys like me?"

"A patrol car out front for a few days is a good idea." She leaves my question unanswered. "That okay with you?"

How will I explain a parked police car to Nathan? I'll have to make something up. Detective Henning hasn't given me much choice. "Sure, yeah."

"They'll be by later today. They won't approach you or the home without a good reason. No need to interact with them either. Understand?"

In the corner of my eye, Kimberly walks past reception, Teal-framed glasses and a snow-white coat. "I've got to go. Will you message me if you find anything else? If you locate him?"

"I'll keep you posted," she says, and clicks off the line.

Kimberly speaks, but I don't hear it. Not well enough to answer. I stare at the blinking cursor on the screen of my computer, open to today's calendar.

"Oliver?" Kimberly repeats, and her studied face comes into tight focus. She's leaning down, eyes grazing my bruises. "These neck abrasions, they look violent."

"Hi. Good morning." The phone cord still wraps around my index finger, purpling its tip. I hide my hand under the desk. "It . . . Yeah, it was."

"If you locate who?" she asks.

"Huh?"

"I didn't mean to eavesdrop." A brief pause. "Were you talking about Nathan? On the phone just now?"

"Oh. No, something else. Nathan's home from New York."

"I reached out to him after your email. He never called me back." Kimberly is, of course, Nathan's friend before mine. "How's he doing with all this?"

"Okay, I think. Overreacting, but—"

"Has he looked at your injuries?" she asks with what could be mistaken for suspicion. Though of what, I can't be certain. "You sound hoarse. Is your larynx tender?"

"He looked everything over." I skirt her question and hope she doesn't bring this up to Nathan if and when they chat. "It looks far worse than it is. Was."

Lips parted, she seems to want to ask further, and I don't blame her. She closes her mouth and smiles. "Why don't you take a half day. It's a light schedule. The nurses can cover for you."

"Thanks." Bile scales my throat, and I swallow. "I'll do that."

She gives my shoulder a squeeze and makes for the chart room. My eyes fall back to the blinking cursor. The tiny, flashing line becomes the point on which I focus my thoughts. The anchor to reality I grasp with whitened knuckles.

How long can I keep this up? Police cars. Missing records. Liars. Stalking.

How long before it all comes apart like rotten wood?

•   •

No point bothering with headphones on the trip home. The voices screaming inside my skull drown out everything. Kristian's taken my ID. The Cheshire Cat lied. His bottom line more important than my safety and that of his customers. Or patrons or clients or whatever he calls us. That man couldn't have forgotten me. Not the horror in my eyes or my strangled words.

His is a cowardly omission that might cost lives. My life. Tiny spiders skitter down my arms, my shoulders.

Nathan aside, a big part of me is grateful for a cop car by the house. Until we get a handle on things, as Detective Henning suggested. A police presence must be a deterrent, right?

I emerge from the Metro like a locust. An entirely different creature, and the air shimmers. Heat wafts off the sidewalk like gasoline fumes as the sun bears down with oppressive vigor. The back of my neck reddens, and my pits grow wet.

I undo a second shirt button as corner stores and bodegas and laundromats give way to apartment buildings and rows of stately townhomes. The vaulted branches of hundred-year-old oaks, verdant and full, form a ceiling of shade, and my eyes relax.

When I round the corner onto my street, I'm jarred.

Wide yellow tubing, papery and collapsible, snakes from a parked van. It winds through our open front door and inside. Darryl's gotten started like he promised.

The relentless hum of an engine in the van's hold grows louder. A man props the rear door open with one hand and smokes a cigarette with the other. Leather boots flecked with paint. Stains streak his jeans. His white tee's sweat-wet and entirely see-through.

He nods and I inhale his secondhand smoke. A habit ever since I *quit*. I step into the foyer in time to catch Darryl coming downstairs.

"Hello there." He adjusts the bill of his Clemson cap. "Didn't expect anyone home."

"I left work early." I clutch my throat to mask my *neck abrasions,* as Kimberly described them. "Wasn't feeling great."

"Sorry to hear that." He smiles. "We're just cleaning up. All done for today. In fact, I suspect we'll finish by tomorrow or Thursday. Not so bad once we opened everything up. A day to dry, then another to put it all back together."

The tube's sucking moisture left from my mistake. If only it could suck the poison out of all the others.

"That's good news." I set my things on the entryway table and take a deep breath. I'll take good news wherever and however I can.

"I'll bring the boys over same time tomorrow. Just leave the key out like usual," he says, making his way past me and outside. Footsteps stomp across the ceiling before appearing by the second-floor balustrade— paint-spackled work boots like the other guy's. Their owner collects and spools the hosing on his way down the stairs.

Behind prisms from the foyer chandelier, the boots take one slow step at a time, careful to keep the tubing untangled.

Knee-torn jeans next. Sweat-soaked wifebeater. He's nearly to the bottom before I catch a glimpse of hair. Face pointed down, long bangs hanging loose. I give him a wide berth to leave through the front, and he lifts his chin.

The stitched wound on Kristian's cheek seems to smile.

14

NATHAN

A tiny washroom serves the suite of offices in the trauma department. Soaping up shaky hands, I appraise myself in the mirror. Whispers of gray hair look even grayer, and bloodshot eyes even bloodier. Red like marbled meat—which is no surprise. All night, lucid dreams struck with horrifying clarity. A vague recollection that I hadn't pulled that writhing scorpion out, that it's still somewhere inside. Burrowed deep in the lining of an organ, spooling sinew through its pincers.

I exit and—making for my own office—find a person standing by the door. Dark jeans, casual blazer, and my gut clenches.

The scorpion stirs. Spindly legs skitter beneath my sternum.

"Hi there." The woman investigating Oliver's assault squares her shoulders and smiles. "Nathan, right?"

She appears pleasantly surprised to have caught me. She flashes a badge. I brush wet palms on my white coat, take her outstretched hand. "Yes. Dr. Klein."

"Detective Rachel Henning. We met briefly at the police station."

"I know." An odd reminder. Does one often forget such encounters?

"Your admin said today's your desk day, so I thought I'd . . ." She hesitates, eyes narrowing enough to register as suspicion. "You okay?"

"Tired." I puff my cheeks. "Work is always work, but home's been better. As you know."

"I do," she replies. "And I hate to be a bother, but I'd like to chat for a minute. If you're okay to?"

"Of course." I reach past her to open my office door. A tremor rattles my hands. Partly nerves, partly the hangover. I'd gone a bit too far last night, but today's all paperwork, no procedures, and I didn't sweat it. Only so many ways to blunt the combined edges of both Oliver's attack and his lies. But now, Detective Henning tracks my hands in the way all people do in a surgeon's presence. The unsteadiness she sees can't inspire much confidence.

Breathe, Nathan. In through your nose, out through your mouth.

The detective claims a chair in front of my desk. I make for the beverage cart against the far wall. A sleek antique that adds a slice of civilization to an otherwise sprawling, brutalist hospital. "Coffee or tea?"

"Tea would be lovely. Something *fruity* if you've got it."

"I do." I couch my reply in pleasantness, but I'm bothered by her word choice. It feels both deliberate and degrading. Something about her presence skews everything in my office toward hostile. The teakettle hisses like a tightly coiled viper. The room lists. The wallpaper and warm desk photos of Oliver and Mother and Father and Tilly seem to melt like hot wax.

I tighten my jaw, tip the kettle over a porcelain teapot.

"Have you learned anything new?" I ask.

"Can't say." Detective Henning sounds genuinely apologetic. "Open investigation."

"I'm his husband."

"Actually"—she tilts her head as if offering charity—"you're not."

"Right." I grin, but my plaster veneer is undoubtedly cracking. "Milk, sugar?"

"A spoonful of sugar's perfect."

Office air is never refreshing, but it somehow grows even staler. I stir a cube into her orange pekoe. "What would you like to chat about?"

"I have a few questions." She cups the scalding tea with both hands.

I've turned my back to her, like Oliver and I have done so often to each other. My motions are deliberately slow as I fix my own drink. I'm not eager to face Detective Henning because she reminds me of, well, me. Cunning always recognizes itself. The question is, what's her agenda? "Fire away."

"I appreciate you being so supportive of Oliver. Bringing him down to the station. Really speaks to your character."

"I love Oliver." The tip of my tongue burns. My cautious sip turned into a hot gulp, and I hope she didn't notice. "What happened to him, it broke my heart."

"He's very lucky. To have survived and to have you." Detective Henning's gaze has taken on a studious quality when I finally turn her way. She's unpacking my appearance, my demeanor. "For support. Given he never called Victim Services."

"Excuse me?"

"Social workers, therapists, they help people cope in the wake of these things. A sliding pay scale for folks who can't afford it." She motions to the art gallery of framed degrees and certificates behind me. "Not that you two need it. In any case, Oliver never reached out. But at least he has you."

"He does." I nod but recall zero talk about social workers or therapy. Oliver and I were together the whole time at the station. Had Detective Henning spoken with him since? And if so, why haven't I heard about it?

"I can't imagine enduring this alone." Detective Henning's approach seems to soften. "Oliver has no family. No friends either, it seems. Nothing undoes a person as efficiently as loneliness."

Her words, the irony in them is rich. Loneliness, the urge to feel alive again. Wanted and loved and like I still had a life worth being lived. One Oliver was capable of loving. It seems I've been undone by all of it.

I expect our tea party talk to continue—but it doesn't. An unnerving quiet as Detective Henning stares, eyes tightly focused. She runs a nail on the rim of her cup, and metallic notes pinch my jaw like sour candy.

"Do you trust him?"

"What?" I clear my throat. The question's a wild departure by itself, but her tone has also turned. It's almost accusatory.

"Oliver. Do you trust him?"

I scoff. "What kind of question is that?"

"Look, Dr. Klein, I've been at this awhile." Her cup strikes the desk with a thump, and she steeples her fingers. "I've engaged with just about every personality out there. This gives me a certain kind of talent. I can read people. Quickly and in most cases, accurately."

"And?"

"I'm not sure I trust Oliver. Not entirely, but nobody knows him better than you. So naturally, I'm curious."

"Yes." *No.* "What reason would I have to distrust my—my partner?"

"What happened to him, it's quite serious."

"Got that right." No question, she's working an angle. Does she suspect Oliver of something? I was decidedly and empirically hundreds of miles away; she can't be here to interrogate me.

"Oliver strikes me as a guy that keeps secrets."

"I'm having trouble following you, Detective Henning"—despite my best efforts, my chest swells with heat—"and comprehension isn't typically a challenge for me."

She grins. "For self-defense, to cope, whatever the motive, my take is that Oliver's default is to withhold truth. Do you agree at all?"

"You know what he just went through?" My heartbeat quickens. "Can you even imagine how—"

"Nathan—"

"Dr. Klein," I correct. "Oliver grew up closeted in a very conservative community. Of course his default is to hide. It's how he survived. For years."

"Just wanted to get your read," Detective Henning says. "That's all."

"I have absolutely no reason to distrust Oliver," I lie.

"You two been together for a while?" Detective Henning reaches into her blazer for a notepad.

"We have."

"How are things?" She clicks the butt of a blue pen. "Lately, I mean?"

Why does she care? She saw my boarding pass, my expense receipts. It made sense to request them, because if Oliver's been assaulted, statistically I'm the most likely to have done it. Rising discomfort meets my headache from last night's liquor, and the truth carelessly spills: "Things have been better."

"Sorry to hear that." Detective Henning's poised to write. "Mind sharing?"

Her predictable reply spikes my pulse. Do I tell her about my own suspicions? The high likelihood Oliver's cheating? That my only remaining questions are how many, how often, and who, exactly? I opt for a vaguer track. If she wants details on the do-not-resuscitate status of our marriage, she'll have to pull them out with pliers. Tooth by bloody tooth. "A rough patch. Not unusual. Nothing special."

"You both wear rings." She gestures to my left hand. "Can I ask why you haven't married?"

"Our situation works for us." It's the truth, but it must sound like something else. "And until recently, marriage wasn't an option since, I don't know, the Constitution was ratified."

"Sure it doesn't have anything to do with finances?" She flips back a page or two. "Your family does quite well—"

"How do you know anything about my family?"

"Nice pictures." She points to my desk photos instead of answering. "That the Williamsburg Bridge you two are standing on?"

"It is."

"Oliver's dressed sharp. He could almost pass for a Klein. If he was included in that other one, I mean." She refers to the next frame over. Me, Mother, Father, and twelve-week-old Tilly on a beach in East Hampton. "Any complete family photos?"

"Plenty." *Complete* lands hard because there are none.

"Your mom," she says, and my jaw nearly drops. "I rang her up yesterday. Same as you, I wanted her thoughts on Oliver."

Sweat gathers on the back of my neck. "I'm sure she had many."

"No. Surprisingly," Detective Henning says, which in itself is surprising. I peak my brow. "I mean sure, she had emphatic opinions on Oliver and yourself, generally. But regarding Oliver's assault? The woman had no clue what I was talking about."

"I don't appreciate where this is going." As if summoned, the phone in my coat pocket buzzes. I must've finished a final, thirteenth Bloody Mary chant because it's Mother. "I'm also entirely unsure how this brings us closer to finding Oliver's attacker. It's irrelevant and invasive."

"How bizarre that she wouldn't know. Given how frequently you speak."

"Because women like her worry, so thank you for this." I show her my phone. "You know what's bizarre? Bothering her over a mugging. Eighty whole bucks."

"You don't think violence merits a follow-up?"

"Sure do." At this point, I'm grinding my teeth. "So why is my family a priority over actual investigatory work to hold actual violence accountable?"

"Women like her," she parrots. "Tell me, Dr. Klein, does being questioned by a woman bother you?"

"It's the content of your questions, Detective Henning, that bothers me."

"All right." She raises both hands as if to say *I give up*. She follows this stupid gesture with: "I know you're a busy guy, and I'm genuinely grateful for your time."

I give a smirk and unlock my phone to catch Mother's missed call and its accompanying texts.

Father and I are in Washington right now. Awards gala tonight. Call soon please. Mother has attended exactly zero DC galas, and the timing of this one is highly suspect given Detective Henning's reveal. Seems there are two Kleins telling lies now. But it's her second message that holds a hook: **Also need to discuss the Georgetown property.**

"Before I take off"—Detective Henning stands as I return my phone to my coat—"I do want to remind you of one thing."

"What's that?"

"Spousal privilege."

The second curve ball in a row I didn't see coming. And I see all curve balls thrown my way. Bringing that up implies suspicion of not only me or Oliver but of *us*. Said suspicion intrigues me as much as Mother's gala–slash–sudden need to talk real estate. "Are you serious?"

"The notion that conversations between spouses are shielded from law," Detective Henning says, needlessly. I can't tell if she's more interested in actual answers or my reactions, but no question, she's both good cop and bad cop. Something stirs deep in my chest. Something alive and quite like a scorpion.

"I know what it means."

"Then you know Oliver and you don't have it."

OLIVER

I stand frozen in the foyer. Locked in place and position from the moment Kristian's face blurred by, in the flesh, *inside* my house.

As if my motionlessness would halt the march of time, give it a chance to correct its mistake. Because that's what it must have been. That's what it has to have been. A mistake.

My hands are trembling fists.

There's no way, no possible way, Kristian could've walked past me just now.

The front door closes behind him. Behind whoever the fuck just strolled out of my house. With ice-cold ocean eyes and an inflamed slash through his left cheek, threaded with black stitches.

The quaking spreads up my arms and swallows me whole. I turn slowly; the blinds still dance on the shut door.

An engine cranks, lighting my blood on fire, and I leap to the drawing room's bay window. I part the blinds and realize with horror that I've made myself visible to him, vulnerable to him. I drop to the floor. Through a crack between the windowsill and the bottom slat, I peer into the street.

The van backs up, turns its front wheels, and pulls from the curb. The driver wears a cap. Darryl. The man in the front seat is the same one smoking outside. Kristian must be in the back.

I fall and catch myself before my skull strikes the coffee table. As I sit there, silent and shaking, a second engine hums and I crawl on my knees to the window.

A police car pulls into the space vacated by the van. The marked patrol car, courtesy of Detective Henning. Meant to impart security, a sense of safety and protection. Instead, it mocks me. The patrol's timing, a malicious joke.

Kristian's been inside my house. He saw, smelled, touched my life with Nathan without my knowledge or consent. Despite the thrumming heat of my pulse, coldness settles over my shoulders.

Panic blooms.

I crated Tilly upstairs in our bedroom because Darryl would be working today. Men would be coming in and out. I spring from the floor and fly up to our room.

I round the second-story landing, push off the railing, and catapult down the hallway. The door to our bedroom is shut. I didn't close it. Tilly gets anxious when she's in the crate and it's closed. When she can't see what's going on around her.

I nearly tear the door from its hinges. My eyes find the crate. Its occupant.

Panting, Tilly bolts upright. Her bobbed tail wags wildly. Little paws eagerly padding about. She scratches at crate wiring, and I undo the latch. She leaps, front paws propped on my shoulders, tongue lapping and licking and searching my face.

I exhale. She's okay. Nathan's dog is okay.

"Hey there," I coo. "That's our good, safe girl."

She pushes off and gallops, nails clicking against the hardwood, downstairs. Next, the sound of lapping water from the kitchen. *The water*. Paranoia spikes again, sends me racing downstairs.

Terrifying thoughts of Tilly's water. Horror stories of hateful people, irritated neighbors, poisoning dogs because they bark too much, too often. Antifreeze tastes sweet, and an unsuspecting dog would drink it till they're dead.

Sliding into the kitchen, I snatch Tilly's bowl from under her, spilling most of it. Making for the sink, I sniff what's left. No odor—chemical or otherwise. I dump it, start to rinse and refill it, but shove it in the dishwasher and grab a clean bowl from the cupboard.

"Here ya go, girl." I thread my tone with gentleness. Tilly perks her ears and cocks her head. She's baffled, and I don't blame her. I'm baffled by my behavior. I'm baffled by why and how Kristian was in my house.

I monitor Tilly as she bounces around my legs for another minute or so. When I decide she's okay, that she's not ingested anything dangerous, I pace. Same as my first homecoming from Haus. When I escaped from Kristian's grip. His attempt to crush my windpipe and snuff my life out. Now he's been here.

Inside my house. Walking where I walk. Sitting where I sit. Breathing *my* air.

Nausea churns, and the room lists. A spring of bile bursts into a geyser. I almost don't make it. Cupping both hands over my mouth, I start to vomit just before flipping the porcelain lid in the bathroom.

I heave, blood rushing to my head, straining as though my cheekbones might pop out of my face and fall into the toilet water. I gasp between violent heaves. I've eaten nothing, save a few sips of coffee coming back up as hot spoonfuls.

I wipe spit from my bottom lip and prop myself against the toilet. How did he do it? It's too much of a coincidence to consider he worked for Darryl by chance. But how did he know I'd called him? Needed a job done? How did he know to approach Darryl for work?

Has he been watching me at home ever since?

Flush, wash my hands, splash water on my face, gulp straight from the faucet. I leave the hand towel crumpled on the floor and stagger back down the hallway.

Tilly trails behind me as I make my way from room to room. First downstairs, then up. Looking for anything out of place. Anything missing or moved. Anything suggesting Kristian's long fingers may have touched or brushed or prodded.

A crushing sense of betrayal and invasiveness replaces nausea. Of soiled surroundings. For the second time, the wretched feeling of being attacked—strung up and splayed open for all to see—takes hold. Kristian's seen me naked. At Haus, without my partner, thirsty for anonymous sex. And now he's been inside my home. He's explored my life. He's penetrated my privacy, befouling and defacing it.

It's poisoned now. Our home, our things, all poisoned. Sown with salt and there's no one to tell without losing everything.

Back in the master bedroom, Darryl's work in our en suite is hidden behind closed doors. The sheets are neatly tucked beneath the mattress.

The duvet pulled tight by Nathan same as every morning. No impression or shallow groove from a man's weight. In the dresser mirror, a stranger peers back.

Bloodshot eyes. Deep shadows beneath them. Pants hanging loose at my hips, wild hair. I'm unraveling. My chest heaving from running and vomiting and running again. The man glowering from the mirror's far side is a cruel image. Insult to injury, but I've done nothing to deserve an empathetic reflection.

Something else steals my focus. Something I hadn't noticed when bursting into the room for Tilly. Each and every dresser drawer sits flush in its place. Except one. One is pulled out an inch from its mooring.

My underwear drawer.

I step back, heart thumping. My gut moves like I've swallowed a teeming knot of hornets. Kristian's been through my drawer. It's been left ajar to call attention to itself. As though Kristian wishes it known he's been through that specific drawer.

But Nathan and I share a dresser. There's no way he can know . . . only, he can. My black briefs—the ones he pulled down my trembling, eager legs. I'd diligently washed, folded, and returned them.

I yank the drawer open and there they are. Clean briefs. Except they've been unfolded. Deliberately strewn atop neat garments. I pinch their elastic waistline with my thumb and forefinger.

Under them, something else beckons. A USB stick, tiny and neon and terrifying. *We're dealing with a dangerous person,* Detective Henning cautioned. And now a flash drive has been tucked beneath my briefs.

His whispers hot on the back of my neck, before I'd even seen that face, those eyes. Now a fresh heat crawls my spine, and I hear that same question that thrilled me at Haus.

What are you looking for?

16

I sink into the duvet. Nathan doesn't like it when I do. The way my weight tugs and wrinkles the smooth cover is irksome. My clammy fingers pinch the flash drive. The device now includes my prints alongside Kristian's—unless he wore gloves.

My first instinct is to smash it and scatter the pieces in the dumpster out back where my wallet met its fate. My second, to flee from what frightens me. And I am *very* afraid of what waits on this USB stick. Afraid enough to lock it away without looking. Unscrew the downstairs duct grate and push it deep inside with my other secrets.

Most people would have to look. That's not me; I can live without knowing. I did it before. Reinvented myself nearly a thousand miles away.

Never confronting Hector because that's what running away is. No matter how many times he called, how many texts and emails and DMs. Voicemails deleted and not listened to. Maybe they were conciliatory or even heartbroken pleas. They could've been, probably were, violent. The point is I don't know. I erased them, one after another, as they came through. Killing off each and every chance for a future that included him. A vast departure from my life with Nathan in that now there's a life worth living. If only barely.

TYRE, IN

New Year's Eve, and Hector sat at our shitty kitchen table in our shitty, prefab apartment. Hector, somehow sun-kissed even in winter. The whole place reeked of liquor. Sweet like stale Skittles.

"It's almost midnight," I said from the sofa. "Blaire's texted like a hundred times. We gotta go."

Blaire, the obligatory girlfriend–turned–best friend TV sitcoms required me to have. A hangover from high school, but a welcome one. New Year's was her thing. Backyard binging behind her family's farmhouse. Firepits. Cases upon cases of piss-cheap beer. Backslapping and smoking—cigarettes, pot, whatever else—till the sun came up. This would be the first time I'd gone with someone.

The thought of bringing Hector, my boyfriend, cranked my anxiety to eleven. His lack of interest wasn't helping. I re-scrolled through Blaire's texts as he prepped another suspension.

"Jesus, Hector, let's go." I made for the kitchen. The mildewed linoleum was so sticky, every step took effort.

"Hold on a goddamn minute." Hector's eyes, bold and dark, fixated on a ziplock bag of white pills. Dozens of them that he slid into a stone pestle. Percocet.

"It's been, like, not even an hour since your last one. We're gonna be drinking."

"I won't drink much," he promised as he made pill powder. Veins in his forearm swelling with each pestle turn. He poured the mixture into a glass of cold water, which he delicately placed in the freezer between a half-empty handle of grain alcohol and oven-ready waffle fries.

Cold-water extraction. Hector taught me that Percocet is a simple combination of two drugs: a narcotic—oxycodone—and acetaminophen, aka Tylenol. The latter is incredibly dangerous in high amounts. Brutal on the liver and added to discourage overdosing on the first ingredient.

In a clever moment revealing his squandered potential, Hector told me oxy was soluble in cold water but acetaminophen wasn't. Crush the pills, stir them in water, stick them in the freezer. And when you strain the suspension through a paper towel? Almost pure narcotic ready for drinking.

All high, no liver injury, no death.

As soon as he shut the freezer, I opened the fridge. My buzz was kicking up, but now I'd have to wait around even longer. I popped open a PBR and took a healthy gulp. When I lowered the can, sadness bloomed. I'd never watched anyone crushing and filtering pills as a passive observer.

Hector's hands, trembling with anticipation, worked diligently to recover every last powdery pestle speck. I must've looked just as tragic the countless times I'd done the same.

On her deathbed three months earlier, eaten from the inside out, Mom said she'd always be there. Breast cancer had turned into everything cancer, and she knew our time was drawing to an end. She said she'd always watch over me. We never really found time for church with her carousel of shitty jobs, but she meant from heaven. Grinding my teeth, I hoped she couldn't. I prayed she'd be blinded to my earthly bullshit. She shouldn't have to see this.

"Let's go." Hector coughed, chugged the bitter cocktail, coughed again. We grabbed coats and a fresh sixer of PBR and headed out.

WASHINGTON, DC

That moment of self-awareness wasn't what did it. It wasn't what spurred me to run and to hide from his texts and voicemails. But the courage to leave him, afterward, may have never come had I not seen myself in Hector at our kitchen table that night.

The USB pinched in my fingers snaps into sharp focus.

New surroundings. Furniture, decor, things inconsistent with my past. Expensive and smelling of well-adjusted decision making. Notes of Nathan's Tom Ford cologne—vanilla and tobacco—not Hector's corner-store top shelf. Nathan's controlling, but he has every right to be, given my behavior. And now this? Lashing out like a child, going to Haus. As if it'd be worth it.

And running away is no longer an option. Not like before. I have to see whatever's on this. Flash drive in hand, I make for the upstairs office.

Centuries-old stairs shrieking under my feet, I game this out: a threatening clip? An accusation? My tightly coiled gut says it's media of some kind. Maybe homemade porn—

Haus-made porn. I stop. I would not have noticed a camera. Not in *that* room in *that* moment. Reliving *that* night is suddenly possible.

A memento left in my underwear drawer, because what's the point of Kristian sneaking inside my house if I don't know it? And if I hadn't come home early—which he couldn't have known would happen—he wouldn't have been caught. How or when he'd entered would have been a mystery. I'd only know he had, and fear would make him a mythic evil. My life, a porous thing Kristian slips in and out of at will. No way to stop him. Or be certain I'm ever truly alone.

The PC's fan whirls to life. Entering the PIN to our shared account takes two tries because whatever I'm about to see has my whole body trembling.

My phone vibrates. A text from Nathan.

Dinner tonight?

Just us, then drinks with Tom after?

The question marks mean nothing; he's already decided. Reservations have been made.

OK.

His timing is spectacular, and maybe he can see me? My every move. Constant control might be impossible, but he can erect guardrails. Keep me in my lane beneath a veneer of self-determination. This is what pushed me in the first place. Made seedy corners online and in bath-houses so damn appealing. He knows what I'm doing and when I do it. Strategically timed texts keep me uncomfortable. Payback for my mistakes. For bringing a killer into my life and now into our home. His life, his home.

Paranoia, Oliver. Don't avalanche.

I slip the USB stick in and a media player launches. I hold my breath. Panic stirs, snakes up my back. The contents are organized into chapters. Sixteen of them for sixteen scenes, and I play chapter one.

A Caucasian man sits on a half-gutted sofa. Fit and young. Hair so dark it's nearly black, so it's no one I recognize—though I'm unsure why I would expect otherwise. The camera zooms, fixing on a close-up.

"Devin," he says, then: "Twenty-two."

He must be answering offscreen questions, but *what's your name?* and *how old are you, Devin?* are too muted to hear.

"I'm straight." Accent's vaguely Jersey. "I have a girlfriend."

He hammocks his chin in the groove of a thumb and forefinger.

"Nope. Never done anything like this before."

His cheeks dimple when he smiles.

"I'm nervous."

He brings a glass into frame and takes an anxious sip.

"Okay. Sure." Devin pulls his shirt off, and a hand reaches from behind the camera. Long fingers run over his chest, tiptoe across his clavicle. "You got my cash? Just gotta jack off, right?"

Amateur porn. My pulse settles because I'd braced for something else. Shit like blackmail. Or worse. Maybe Kristian had filmed our encounter.

"Her name?" The same hand forks over a wad of bills, and Devin rubs his exposed biceps like he's suddenly cold. "Ashley."

Another sip. Beer by the foaminess, and his eyes seem to go glossier with each gulp.

"Uh, soccer. Sometimes, but not so much lately." Devin massages a bare shoulder. "Mostly studying a lot, I guess?"

He polishes off the drink.

"Nursing. Probably pediatrics."

He's starting to slur. Maybe the on-camera beer's not his first?

"Nah, no tattoos."

Devin nods, and hesitates before standing.

"Sure."

He slips acid-washed jeans to his thighs. Ditto a pair of neon boxer briefs.

"Like this?"

He stumbles once, twice while spinning slowly for the camera, and maybe it wasn't beer in that glass. Or *only* beer. After a second three-sixty, the screen fades. For thirty excruciating seconds, nothing and I bite into the inside of my cheek. Then chapter two plays.

Blackness resolves into a mop closet of a room. The quality's poor, but the walls look like cinder block. No windows. The camera seems fixed high in a ceiling corner. Pointed downward like closed-circuit surveillance.

Not a thing in the space but a mattress. Mottled with spilled whatever and thrown on a concrete floor. The scene holds a filthiness that's not the video's fault. It reminds me of Haus. Of the room I followed Kristian into so naïvely. Not exactly the same, but sparse and similar enough to wonder. A clock at the frame's bottom keeps minutes.

The same dark-haired guy from the first scene—Devin the maybe-nursing student—walks in. Stark naked. He stumbles around almost aimlessly. His gait, hapless, off-putting, bordering on unsettling. He's drunk or otherwise intoxicated. He bumps into the mattress two, three, four times.

Something about this is wrong. Very wrong.

A second man enters. Likewise naked, and my chest knots. Kristian. No mistaking it. He even flashes the camera a knowing smile. Acknowledges its presence for the benefit of the audience.

It suddenly occurs to me that Devin hasn't gazed up once. When people know they're being filmed, the natural compulsion is to look at the camera. He isn't aware of it. The footage is surreptitious. Either the camera's hidden or he's too inebriated to notice. Regardless, Kristian hasn't alerted him.

But he has alerted me.

A sudden chill sweeps up my arms, raising bumps on my skin. My cheeks grow warm and my scrotum tightens. Something deeply, profoundly, *primally* wrong is unfolding here.

Kristian whispers inaudibly into Devin's ear. Then he embraces the man, kisses him, cups and fondles him.

Devin might reciprocate, but nothing about his mannerisms scream consent. To the contrary, it looks like he's been drugged. Heavily. Movements are staggered, exaggerated in ways that don't make sense. Kristian takes his hand, leads him to the mattress. He shoves him backward onto it. A hard push to his chest that reverberates in mine.

He climbs on top of him, dick hard.

A series of memories pop off like a string of firecrackers. Images, smells, feelings, all visceral and raw. Kristian's grip. His touch. His tongue traveling over me. Spinning me, coming from behind, positioning me the way he wants it. The way he wants to fuck.

Fear crawls up my spine, and I clutch my chest, my throat. I can't breathe.

Through invisible ducts, billowing steam pours into the office. Obscuring, masking, suffocating. It blots out the window's sunlight, and the room draws dark. Jungle humid and sweat gathers on my arms, under my pits, between my legs. Beads roll down my face.

I already know what happens next.

Kristian kisses Devin's ear. His fist finds his throat.

The struggle is instant. Twenty-two-year-old Devin flails, jerks, and jitters like a harpooned fish. I know what's racing through his mind. The horrifying conclusions he's drawing. The inescapable reality. No more Ashley. No more soccer. There will be no Devin, Registered Nurse.

He grows more fitful, spiking adrenaline pushing through whatever roofies he's swallowed.

Kristian presses hard against both our bodies. My lungs collapsing beneath his weight. My sternum fracturing and buckling inside my chest. The man on the tape can't breathe. I can't breathe. No physical penetration. Only mindfucking during the few minutes asphyxia lasts.

Despair distills itself into a concentrated resin at the bottom of my heart. Devin's time is ending. His face blues and he froths. A last jerk this way and that before he accepts what's happening.

He seizes, then stills.

When Kristian stands, he shudders and I wonder how intense his high is.

He runs fingers through sweat-wet hair and smiles into the camera a second time. Grins at *me* once more. He doesn't glance behind on his way out of frame. The lifeless body he's left on a mattress. Devin, who mere minutes earlier moved and breathed and lived. The clip dissolves to black.

A snuff film. Kristian has left me one minute and fourteen seconds of snuff film.

No! One minute and fourteen seconds of snuff *scene*! I punch the space bar before chapter three starts. Jesus, there are sixteen of them!

It's the worst fucking kind of personal message. Showing what might have been, what still might come to pass. He's sharing what comes next for me.

I'm petrified, an inanimate extension of the chair I sit on. He raped my mind, plunged me into a darkness unlike, Christ, unlike anything imaginable. How do you, how does anyone make sense of this? A whole life discarded for the sake of an orgasm?

I'd struck the keyboard like a mallet just as another clip queued up. Another interview, another man, another murder. My paranoid nightmare—the one I've fought and rationalized and bald-faced lied to myself about—isn't. It's reality, and there are others. Others who didn't escape. Others whose lives were taken, begging silently as Kristian shattered their windpipes. Entire lifetimes, entire worlds, faded to black.

The image, the hidden bodies, rotting, melting into wet piles of corruption. They're all real. Somewhere, right now, Devin's remains are as real as the shallow grave he's buried in.

Sixteen whole chapters, and I could've been one of them.

The tiny dot at the top of my own monitor—the camera—spurs a fresh wave of panic. I spent exactly zero seconds appraising Kristian's room at Haus. An entire film crew could've stood in the corner, and I wouldn't have noticed.

Not while we kissed. Not while I stood against the wall. Not while he pressed his chest to my back.

Sixteen chapters.

However many men.

I very well might be one of them.

17

It takes all of me, all my willpower, any strength that remains, but I push the chair from my desk and stand. Dazed, I grab the USB stick and stumble downstairs, where I pluck a ziplock bag from the kitchen pantry.

A surreal hallucination. Brief. Maybe too brief to be an actual hallucination. The baggie is suddenly filled with pills. Piles and piles of white pills. Then it's empty again. Then the flash drive is slipped and sealed inside it.

I wish it did hold pills. For the first time in a very, very long time, I crave them. Not like a once-habitual user craves them, but with a sense of frightening urgency. The bitter taste on my tongue. Swallowing one after another after another until a warm euphoria blooms. A crawling numbness that flowers and crowds out everything else. A mind at peace is impossible, but I'd settle for fake peace. Beautiful and fragile and false like wrapping paper.

Deep breath in, deep breath out. In a bizarre way, I'm grateful for the baggie's contents. If they were pills, I'd swallow all of them. I might not wake back up to this nightmare.

I grab my keys. Baggie in hand, I make for the marked cop car out front.

•   •

This time I sit in Detective Henning's office. A foam cup of orange juice ripples each time Detective Henning touches the desk. First, when she opens her laptop. Second, when her elbows come to rest. Third, when her boot strikes the desk leg as she shifts uncomfortably.

"Devin. Twenty-two."

"I'm straight. I have a girlfriend."

As hard as she tries to stay stoic in my company, she fails. Tiny movements, her jawline tensing, the way she runs her thumb over her fingernails over and over again, betray her.

"Nope. Never done anything like this before."

When she stops the clip, she exhales loudly. Then we sit in silence for an uncomfortable length of time before she breaks it: "You have to tell him."

Not what I expected. "Nathan?"

"Yes." She squares her shoulders. "You're going to have to tell Nathan what's been happening."

"Why would I—"

"What you're trying to do here? It's unsustainable." Her tone is conflicted. She's empathetic. She doesn't want Nathan to find out, but I can almost see the foregone conclusions surfacing in her mind. The narrowing and winnowing of possibilities. Of ways to do her job and help me maintain my charade.

With every passing moment, my safety and my relationship inch closer to mutual exclusivity. They may never have been reconcilable. I lied to myself. It's funny, really. I've lied to nearly everyone else in my life, and yet somehow managed to save the biggest untruth for yours truly.

"No." I'm completely unmoored, and she must see this in my eyes. "I can't."

"I received the membership list from Haus." She skirts my entrenchment. "We've completed a very thorough cross-referencing of each name with publicly available data. Photos, social media, everything."

I ball my hands into fists beneath the table.

"We've come up with nothing, Oliver."

"How is that possible? There was blood. And you talked about cameras and canvassing."

"There's nothing." She leans forward, crosses her arms. The day's heat has coalesced into a storm. Drops from the summer rain collect on a window before streaking down like comets. "There's nothing placing you there. Every room came up negative for blood with luminol. Is that suspicious? Given the expected kink, sure. But we can't find your records. We can't find Kristian's either."

My questions keep pace with the pelting raindrops on glass. "Do you believe me? Do you believe I was there? That I was attacked? That someone tried to kill me?"

She pauses, weighing her next words carefully. "I'd like to believe you, but that's not enough. That's not going to locate this man, nor will it keep you safe." She closes her laptop harder than necessary. I imagine to excise the video's images from her mind.

"Let me explain how this is working so far. I can't place you at Haus. Traffic cams put your vehicle, or I should say, Nathan's Range Rover—his is the only name on the title—in roughly the same neighborhood, but the parking lot isn't covered by surveillance. Both the owners and the receptionist refuse to corroborate your story—dispute it, in fact. I've got no other cases resembling yours to suggest a pattern. And, Oliver, I know you're sick of hearing this, but you've reported two entirely different assaults. Your credibility is tissue-paper thin."

"My credibility?" My throat's covered in finger-shaped contusions, and Detective Henning's questioning the veracity of my story?

"Yeah."

"Witnesses," I protest. "The other men. There were so many, and they all saw me running out. They must've seen Kristian. Pretty sure only one guy was cupping his bleeding fucking face."

"Nobody on that list will come forward. No one wants to admit they were there. Someone in your position should understand that. You claim the same pressure forced you to file a false report."

"You are absolutely right. But there is a pattern. The tape shows it. You just watched him murder someone. Exactly like he tried to kill me. And god knows how many others are on that flash drive!"

"Were you drugged like this guy appears to have been?"

"No."

She speaks slowly, takes care to enunciate each word to completion. "I *think* I just watched someone who's similar to the man in your photo drug and murder someone. But I can't know this. I can't know this wasn't acting, a work of fiction. We *think* it occurred years ago, but timestamps are easily manipulated. The scenes transition with a dissolve effect, meaning they've been edited. And we have no idea where it was filmed, whose jurisdiction."

As Detective Henning ticks through each obstacle, from speed bump to dead end, my heart falls deeper into my chest. This was never going to be easy, I figured that from the start, but my duplicity and lying have made it damn near impossible.

What a stupid thought! What a stupid fucking thought. My duplicity and lying are why this happened at all. I wouldn't have downloaded the app or gone inside Haus. I'd never have run into Kristian. It's my fault. I'm not supposed to say it but it's true.

"Kristian is in your jurisdiction right now. He's working with our fucking contractor. I want to know what you're going to do about it!"

"Oliver. Lower your voice." Detective Henning folds her arms.

"Wait," I say. A sudden recollection bursting to life. "My credit card!"

"I thought you paid—"

"Cash. I did, but not for the drink."

"You were drinking that night?"

"No. I mean, yes. Not really. Just one in the bar at Haus. They took my card at the front, but I never cashed out." I open my banking app. "The drink charge should be there. Timestamped and everything."

Detective Henning sighs, purses her lips.

I scroll, but my first pass at pending charges comes up empty. I must've missed it, so I start again carefully at the top and—fuck. My heart, my chair, even the ground under me, they all sink.

I didn't miss the charge; it's right there. The Saturday timestamp. The amount. The expense.

10:48p | $14.12 USD | Dry Cleaners

"Well?"

"The charge, it's—" I stutter and turn my screen around. "It's listed discreetly, but it has to help. You can confirm it's their standard practice. It matches the timeline."

"Uh-huh." She looks up, rightfully incredulous. "Maybe if the name was notable, but Dry Cleaners? Circumstantial is too generous."

"But the time. It substantiates my story or at least part—"

"Look, I'll bring in the receptionist at Haus for formal questioning.

Compel him to make another statement. It's one thing to mislead or cover up when questioned on friendly turf. It's quite another to deliberately lie on an official investigatory document. While sweating bullets in a police station."

This makes perfect sense—to bring him in. So much sense I wonder why it's taken until now to do so. Why it took a snuff film to needle the man—the Cheshire Cat—who clearly lied to her once already.

I keep this to myself. Victim or not, I'm not entitled to the inner workings of police matters. And cops often mislead. To trip up persons of interest, to get to the truth. *Lying to discern truth.*

"Two, I'm going to follow up with your contractor, Darryl. I suspect his crews are all under-the-table. Especially given the short time it took your attacker to land the job. Hopefully the manner in which Kristian found and contacted him will be revelatory. You mentioned you'd left a key for Darryl?"

"That's right." I eye the orange juice. The inside of my mouth tastes like sidewalk chalk, but the cup looks to weigh a metric ton.

"Did he leave it behind when he left?"

Shit. I didn't look. Between panicking over Tilly and discovering a fucking snuff film, I completely forgot to check if the spare was returned.

"I don't know. I'm not sure if he left it in the mailbox on his way out or not."

"You need to find out. If he left it, then it's unlikely Kristian had time to make a copy. If Darryl took the key home with him by accident, there'd be plenty of opportunities to slip it from him. I suggest changing your locks. Today."

A good idea. I'll tell Nathan the mugging has me on edge and changing the locks will make me feel safer. I'll phone Darryl and cancel the work for now. Alert Kristian to the fact he's been busted again and cops are closing in. The latter might be a lie, but he doesn't know that.

"I'll call a locksmith."

"We also need to prepare for another challenge," Detective Henning says. "From how you describe him, Kristian's likely foreign. Perhaps Scandinavian, perhaps not. We need to confront the possibility he's here illegally. If that's the case, there may be no records pointing his way. No IDs. Nothing."

"If we can't find him"—the insides of my cheeks stick to my teeth—"how do I protect myself?"

"We'll find him. People slip up. It's only a matter of time before he does too. In that regard, we've got something going for us."

Doubtful is an understatement. "What could we possibly have going for us? After everything you just said?"

Detective Henning's tone sharpens. "He's bold. Incredibly—recklessly—bold. To enter your home and leave behind evidence with the intention of tipping you off is brazen. Evidence perhaps depicting homicide with no attempt to mask his identity—quite the opposite, actually. From a law enforcement perspective? It borders on insane." She reaches across the table and takes my hand. It's meant to instill confidence. That she truly empathizes and is still my ally.

Detective Henning's eyes haven't once left mine, but her stare strengthens. "I know it doesn't seem like it. You're scared, and this isn't going to make you feel better, but trust me. Guys like this get caught. Guys like this get caught sooner rather than later."

Trust me, she says. Two words, but I have a fraught history with both.

Do I trust Detective Henning? I don't distrust her intentions. But I don't know if I trust her abilities to help me. My doubt is no libel against her gender.

She squeezes my hand. "Oliver?"

It's fear of a monster.

18

NATHAN

Nathan?" A voice asks from the street outside Walter Reed. A familiar voice and a subtle cold climbs my back. The prowling sedan had pulled up curbside and rolled down a back window like in a mafia movie. "Can I give you a lift?"

I've been intercepted leaving work. By a Bentley Mulsanne in an oily Windsor blue. Its feline lines almost as predatorial as its passenger. "Mother?"

"Get in," she beckons. The sidewalk's hot with steam from a summer rain. "I'm in no hurry. Let me take you home."

My SUV waits in a staff garage one block over, and I almost decline. Then I remember Mother's loaded request to talk real estate and I'm in her car, wrapped in camel leather, burled walnut, and a thinly veiled agenda. "What are you doing here?"

"If you'd answer the phone, you'd know." She removes her vintage shades and—despite an idling AC with the carbon footprint of a 737—tugs her blouse as if to cool down. Her eyes aren't nearly as flippant as her tone. "Awards gala."

"You loathe the New York gala circuit." I buckle up as the car swings into the street. Her driver stays silent. Kept quiet by the Gilded Age sensibilities Mother carries like an Hermès handbag. "I'm supposed to believe you flew down for one?"

"Your father and I have been given a very prestigious award. Thought Leadership in Philanthropy. Victor had business anyway, so we're accepting in person. Tonight." Mother plucks a tissue and touches up stray mascara in a back-seat mirror. "It's a tremendous honor—"

"Again. Something you detest."

An uncomfortable quiet settles. I trust Mother will break it the moment she's ready.

"I took a call yesterday." Her clutch snaps shut like something hungry, and here we go. "Detective—"

"Henning."

"Then it's true?" She jolts, and both bag and jaw drop to her lap. "Jesus, Nathan."

"Oliver is fine."

"I'm certain Oliver is anything but fine." She pronounces *Oliver* like a vaguely French *Olivier*. She can't resect him from my life, so she cuts away what bits she can. His name, low-hanging fruit. "Why didn't you tell me he was mugged? Or assaulted, rather."

"Because." Her peculiar qualification after "mugged" is off-putting. "This conversation right now?"

"She asked very pointed questions," Mother starts. "About you."

"That's protocol," I say, though the conversation veers in a direction it most certainly should not. "Following up with me is justifiable. I'm his husband. Statistically—"

"I know the numbers. I cut my teeth in clinical psychology." And what sharp teeth they are. "Married or not, I know exactly what the woman, Henning, was after."

"What are you after, then?"

"Honestly?" We glide to a soft stop at a traffic light, and Mother pulls her shoulders back. "My son. The very one I assured the detective was with me in New York. At the Millennium Hilton. One UN Plaza and, oddly enough, during the precise time she inquired about."

"Fabulous." I shrug. "You should both be satisfied, then."

"I suppose." She fingers the knot of Tahitian pearls dangling from her neck. Slick and so black I can almost see myself in each one. "If Oliver's injuries happened when Oliver says."

"What are you trying to imply?"

"Easter weekend. Last time you came down to the coast." By "the coast," she means the family getaway nestled in the South Carolina Low Country. We've always kept a winter house on Bald Island, just south of Charleston. We also keep the entire island. "Oliver's behavior there, it bothered me."

"Breaking news," I scoff. "You're never not concerned by Oliver's behavior."

"He was withdrawn, he barely seemed to sleep. I heard him walking about in the night. Everything he said was vague, excessively private." She turns to her window, to the regal homes and tony mid-rises breezing by. "Now he's apparently got bruises, according to the detective."

"He's always withdrawn around you," I say. "I hardly blame him."

"I'm trained to recognize signs." She skirts my sarcasm. "You favor Victor, you know. Your father's sharpness. His tenacity."

"Mother—"

"His temper," she whispers, and my face warms. "Sometimes people disappoint you, frustrate you. People like Oliver? I can only imagine—"

"Fucking Christ," I interrupt as the Bentley closes in on the house. "I must be batshit crazy."

We brake hard out front, and I unbuckle.

"Nathan."

"Because a more lucid me might think you're the one asking pointed questions. We're done talking about Oliver." I start to unlatch the door when three stories of exquisite Georgian brick come into crisp focus. A singing sparrow takes to the air from tall hedges. "You said you had something to tell me? About the townhome?"

"I do." She tightens her lips, recrosses her ankles. It's evident whatever *this* is, it won't be easy. I sink back into hand-stitched leather. "You'll be thrilled to learn your father and I are ready to sign it over to you."

"Sign what over? The house?" My heart flutters. Though I advertise it to exactly no one, I don't own the property Oliver and I call home. The salary leap from the top 5 percent—a surgeon's earnings, for example—to Mother and Father's top 1 percent club is astronomical. The truth is, as surprising as Oliver might find it, I could never afford our house. Nobody deftly baits me quite like Mother. "Go on."

"But," she says, drawing in breath because she always hides her knives in velvet, "I'm not sure you appreciate what that entails."

"It was a gift." *What's your angle?* "From a Klein Foundation donor."

"Not per se." Despite a fresh round of botulinum toxin for a suspiciously timed gala, she somehow peaks an eyebrow. "It was left to Victor—not the foundation—in the late senator Dick Howe's will.

Funny way of doing business back then. Legacy gifts in kind for favors in kind, such as it was."

Nothing about Mother suggests she ever stopped trading in favors. Almost exclusively. I may not own the place outright, but I've done my homework. Pulled the papers because no Klein Foundation staff questions a directive from anyone with said surname. "Our charity is listed on the deed."

"Now it is. What with skyrocketing property values in this little community?" Her sharp eyes travel the ancient oak-lined street. "Transferring it made fiscal sense. The taxes on this one here?" Those same eyes land hard on the house, and she punctuates her point: "Cosmic."

Why am I not at all surprised? "My home is a tax shelter."

"It's not your home," she corrects. "Of course, it could be. Though I imagine you'd find upkeep a challenge. Without any help."

My heart thrums as I brace for her knife. "Help?"

"You and Oliver are a family now—of sorts." Her weapon finds its mark. "It only makes sense you and he should take it."

"You're threatening me." It plunges through my flesh. Deep into something vital, and I choke out: "I cut him loose or you cut me loose?"

"Please, you're always so dramatic. If it's worth keeping Oliver over, your father and I will support your decision." She plays with her own ring like an eight-carat exclamation point. "Emotionally, that is."

"Did you practice this speech on the ride over, or does Joan Crawford just come naturally?"

"You want to keep playing house with Oliver?" She twists her blade. Needlessly and cruelly. "Buy the dollhouse you've made such a mess of."

"Wow." I shut my eyes. She's stabbed me and I can't help but laugh. "This is fucking rich."

"Victor has his playthings. But Victor puts them back in the toy box when he's done. He doesn't live with them." An unsettling pause. "He certainly doesn't *break* them."

"You actually think I hurt my husband, don't you?"

"Husband?" She sneers. "This foolishness stops now. If and when that detective—or anyone else for that matter—contacts you, you're to call me first, understand? I'm the psychotherapist. I know what subtleties she's hunting for. I can help you."

"You booked a flight," I say. "Lurked outside the hospital in a limo like the fucking Godfather or -mother or whatever. Just to—"

"I love you, Nathan." She veers from callous to emotional, and the whiplash nearly snaps my neck. "More than you can know. I will do whatever it takes to—"

"Did you come down to help me or threaten me?"

She burns in silence for a beat, then: "Both."

"An ultimatum, huh?" If I'm gasoline, the cold human calling herself my mother just struck the match. "Tell me, would you be this bold if Oliver was a woman?"

"Don't." Her jawline tenses. Tighter than I've ever seen it. "You know goddamn better than that. Don't go there with me, son."

"If Oliver was my wife, your whole take would change."

"How dare you!" She nearly pulls her pearls apart, and the driver flinches. "I'm a bigot, am I? Thank god you have no clue what that experience would actually be like. If your father and I were so narrow."

"If Oliver was a woman, your *Town & Country* dreams would all be intact." My climbing voice keeps pace with my anger. "Bonnets and driving gloves and grandchildren—"

"How different you'd have turned out," she cuts me off. "If you'd had, say, Oliver's parents."

"His parents are dead."

For a painful stretch, heaving chests and heartbeats are the only sounds.

"You and I both know where this is headed," she grits. "The longer you hold on, the more trouble he'll get himself into. Sometimes the best way to love someone is to leave them."

"Bummer you spent your life as a therapist. Sounds like you missed your calling as a songwriter."

"I'm not asking you to do this for me. Or you, for that matter."

"I've heard all I'm going to hear."

"Do it for him. Before something worse happens, and it's too late."

"The only thing that's too late is you. And this little proposition?" I shake my head. "It's monstrous."

"Speaking of monsters." Her tone abruptly turns again. Suddenly light with a jarring hint of whimsy. It grabs me as I throw open the door.

"What!?"

"I had hoped Oliver's incident might scare him off. Frighten him into leaving because you're far too weak to do it yourself."

"What a shitty thing to say." I step out onto the sidewalk.

"Funny, isn't it? The two of us relying on Oliver to make the right decision."

I lean down to shut the door to the car and the conversation. "We're finished here."

"No, Nathan," she says, nodding to the townhome behind me. "You're finished *there*."

19

OLIVER

On the scale of dumb shit I've done, leaving my card behind the counter at Haus is almost transcendent. I ordered replacements for everything in my junked wallet—including said card—and yet, here I am. Nathan was right to question why I'd even go running with it in the first place. Can't even clean up mistakes without making things worse. And making his life needlessly harder.

"This is good," I say. The patrol car driving me back from the station brakes hard. A few blocks from an address that's now cauterized in my memory: Haus.

"You sure?" the cop at the wheel asks. "Not much around here, kid."

"Yeah, I'm sure. Thanks."

My credit card statement was of zero value to Detective Henning, but to me, it's something far more dangerous: a loose end.

"All right, then," he says, popping the locks. "Take care of yourself."

Kristian might've stolen my card just as easily as my license. It may be canceled, but he's nothing if not creative. I can't begin to predict the ways it could still be used against me.

I slam the passenger door too hard. Daylight dulls the edge, but it can't stifle my anxiety much. The brief rain's vanished, leaving a scalding wetness behind. Anxiety, not panic. I can do this so long as anxiety's all I must contend with. Panic will unravel me, garble my words, make me useless.

I have to get my card back.

As the police car peels off, I squeeze my pocket pepper spray and find landmarks. A bent street sign, a graffitied dumpster screaming DICK CITY! in red spray paint. Trees—intentionally obscuring—thick with stringy creepers. No cameras. Nobody out and about. Broken glass under my sneakers.

The front lot, however, is full. My heart rate spikes and my skull buzzes from the inside out. In a visceral way, it's all the same as last time. Standing here, working up the nerve to go inside. Only then it was anticipatory, transgressive excitement. Now? Unadulterated fear. Self-preservation.

Keep moving, Oliver. Lingering will cause me to turn tail.

The cinder-block building looms with a grimness that's almost spectral. Bone gray and the same paint covers that windowless door.

I need to know if my card's gone *before* Kristian slips it under Nathan's office door—accompanied by a love note or god knows what else. At the very least, I'll force the coward, the Cheshire Cat, to look me in the eyes when he lies. To see my throat. To know who he's hurting and who he protects.

When I step inside—when the solvent reek of lavender pulls bile from my gut—I find the Cheshire Cat right where I left him last.

My hands, my legs, my fucking spine—everything trembles. From behind plexiglass, he doesn't even look up. "You a member?" he asks, distractedly thumbing through papers.

"I am."

"I'll need to see your—" His eyes meet mine. His sentence, unfinished.

The silence between us is oddly intimate. A connection that teeters on the brink of adversarial. Walks the line between conflict and camaraderie. The two of us have a past. We've experienced something together we'd rather not have.

I've bitten into my tongue without knowing it and taste metal.

"You know who I am," I start.

"I don't." A tiny quiver takes his bottom lip. "You say you're a member?" Another pause. "I need your ID."

Anger blooms, spreads as a tingling numbness down my back. I can't stop it. "You know who the fuck I am!"

His shoulders jump. He swivels back a foot or so in his chair, eyes shooting to a desk phone.

"You know exactly who the fuck I am," I scream. "Huh, liar?"

"I don't, I don't know," he stammers. Phone off the hook, thick fingers perched to dial.

Tears well. Flecks of spit spray the glass. "Why would you lie to the police? Someone tried to kill me, strangled me." I thrust my arm at door number two. "Right through there!"

"I'm sorry," the Cat stutters. Eyes glossy, crowded face a hot scarlet. "I'm very, *very* sorry."

A thought strikes and I tear my phone from my pocket. Scrolling with wet thumbs isn't easy, but it's the first picture in the roll. Ocean-deep, mocking eyes. I press my phone to the glass.

"Him! He tried to kill me!" My voice catches. "This man, do you know him? Is he here a lot?"

My last question spawns a far darker one: *Is he here now?*

The Cat's narrow eyes fix on my screengrab. "Never seen that man," he whispers, one hand still hovering over the shrieking phone.

"This man you've never seen? He tried to murder me." I've gone full-blown raving, but no easing up on the gas now. "Here. He's killed before. Guys that didn't get away. He'll kill again. You know him. You saw the blood. How long did it take you to bleach all that shit out?"

His chair yaws like a sinking ship as he shifts his weight uneasily.

"Look." Shaking, I point to my purpled throat. "You see this? See the marks he made?"

The Cat wipes his mouth, hangs the phone up, and pushes his chair back. Then he finally says something useful: "Outside."

•   •

Back in sobering daylight, the Cat turns his door key. "One-way lock. Guys can leave, but nobody else gets in. Let's go around."

Now the sudden fixation with safety?

The rear lot's the same as the front, only the tree line creeps closer. Whatever space the thicket's not threatening to reclaim seems like staff parking.

Only now do I appreciate the Cheshire Cat's size. He could easily, well, kill me. Gray tee, floral board shorts, and lime flip-flops. He packs menthols on his palm and slips one between his lips. When the tip turns into a hot cherry, I breathe in deep.

"Don't know who that guy is." After drag number three, he starts talking. "I'm sorry about how this shit went down." Drag number four. "But look, I was freaking the fuck out. I called Jimmy and Bill—the owners, old queens. By the time they got here, that dude was gone. So were you."

Why the hell didn't you call the cops? I don't ask this because it wasn't until the following day that I'd gone to the police. And if Kristian hadn't found me on MeetLockr, I wouldn't have made a report at all.

"They made the call. Said if something happened, it was on you guys to work it out privately. Made me"—he pauses—"made me clean up everything. Then came behind and cleaned again." He sucks what's left of his smoke. "I'm Theo, by the way." He extends his hand, and I shake it. Both our palms are clammy and wet and uncomfortable. "I'm really sorry this happened to you."

"Oliver."

"I know." He nods. "Jimmy and Bill, they made me find your membership info, license copy, and get rid of it. Over there." He gestures to a back corner where a metal bin's been blackened by a trash fire.

"My credit card, I left it behind." I rub my scalp. "Did you destroy it?"

"I mean, yeah?" He takes my epic sigh of relief as frustration. "Look, I'm sorry—"

"The other guy?" I ask. My card's gone for good, and fresh optimism swells. "His name's Kristian. Did you find his info? They must've asked you to destroy both."

"They did." Theo shakes his head. "And I checked like a hundred times over. I knew what the guy looked like. Enough to promise Jimmy and Bill he wouldn't be let back in. He was fucking hot compared to the usual crowd, and no way I'd forget his face. I got a good look when he ran out past me too. Covering his cheek."

"And what did you find?"

"Nothing." He slips a pin through my ballooning hope and it pops.

"Must've used a fake ID. Or stolen, maybe." He looks at his feet. What he says next seems to embarrass him, as though he's ashamed of phoning in the job he does for Haus. "It's dark. A lot of guys coming and going. A lot of faces. I don't really match the ID to the person. Just make the copy, take the cash, provide the towel, the key. The condoms and the lube."

I recall what Detective Henning said, that Kristian might not be in the country legally. "The police. They're going to bring you in for questioning."

Theo tightens his cheeks like he's sucking sour candy. What I've said makes him afraid, and I don't blame him. Kind of feel for him, even. Lying to the cops, destroying evidence. We're both textbook nefarious.

"You need to tell her, Detective Henning, exactly what happened. She needs to place me here. She needs to place me and Kristian at Haus on Saturday night."

"Jimmy and Bill—"

"Told you to do the wrong thing. You know they did." I'm struck by shame as I say this. Blatant hypocrisy. I'm lecturing this man on the importance of being transparent. Truthful.

"This gig is the only thing keeping my head above water. Student debt is fucking brutal—"

"Blood," I counter. "Blood on your hands is fucking brutal."

"Okay," he says. "I'll tell her. I'll change my story. But the owners, you gotta understand, they're good guys. Good people. They just come from a different time."

I'm uninterested in the owners of Haus or the excuses Theo makes for them, but I've got a tenuous grip on his cooperation. I don't want to screw that up. The more we bond, the deeper he forms a human connection, the more likely he'll give Detective Henning what she needs.

He pitches his cigarette into a puddle. "One where getting caught meant getting curb-stomped. Killed. And if homophobes didn't do the job, well, gays didn't grow old back then for lots of reasons.

"Point is, they're used to living underground. When park cruising and bathhouses were the norm. It's all they know. Now, with apps like Meet-Lockr? Pop a PrEP pill and HIV's knocked halfway off the table. Everything's normal. And normalized makes people safe. Jimmy and Bill, they don't trust the progress. And plenty of other folks don't either—that's how we're in business. I mean, even you . . ." He lets this last bit hang unfinished.

"I don't doubt their intentions. They cater to a community; they're protective of Haus. But when they cover up, when they *burn evidence,* ask yourself who they're protecting." Again, creeping hypocrisy rears its head, but this time, it's harder to club back.

"When they come asking, I'll tell the cops you were here." He looks over his shoulder. "I was confused or some shit. But I need to get back to the front."

"Yeah." I give him a smile. "Okay. Thanks."

We shake hands a second time. "Glad you're okay."

He vanishes back into Haus's darkness, but his parting words are a cruel joke. He's glad I'm okay, which couldn't be further from the truth. As I send for an Uber, another thought emerges, edging out the hypocrisy and guilt: I've gotten somewhere.

No more needless panic over a lost card, but that's not my only progress. Because of my coming here, confronting the Cheshire Cat now named Theo, Detective Henning's investigation takes a solid step forward. She has a witness willing to place me—and an injured man matching Kristian's description—at the scene of his crime. On the date in question.

I don't have to be a passive participant in Kristian's sociopathy. While he stalks my life. Enters my home. Scares the shit out of me.

Who else can I confront?

20

Nathan and I sit at a back table inside Leek. A chic restaurant wrapped in warmth and soft lighting and the earthy umami of roasted flesh.

We await the bill to a soundtrack of clinking glasses and muted laughter. The table linen. The dancing flame of the tea light. Our plates, remnants of balsamic asparagus and drawn butter and pan-seared wild tuna. We've both had the tuna. Nathan ordered for us because it's rich in omega-3 fatty acids. It's good for me, and Nathan's a doctor. He knows what's good for me.

Sensing my detachment, he asks, "Is everything okay?"

"Yeah." I bite the inside of my bottom lip. "No. I'm still a bit jarred from Saturday. To tell the truth."

"That's hardly surprising." His voice holds a sardonic edge that doesn't sit well. He takes hold of his wineglass and drains the last drop of cabernet. When he speaks again, his tone is milder. "Have you thought any more about my suggestion? Heading back to NA for a bit? It'll help."

I turn my used fork—crusted with sea flesh—over on the linen. Then over again. And again. "I'll think about it."

"I hope you do, Oliver, I really hope you do." When he says my name like that, it bothers me. It's patronizing. But, everything I've done, everything Nathan knows I've done and everything he doesn't, warrants parenting. I've brought this on myself. I've made a trade-off. Decided long ago I needed guardrails, and Nathan provides them. Fulfilled the expectation. Our unspoken agreement.

Nathan's phone vibrates against the tabletop. Tom. We're due to meet him at Trance next. A clichéd gay bar with a clichéd name.

As Nathan's fingers tap-tap-tap, a server drops off the check. Not once looking up, not stopping to think or missing a beat, Nathan tucks his card into the leather billfold.

This tiny action is as bothersome as the parenting, if not more so. There's zero expectation for me to pay. Sure, Nathan makes more—and any outsider would conclude I benefit handsomely from it—but it serves as a stark reminder of my place. In every way, I need Nathan. I need him to keep me from drugs. I need him for shelter, for food. Most important, I need him for life. Nathan is the reason I breathe.

It's not perfect, but it's a need. Not a want, not a desire, but a must-have. Risking it with a visit to Haus was one of the worst decisions of my life. Why did I give in? Why did I let Nathan burrow so deep under my skin? Push me into acting out?

What Detective Henning said earlier today about having to tell him, I consider the meaning of that. The painful opening up, the admission of lying and infidelity. I could lose him. The concussive shock waves that would detonate through my life, the important things it would destroy. My sobriety. Could I survive it? Could I *physically survive* Nathan leaving me?

That I once thought it'd be worth it is laughable. Casual Encounters, MeetLockr, Haus. An escape from a stifling cage beneath an all-too-perfect veneer. A guilty conscience was supposed to be the worst of it. Worth enduring for a fleeting reprieve, and I couldn't have been more wrong.

"I want to change our locks." I drop my fork clumsily and it rattles on my plate.

Nathan hesitates. "Change our locks because you were randomly mugged on a jog? I gave you my pepper spray."

"I haven't slept well since Saturday. It's irrational, but it'll help." My next words are designed to manipulate, to use my own past as leverage. "I don't want to keep taking pills to sleep."

"Of course." Nathan takes a deep breath. "We'll change the locks, then."

An invisible weight on my shoulders lessens. Not much, a pebble removed from an enormous pile, but I'm better. Lighter.

"Thanks so much." Nathan smiles as the server swipes his card. He clicks the butt of a pen on the table and I picture him signing my death warrant.

It all plays out in my head—Nathan's response to the truth. He would be furious outside and in. I *think* I've seen him mad like that before. Not at me, and each time I was grateful to not be the object of his fiery ire. I don't think he'd put hands on me. I don't think he'd hurt me. That's not who he is, and I chose him—or let him choose me—specifically because of who he isn't.

But he might very well hurt me in other ways. He almost certainly would. Emotional wounds burn hotter. Something Nathan knows. But the ultimate question, the question of whether he would leave, whether he would lock me out of the safety and security of our life together— that, I can't answer.

Another vibration. This time it's my phone. My eyes dart to Nathan first. He's returned his attention to his own and hasn't noticed. *Kristian*. The first place my thoughts stampede anytime there's a call or a text.

I turn it over. An incoming call, but the number's unrecognizable.

"Ready to head out?" Nathan's already half standing.

"Sure," I say, and follow his lead.

Typically, I'd use the time between dinner and drinks to mentally prepare for the forthcoming company. I'd tick through anything interesting or new that's happened. Come up with talking points to fill shallow conversation. When said company will be Tom Vogt, this ritual takes on new importance. Anything that mitigates my own insecurities.

But this time, as the lights of bodegas and bars and coffeehouses whirl by like neon river water, I think only of that damned phone call.

Whoever it was left a voicemail. Has Kristian discovered my number? It's not on my license, but it's on plenty of documents at home. And if he's the competent stalker–slash–homicidal maniac I think he is, he's got everything.

Still, there was something familiar about those digits. Something that scratches at an itch in the back of my brain.

"You wanna get out?" Nathan brakes. "See if Tom's already here? I'll find parking."

The idea of sitting alone with Tom for any stretch of time hits me somewhere behind the eyes. Like the last time I saw him. The miserable experience of sharing a drink the day after Kristian tried to kill me.

"I'd rather go in together."

• •

We walk to the entrance of Trance. Bass thumping. Boys in tight-fitting clothes smoking out front. Gesticulating wildly, dramatically. Guffawing and touching and slurping up the twirling parade of men.

Nathan doesn't seem to mind or care, but I cast my eyes downward.

Inside, the noise doubles, triples. Ace of Base—the electronica drumbeat of a "Cruel Summer" remix pulses like a pink heartbeat. The collective volume of conversation raised to combat the music is almost unbearable.

"I see him!" Nathan half screams.

As we plunge deeper into the bowels of Drinks with Tom™ the voices grow sharper, like bedazzled kitchen knives. A crowd that's almost exclusively white and either rich or pretending to be. Laughter and *oh my god, he's fat now* and *oh my god, that bottom is sloppy* and *oh my god, his bussy's worn the fuck out.* Toxic snippets spoken or whispered or shrieked from behind copper Moscow mules and martinis screaming for help through olive eyes.

I trace Nathan's steps to a corner table where Tom sits. Standing room only, and Tom's got a whole table—bottle service and enviably elevated—to himself. Tom Vogt, the Emperor of Trance.

He's in denim, a pressed shirt patterned with interlocking something or other. A navy sports jacket. As usual, he's effortlessly chic. Successful. Comfortable navigating the hallowed halls of Capitol Hill and the sweat-soaked dance floor of a gay disco.

Nathan and Tom hug first, kissing cheeks. Then it's my turn and I gulp.

"It looks so much better." Tom starts the conversation at the last place I'd prefer—my throat. "I can barely see it." This is a lie, but it's a polite lie. I shouldn't hold this against him.

"Thank you," I say. "Feels better."

His attention turns to Nathan. "I've got drinks coming. Vodka tonics for the girls." *Himself and me.* "And warm bourbon for the ninety-year-old robber baron. I swear to god, you could wear a monocle with the shit you drink."

Nathan laughs, but there's a kernel of truth in Tom's assessment of Nathan's drinking. The joke is too on the nose, especially for Tom.

"So how was New York?" Tom asks as drinks find their way to our table. "At least it wasn't *Cleveland* Clinic again." His pronounces *Cleveland* with the usual blanket disdain he reserves for the entire Midwest. For my home and, by extension, me.

"It was okay," Nathan answers. "Not a lot of downtime, and of course, I had to see Mother."

"Mamma Klein gives me life!" Wide eyes and a predictably overzealous reply. Tom's been fixated on Nathan's mother since the moment he saw her splashed across the pages of *New York Social Diary*. "I'd literally kill to be Mother!"

"Feel free to literally kill her."

"Please," Tom scoffs.

"Anyway, I'm glad to be home." He takes my hand as he says this. A genuine expression of love. He is happy to be back in my company. I hold on to small moments like these. As Aqua's "Barbie Girl" thrums like a lucid dream, these moments remind me that, at the end of the day, I'm luckier than I often appreciate. They remind me of what I stand to lose.

"I'm ridiculously glad Oliver's okay. Scared the shit out of me." His hold on my hand tightens.

"This city's fucking violent." Tom turns my way. "You're, like, the tenth person I know that's been mugged. Three at gunpoint."

"Speaking of guns," Nathan says, "saw Ted Rucker on *Hannity* at the hotel. Your boss was a piece of shit, as per usual."

"Why were you watching fucking Fox News?" Tom asks. "It's my job to watch. I have to. You don't."

"Pulse check on Senator Turd Fucker and everything you support."

"A paycheck's not support."

"A paycheck's the most ardent support there is."

Tom counters with something, but it barely registers. My mind crawls out from beneath a discussion veering political and toward my waiting voicemail. Patient like a crocodile at the surface. Elliptical eyes and reptilian nostrils, tiny iceberg tips.

Nathan and Tom grow muffled as though acid-lit Trance were submerged in swamp water. I forgo listening and search blurred faces like I did on the morning Metro. I look for Kristian's wound and those arctic eyes in each one. I turn up nothing in the glittering room, but what about in my back pocket?

"I'm going to the bathroom."

Nathan and Tom say nothing as I stand and make my way to the back. This is—tragically—not my first time at Trance. Past the corridor and the bathroom—each urinal painted like a pair of lips—sits a deck with an outside bar. Beyond that, an exit to a side street. Where guys gather to smoke and where I've bummed countless cigarettes. Reeking of Marlboro post-bar isn't incriminating and I've repeatedly exploited the loophole.

I expect cool relief from a stifling, heat-swollen Trance, but the District's humidity has other ideas. I push through the crowd. The leering I enjoyed within Haus's wet walls is now unwelcome. Someone cups my ass, and it takes everything not to sink teeth into his wrist.

Finally on the street and alone, my spine meets cool brick, and I draw a deep breath. *You can do this,* I think. *You must do this.*

Phone to my ear. The voicemail plays and something clicks.

Lots of things click, actually. Everything fits into place suddenly like a self-solving puzzle. The elusive familiarity of the number. The unresolvable déjà vu.

"Hey, Oliver, it's me. Sorry to call like this, but I, I'm in DC, and thought it'd be nice to see you. Catch up over a drink. Or whatever. Anyway, call me back. I'm here for a bit."

The number, the area code attached to it. Indiana. Tyre, Indiana. A hint of laughter punctuates the message. Though there's not a damn thing funny about it.

"This is Hector, by the way."

21

NATHAN

The empty cocktail glasses on our table have multiplied, and despite Oliver, I've managed to pry fun from the jaws of defeat. I'm enjoying myself for the first time since his assault. Since Detective Henning's bizarre third degree. A lecture on spousal privilege like she suspects both of us of something. Since Mother held her own theory to my throat like a switchblade. Drawing just enough blood for her threat to go unquestioned.

As soon as Oliver excused himself, Tom ordered shots and led a game of Would You Fuck Him? which he clearly had just made up. The subtext in his timing, however? Strategic. As he pointed around Trance, he gave eight yeses—though each with specific caveats like *only head* and *might jerk him off* and *girl, that man could* wreck *me.*

I gave zero, and Tom couldn't have been more disappointed.

I'm not aloof—or worse, puritanical. But I honestly could not imagine sleeping with any of Tom's strangers because none of them are Oliver. After five years of dwindling emotional investment from him, do I have some kind of psychosexual issue? I should ask a therapist not named Kathy Klein.

"Seriously? Not even that one?"

I shoot silver Patrón like fiery butter and follow Tom's gaze to a man spinning a tumbler alone at the bar. Blond bangs, husky blue eyes, and maybe . . . maybe I just might. He lifts a sharp chin and catches me staring. I quickly turn. "No."

"We should ask Oliver." Neon glistens in Tom's eyes like something devilish. "Maybe he's feeling more peckish than you tonight."

"Oliver's not hungry." I drain a last finger of bourbon. "But speaking of, I also need to leak."

"Let me know how fresh the bathroom buffet is." Tom's got the start of a slur.

I stand, push my chair back. The blood falls from my head a little too fast, and the room skews crooked for a moment. Turning down a narrow hall wide enough for maybe two people, and Oliver's nowhere to be seen.

As I wait for a free toilet, my eyes briefly meet those of a twenty-something running product through thick hair in the mirror. Like the blond at the bar, he's quick to look away as though it were an accident.

"Blake?" A disembodied voice whines from an occupied stall.

"What?" the twenty-something at the sink says.

"Got any Adderall?"

"Yeah," Blake calls back, his middle finger now painting his lips with balm. "Give me a sec."

I seriously doubt either Blake or his toilet friend have attention deficit hyperactivity disorder, but the apparent bathroom drug of choice calls uncomfortable attention to my age. ADHD drugs? Whatever happened to good old-fashioned blow? I never really partied, but the gap between *then* and *now*—between me and Oliver—grows wider. A gap to me, anyway. To him, it's a chasm as deep as the Mariana Trench. What Mother said set my soul on fire. I was furious because that's how we respond to brutal reckoning. When denial's that thick, you can suffocate yourself with it like a pillow.

He's ungrateful.

A stall finally frees up. I go quickly, wash my hands for the same twenty seconds I would before any surgery, and decide this night's nearly done.

The hall outside the door is more crowded than it was minutes ago. I shoulder my way through small gaps between tanks and tight tees. To my left, the patio door swings open, and I catch a sliver of Oliver. He's on the sidewalk just beyond the deck.

And on the phone.

A knot of something—something like tears or sadness or anger or all of them bound together—builds in my throat. *Ungrateful.*

"Excuse me, *sir*." Blake and company exit the bathroom and push by. I hold my ground and shoulder-check one of them. Hard. "Ow! What the fuck's your problem, guy!?"

He waits for an apology. When he accurately perceives one's not coming, he meets my eyes like he just might leap. I shove a finger deep in his clavicle, and he squeals.

"You can fuck right off," I say.

Opting to swallow his pride over his own teeth, he does just that. I fix my eyes back on the street outside. Oliver runs a hand through his hair, pacing. My cheeks still simmer and maybe Tom's right, after all. Who are you talking to, Oliver?

You're ungrateful, but are you also peckish?

22

OLIVER

TYRE, IN

The grass smelled sharp, as if Blaire had cut it just for the occasion. Dew gathered like a sparkling carpet as dawn crept closer. Threatening to end one stage of revelry and usher in another—grease at the highway Waffle House where Mom sometimes pulled shifts when she was alive.

The once-towering firepit blaze was nothing but a smolder now. White smoke, tangy and woody, touched the air.

I was in a good place. The nervousness over showing up with Hector had proven unnecessary. Of course Blaire would be fine with it. Her parents likely not, but they'd been banished to their double-wide's interior. Some of the others knew, mostly the girls. Some didn't. Mostly the roughnecks with Browning-branded hats and Dixie Outfitters belt buckles—which I always found so stupid. Indiana's never been part of the Old South, but white cis-het male entitlement gets to pick and choose through history like a lost and found. Taking whatever it wants and turning a blind eye to the rest.

Hector and I made no obvious show of togetherness; we'd all screamed the countdown to the New Year together like drunk howler monkeys. Happy, drunken howlers sending half-feral barn cats skittering.

Hector hadn't kept his promise. A fresh beer was in his hand the whole night. Glazed pupils the size of saucers. Slurring from booze and oxy.

A corner of me was jealous. Beer had done okay, but a familiar itch burned between my bones. I hadn't popped a pill since noon. I'd wanted to keep control, given that Hector and I were coming here as a couple. I didn't want to say the wrong thing. Tip off the wrong person to the fact that Hector and I were a thing. A gay thing.

Shame dictated my decisions, but what I felt for Hector, the consuming attachment? Love or a close-enough cousin to it, and I didn't want us reduced to sexual terms. Base, demeaning, ignorant. Stupid questions about pitching and catching, who's the woman, and how we fuck. I didn't want it sullied like that. So I didn't take any oxy, and now I wished different.

I told Hector I had to piss, and he nodded. I was unsure if he was nodding in the affirmative or literally *nodding*. As in, what folks on too much oxy did. A teetering between awake and asleep.

The trailer was off-limits, so I made for the tree line. Which was fine by me because I can't pee around people anyway. Only ever stalls in public restrooms—never urinals. And despite the fact the woods are dark and whispery, it was this first fear that drove me far from glowing lights.

When the yard lanterns dimmed, when the laughter muffled, I undid my fly and leaked on a tree trunk. Back to the party so I could face the thicket's shadows. Threats, dangers imagined or otherwise, come from the dark. Where I saw and heard things that weren't really there.

Trickling piss against foliage masked careful steps. Careful steps I swore I almost heard but told myself I didn't. But leaves and twigs did in fact snap and crackle beneath heavy boots. I was almost finished when the steps drew close.

A pair of arms wrapped around my stomach like a seat belt, and I leapt.

The sleeves were Hector's. He'd followed me into the woods. "Jesus, Hector, what are you doing?"

He said nothing. But his hands groped. He was drunk and high and he reached for my dick. I jolted and peed on his hand by accident. He didn't seem to notice. Or he was way too fucked up.

"I wanna fuck," he drawled. It was dark, but his belt buckle clicked open.

"What?" I pivoted, and he grabbed my arm. The speed at which he did this was surprising, all things considered. "We're not fucking."

"I wanna nut," he said, bringing his face close to mine. Through the beer, his breath reeked of metallic tin or copper. "I wanna nut in you."

I pushed away. He wobbled, but his grip tightened. His strength as surprising as his speed. I was unsure if he grasped my arm to steady himself or to stay me. Didn't matter which because he wouldn't let go.

"Stop it." I wasn't shouting. I wasn't mad. He was intoxicated, and honestly, so was I. He just needed to let me go.

Holding his ground and my arm, his other hand plunged into his pants. He was serious then. He was pulling his dick out. Right here, within earshot of a backyard full of wasted rednecks.

"Hector, no." I threw a sharp edge in my voice, and he traded my arm for my groin.

"I wanna nut." It was all he could manage to spit. A skipping record, and it was such a stupid thing to say. "Remember Barceloneta Beach? We jacked each other underwater. In front of the whole—"

"We're not in fucking Spain!" When I turned again, he grabbed the back of my shirt and I spun.

I started to scream, to yell *stop!* but nothing came out. For a moment, not longer than a fraction of a second, our eyes connected. Mine, dry from cold wind. His, the size of dinner plates.

Clouds parted, and the moon set the forest aglow. It lit his eyes with something I'd never seen before. Something hot like firepit flames. Something furious and swallowed by heat and rage.

The fire in Hector's eyes, it burned. Then my cheek burned. My cheek was on fire. Hector had slapped me across my face.

I was frozen, stunned. The slap paralyzed me head to toe. He couldn't have known how hard he struck me. He was too fucked up. Before I could process what happened, he was on me. I choked on the staleness of his heavy jacket.

My cheek throbbed with neon pain. He held my face. His thumb dug into one cheek. The rest of his fingers pushed into the other, and he puckered my lips like a fish. He squeezed, brought my face so close the tips of our noses touched.

"I'm gonna fuck you the way you like." Metal breath. "Hard."

"Please," I groaned through smashed lips. "Stop it—"

He pulled my pants to my thighs, shoved me onto the thicket floor. Wet leaves on bare skin set off a firestorm of thoughts.

The whole of his weight pressed me into frosty dirt. I felt him on the inside of my thigh.

"What the fuck?" A new voice.

Hector jumped to his feet. Pants up just as quick. Heaving on the ground, I rolled over and did the same. One of the guys from the party—Dane or Dave or Donnie—must've had to go too. He stood yards away, fists by his sides.

"It's fine," Hector slurred.

"You okay?"

"Yeah—"

"Not you." He flicked his chin my way. "You?"

"Yeah." Staggering to my feet, I coughed into cold air and zipped my jeans. "Fine."

Hector said something. Maybe to me, maybe to Dane or Dave or Donnie, but I was spinning. I stumbled and started the long walk out of the woods. A far longer walk than I could've imagined at that time.

Hector shouted from behind, and I sped up.

"Oliver?"

He couldn't have known. I was jogging now. He couldn't have known how hard he slapped me.

"Oliver!"

I broke into a full sprint.

Was he going to do it? That? I said *no*. I told him no!

I took to the country road winding from the farmhouse.

No!

The wild brush to both sides became walls. Mighty and impervious. Every breath briefly fogged before it was whisked away, dashed in my wake.

I started to cry. Slow tears turned to sobs, and I was forced to stop for breath.

Hands on my knees, I stared at scuffed sneakers. My pant leg was wet with piss from Hector's groping. Hector who tried to fuck me. Hector who slapped me. Hector who liked to choke me from behind. I had told Hector I liked it—being choked—even though it scared me shitless.

Hector who had once kept squeezing until I passed out. For a tiny instant, but long enough to know he'd gone too far. And long enough for him to paint my back with drops of warmth because going too far really did it for him. Hector who saved his softer touch for crushing pills.

Did Mom really see me? Did she somehow know what I'd become? Was she watching this right now?

Cancer had shrunk her to a gaunt woman with no hair and yellowed skin. Pain so deep it bled into her marrow. And this was what I was. This was the son she raised. The son she loved and dressed and celebrated birthdays and Christmases for. The son she read to. The son she taught never to touch a woman like my father touched her. The son who was afraid, always afraid, of the day he'd lose his mother when Dad finally went too far. The day that came early anyway.

This was her son. It turned out I was just like her. Touched in all the wrong ways by men. Strung out. Piss on his pants. Face burning from being struck. From being betrayed by the same person who had convinced him to betray her. To park down the street from our tiny blue house with white shutters so she wouldn't wake from the car crunching gravel. So she wouldn't think this was a visit as I slow-walked up the porch and passed her flower boxes covered in hand-painted magpies. To creep into her bedroom, the sanctuary hospice had built for her to die in. *Just once,* he'd said. But that first time was the last I saw her alive.

I chose a few hours of high, chose myself, chose fucking Hector! All over the jaundiced, bleeding, moaning woman departing life as torturously as she lived it. I stole my dying mother's pain medication.

I chose myself over the woman who only ever chose me.

III. Unconsciousness

*Respiratory arrest. Awareness of self
and environment ceases.*

23

Nathan's alarm clock goes off. A shrieking banshee that leaves no room for excuses. He wipes his eyes, and his lips meet my forehead.

I see all this because I haven't slept. I hold on to a vague sense that perhaps I have. An ephemeral dream maybe, but a part of me is happy I haven't. Memories of my attack can't strike in the morning like a billy club because they've beat me all night. Kristian's fingers tight on my throat, traveling my dresser drawers, crawling the shoulders of a man named Devin. The one he'd later strangle on film.

The light in the hallway comes on. Farther down, Nathan shuts the guest bathroom door, and Tilly stirs in her bed. She begins to pace the room, anxious for breakfast.

A knot burns in the pit of my stomach. I'd switched my phone to silent—no vibrating—because I didn't want to know if, or when, it went off. But now's the time. Nathan's up. The day beckons, and I must look.

Confront, I tell myself. Confront.

Three texts wait patiently. Each from Hector's number and the first two timestamped at 11:03 p.m.:

Hey

Not sure if you got my message earlier. I'm in town. Want to see you. Call me back.

I scroll for the last message—the one that will reveal much about Hector. About where he's been since I left his life. Whether he's continued the bottomless descent on our once-shared elevator or at some point stepped off. Maybe even climbed the stairs back to sobriety like me.

Timestamp says 3:17 a.m. A large block of text. Not a good sign of things to come.

Oliver, please call me. Please. I wanna see you. I don't want anything else. I don't want you. I'm happy for you. I'm just in town. For work. Got a job. It's great. But I want to see you. Want to catch up. We have so much history. No reason we can't be friends. Heard a song tonight & it made me think we could be friends . . .

The message goes on, covers the same ground repeatedly. Endless iterations of a handful of sentences. Hector's still on the elevator. Maybe he does have work, and maybe that's why he's in the city, but he's still using. He might've cleaned up enough for gainful employment, but that's a stoned text. Not a drunk text rife with misspellings and nonsensical sentences. He's high as fuck.

Nathan re-enters, wet towel loose around his hips. "Still in bed, sleepyhead?"

"I'm up," I say, and roll over. Sitting on the bedside, I rub my eyes.

"Anything interesting?" He pulls a pair of scrubs from his side of the closet.

"Oh, no." I slip my phone into the folds of the top sheet. "Not really."

• •

I struggle to focus on the tasks at hand. Kimberly's patient calendar. Resolving appointment conflicts. The birthday card awaiting my signature. A pink Grim Reaper on the front because a technician turns the big five-oh today.

These tasks feel overwhelming, which is bizarre because I'm too smart for a job like this. My self-awareness and self-sabotage have made it a slow-drip water torture.

But this morning, it's a hundred times worse. Kristian has destroyed my sense of security and possibly my relationship, and now Hector—Hector!—has surfaced like the undead. The psychological distance between us is tenfold the geographic space. Yet, here he is. Here's Hector, and I'm overwhelmed by signing a fucking office birthday card.

"They look better." Kimberly tosses a meaty folder into the tray marked RETURN TO CHART ROOM. "Your bruises."

"They look worse." This morning, the mirror gave me yellowed, sour green.

"That's how bruises go. They take on more menacing colors and shapes as they heal," she says, and I guess she would know. "How's Nathan handling it?"

"He never got back to you?" I ask. Kimberly's also never pried like this before.

"He did. To rant about that fight with his mother. He was dismissive about everything else going on." She scrunches her face. "Kind of worries me. We usually don't keep things from each other."

The same can't be said of Nathan and me; he certainly never mentioned *that fight*.

"He's doing okay." I offer a smile, which Kimberly returns before checking steps on her watch. Thankfully, her attention is elsewhere for the rest of the morning. She's always on her phone between patients, but now I wonder how many of those back-and-forths are with Nathan.

The two of them must keep plenty of things from each other, I assure myself.

Right?

•   •

It's nearly noon when I see Hector behind my monitor. Standing before my reception desk in the lobby of First Choice Internal Medicine.

I'm speechless. Shocked by the sense of invasion. The expectation, the entitlement. *How the hell did he find me?*

"Hey, Oliver." He parts his lips in a vague smile. The intent is that it be warm, gracious even, as though he's to be applauded for taking the first step in our reconnection. It doesn't help that he's standing and I'm sitting. He's literally the bigger person.

My heart climbs my throat, and I'm suddenly cold behind the chest bone.

"What are you doing here?" I stutter.

Hector's dark hair is gelled into a side part. A loose lock, fallen from his bangs to that still-tanned brow. His clothes look expensive, fine, and contemporary, like they might be tailored. Nothing about this look squares with the man I know. Maybe I don't know him. Or maybe it's a front—in which case I very much still do.

"I'm in town like I told you. A work conference." Hector emphasizes the word *work*.

"Said that a few times in your messages," I reply, clearing my throat to make my appraisal of his sobriety plain. "Where are you working?"

My cheeks redden because I've asked Hector a follow-up question. One that can't be answered with a simple *yes* or *no*. I'm already fucking this up. Paving the way for discussion. For the reunion I want nothing but to avoid.

"Pharmaceutical sales." Even he can't skirt the self-styled irony, so he adds: "Diabetes medication."

"Wow." I feign sarcasm, struggle to gain a foothold. "Congrats."

"It's been a while, Oliver." It's the second time he's said my name in under a minute. Like he's staking a claim. "You wanna grab lunch? I'm only in town for a few more days. No hidden agenda. I only want to see you, talk to you. Then I'm back to Indiana. Gone."

Gone. I like that word. As far as he's concerned, I'm gone. Been gone for quite some time. And from my perspective, he's gone too. Tyre, gone.

I'm unsure if it was Hector's intention, if he has the mental where-withal to manipulate my feelings anymore, but no denying it works. Maybe he knows I'll do anything to put him back there. Maybe he knows I'll give a little to make him *gone* sooner.

"Starbucks." I draw in a staccato breath. "There's one in the lobby downstairs."

"You don't want to get a bite to eat?" He checks a leather wristwatch. "It's lunchtime."

I've given in to Starbucks, but he wants an entire meal? Hector's never met a healthy boundary he's failed to push.

"Coffee, Hector." I use his name this time, let him see what that feels like.

Grinning, he gestures to the door as if he's the host and I'm the guest. A quick scan for Kimberly because this is one thing that most certainly should be kept from Nathan. She's nowhere to be seen and hopefully I'm the same to her. An imaginary breeze of vinegar and metal—the last smell memory holds of Hector—reminds me to call the chart room.

"Ten minutes. Tops," I tell the nurse on the other end, but the message is meant for Hector. I'll be missed if I don't come back.

As I follow his footsteps out of Kimberly's office, it occurs to me that Hector hasn't mentioned my throat. His sudden appearance, out of nowhere like a malicious magic trick, made me forget. The bruises are conspicuous and finger-shaped and Hector hasn't said one word about them.

Must be vindicating for him, something dark whispers. *He always knew you liked being choked.*

· ·

The lobby's an open space with plenty of glass for sunlight. Plants everywhere—the usual indoor kinds like peace lilies, white orchids, and majesty palms. The requisite Starbucks is tucked into a corner by a row of revolving doors.

I point to a table, the implication being that he sit while I go to the counter. When he fails to get it, I add, "Drink's on me."

As a barista preps two house brews, I keep Hector in my peripheral vision and fight against a hummingbird pulse. Turning my back to him feels no less dangerous today. When I return with coffee and claim the opposite chair, his first comment is on the blond joe: "I take coffee black."

I was liberal with cream in the needling way I suspect Nathan is. It's not as though I've learned nothing from him. "How'd you find me?"

He shrugs, takes a slow slip. "You live in DC. I'm here for a work thing. Thought why not try your number?"

Bullshit.

Crazy thing is, I've shared coffee with Nathan in this exact seat at this exact table. Hector was so fucking large in my life. All-consuming and abusive. He made me *think* I wanted his hands on my neck. He made me *think* his yard was where I belonged, and he wasn't afraid to collar me. And sitting where Nathan had? Nathan is nothing like him. Nathan would never put his hands on me. Nathan who has never once touched me, entered me without a *is this okay?*

There is one man on Earth who can keep me grounded, and I was lucky enough to find him—and stupid enough to risk losing him. All the world's relative, but Nathan definitively unmasks Hector for the abuser he is.

"How'd you find me?" I repeat. He knows I'm not going to let him skate by this question.

"It's funny, really," he begins, but it'll be anything but. "Facebook."

Again, bullshit. I have an account, hardly active, but I have one. Besides the odd online "Happy Birthday," I haven't engaged with anyone back home. My place of work and number aren't listed in said account. But I'm positive of something far more relevant: "We're not friends on Facebook."

He buys time with a second, lingering sip before rolling up his sleeves. Instinct spikes, and I scour exposed flesh for signs. Bruises. Punctures. Track marks. It's been years, and I want to know if Hector's escalated to the needle yet. I think *yet* because that's what they say in NA. Everyone makes their way to the needle. Fear of skin-piercing syringes can only hold off promises for so long. The false promises of harder, quicker drugs. Delivered straight into the bloodstream.

"I know we're not friends." On the underside of his wrist, the mark I already knew about says *hello*. I once sank teeth into him like something feral. "But you are friends with Blaire, and she told me."

Blaire? The name snaps the present into sharp focus and the back of my neck frosts. Blaire didn't know what happened because no matter how many times she begged, I never told her. Blaire never learned what happened in that thicket.

Hector follows my eyes to his wrist. "If you're finished being cagey about how—"

"You message me out of nowhere. Show up at my work—"

"You finished?"

I'm not finished. Nowhere near it, but I don't say this. "What do you want?"

Hector leans back, and the top of his chest peeks out. Black hair—just a stray strand or two—invites memories, transient and ephemeral. Hector shirtless. Hector naked. Sex with Hector. Lying languid on a floor mattress soaked in sex. While the bite on his wrist drips blood on bad sheets. My dick moves.

"It's been a long time since we've seen each other." He tugs his collar like he knows my groin's swelling. "I dunno about you, but I'm past everything. I thought it'd be nice to see your face once before I go back."

Guilt blooms. What does he have to get *past*? I'm past everything! Time has done what willpower wouldn't or couldn't. Dulled the blade of Hector's betrayal. Reframed that place in my life before I made the decision to save it. Before Nathan reached down into the darkness and grabbed my hand with his. "I'm doing okay."

"Seeing anyone?"

"Yes," I reply with a sureness meant to leave no room for doubt or footholds for Hector to grip.

"Me too." He peaks an eyebrow. "Local guy here, if you can believe it."

Quite the speedy accomplishment so no, I can't. But the numbness in my chest overtakes curiosity, and Hector smirks as if reading my silence for blood in the water.

"Bit older than I usually go for." He spins his cup and fixes his eyes to mine. "But hey, if somebody wants to take care of me, who am I to say no?"

Nathan couldn't be more different from him, whispers that same taunting voice, *but just how different from Hector are you?*

"I'm happy for you," I say, scratching both my arms. The sudden lust was a flash flood. As it drains, I'm thankful my hard-on didn't mean a damn thing. "Glad you've gotten along so well."

An awkward pause further stilts our conversation, and I remember it was always this way. We were never the furious lovers my mind tricked me into recalling. In this small way, Hector reinforces something important: No matter the lack of bedroom chemistry between Nathan and me—the endless comparisons to Hector's heat and kink—the truth is Hector's as dull as dishwater. Still strung out, probably, and not half the man Nathan is. A surgeon who saves lives while Hector only destroys them.

"So, where are you living?" Hector asks.

"Georgetown."

"Fancy."

In that moment petty bragging gives way to fear. Fear of giving away too much, fear of being vulnerable in my own home. Why did I tell Hector where I live?

"Sounds like you can't say no either." He sneers as I start searching faces again. "To being kept."

The people in the queue to overpay for bad coffee and stale croissants. The sharp-jawed suit spilling cream. The couple talking mutual funds one table over. None of them are Kristian. None of them are ever Kristian. None of them are, until one of them is.

Hector shifts in his chair like my inattention irks him. My distraction and my accurately perceived disinterest. I don't owe Hector a damn thing. In fact, simply talking to him is giving too much. He's not Nathan. And I'd like to see him try to hurt something Nathan loves.

*Some*thing *Nathan loves.*

"So." Hector drags a line across his own throat; the universal gesture for *kill.* "What happened?"

I want to lie, to mask any weakness. That I don't want to admit I was mugged is richly ironic. Decadent even! I want to lie to Hector about my lie to Nathan.

"I was robbed." Common sense over pride at last. "Last weekend."

"Wow." Hector narrows those dark eyes. "Sorry to hear that."

"People who physically hurt others are weak." I slam my cup on the table too hard. "I'm not worried about it."

Thick silence grows between us like kudzu. Maybe Hector realizes it was a mistake to reach out. I hope this is what's scrolling through his mind now. Our conversation is awkward and uncomfortable, and whatever he thought might be accomplished? Not happening.

"Well, this was wonderful." I slide my chair back. "But I've got work. Hope you have a nice flight back—"

He grabs my arm, and I jolt. Fresh heat crawls up my back.

"It was good to see you."

His eyes are knives. "Let go—"

"Too bad." His grip tightens. My skin burns beneath his fingers. "Maybe I'll see you again before that flight."

I tear my arm from his hand and make for the elevators. Heart humming like it's horse-powered. While the elevator dings its way down, those sharp eyes slip in and out and in and out of my back. So much so, I worry I'll leave some of myself behind on the slick lobby floor.

• •

I collapse into my desk, breathless.

I don't accept his explanation for finding me. My arm's reddened from Hector's grip and not for the fucking first time. I don't accept that Blaire gave my info to Hector like, no big deal. She didn't like him for all the right reasons. *That boy's got a meanness in him,* she'd said once over a shared basket of food court cheese fries. *He walks in a room and I get ten kinds of chills.*

I scroll Facebook on my phone, search *Blaire* in my friends list. What I find gives me ten kinds of chills.

Two profiles. Same profile picture, but two Facebook accounts. I'm friends with duplicate Blaires.

The first contains endless posts. Check-ins. Vacation photos. Inside jokes and motivational memes and apparently a toddler named Gabriel. I open our private messages. One from me wishing her a happy birthday. One from her wishing me the same. A few iterations of *we should catch up* neither of us followed through with.

I open the second profile. The profile pic is the same, but that's it. This second page has no wall or timeline posts. No photos. No details. No children. I open the private messages. A single, brief exchange between this Blaire and myself not even a couple of weeks ago.

Hey Oliver! Lost my phone. Need your number again!

Blaire! Sure thing and no worries! Hope you are well!

Deep in my chest, panic uncoils and the tips of my ears burn. Because I know exactly how Hector found me: I gave him my number.

24

NATHAN

D r. Klein." A third-floor nurse rings just as I ready myself for my next case. "Jeremy Mackey's out of post-op and recovering in room 314."

"Great. Thanks."

Mr. Mackey's airbag deployed on the George Washington Memorial Parkway when he mistook an off-ramp for an on-ramp and veered into a barricade to miss oncoming traffic. The airbag kept the steering wheel from opening his chest but buckled his face inward because high speeds and concrete do things like that.

"Pain control?" she asks.

Mackey's mistake was wholly due to a blood-alcohol level of .32 and however many tabs had been in the bottle of hydromorphone on his floorboard. Likely a lot, since the script was filled yesterday.

"IV morphine as needed." Pen uncapped, I note my instructions on his chart. "Send him home with three days of Lortab, thiamine for vitamin B deficiency, and—"

"Patient's intermediate-stage liver cirrhosis. Lortab has acetaminophen," she says warily. Right. Acetaminophen's brutal on anyone's liver but especially one on the cusp of failing.

"Guess he gets the good stuff straight, then. Five milligrams every four to six hours. No more than three days."

"Roger that, Dr. Klein."

I hang up and return the chart to the pre-op tech for data entry. Like Jeremy Mackey, Oliver's also an addict. Unlike Jeremy Mackey, Oliver doesn't have the excuse of losing his leg to an IED outside Mosul. The phantom pain's got nothing on the emotional fallout, and grain alcohol and narcotics relieve both with tragic efficiency. I get Jeremy, but Oliver? He was bored. Nothing but a bored fucking kid in Tyre fucking Indiana.

No question, forty-one-year-old Jeremy will burn through three days of pills in his first three hours at home. Had I not saved him, Oliver would've done the same. Or Oliver would be dead.

Most might judge my relationship as recklessly unethical. Misguided at best and unquestionably wrong at worst, like divorce attorneys fucking clients fresh from bad marriages. You don't mess with people in recovery. The power dynamic is far too unbalanced to ever form a healthy foundation. When one's into prescription pills and the other writes for them all day long? If I didn't maintain control, Oliver would discover what vomit settling in his airway felt like.

Undoubtedly, he was also warned against relationships without a full year of sobriety under his belt. But he needed far more support than outpatient detox provides. That was immediately clear to me. Helplessly lost as I was in Oliver Park's eyes, I still observed a weakness that both scared me shitless and strengthened my resolve. Twenty-four hours in a day, and no one to hold him accountable for the twenty-two he wasn't at the hospital.

He would need love. And he would need to be watched.

He was a cafeteria regular and it wasn't difficult to determine why. One slice of pizza and a Diet Coke courtesy of a free meal ticket the same time every day like clockwork. Way too early for my own lunch, I began showing up for coffee instead. He cycled through three T-shirts—solid pink, solid black, and white with thick blue stripes. One pair of jeans because the tear in his left back pocket gave the game away. He was in trouble, but I let him catch me staring exactly three times on three separate days before making a move.

"Nathan." The first thing I ever said, hand extended.

"Oliver." He smiled nervously because Oliver had never met a man without an agenda. Not one that looked at him the way I did. He lied at first: "Mom's on the sixth floor. Breast cancer so I'm here every day."

It never occurred to him that cancer patients stay at cancer centers and this cafeteria serves exactly zero of those. But it didn't matter; I'd already pulled his file from Psych. No admin questions a request from a white coat, stethoscope, and badge reading MEDICAL DOCTOR.

"Let me know if there's anything she needs that she's not getting, okay?" I twirled my coffee cup on the table. "I'll take care of it."

"Thanks." He was fidgety, nervy, and restless because his psychiatrist had tapered his methadone again earlier that morning. His body shrieked for drugs that weren't coming. "I'll do that."

"You too."

"Huh?" Like crushing a thumb to save a life, kindness doesn't always look kind. The *means* might've been forbidden by every therapist or physician or review board ever. But the *ends* were binary: Oliver could struggle through this by himself and die like the millions of addicts just like him. Or Oliver could choose life. With me.

"If you need *anything*." Our eyes met, my words steeped in intention. "Let me know."

When I asked him for his number, the confessions came. He was sorry for being dishonest—his mother had already passed—but he was in recovery and his phone had been stolen by a halfway house roommate. There was no number to call and because Oliver was a bottomless pit of need and Oliver didn't know better and Oliver repaid favors with the only currency he had, we drove to AT&T that night and he sucked my dick in the car before I bought him a prepaid phone.

Not exactly a meet-cute.

Something chimes. The bleeps and banter and squeaky gurney wheels and a vibration in the back pocket of my scrubs. Another call's coming through, but not from any third-floor nurse asking how best to enable Jeremy Mackey's sustained substance abuse. This call is from a number that pops with electric panic.

"This is . . ." My voice catches. "Dr. Klein speaking."

"I'm with Vigilance Alarm Systems," a rep says. "Please provide your security phrase to receive an urgent message."

"It's *Tilly*—what happened?"

Oliver's careless, but he's not currently at the house.

"We've detected unusual activity inside your home."

His thoughtlessness can't be behind this call.

"The glass-break detector at your rear kitchen door was triggered."

Shit.

"Would you like us to contact the police?"

25

OLIVER

I take the running path at high speed. A meandering trail and paved with rubber that gives a bit underfoot. I've now left work early twice in as many days.

A leafy thicket rambles along on my left. To my right, a grassy bank rolls into the slow murk of the Potomac. Midday sweat beads on my brow, slips down my neck. My collar and pits, soaked. Most folks save summer runs for cool evenings or even cooler mornings, but not me. I want the heat, the sweat.

I need to punish myself.

I've heard nothing else from Detective Henning, or Kristian. The locks have been changed, the snuff film was an awful goodbye, and maybe it's all over. I held on tight to Detective Henning's doubts about both the USB stick and its alleged contents.

I think I just watched someone who's similar to the man in your photo drug and murder someone, she'd said. *I can't know this wasn't acting, a work of fiction.*

She's right about the scene transitions too; the clips are edited. Is my fear unwarranted?

Then there's Hector. Hector and his clever little ploy to find me. I reported the second Blaire profile as fraudulent to the Facebook police— whoever the hell they are. Then I DM'd Real Blaire, who mistook it for a hello at first.

OLIVR!! Omg how are you??!?

I replied with a vague "pretty good" and got to the point. My circumstances might seem grand to her, but dig any deeper and she'd unearth a needy, kept guy who's wildly insecure about it. I gave Blaire no chance to dig, but sure enough, minutes later a new post appeared at the top of her timeline. The expected public proclamation.

Hey guys, there's a fake profile with my picture out there! Please don't accept any requests from it. Report it if you can!!!

Hector now knows that I know. Hector, who's presumably on his way back to Indiana. Not only did he fail to accomplish whatever it was he planned, but his bullshit's been exposed online.

The path follows the bending river and DC looms. A sandstone silhouette beneath a high sun. A rotunda and an obelisk and a skyline of mid-rises where important people like Nathan and Tom do important things.

Industrial rock screams from my headphones. Nine Inch Nails to outpace my pulse and stay a step ahead of anxiety. A release valve for fear. The vacuum emotion leaves, filled by endorphins. Neurochemicals that are structurally related to opioids. They act on the same receptors, and this is a high Nathan doesn't mind me chasing.

The pounding beats break for an incoming call; my phone reads *Nat*.

"Hey," I answer in a breathless gasp and sidewind off the trail.

Nathan's out of breath too, but unlike me, he hasn't been running. Something else has stolen his air. In fact, he might even be crying.

"Tilly is gone."

• •

I don't remember the time it took to get home. I lost it all in the ensuing explosion after Nathan's call. A detonation in my brain blowing everything to pieces. Searing heat consuming all reason and sensory detail.

Two marked patrol cars are parked out front. A cop sits inside one, typing on a dash computer. The flashers of the other are on. Muted in daylight, but the strobes still scream that something horrible has happened in a corona of red-and-blue light. An unmarked Dodge with city plates might be a third.

The front door's wide open. I slow my pace as the icy foyer AC swallows me. Resisting forward momentum, I want to hold off whatever truth I'm about to learn. Several sets of eyeballs stare from the drawing room.

Nathan shakes on the couch, tissues twisting between trembling fingers. His face is swollen, his eyes yellowed. His skin, almost bloodless under seafoam scrubs.

I leap to him. "What's happening?"

"She's gone." I fold Nathan into a tight embrace, and he cries into the crook of my shoulder: "Tilly's gone."

The room blurs, fragments along invisible faults. That's when I notice Detective Henning in an opposite chair. She brushes her jeans and stands.

"Oliver." She holds out a hand, but her voice is cold. Devoid of all empathy. She motions to a tall man who enters from the dining room. "This is my partner, Detective Bowerman."

"Detective-Sergeant Lucas Bowerman." When this new investigator shakes my hand, his firmness bends my entire arm. I've spoken to Detective Henning more times than I care to count. Why hasn't she mentioned a partner during any of them?

My thoughts streak by at light speed. No processing or interpretation. No unpacking of feelings, just comets hurtling by. I snap meaning from the debris:

Tilly's gone.

Detective Henning's in my house. She has a partner.

What have they told Nathan?

Nathan, who pulls me closer and into a cloud of latex hospital reek.

"A break-in." His eyes scream for help. As if I can do something when I don't even know what's happening. As if he's not the one who helps me. Always. "That's why the police are here."

"Tilly—"

"She's gone." Nathan coughs into a fist, pulls his shoulders back. He's desperate to regain control. Of himself, if nothing else. "Someone broke a glass pane in the kitchen door to undo the lock. They left the door open, and Tilly escaped. At least I hope she—"

"The back gate—"

"Open too."

"Oliver, I'm concerned this is related to your other incident." She says *other incident* like it's coded language. Is she still speaking in euphemisms? It's Nathan's house, after all. My name's in no way attached to it. Legally speaking, I have no rights here whatsoever.

An uncomfortable—if odd—thought blossoms: If Nathan wanted to, he could tell the police I'm trespassing, that maybe I broke in. They'd have no choice but to arrest me; I own nothing in my life.

"This is related to my mugging?" I prod Detective Henning. She arches an eyebrow, but I need to know what Nathan does and does not know. My question perks his ears and my pulse climbs.

"Mugging?" Detective Henning asks. Rhetorically, and I hold my breath. Can Nathan hear her sarcasm or is it a dog whistle?

"None of our *material* possessions seem to be out of place," Nathan says. "A mugger would steal, right? And how would a random mugger know where we live?"

"Oliver's wallet was taken," Detective Henning replies, and I nearly gasp in relief. "Even still, you both need to go through everything, make a detailed list. The coincidence doesn't sit right with me."

"What about Tilly?" Nathan teeters on a fresh round of tears. He loves Tilly. She's *his* dog. Same as everything else in this house. "Are you going to canvas—"

"In all likelihood, she ran off," Detective Bowerman says, his accent full-blown Boston. "Dogs are never the target of break-ins. They're an obstacle, a nuisance. It's quite common to get 'em out of the picture as soon as possible, and there's no blood so—"

"We don't canvas for pets, but she'll turn up," Detective Henning interrupts. "It's summer. People are out and about. She's probably with a neighbor."

Tilly has always been a runner. She'd bolt any chance she got, and it's one of several things we have in common.

"They got Facebook groups you can check. Missing pets and stuff . . ." Detective Bowerman starts, but his voice trails off as my heart falls deeper in my chest.

Detective Henning's reassurance is hollow. She knows this isn't just a break-in. She knows this is personal. She's the one who suggested changing the locks! That's exactly what we did, and now Kristian's let me know he can get me whenever, wherever, however he wants. He's never stopped toying with me, and I'm a fucking idiot for thinking otherwise.

"Can I speak with you in the kitchen, Oliver?" Detective Henning asks. Her tone is even, but still cold like stainless steel. There's nothing to hang on to. No trust, no benefit of the doubt. Only slippery metal.

I stand. When Nathan looks to follow me, Detective Bowerman holds out a hand. "Mr. Klein, I'd like to run through a few things with you."

"*Doctor* Klein," Nathan corrects. Even in the midst of catastrophe, the innocent slight irks him. But again, Nathan's comfortable in catastrophe because that's where trauma surgeons thrive. Maintaining a steady footing is as important to him as it is to Detective Henning. And Detective Bowerman, who's cleverly wedged himself between Nathan and me.

A dynamic between Detective Henning and her partner crystalizes as they successfully separate us. It's manipulative, but I appreciate it. It gives Detective Henning space to question me without Nathan's rapid-fire mind to contend with.

They know I can't tell the truth around him.

• • •

I see the broken glass and a pressure drop plugs my ears. Jagged triangles and curved shards cover the floor beneath the back window. The all-too-familiar vinegar bubbles up from a well in my stomach. A sour spring tickling my tongue.

"If you don't tell him, I will." Detective Henning's razor words cut deep; she intends to do exactly that.

"I get it," I interrupt. Of course, I don't *get* anything. Except the fact that Nathan can't know. "I know I need to tell him. Can you give me time? My dog's missing, I'm going crazy. I just need some time. Please."

Detective Henning's eyes stay fixed on mine, but she hesitates like she's tussling with something.

"Please!"

"The man we're dealing with is dangerous."

"Then you've found something?" I ask. A muffled conversation drifts in from the drawing room. Nathan's tenor and Detective Bowerman's baritone. He's doing his job—effectively keeping Nathan distracted. Or maybe that's not his job at all. Maybe he's plying Nathan for information about me. The drug addict. My arrest record. Details a liar like myself can't be counted on for.

"Haus revised their story. A 'sudden recollection' puts you and a man matching Kristian's description on the premises Saturday night. They're corroborating your allegations." The Cheshire Cat—Theo—he's come

through for me. The relief such a revelation should stir is canceled out
by the glass on the floor. It changes nothing and now Tilly's gone.

"Okay." I palm my face. "What else do you know?"

"The flash drive is FBI jurisdiction, so they've got it. What happens
next, how seriously it's taken, is out of my hands. But I'll tell you this:
I'm worried for your safety. It's possible this break-in's wholly unrelated,
but I don't buy it."

"But it is possible."

"How long have you and Nathan lived here?"

"A few years."

"How many break-ins have you experienced?"

"None."

"What are the chances your assault and your first break-in go down
side by side? I don't have to remind you the man's been inside this house
once already."

"Give me a few days," I say. She's right, though. This is Kristian's
doing. "A few days to tell Nathan. That's all I'm asking for."

"What do you really want, Oliver?" Detective Henning's question
flies in wild from left field. Heavy and loaded and it hits me behind the
eyes.

"I want this to end." Deep down, a fire catches and the heat pulls tears
from me. "Kristian. Tilly. All of it."

"So end it." She crosses her arms, and I gird for wherever the hell she's
going. Someplace not good, that's for sure. "Tell Nathan the truth and
confront this *with* him."

"I can't." A sob gathers, swelling and coming fast.

"What scares you so shitless that the lies are worth it?"

"Because if he knew . . ." I lower my voice to a choking whisper,
search for a better way to put it, and come up empty. "It could kill me."

"You're scared of him." Her eyes sharpen. She's silent for a beat, then:
"Are you in physical danger?"

"Of course I'm in physical danger!"

"Not from Kristian." Detective Henning's agenda starts to take shape.
"At home. If Nathan knew the truth, are you afraid he'll hurt you?"

"Jesus Christ. No," I scoff. "Nathan only ever helps. His savior com-
plex is annoying, but he's a surgeon, so I deal. Not to mention I owe him

for my life and literally everything else. For taking me out of Indiana. For quitting the oxy and the bullshit."

"Oxy?" Her question brings blood to my face like I've been caught. Detective Henning's kicking over logs and no telling what truths might slime their way out. The heat behind my sternum burns hotter. "You answered *no* to drugs on your report. Both of them."

"I'm in recovery. Five years," I say. She purses her lips like nothing about the shivering man before her suggests he's recovered.

"Huh." She squints. "Five years with Nathan. Five years in recovery."

"Yeah, and if he finds out about Haus I'll lose both."

"Listen to yourself."

"It would destroy him." My eyes widen, and I'm squeezing both my arms. "And us. He wouldn't get it. He grew up different and privileged and me cheating would destroy everything."

"You're doing a bang-up job of that already," she mocks. "Admitting infidelity has nothing on losing your life."

"They are the same goddamn thing." The sob finally crests, and I break. I see that future as plain as if it were projected on the wall behind Detective Henning. "If Nathan kicks me out, I have nowhere to go"—I wipe my face, teeth chattering—"and nowhere is exactly where recovery goes to die."

"If Nathan loves you that much, don't you think he's got a heart to forgive you?" she asks, but all I feel is the rush of air as Nathan slams the front door behind me. The walk to a motel. The hours I'd spend sweating up the courage to tell Kristian exactly where I am because he'll kill me way faster than I'd passively kill myself.

"Nathan saved me once." I squeeze blood from my biceps, so tight my knuckles whiten. The blowtorch inside me cooks my flesh from the inside out. "He won't do it twice."

Silence settles as Detective Henning considers my case. I tighten my jaw and wonder if she appreciates the power she holds right now. My death warrant already drawn up, and she need only sign it.

"Three days," she relents, and I want to collapse or scream myself hoarse or both. "No promises. If something happens to force my hand, Oliver, I'm going to do my job. I have a responsibility to report to Nathan that he's in danger."

Detective Henning's setting a timer. I've got until it reaches zero to find a way down from this window ledge.

"Tell me, Oliver. Tell me you understand what I'm telling you."

"I understand."

"You've committed a crime." Unblinking, she's not one for empty threats. "You've filed a false police report. Perhaps lied about drugs on both. Maybe obstructed justice. I don't want to use that to force you to do the right thing. But I will."

"I said I understand."

Detective Henning nods and rejoins the others in the drawing room. She still hasn't told Nathan the truth, but how could I feel any better? Tilly's missing and my insides retch at the thought that Kristian took her. What he's planning if he did.

I slam my fist on the counter, try to swallow another wave of tears that come anyway. I'm a rope. A rapidly fraying, unraveling rope. How much is left? What happens when it runs out?

"Oliver?" The front door locks behind the police, and Nathan makes his way to the kitchen. His heavy steps hardly register as I chew over everything. "We need to take inventory."

What are the chances? Detective Henning asked. Coincidences like assaults and break-ins back to back. But what about Kristian and Hector coming into my life in rapid succession? That's crazy, but what isn't about any of this? Is the timing intentional or am I simply losing my goddamn mind?

"We need to let the police know if anything's missing." Nathan pauses, swallowing. "Besides Tilly."

Hector tricked me into telling him where I live. Not an address, but enough to find me. He stalked me in a way Kristian might.

"Did you hear me, Oliver?"

But Kristian has a reason to hide too. To obscure and muddle. To keep his identity masked. Or his location secret, at the very least. Kristian followed me out of Haus's darkness. He followed me into daylight, snaked into my life like an asp. Taunted and terrorized. Maybe fucked with Nathan's dog.

"Hey?"

A thought strikes, an inkling, tiny and amorphous. But the way my heartbeat, already quick, races faster says there might be something to it.

"Yeah." I cough. "Yes, Nat."

"You wanna start on the third floor?"

The inkling grows, hardens. The app—MeetLockr. It's where Kristian found me once. A way forward takes shape like molten iron cooling in a mold.

It's where I've decided Kristian will find me again.

26

TYRE, IN

When something bad has sharp teeth in your heart, you've got a choice. Let those canines sink deeper and deeper until they kill you. Or tear free—and hurt like hell when pieces of flesh are left behind.

Hector struck my face, squeezed my cheeks as though trying to collapse my skull. But his betrayal was the catalyst for what came next. I used to underestimate how much blood abrupt change can draw. How slippery the slope is from *transition* to *trauma*.

Somewhere along an empty Indiana highway, I ran out of breath. On the thinnest of fumes, I slowed to a staggering stumble. One foot on the asphalt. One foot in the dirt.

That's when I saw it. A young deer—knobby velvet nubs starting to protrude from its skull. Perfectly intact, pristine, beautiful. Save a neat rupture of the belly. A knot of intestine peeked from inside. Steam breezing out marked the carcass as fresh.

Vehicles whirled by every now and again. High beams burning into early morning mist, and I knelt close to vacant eyes. How quick was it? If I step out before a semi can stop, would my insides look the same?

Brakes squealed from behind. I spun to find an old pickup flashing its hazards. A shadow leaned out the driver-side window.

"Got somewhere to be, son?" The shadow drawled like emphysema and sandpaper.

"Yeah," I called back, not thinking. "Tyre."

"That's a long walk." A featureless face, but his chin gesture was unmistakable: an invitation.

A parade of horrors flickered by in black and white. Rape. Murder. Cannibalism. All of the above and in god knows what order.

"Go on. Get in," he rasped. I saw no choice. Behind me was pain, and before me was a dead deer and an endless road. I drew a long breath and climbed into the passenger seat.

"Which street?" The truck reeked like raw chicken gone bad as it gathered speed. Something about the way air whistled through his teeth said he didn't have all of them. Whatever was left, the color of corn.

"Vidalia Avenue." Highway signs ticked by as though my life depended on it.

"Bad side of the tracks."

He chuckles. I don't.

As the distance to town indicated by road signs dwindled from twenty miles to ten to single digits, the vise in my chest began to unwind. He was, in fact, driving me home. Or closer to home. I recast him from Jeffrey Dahmer, eager to stab me, bury me, eat me, and whatever else in some shit cornfield. But what does he want then?

Who picks up young men crawling the highway alone? In the dark? He'd have seen no broken-down car. And folks traveling the shoulder by foot were never in a good place. I needed to decide what this ride was worth and fast.

If he asked me to jerk him off, I'd do it. I'd probably suck his dick too. I wouldn't let him cum in my mouth. And nothing else. Absolutely nothing else.

"All right." He pulled over on the corner of Vidalia and Anderson. A block away from home, but I kept my eyes from revealing that to the stranger breathing heavy beside me. I hesitated, still unsure how this was going to play out. *Please don't ask to come inside.*

He angled his body toward me, and my heart caught fire.

"I don't want you to touch me or anything like that." A streetlamp lit up cheeks as pocked as the road, and for a flash those crooked teeth were filed into fangs. "Just pull your drawers down and let me see."

Fear tickled my neck with curled fingernails, and I unbuckled with trembling hands, pulled my zipper. The vinegar odor of urine still clung to my jeans as they fell to my thighs. The man began to grope himself through worn coveralls.

"Pull 'em down too." He nodded to the oversize boxers that joined my pants around my legs. The cold shrank everything, but the man just kept breathing heavy. Mouth clamped shut, air pushing in and out of wide nostrils.

His eyes on my exposed crotch, I fixed mine to the door handle. So close, and so soon, I'd grab it and leave this—all of it—behind. The moment he held his breath was the moment I released mine.

"Get out," he spat. I scrambled to pull my pants up, my right hand on the sweet coolness of the handle. The longer I dawdled, the longer this stranger steeped in the shame of what he'd just done. "I said get on out!"

I pushed open the door and nearly fell to the pavement.

"Thank you," I whispered as if gratefulness were still warranted. He sped off the instant the door slammed, and I gathered my footing, shook my head. No doubt I was in shock. What Hector did in the woods dulled what I'd just done in that truck. One of which was not being eaten by corn-colored teeth.

No lights on in our place. Hector was so fucked up; he was undoubtedly passed out by Blaire's firepit. Come morning, the lucky bastard would have no recollection of this night.

Unlocking the door was a challenge. I was wound so tight any wrong move might snap me in two. On the way to our room, I flipped every switch, cold light exposing our loving home for the rat's nest it was. Most people would go straight for their clothes. Their toiletries and whatever meaningful items life would be unimaginable without.

I couldn't imagine life without the contents of a sock drawer in the dresser we shared. When I yanked it open, it rattled like a diamondback. Bottles and bottles and bottles of pills rolled like spinning tops. Oxycodone, hydrocodone, hydromorphone. A blister pack of emergency Ativan—to chill the fuck out when we couldn't scratch the itch with anything better.

I gathered them all into a gym bag. Not really a suitcase, but the only luggage I'd ever owned. I swiped the pad too. Hector wouldn't say how he'd stolen a prescription pad, and we'd only ever used it with utmost caution.

I put on fresh jeans and shoved a fistful of cotton tees into my bag. Pairs of socks and underwear. My winter coat was already on, and as I started to flip off the lights—to shut the door behind me and never look back—I stopped.

Not to reconsider, of course. Or to wistfully take a last flaccid look at the shit home we shared. No, I hesitated because cough syrup with codeine sat on the bottom shelf in the fridge.

I decided not to take it. Hector would need it when he came to, and I'd leave him that much. Not that he deserved it. And maybe I'd leave him something else too. A token so there'd be no mistaking it; Hector would know he'd lost me. No debate. No questions. Case fucking closed.

I shoved the cough syrup aside and left my piss-soaked jeans on that very same shelf.

WASHINGTON, DC

I hold my breath and listen for Nathan downstairs. When the fridge door opens and shuts in the kitchen, I grab my phone and make for the third-floor study.

I scroll for MeetLockr in the app store. In place of a download arrow is a stylized cloud—my data was stored and still easily retrievable. A reminder that nothing deleted is ever gone.

An anticipatory anxiety fills me top to bottom as it loads. My heartbeat grows swift. My palms, a sticky damp.

An undeniable curiosity rises. Through everything, in the face of all that's unfolded since last Saturday, I'm still interested to learn if I have new messages. Not from Kristian, but from other guys. I hate myself for it, but I'm counting this as a silver lining. I get to have another look.

Have another look? I shake my head. Tilly's gone, maybe dead. The price of my second look. Silver lining? *Fuck you, Oliver.* Maybe Kristian's nothing but an instrument of karmic justice. And the fact that I escaped him once already? Another universal mark against me because the wicked are undeserving. Whatever I've lost and whatever I've yet to lose are all undeserved.

MeetLockr appears, no longer hidden inside a fake vault app. Instead, the orange-and-black icon sits pretty between Gmail and the weather. Like it appears on millions of phones. Gays with nothing to hide and full of pride.

I swipe it open but haven't truly gamed this out yet. I have a plan, sure, but it's more like the talking points of a plan rather than detailed machinations. A vague outline. I know what I want, but little else. I have a beginning and a desired end. The middle? An uncertainty. A foggy bog laden with quicksand and razor traps and venomous mist. I'm navigating it blindfolded.

My profile appears just as it had before. As if nothing had changed.

A ping chimes for my unread messages. Dozens of them and all collected since I last swept the app into my phone's dust bin. I open one after another, and the knot in my chest comes undone one sinewy thread at a time. They're all strangers. Some faces. Some headless torsos. Some crotch shots. Nothing from Kristian or the *!* he masquerades as.

"Okay," I whisper. "Do this. Confront."

I tap *Account Settings,* then *Name.* Currently it reads *O.* Not terribly creative, but it did the trick of both hiding my name and providing a double entendre. O is for Oliver, O is for orgasm.

I type the rest: *Oliver.* I even add a *P* for good measure. *Oliver P.*

Next, I thumb over the profile pic slot. The camera activates, and my face stares back. I draw in breath, deep and hot.

Confront. Hollow eyes. Bagged and dark against the pallor of my face. I angle the camera until my bruises, still painfully evident, vanish out of frame. And then I glower, boring into the tiny lens as if to make eyes with each and every gay man on MeetLockr, one most of all.

I unclench my jaw, smirk, and snap the photo.

Just like that, Oliver P joins the sea of faces and torsos and landscapes and bulges. All thirsty to have and be had. Likewise, I've skewered myself, braided my writhing body through a razor-sharp hook, and cast the line. Now I wait for Kristian to find me. To feel peckish. To take a bite.

When he does, steel will sink into his flesh for a second time.

The shower stops, and the ensuing silence suggests Nathan's toweling off. I flip to *Privacy Settings.*

The PIN for "Oliver's iPhone" has been successfully reset.

From here on, I need to be even more careful about where and when I leave this. Nothing's more damning than a password change.

So much of Kristian remains unknown, but at the same time he's predictable. Patterns work both ways. Kristian can't resist because he plays with his food. He's a cruel cat pawing at a wounded sparrow. He's been toying with me for a week now. It's why he let it go so far in his rented room at Haus. The kissing, the fondling. Skin contact, the perspiration on our bodies mixing and melding. But Kristian's about to discover he crossed a line with Tilly. My teeth grind.

Kristian's food is about to bite back.

27

Early evening, I sit uncomfortably in the breakfast nook. A square of cardboard covers the missing door pane perfectly. Cut by an X-Acto knife with a surgeon's precision. Just outside it rests a lawn bag, filled with sharp glass and waiting to be taken to the alley bin. Nathan—who never leaves garbage—has left it for me. *Your crucifixion,* I imagine he thought. *Carry your own goddamn cross.*

A gulp of beer and Nathan appears as I set a sweaty bottle on the table.

"Coaster?"

"Sorry." I walk to a kitchen drawer. One cork coaster later, I reclaim my chair.

Nathan's fixed his eyes on me since entering the kitchen. They bear down; I sense them in the same way all creatures know when they're being watched. The same sensation that tap-danced down my spine in the Metro station. On the train. At Trance. The feeling I'd chalked up to paranoia until Kristian materialized inside our home.

Now I feel it again as Nathan glares from across the room.

"What?" I finally ask. The edge in my voice surprises even me. If Nathan's taken aback, his stoic face betrays nothing. He's the person I'm closest to. He's seen every part of me inside and out, and he's the person I can never seem to read.

A heavy stack of paper falls to the counter with a thud. "Missing posters. For Tilly. Phone number, her info, a reward." Something in his voice raises my hackles. An unsettling little thought pricks. He didn't come down here to talk about Tilly.

Quiet drops like a thick curtain, then: "Question for you."

I cringe, clench my gut. I don't like questions. Questions are frightening. I gulp my beer, stiffen my spine, and brace.

Nathan reaches into the back pocket of his jeans. As he retrieves whatever the *something* is, seconds stretch into seemingly endless expanses of time. I have no idea what he's fishing for, but it's a threat.

And then I see it.

Pinched between his thumb and forefinger is the wallet-sized picture of Mom. My heart sinks. Blood falls from my face, down my body, pools in the soles of my feet. I've made another mistake.

Nathan delicately rests it atop the stack of Tilly posters. He knows how much the photo means to me. He's careful with it. He treats it with the deference of a religious relic.

"Your wallet was stolen." Succinct. To the point. I'm grateful for this because each word impales me on spiked vowels and razor consonants. One after another.

A frightening silence creeps through the air, blooming poisonous black flowers. I have nothing to say. Watching Nathan produce the photo from his pocket grinds thinking to a hard stop. Even I, good, swift liar that I am, can't conjure an explanation. Nothing I say will keep my lies intact. To refute what he knows. What he *thinks* he knows.

"Your wallet was stolen," he repeats for good measure, "and you won't believe where I found this."

I edge forward in my seat, attempt to stall. "I took it out when I went—"

"You've never taken it out. Never. Not once."

"What are you saying? That my wallet wasn't stolen?" Self-preservation kicks in. I grow defensive, accusatory. I wrap myself in a shroud of offense. "That I lied about being mugged? Have you seen my throat lately?"

"Went down to the cellar to account for anything a burglar might've taken," Nathan says. He grazes the tiny photo with his finger, then taps the counter. "Realized I forgot to shut down the furnace for summer, so I did. Checked the flue by making sure our vents weren't sooty."

Fuck.

"I know you keep this in your wallet, which you said was stolen when, strangely, you went jogging with it. And on second thought, maybe you *would* believe where I found this."

"You calling me a liar?" The question sours like curdled milk, and Nathan undoubtedly sees me wince.

"Whether or not you lied about the wallet, you did lie."

"Yeah? How so?" Still couched in defensiveness, I bite the inside of my cheek and taste wet iron. My cigarettes too. The pack was almost empty, I think, but did I finish it off? Was it still in there?

Nathan's thumbs dance across his phone, and the whole kitchen draws dark.

I swallow. Has he found out about MeetLockr? Already? Jesus, my face has been posted for a matter of hours! Well, if he has, Nathan—stalwart, well-adjusted, always-makes-the-right-decision Nathan—was on the app too. Like Mormons bumping carts in the liquor store, to challenge me on this implies a stunning confession on his part as well.

Unless he was only lurking.

"The cigarettes," he starts, and I'm confused again. I have no idea where this is going, and there's an element of relief in this. "You told me you bought a pack of cigarettes after the attack. You told me you smoked one and tossed the rest."

"Yes." My jaw clenches so tight its hinges might snap. "I did."

He flips the screen of his phone my way. It's a bank statement of some kind. He's standing too far away for me to discern any of the numbers, but it's not our bank's mobile app. That screen is wreathed in neon blue and hot orange. The app on Nathan's iPhone is lime green. I squint and make out a logo at the top: *Wealth Wallet*.

"You didn't charge any cigarettes this month."

"So? What are you trying to tell me?"

"I'm trying to tell you that you lied. Maybe you bought them earlier, maybe you found them. How the hell should I know? But you lied about them."

"I used cash—"

"You said eighty bucks was stolen?"

I nod *yes*.

"Well"—he scrolls—"here's an eighty-dollar withdrawal. Plus a three-dollar fee for using a 7-Eleven ATM. But that's it. No other cash transactions."

"Is this goddamn 1984?" I slam both hands on the kitchen table and shove my chair out. "Nathan, for fuck's sake!"

He cranks his voice to match mine. "Which means either eighty dollars was in your wallet when it was taken—sans the picture of your mother, oddly enough—and you lied about buying cigarettes. Or, eighty dollars *minus* the cost of cigarettes was stolen, and you lied about the amount." Nathan's face remains stainless-steel cold. Utterly and frustratingly unknowable.

"You're really trying to litigate this, huh?"

"The cops might. If you lied about the amount to me, then you lied about the amount on a police report."

Ire swells behind my chest bone, and I make a last-ditch effort to redirect. "I was robbed, Nat. Fucking robbed. And you want to nickel-and-dime me over how much was taken? You want to reconcile my story like receipts for fucking travel expenses?"

Nathan exhales, his tight cheeks relax by a hair. A narrow, razor-thin hair. "You never take this photo out of your wallet."

"Nat, I—"

"One other thing." He reaches into his pocket and slams a pack of cigarettes on the counter with all the force and anger and sadness in the world. "Trash these. Now."

I open my mouth, but he's already turned away. He's abandoning me and my Marlboros in the kitchen to steep, and no way I risk pulling him back.

"Put up the posters for Tilly," he calls out, vanishing down the hallway. Heavy steps up creaking stairs, then thump-thuds on the ceiling.

I drain my beer, start to place it on the coaster but hesitate. Instead I set it directly on the table like a petulant child. Ridiculous, the petty pleasure this conjures, but there's no denying it: I revel in the watery circle it paints.

And I want a fucking cigarette.

• •

It's too hot outside. I wipe sweat from my brow. A single beer down the hatch, but hops breeze off my skin nonetheless. The masking tape I'd brought didn't stick to iron posts and wooden poles, so I'd gone back in for duct tape.

During this second trip, I listened carefully for Nathan upstairs, heard nothing, and pulled a single cigarette from the garbage bin under the sink.

Now I set my stack of papers on the splintering pavement and put a Marlboro between my lips a few blocks from the house. A side street Nathan has no reason to travel. Even if he suddenly decided to run errands in my absence. Certainly far enough from our neighbors and their goddamn open windows. The cherry on my cigarette glows like a tiny heartbeat when I take a drag. Smoke sweeps my lungs. The tension in my spine and shoulders unwinds.

Tilly's photo at my feet is large in proportion to the text Nathan's typed—MISSING across the top, our number and a cash reward of five thousand dollars at the bottom. Not *lost* like a dog but *missing* like a child. Because that's what she is to Nathan. Tilly is mid-pant, her pink tongue hanging lopsided from wet jowls. Black eyes so damn eager to leap into the lap of the photographer. Nathan.

He'd snapped the picture on a grassy knoll in an off-leash park not far from the telephone poles now advertising that she's gone. I whisper that I'm sorry, but something mean inside me says Tilly would never accept my apology.

She's like her owner that way.

●   ●

At home, Nathan and I hide from each other. As far as city homes go, ours is enormous. The kind of place you only inherit. Imposing brick and elegant gables and a front door that seems to gag every time I pass through. Silver lining: it's deep enough to avoid someone.

He's staked out our bedroom for himself, and the door's been shut ever since.

Fine by me. Let Nathan have it. It's hardly a good spot to hunker down. The kind coveted by someone who's never wondered when a meal's coming. Never shut his five-year-old eyes and wished the malt liquor in the fridge would turn itself into bologna. Never ate ranch fucking dressing for lunch when it didn't. I've claimed the kitchen. A second beer sits open on the table. Nathan's wiped it down from earlier and returned the coaster to its drawer.

Where it's stayed because I refuse to use it.

It's well past five in the evening, which means Nathan can toss back the bourbon he loves so much. Except the bar cart's downstairs too, and this drips a drop of pleasure. Which does he love more—his pride or his liquor?

I unlock my phone and open MeetLockr. I have messages, though a quick perusal tells me none are what I'm looking for.

Be patient, Oliver. Traps hinge on patience.

My restless mind leaps to something else: the app Nathan advertised when hurling his accusation—his correct accusation. Wealth Wallet isn't mobile banking, and I pull it up.

A budgeting app. The sort of thing that would appeal to Nathan's sense of fiscal responsibility. I skim the description. *Manage your finances, from daily expenditures to long-term savings, easily and right from your phone. Set daily caps on spending by category. Earn praise when you meet your goals, and get instant notifications when you spend too much.*

Instant notifications when you spend too much. I bite my bottom lip. The day's second beer, and an empty stomach and heat exhaustion from taping Tilly's missing posters all over our neighborhood renders a considerable buzz.

Instant notifications.

Pushing back from the table, I head for the hallway, pass through the dining room, the drawing room, the foyer. One hardwood step at a time, I stalk upstairs.

Instant.

We may be fighting, we may have divided the house into wartime territory, but ultimately, I have every right to enter my own bedroom. I turn the knob slowly, but the brass handle still whines.

Nathan's asleep. I hadn't heard him stir for quite some time and hoped he would be. His black iPhone is facedown on his nightstand, tethered to a wall charger. Careful steps take me close enough to reach it.

Nathan doesn't move as it unplugs. He breathes through his mouth but hardly snores. His eyes twitch as though he dreams.

What do you dream of, Nat? I unlock it with his PIN.

I know his password because Nathan makes such a goddamn show of his own transparency. He advertises it—no, blasts it at full volume—

nonstop. In the past, I suspected this was to undermine my own compulsion for secrecy. I chalked up this perception of a hidden agenda on Nathan's part to my own paranoia. A guilty mind makes somethings out of nothings incessantly.

Sure enough, I find Wealth Wallet there. It asks for a PIN, and I simply repeat his phone's. Ta-dah. It takes a moment to figure out the interface, but the designers have done a bang-up job. I make my way to Nathan's budget settings.

And they're each set to zero.

Daily budget for fast food: zero dollars. Daily budget for clothing and accessories: zero dollars. Daily budget for alcohol: zero dollars. Daily budget for recreation, for toiletries, for gasoline: zero, zero, zero.

Why use a budgeting app if you set daily limits to zero for every expense? It literally defeats the entire purpose.

Unless keeping a budget *isn't* the purpose. Something cold tickles the back of my neck.

In *Settings,* I scroll for a list of accounts. Only one is linked. Most of the numbers are masked, but the last four digits send gooseflesh up my arms. I recognize them as my own.

Instant notifications when you spend too much.

Nathan's linked my credit card—and only my card—to Wealth Wallet with daily spending limits at zero across the board. He gets notifications sent directly to his phone each and every time I spend money. On anything. The room sinks further into eerie coldness. Nathan's been tracking me in real time by my spending.

Sheets rustle and I spin.

"Why are you on my phone?"

28

My heart thrums and I swallow something dry like cigarette ash.

"I wanted to see if anyone had called about Tilly." My voice shakes. A cracking tone that screams dishonesty. "You listed both our numbers."

Nathan falls back on his pillow. "Did you put all the posters out?"

"I did." I draw closer to the bed.

His eyes find mine, and he offers a tiny smile. I drink relief like ice water and accept his invitation to lie beside him. His hand crawls under my tee; his palm traces a circle on the small of my back.

"I shouldn't have come after you earlier," he says. "I'm crazy over Tilly. And other things."

"I know. Kimberly said you'd fought with your mom."

"I'm sorry." He sighs and ignores that last bit, which is fine by me. "Tilly going missing, it's pushed me to the edge."

"Me too." My reply's ambiguous. I could mean that I'm sorry too. Or I could mean that Tilly's absence has also pushed me to the edge. It's not that I've meant it to come out this way, it's simply habit. A survival technique I'm too good at. Equivocating. Focusing on the literal meaning of my words the way a child might.

"She'll come home." Nathan gazes at the ceiling fan. "The detective's right. Lots of people are out. She's collared and microchipped. We'll find her."

"The chip!" I say. "You can track—"

"There's no GPS. Someone has to scan her," he interrupts. "A vet or a shelter. It's not a hookup app. It's not Grindr or MeetLockr."

"Sure," I whisper as heat flames up my body. He was joking, of course. His word choice coincidental like all the other coincidences I've collected. I grip his hand; his fingers are cold in mine.

What he can't know is how dangerous this situation is. Why we experienced a break-in. Kristian knew about Tilly before he punched through the back glass. He heard her barking while he worked with Darryl's crew. Saw her crated as he hid his sick movie in my underwear.

His long fingers, the very same that wrapped so tight around my neck, that squeezed it, might've reached inside the crate. Tilly might've licked them.

I shut my eyes. She might've escaped like I had. But if he's taken her? My throat tightens, and the room darkens with metastasizing shadow. How many boxes will he use to mail her pieces back to us, and over how many days? I drag both hands down my face. Then what will he do next? My shoulders shake because that last *he* applies to both Kristian and Nathan.

"It's okay." Nathan sits up again. "It's gonna work out."

"Nat." I squeeze his hand, wade deeper into those sad eyes. In my head, I confess. *I cheated. This is my doing. All of it. I betrayed you.* But my lips whisper another thing entirely: "Would you ever leave me?"

"We're stronger than this," he says as if I'm silly. "Assaults and Tilly and parents."

He could mean anything by *parents* but I say something honest for a change: "I need you."

"I know." Nathan blinks. "That about Tilly?"

"What?"

"Check your phone." He gestures to my lap. "It vibrated."

I don't check it. Not in front of him. Instead, I tell him to go back to sleep. I'm sorry I woke him, but this message is a "work thing" and I leave the bedroom. If Nathan finds this odd, I don't have the luxury of caring.

When I'm down the hallway, I flip my phone over. A notification from MeetLockr. I've got a message.

I pivot into the guest bedroom, past the four-poster bed, the framed black-and-whites from Nathan's favorite art gallery in Frederick, Maryland. I close the bathroom door and take a seat on the toilet. My gut clenches and my pits dampen. My palms itch because it's never Kristian until it is.

Our home is old and our walls are thin. I let the toilet lid fall hard against the porcelain tank for Nathan's benefit. I open MeetLockr and scroll for my in-box.

My pulse spikes.

Oliver?

The profile pic is a man's chest. Fit, but not cut. Another headless torso among dozens like it. The distance reads *4.5 miles away* and the piano wire around my neck loosens. My username is now Oliver P. It's not weird that someone might greet me that way, but what's up with the question mark?

A face pic comes through. His arrogant smirk taunts me because I've seen it and felt it dozens of times. In restaurants and cafés. In bars like Trance. In my own house.

Tom Vogt has dropped me a line on a hookup app.

I leave his question and his photo unanswered while the cogs in my mind spin. How will I play this? Why the hell didn't I consider this could happen?

Instinct says to lie. No, this isn't Oliver. You must be mistaken, you pretentious dick. But of course it's me. My face. My name and last initial.

He'll correctly interpret silence as panic. I must answer him. Say something.

Hi Tom.

Not nearly enough of a reply, but it buys time and keeps my options open. No matter how I spin this, a simple *hello* is as good a start as any.

What are you doing on here?

So much for stalling.

Think. What am I doing on here? I have no defense. Offense won't work either. Earlier, I worried Nathan had discovered this account and pictured Mormons in a liquor store. My metaphor doesn't apply here. Tom's single; I'm not. Neither of us is Mormon.

Open relationships are a dime a dozen these days. Nathan and I might plausibly have one. Not quite polyamorous or open romantically, but solely for physical gratification. A step removed from casual porn consumption. Masturbating with the body of a stranger. But wouldn't

Tom know this already? Wouldn't Nathan have mentioned it during the literally hundreds of times they've been drunk together?

I won't tell.

I can almost hear Tom's voice as he says this, and it riles my pulse. Cherubic, taunting Tom in playground pigtails and smacking of entitlement.

My secret's safe with Tom, he assures me. Bullshit. He's never arrived anywhere without an angle. A bouncing ellipsis says he's typing something.

Oliver??

Tom—who's never fucking patient—is growing less so. I'm out of time.

Hey, sorry, got distracted with something. How are you?

I brace for his reply. I will him to simply tell me how he is in a casual sense, but I know he won't let me go so easily.

As if reading my mind, Tom says exactly what he's getting at: **I've thought of you before.**

Me?

I pretend to not know where this is going.

When I play with myself.

Why does this surprise me? Coming from someone like Tom, someone with the principles of a Capitol Hill staffer. The moral resolve of a soggy sandcastle at high tide. The thought summons a glitter of guilt. Am I really taking the high ground here? Even for an audience of one, it's laughable. Still, Tom's willingness to betray Nathan—his best friend—is uncomfortably surprising.

Really?

A stupid response, but what am I supposed to say? Great, Tom. That's great. Glad I can be of service during your coveted toilet time.

Yeah. I think of you a lot. You ever wonder what it would be like? Me and you?

No, but I'm reminded of Kristian, of why I'm back on MeetLockr in the first place. I'm taking control. I'm confronting. I'm finding out what happened to Tilly. I'm finding what I can about the man terrorizing me. I'm going where Detective Henning cannot. Now is not the time to unfurl angel wings.

You're no fucking martyr, Oliver.

If this ruse—this plan I've deluded myself into thinking is clever—is to succeed, Nathan's ignorance is vital. And now I have my first loose end. If I become sanctimonious, there's no stopping Tom from tipping off Nathan. He'll have screengrabs just like mine of Kristian. No room for debate when Nathan sees hard evidence. Only cold truth.

Tom must be engaged; he needs something to lose.

I reply: **I haven't. But I am right now.**

Nice. You're so fucking hot.

Go on.

Tight ass. Let's do something about it. I do discreet really well.

He's lying. Nothing about the man suggests he does discreet well. But then again, he works for a Republican. A family values pro-lifer who paid for a staffer's abortion because he already had one family he valued. In politics, the ability to keep secrets is the difference between pillar of the community and prison. Besides, I must secure Tom's absolute discretion.

I write: **To tell you the truth, I haven't met anyone from here. I'm just figuring this app out.**

You exchanged pics?

I lie: **No.**

Boys on here expect pics you know.

Guess I do now haha.

LOL. So what are you wearing?

I draw in breath. This is good. Tom's focusing on the present instead of any possibilities the future might offer. I encourage this new direction.

Jeans. T-shirt.

Underwear?

Briefs.

I hesitate, then for good measure: **Andrew Christian. Backless. You?**

I'm in bed. Naked.

Of course he is.

You said you think of me when you play with yourself.

;)

You playing with yourself right now?

Yeah. Want to know what's in my head?

No, Tom. Not in either of them.

Tell me.

You on all fours. Back arched. Ass up like a bitch in heat.

Mmm.

I'm fucking you. Hard.

What's happening starts biting into my heart. I'm duplicitous, which is nothing new, but in a more bothersome way at the moment. I'm exposed. I've given Tom permission to take pieces of me.

You're hurting because I'm big, but you don't want me to stop pounding you.

Don't you dare fucking stop.

To type that takes considerable strength. I want this to end. To be over. More than anything, I want this conversation to die. Time to kill it.

Can I see?

Sure ;)

A few seconds later, a picture of his dick comes through. Hard in his left hand. One obnoxious gold-and-garnet college ring and one pecker. He angles the camera with his right hand and there's something shiny in the background. A mirror, and a new idea sparks like a pricy lighter.

I wanna see everything.

Lol huh?

The mirror. Stand in front of it. I want to see all of you.

Another pause. Excruciating in length, and maybe Tom's texting Nathan from another device right now. He never has fewer than two phones on his person. *Better check your boy toy's leash, because he's wandered out of the yard* or some shit. Or maybe he's having entirely justified reservations about giving me face.

Panic pushes me to seal the deal: Give it to me. Give me your body and your cum face and maybe we do something about it like you said.

Downstairs, the doorbell chimes. I jolt, then listen carefully for voices. When someone asks Nathan to sign for a package, I return to my phone to find another bouncing ellipsis. Tom sends it. It's perfect.

Phone at waist level. I've got everything from salt-and-pepper hair to his kneecaps. Bet you count that smarmy-ass smile as a selling feature, don't you?

Now, I tell myself, *Tom has something to lose.* I have no intention of sharing it with anyone, but for everything Tom isn't, he is intelligent. He

won't forget I have this, and it may very well purchase his cooperation.
Total silence.

You?

He wants reciprocation, and I need to deliver something.

I couldn't hold it. I came when you sent me the second pic, but . . .

I undo my zipper and snap a quick—and plausibly deniable—shot
of my flaccid dick.

Here.

Nice.

Again, a stupid reply. I hear the front door lock and Nathan's footsteps on the hardwood.

I gotta go. You do discreet well right?

Yeah.

What Tom says next has an unsettling ring of truth to it.

Secrets are my specialty.

29

NATHAN

Deep into the evening, I shut the library door and carry a fresh bourbon over to my desk. The weighty envelope sits in the exact center. Where it's been since it was diligently couriered to my front door hours ago.

ATTN: DR. NATHAN KLEIN. It's from a DC law firm, but the label contains another detail. One that called for a stiff drink or three before contemplating opening it. RE: KLEIN FAMILY FOUNDATION TRUST.

I sink into the leather high-back and breathe heavily.

All afternoon, I told myself that Tilly is fine. She's collared and chipped and making some kids' day at Rose Park, where they came across her. Rock Creek Trail runs right through it and along the water. Plenty of green spaces and quiet streets in our corner of Georgetown. It's not winter, she's not fearful or aggressive, and like the detectives said, neighbors are all out and about.

But as night fell, my hope did the same. Now I've got this goddamn envelope sitting in front of me because when it rains, it fucking pours. I tip my glass until it's empty and set it down harder than intended. Humming that song by the Clash about Monty Clift, I point my chin to the ceiling. Nembutal might numb it all, but we both stick with alcohol.

I pull a letter opener from my drawer. Silver and sharp.

I have a thing for tragic stories—Oliver is evidence of that. But Monty Clift, there's a tragedy! Pioneered Method acting and then drove into a telephone pole. He'd just left Elizabeth Taylor's place, and she was first on the scene.

I cut into the envelope, slicing lengthwise.

Elizabeth Taylor, paramedic, pulled his tooth out of his tongue before he could choke on it.

A bound stack of paper slips out with a thump.

Smart people like Monty and me are more fragile than the Mothers of the world appreciate. The car accident didn't kill him, but it turned him into an agoraphobe, which itself was a slow bitch of a death. This society, it swallows up smart people. If you're smart—and not a sociopath—you don't stand a chance.

I unclip the pages of what is clearly a property deed. A cover letter says it's only a copy for careful review. Signing will occur at the firm's office before a notary and witnesses.

The address—my address—printed in black and white pulls tears from my eyes. As I flip pages, a heaviness in my chest hints at everything I'm losing. I'm no longer the surgeon in command but an unraveling next of kin in the waiting room. I'm not the pilot but a back-row passenger bouncing through turbulence. Terrified as we fly into a storm of unknown scale and utterly powerless to stop it.

I'm fragile, Mother!

My dog. My house. My husband. My control. My mind. I'm losing them all. My grip around the blade tightens, and my knuckles go bloodless.

I scroll for Mother's number but stop short of dialing. No, that's what she wants. She wants me to beg. She wants me to account for my mistakes, Oliver first among them. There's no way she and Father intend to go through with this bullshit. Except my love and my happiness mean nothing to either of them and they very much already have. On my desk sits the final product of a work order that's been executed. And as a psychotherapist with a strategic talent for passive-aggressive tactics, she's framed it as a gift.

I turn to the painting hung over an ivory mantel. A family portrait done a few years before I was born. Father appears effortlessly disinterested even then. But stoic Mother in Jacqueline Kennedy Chanel seems to taunt me. *I'm giving you the home, darling! An opportunity to prove Father and me wrong. If you can afford it.*

I laugh, quietly and to no one. When I toss my phone across the desk, the swollen vein on my wrist is suddenly magnetic. Once again, the letter opener is in my hand.

How destroyed would she be? The delivery of her paperwork and her son's suicide happening in rapid succession. How many years of her own grueling psychotherapy would it take to convince her that, surely, it was a coincidence. That underlying issues were at play, and Dr. Nathan Klein was always going to do it. She can't blame herself for something she had no control over.

Under my skin, I push that fat vein back and forth with the letter opener.

I have a thing for tragedy, but something tragic says Mother would unburden herself the second the funeral ended. What's the point of knowingly bemoaning your misplaced guilt without an audience to feed the narcissistic histrionics?

Mother would be fine, but my husband is another story.

Pull it together, Nathan. I run both hands over my face. *Maybe you can't afford* this *house, but you can certainly afford* a *house.* If we're forced out, I'll need to come up with messaging for Oliver. No telling how he'd handle a lack of stability on my part. I'm his foundation, but I should start reinforcing things on his behalf. Abrupt change could very well trigger him.

It's certainly triggered me. I pull my briefcase from the bottom drawer and twirl the spin lock. Control may be slipping through my fingers, but it's not gone yet. I dig for my prescription pad.

Poison might be a woman's weapon, but gays take liberties with what is and is not a woman's anything. I click a pen and write for a very specific drug. A narcotic I won't ever use but will feel better knowing is at arm's length.

An off-ramp, so to speak.

I rip the paper from its mooring and stuff it in my pocket. Before I leave the library to join my husband upstairs, I grab my letter opener one last time. I walk over to that ivory mantel—African ivory and original to the very home I can't pay for—and catch scorn from eyes in the portrait above it.

When the blade sinks into canvas, it's me—not Mother—who's suddenly unburdened.

30

OLIVER

As best I could, I'd avoided Nathan for the rest of the night. When he finally crawls into bed, there's bourbon on his breath. He asks if I'm still angry. I tell him no.

He opens his nightstand and a familiar pharmaceutical rattling calls.

Nathan pops an Ambien and nudges my shoulder with his. In his palm rolls a tiny pill. A calming light blue. "How does some sleep sound?"

I could be forgiven for thinking he's offering it. "That for me?"

"You're not getting rest, babe. The mugging already had you paranoid, but after today? I'm worried, Oliver. Sleep is something I can give you."

"You always talk about how triggering these can be."

"Ambien's not a narcotic. I trust you." He winks. "Besides, I'm a doctor. I won't let you slip."

"Okay." I sit up, surprised by how easy he's made this. "Thanks, Nat."

Surprised and guilty because my "conversation" with Tom's been on a loop in my brain all evening. Tom exploited me. He took advantage of the shitty hand I've been dealt. But again, he doesn't know the truth, does he? From his perspective, I could easily be the bad guy. Betraying Nathan's trust while cruising hookup apps. Looking for just the sort of thrill Tom provided.

Nathan starts to drop the pill into my open hand but stops short. "I do want you to do something for me."

I choke down a laugh. Why the hell did I think this would be easy? That Nathan would do me a favor and that would be the end of it? It's never the end of it, and to think otherwise is foolish.

"What?" An undeniable edge to my tone, and my cheeks flush.

"NA," Nathan starts. "I want you to go back. A meeting or two. It'll be good for you."

"You literally just said sleeping pills aren't—"

"I know," Nathan interrupts. "But *I* want you to go to a meeting, okay? Promise me you will."

He stares, unblinking. I eye his closed fist, then his no-nonsense face. Stoic, and the only one he's worn all day. Maybe ever.

"I'll go to a meeting."

"Promise?"

"Jesus, Nat. Yes. I promise."

He drops the tablet into my palm. It rolls a half circle, and I toss it back with spit before Nathan changes his mind. But maybe he's right about revisiting NA. Meetings reinforce boundaries and mine haven't been this weak in a long time. Kristian's worked diligently to undermine each of them.

Sobriety is like the surface tension of water. It can only endure the most fragile of pressures, and Kristian's found a particularly dangerous one: me. He's set me against myself. Against Nathan too. I mistrust and resent my partner for acts of kindness. Loving me so much he'd risk a fight to get me back into NA.

"Addicts deceive themselves, Oliver. I can keep you accountable," he'd promised, braking in front of that Unitarian church. My very first meeting had my pulse reeling. Before I went in, Nathan folded me deep in his arms and whispered in my ear: "This is *our* journey."

•   •

When Nathan's alarm chimes, I'm swaddled in a sleep that'd been avoiding me. The buzzing is distant. A foghorn atop the mast of some ship on the horizon. Drawing closer and closer before the sharp siren wails and—

Sheet folds cut creases in my cheek. I reach over to his nightstand and turn the damn thing off. Where the hell is Nathan?

My eyelids stick, but the umami of grease and sizzling fat finds the bedroom. It's Thursday, and Nathan's cooking breakfast. Waking before his alarm means he hasn't slept well. If at all.

No jingling dog tags because Tilly's downstairs biding time for cutting-board scraps. My heart swells and guilt erupts. Tilly!

Maybe someone's found her, called even. I unlock my phone.

I do have a new message, but not from any neighbor saying Nathan's dog is safe and sound. Far from it: MeetLockr. Playing with Tom was a huge risk. Has he reached out for a second go? My mouth is ashtray dry.

Who and what's been sent is hidden, but the notification still sharpens my focus. Blurry lines grow cruelly crisp: Tilly's gone. Detective Henning's investigation is stalled. She plans to tell Nathan the truth. In what? Two days now?

Meanwhile Tom sours my stomach. Yesterday was nothing new. Nothing I hadn't done with MeetLockr's catalog of strangers. Dozens of times, but things are different now. I went to a bathhouse. Someone tried to kill me there. A mistake I've paid for ever since. A mistake Tilly's paid for, Nathan's paid for.

Perhaps that's what angers me most about Tom. I'm cornered. Everything's unraveling. Everyone's paying for my mistakes. Except fucking Tom. Solicitous Tom gets a dick pic from his best friend's partner. He gets to pop one off at my expense. Fantasy fulfilled.

But it's not only Tom. Hector's made a surprise cameo. Nathan's brooding around the house. Tracking my movements with a stupid budgeting app. Every man in my life has turned against me in some way. As though they coordinate with one another. Emerge from darkness to frighten me whenever I've finally escaped whichever one had the last go.

And now I'm projecting blame. Add that to my endless list of flaws. Alongside running, lying, denial, and an unrequited love of self-destruction.

No. *I've* made a mistake. *I've* cheated. But lots of people do it. Lots of people cheat, and they don't deserve to die for it.

I've dug my nails deep into my palm. Four crescent shapes like tiny stab wounds. I open MeetLockr. Scroll for my messages.

The username—the sharp exclamation point—is cold water. Arctic water from ocean-deep eyes.

My chest collapses. I open the unread message.

Like my movie?

Kristian's hungry jaws have taken the bait. This is what I wanted, but getting it still sets my pulse aflame. I skewered and dangled myself, and Kristian's obliged.

I am not ready for this. I haven't processed what contact would feel like. The fear is a knife and impossibly sharp. He's slit my belly, groin to sternum.

A long pause. Kristian's not Tom. He doesn't need the validation of a quick response because he's practiced at his game. He's cut me open to the air—blood turned septic from terror.

My throat tightens. Panic crawls down my arms. When it reaches my fingers, they move on their own. Reflex and instinct. I respond with two words.

Meet me.

The idea of a meeting sparks an idea. Something I didn't do when he last messaged: I thumb to his profile. Where the physical distance between us is displayed. MeetLockr's business model hinges on geotagging.

Eight miles. He's eight miles away at this very moment. My phone jolts.

Where?

I need to be smart. If I truly intend to go through with this—a question I admittedly cannot answer yet—then I need to be fucking smart.

In public, obviously. Someplace with other people but not too many. A thick crowd is as isolating and desolate as a back alley or vacant park. Trance comes to mind, the bar's nonstop party every night. No, that won't do. I need people, but the setting must be quiet. Orderly. Mannered. A place where a disturbance of any sort will be promptly noted. Somewhere privileged.

Jefferson hotel. The lounge.

I've never been, but it's a Washington landmark. A five-star establishment for patrons who require atmosphere. Serviced by people who'll quickly pounce on anything or anyone threatening said atmosphere.

Fancy boy. When?

Good question. I chew my lip. When's the right time to meet a murderer? To pull up a chair and share a drink with Alexander Scares-gård? The answer is never, but time's slipping. Detective Henning will tell Nathan, and I need to find Tilly before that happens. There's also the courage the *immediacy of now* stokes. The more this drags on, the longer a confrontation lingers in the theoretical, the greater the chances I abandon my plan. Or come to my goddamn senses, as literally anyone else would conclude.

Tonight @ seven.

Even if I call out of work yet again, I can't be ready, emotionally or physically, for the lunch crowd. I'll have to catch a supper rush. The lounge must crawl with as many pairs of eyes as possible. WASPy, disapproving eyeballs.

Him: **I'm not into group things. No threesomes.**

???

Come alone. See you soon.

Fine.

Just like that, it's done.

My phone slips from my grip. When I push off to stand, my palms sink into a wet mattress. I've sweated into memory foam like a child pisses the bed. For a fevered second, I fear the latter's happened.

What I've done, the events I've set into motion, finally registers. Sheets might not be soaked with urine, but I'm still a child. Stumbling blissfully through the woods, and I've come upon an enormous wasps' nest. It clings to a dying tree like a malignancy. Layer upon layer upon layer of twisted mulch. Both sinister and enthralling.

I stoop for a stone by my feet and hurl it. Papery walls buckle. The rock sinks deep inside blackness. It vanishes and for a cosmic instant, nothing happens.

But they do come.

Wasps pour from their wounded nest. A whining tsunami of rage. Black with hypodermic stingers. Thousands of needles. Each swollen with venom, and I stand perfectly still.

They envelop me.

31

NATHAN

Morning brings both a hangover and a thunderstorm. Swollen black clouds loom as a saucepan starts to simmer. A capful of white vinegar goes in next. Bacon's keeping warm in the oven, and acidity's the secret to a perfectly poached egg.

"Chives?" I ask. Oliver sits at the counter, phone on the marble, finger tap-dancing across its screen. The Ambien peace offering was against my better judgment. It's not morphine, but it's a scheduled drug, and once an addict, always one. But it'd also mean a deep sleep, a late start, and a chance to skim his phone again.

Because he's still lying to me.

"Sure," Oliver answers as I pull a tray of English muffins from the oven. I sit them on the empty side of the stove, spoon the first egg into swirling water, and recap the vinegar.

That's the taste in my mouth this morning. Oliver had changed his PIN and it coated my stomach in sour vinegar.

"I'm taking call tonight." Didn't need more than five minutes to recover the new one. My card, my account. New PIN, sure, but new security questions didn't cross his mind. I stir the hollandaise, start to plate up. "Got any plans while I'm out?"

"No. Why?" *Because, liar, you're back on MeetLockr. Like nothing has happened.*

"Whole house to yourself." Toasted muffin, poached egg, ladle of sauce. "Not gonna run? Maybe grab a drink with a friend or something?"

Oliver lets half a smile slip. "What friends?"

"Fair enough." My knuckles whiten around the hilt of the butcher's knife. Chives spread on the cutting board, I chop. Maybe too hard.

I sprinkle chives, turn, and pass Oliver a meal he'd have killed for back in Indiana. Now it's all taken for granted. "What are you looking at?"

Finally, some eye contact. "News."

"Anything interesting?"

"Nope." He flips it over, pushes the iPhone aside to make room.

"Okay, then."

When he cuts into his breakfast, a spoonful of golden yolk spills. I smile, privately congratulating myself on an egg well done because not much else warrants celebration. Not with Mother's extortion—now drawn up as legitimate paperwork. Not with my husband's return to MeetLockr. After coming to his senses and deleting it once already.

"Egg looks great," he offers like lukewarm charity.

Cruising the app for sex like it's not available right here. In a six-million-dollar Georgetown dream house that could be gone tomorrow. Barbie's fucking dream house, and all she's gotta do is snap her fingers for some dick. Anytime she wants it! I count the months in my head. Four, five? Has it been longer than that? Not some tepid jerk-off sesh while our shoulders touch but real sex? Pounding, bleating sex that lasts both too long and never long enough? SEX sex.

I saddle up at the counter, and anger pops like a live wire. Everything Oliver has is because of me. Including his own goddamn life. The least—the very least!—he could do is have sex with *me*. It's not a want, it's a need. A billion years of evolution for fuck's sake. As biologically compelled as food and water.

It's only reasonable, then, to conclude that he simply does not find me attractive. Nothing makes him go flaccid faster than predictable fucking stability, huh? Gay men age in dog years, and old Dr. Klein's not so alluring any longer.

I drain my coffee. You know what else isn't alluring? Cradling your sweaty, trembling body all through detox, all through the cravings, sitting through the NA meetings and revising all the cover letters to all the posted jobs on the curated list I diligently crafted on your behalf.

My empty mug strikes the table.

Oliver's eyes flit to mine.

But my thirsty, thirsty husband's gone back to the watering hole.

Missing dog, home invasion, strangulation? None of it kept him away for long. And now Oliver's got nudes saved on his camera roll behind a brand-new PIN.

Photos of himself.

And Tom Vogt.

32

OLIVER

"More coffee?" Nathan asks, pouring himself a fresh one.

"No, thank you." I push the congealing yolk around my plate.

"You're not hungry?" Nathan doesn't look up. He doesn't need to. He's been watching me not eat throughout breakfast.

"Not really." Nathan separates the pages of last Sunday's newspaper— a local city paper more for pop culture than culture culture. *Vibe*. He loves getting it delivered to our doorstep weekly and I'd found this endearing once.

"You sleep?"

"Huh?"

"The pill I gave you. It get you to sleep?"

"Yeah." A headache gathers behind my eyes. "Yes. I did. Thank you."

"You're welcome."

He winks, and I'm back to brooding in silence. At least I've lucked out in one small way. Nathan's on call overnight, so no need to come up with excuses for my absence. No need to lob yet another undeserved lie his way.

He'll take off around five and won't return until well after five the following morning. Haggard from playing god. Doing all he can to stop the bleeding from *this* gunshot. To suture the wounds from *that* stabbing. To inform frenetic parents their drunk daughter struck a lamppost. He'll tell them her spine severed before the airbags even blew, so not to worry, she felt nothing.

That's how we met. The trauma center in South Bend, Indiana, is regional. It catches rural cases from armpits like Tyre. Folks maimed by agricultural equipment. Horrific amputations at unnatural places. Hands and feet and fingers and toes gone ground beef. Kids doing stupid shit on oxy and meth, like diving headfirst into shallow creeks. South Bend is perfect for an emergency surgery resident. Why else leave a city like New York?

He collects his empty plate and my full one. He kisses my forehead and makes for the sink.

"I almost forgot," he says with his back to me. Same as I've turned mine to him so many times. Whenever I'm lying, and again, I find myself bracing.

"Forgot what?"

"Tom's redecorating his condo." He opens the dishwasher, begins organizing utensils and flatware with a diligence bordering obsessive-compulsive. "He mentioned needing new art, so we're meeting up this afternoon."

"Before work?" Seems like I'll have more time alone than I thought. "Where?"

"The gallery we love. The one in Frederick."

Nathan says *we* but he means *I*. Still, it makes little sense. Frederick's more than an hour away. "Really? Isn't that kind of a drive?"

"It'll be worth it."

"Just before a long shift—"

"Called all the shelters again this morning," he interrupts. The sudden switch of topic reads as avoidance, but it works. At once, I'm struck by an inescapable sadness. "No Tilly."

No Tilly. Two words; two blows to the back of my skull. And to his.

He's going to a gallery in Maryland because that's less time spent at home without her. Guilt—unwelcomed and deserved—returns. I shouldn't have questioned it. Not when I've got far worse questions to answer for.

Why do I do this to him? Why let him languish in the purgatory of the unknown? Jaunts to Maryland before fifteen-hour shifts are strange, but maybe that's how he copes. The uncertainty is trauma too. As far as he knows, Tilly might turn up any moment. At a shelter or rooting through a neighbor's garden. It's a false hope, but hope is a powerful motivator. The strongest we humans have at our disposal.

As Nathan heads upstairs to get ready, I fast-forward to an evening I won't ever be ready for.

No question, looping Detective Henning in would've been smart. Maybe she'd even be in The Jefferson's bar too. Undercover to grab Kristian or pump him full of fucking bullets or something. But in what universe would she greenlight this? Kristian also had conditions.

I'm not into group things. No threesomes.

Besides, if Detective Henning had even the slightest hint of a heads-up, she'd go straight to Nathan. If Tilly wasn't already dead, she'd be killed. Then I'd be killed. If Kristian didn't do it, I would myself. After Nathan kicked me out into a world with no room for sobriety.

I breathe deep.

From here on out, every hour brings me closer to the moment when a fresh-pressed doorman gestures me into The Jefferson and the hungry thing that waits there.

And every hour I tell myself it is possible Tilly escaped.

After all, I did.

33

This is a fucking mistake.

A familiar feeling as I cross The Jefferson's checkered floor like a chess piece. A pawn traveling the board for the most high-stakes game of his life. The lobby is elegant, like the White House foyer or the East Room. Esteemed things get announced from podiums in spaces this slick.

I swipe for the time with wet thumbs: 6:35 p.m. I'm early. Very early. I'd consider this a good thing if any part of my plan could be called that. I swallow. None of my plan is certain.

Majesty palms stand like sentinels. Wrought-iron gates cross doorways, and a glass atrium evokes a bygone era. Victorian—no, Americana. An ambiguous word with no tangible definition. Like porn, you know it when you see it.

It was supposed to feel safe, but my palms still itch. The hotel is somehow too sprawling and too intimate. A boutique labyrinth of unknown size and Tom's territory through and through. If he weren't with Nathan, he could be around any corner.

"Hotel bars are underrated," Kimberly had said once. We'd been talking about her Tinder in the breakroom. "They're moodier, never crowded, and *way* more convenient than cleaning up just to get laid." She'd winked, but why didn't I remember this?

Who else could be here that I know? A dangerous voice teases inside my skull.

I draw in breath, brush the front of a twill button-down, and pretend I'm Tom. Not Tom, specifically, but someone like Tom. Someone who belongs here. *You can do this.*

In my pocket, I finger the arming switch of the pepper spray Nathan gave me. Pulled left, the safety locks. Pulled right, it's armed. I tug it left, and then to the right twice. Armed.

From the lounge entry, I scour the room. What I'm doing is ballooning into something too huge, and I can't swallow it.

The bar's even darker. Wood-paneled walls and Persian rugs over parquet. Low yellow lighting and a plushness that's outlasted a stock market crash, a nuclear missile crisis, and god knows what else. I slide out a low-back stool from the counter.

"Hi there." Bartender's a blond woman in a pressed oxford shirt. She'd taken a minute or two to notice me. "Sorry for the wait. We just wrapped up a fundraiser for Senator Rucker in the ballroom."

The name rings an alarm. Rucker as in Ted Rucker who Nathan calls Turd Fucker and who is also Tom's boss. Shit. My cheeks smolder. If Rucker was here for a fundraiser, then Tom might—no. Stop, Oliver. Tom is in Frederick right now. With Nathan who, unlike yourself, doesn't lie about where he is and when he's there.

"Hello?" The bartender breaks my paranoia. "Something to drink?"

"Tonic water." I've never wanted alcohol more. "For now."

"What room are you staying in?"

"Cash, if that's cool." I slide a crisp twenty across burled walnut, exhaling. Can't have The Jefferson popping up on Wealth Wallet.

"Room number was just in case you changed your mind. Water's on the house." Guess bars don't charge for tonic, but she chuckles like my money's no good here regardless. I should be breaking down tables in the ballroom with the rest of the event staff.

The bar top itself is small, and only a single seat faces the entry. A heavy man occupies it. A near-empty draft of lager before both him and his fucking cowboy hat. I will him to leave. Is he finished? Almost finished? I want that seat because Kristian doesn't need to see me before I see—

"What are you looking for?" An unseen whisper. Scandi accent. Warm breath scales my neck like a string of picnic ants. I flinch, spin, but he's already claiming the next stool over.

Kristian's early too.

Cold eyes that somehow burn intensely. Staring into the sun is dangerous. Blindingly hot, but I steel myself. No, I think, molars grinding. *Confront.* "You."

He says nothing.

I sharpen my tone into a box cutter, repeat: "I'm looking for you."

His lips curve. Cheek muscles bend and tense and twist his wound as though it smiles too. An inflamed grin of stitched tissue, taut and damp and just for me. "You're brave."

Not true, Kristian. But we're in a hotel. Posh and protected and you're a caged leopard. I'm simply visiting the zoo. In the wild, you'd have sprung, wouldn't you? Fangs tearing flesh. You'd want me alive when you start to eat me.

The snuff film—the man's face, blurred and pixelated and dying— flashes. His face is my face. You'd make *certain* I was alive before you started.

"Get you a drink, sir?" The bartender's distracted, stacking tumblers. She hasn't a clue to whom she speaks. To the criminal, the killer whose drink she'll soon prepare.

"Vodka," he tells her in his thick accent. The one I'd found so seductive. "Neat."

Her eyes find his, and she lingers there. Does he do it for her too? Or is she startled by his stitches? "Room number?"

"Seven-twenty-one."

Bingo. If he has a room, he used a card to book it. Even if he plans to pay cash, he'd have to provide a card as a deposit. Is it his own? Stolen? Regardless, there'll be a record for Detective Henning.

As a sliver of hope breaks, another thought dashes it to pieces. A dark thundercloud of a thought. Why does Kristian have a room? What does he intend to do with it?

He turns my way. *Or inside it?* His long forefinger runs the length of his thumb. Even his fidgeting is sensual. Carnal and calling.

"You're a brave, brave little boy. Tell me something, Oliver." He smells my fear. I reek of it, and he sips it like a neat pour of vodka. "Does Dr. Klein know you're here?"

"Keep his name out of your mouth."

"Of course he doesn't, but," Kristian teases, "if the good doctor doesn't know you're here, why are you? What do you want?"

The question's a whirling curve ball. Its whistle, familiar. Detective Henning asked that, and I couldn't answer because I've only ever *wanted* by the hour. I want a meal. I want oxy. I want to be safe. I want to be loved. I want to bring Tilly home. I want Kristian dead and I want to live.

I want Nathan, but I keep this to myself and ask the same of him: "What is it you want from me?"

He swallows the liquor now sitting before him. "The truth is, I want lots of things from you."

"What—"

"Oliver, Oliver, Oliver Park," he sings. "Lots and lots of things."

"What the fuck do you want?" Bartender raises her eyes at *fuck*.

Kristian edges closer. His knee brushes mine, and he leaves it there. We're touching; I don't retreat. We're connected for the first time since he strangled me. Since his hard, pulsing dick pressed the small of my back. Since I dragged a key through his shit-eating flesh.

"Your throat looks good." He takes a second gulp. "Healing nice."

I've yet to touch my tonic, and my mouth holds no moisture. My bottom lip quivers, and I stay it with my teeth. "Wish I could say the same. That cut looks infected. Gonna leave a scar."

"I didn't finish." He skirts past my dig. "You gave me blue balls."

This is a game to him. All a big fucking game. I am a wounded bird, battered and broken, and he's caught me. Reveling, no, luxuriating, in my protruding bones and smashed beak. My tears lubricate his glee.

"The police know who you are. They've got your flash drive." My sudden confidence is a thin veneer, but I lie about everything else in life. Why the hell stop when it might save me? "They've got your movie; they know where you work. They're closing in."

He tilts his knee up and down, soft against mine.

"They won't come. I'm not findable." He's becoming an overwhelming force, unstoppable, flooding the space between us. He's proving he really doesn't care about the police. He really is unfindable.

"Everyone's findable."

"You're a selfish date, you know that?" He tilts his head. "How about you get to know me a little instead? What do you think?" My groin swells with warm blood. I haven't moved my knee, and why not? Why let him caress it? He smiles knowingly, his next words perfumed with vodka: "Aren't you curious?"

"Fine." I clench. He knows everything about me, so why the hell not. "Where are you from?"

"Bergen. Know it?"

I shake for *no*.

"Norway." His room number, his place of birth, why is he so forthcoming? "Not so big a city, but lots of sea and mountains and fjords. Quite nice."

"The video. Is it real?"

He nods for *yes*, and perhaps he speaks freely because I won't be alive long enough to share anything with anybody. "Did you watch all of them?"

"No."

"You afraid you might be on it?"

"Did you film me?"

"If I did, you should be grateful. It's why you're here now. Alive."

"What the hell does that mean?"

"The time it takes to pack up a GoPro"—he traces his wound—"while bleeding."

"Why do you do this to people?"

"You want my story?" He laughs in a snickering, tittering kind of way. "Why I'm *fucked up*?"

My drink is well within reach, but turning from Kristian for any length of time is a harrowing prospect. Like flipping the lights off in a closet filled with vipers. The knot in my throat goes down like a baseball. "Yeah, Kristian. Why are you so fucked up?"

"Guess I never had parents to help me unfuck myself." He spins his tumbler as though unwinding memories. "I went from orphanage to foster mom when I was a very little boy."

He's going the orphan route? So cliché it's probably a lie. But static still builds, and the air between us might ignite at any moment.

"I don't say her name, Foster Mom, I mean. She was very nasty. With a nasty little habit."

"Makes two of you."

"Oh no." He gives a taunting scoff. "Far more than two of us. You see, her nasty habit was taking cash from bad men with even nastier habits. So many very bad men."

The space darkens. The lounge, the whole hotel, all of it falls under shadow.

"Men with nasty little habits like"—he brings a finger to his lips, runs his tongue from knuckle to nail—"like putting things inside me."

What little light remains stretches into long, thin rays.

"So, I put scissors inside Foster Mom." He shrugs, but those arctic eyes deepen. Then a smile. Shit.

"You killed her." I break from his face, desperate to find a mooring. I need to anchor myself to reality. To something, anything. A tremor climbs up my arm.

"When I want something, I take it. When I chase something, I catch it. And you're still running, aren't you? Still uncaught."

"With scissors."

"I have a room." His finger taps my thigh. A single, soft rap for each word. Another curve ball that comes so fast, my head might spin right off.

"I—"

"I will put my mouth all over you. For being so brave, I'll make you feel so good. Outside and *inside*."

I need to call Detective Henning. I knew I was jumping into the deep end, but this is way too deep. I'm sinking in panic, and I must find something to push off from. To keep my head above water. His skin, red and inflamed. The laceration. My breath breaks free.

"Did you kill her?" For the first time, my voice is even. Furious but balanced.

Narrowed eyes, he pulls back. "Eventually."

"Not your fucking foster mom." I speak slowly, deliberately: "Did you kill our dog?"

"No." Another pause. His lips and his wound both grin again. "Not yet."

My pulse spikes. Tilly's alive. He has her, and he's using her as a bargaining chip.

"She's upstairs," he says as though reading my mind. "You want to see her?"

The meaning his fractured words hold is brutally clear. I say nothing, and he knows he's got me. My heart thrums in both ears.

"You want, you come and get." He polishes off his vodka like he's had countless chats just like this one. I don't doubt it one bit.

His cruel flippancy, his proposition, sets fire to my thoughts. They rocket in all directions. Exploding, bursting, spreading flames everywhere they land. If Tilly's here, if I can get her . . . No. Am I kidding? Am I fucking kidding? I can't follow Kristian up to a hotel room. I just can't.

I didn't plan for this. Shit, I never considered he might bring her with him. *Alive*. Wait. Do I believe he's telling me the truth? That she is, in fact, alive?

"Prove it. Prove you didn't kill her."

"You got to trust me." He wags that long finger, still slick from his tongue. "Dog is happy. Dog is very friendly." His emphasis falls on *very* in a way that feeds my fear like gasoline. A conflagration as he ups the stakes. "If you brought police friends with you, you will not get her."

I didn't suspect Kristian would bring Tilly, keeping her in a room close by. But I did very much worry he'd kill her should he escape. From cops I brought to our "date."

"There are no police," I say. The truth, and he pushes his glass away, stands. He believes—he knows—I'm alone.

Kristian leans in to my ear, and I brace for something bad.

"I go upstairs. You follow me, play with me upstairs, let me put my mouth on you, and I give you your dog." His words are slow but his breath bites sharp with liquor.

"No," I say through clenched teeth. "You'll kill me up there. Bring the dog down. First."

"You stay here; I kill your dog. I make it hurt very badly. I make her cry for a very long time." His voice dwindles to a whisper. Low, but all promise: "I keep her alive and show her what her insides look like. Do you think she might lick them? If she's thirsty, she might lick her own insides when I show to her?"

A fountain of vomit climbs my throat, and I choke it down. He's splayed his cards atop the table. He's given me options. I never gained a foothold. Never reclaimed control. *I* set the trap. *I* cast the line, dangled the bait. Ensnared *him*.

Yet, here's Kristian. He stands before me, gaping jaw unhinged. Ready to swallow me whole.

He turns and begins a slow walk into the lobby, not bothering to look back. A casual stroll that says he doesn't care if I'm following or not. He's already had his fun. He plans to get off today, one way or another.

"Fuck!" I slam a fist on the counter, and the bartender jolts. I'm out of moves.

"Are you all right—"

Her question is left unfinished. I'm already tracing Kristian's steps, following him up. For Nathan's dog. I can't let him kill her, torture her. Doing that to Tilly and Nathan is not an option!

A row of brass-plated elevators stands at the far end where Kristian waits. He still hasn't glanced over his shoulder once. A chime, doors slide open, and he steps inside. As the elevator closes, both he and his wound smile.

I sprint and throw my arm between the shutting doors.

Inside, instinct flares, and I back into the corner farthest from Kristian. We're alone in what might just be my coffin. I prayed, hoped against all hope someone else would be in here.

But it's only us. Me and my grinning killer.

The doors finally close. The button for the seventh floor glows. Kristian moves close so our shoulders touch. I can't breathe. My stomach scales my throat, and I'm choking on it.

Kristian's arm moves rhythmically against mine. He fondles his groin, breathes heavily through his nose. He's aroused by my terror. Spots form before my eyes, and I might pass out. I'm a fucking idiot.

The elevator ascends.

Second floor. Third floor.

I could mace him. I could mace him right now, get the hotel staff to open whatever room he has. Grab Tilly. Except I can't. We're in an elevator. Pepper spray will blind us both. I reach into my pocket, take hold of my only chance to live. I must be ready.

Fourth floor.

A vibration stirs in my other pocket. My phone. Someone's sent a text.

The floors whirl by. A countdown in reverse. A time bomb to some fate, mostly unknown but sure as hell not one I survive.

Fifth floor. Sixth floor.

I flip it screen-side-up with trembling fingers.

Seventh floor.

The elevator shudders to a stop with a single chime. The texts are from Nathan:

Neighbor found Tilly!

Will you please get her? And call immediately??

I need to see her!

IV. Hypoxic Convulsion

Frothing of the mouth. Blueing skin and nails.

Violent muscle contractions.

34

The elevator doors fold open. Kristian steps out onto the seventh floor, but my feet are cemented to the elevator's plush carpet. I'm so fucking stupid! I asked about a dog. Kristian spied an opening. He took it same as he'll take my life.

He senses he's not being followed, turns as the elevator doors start closing.

His wound thaws me, and I stumble back against the wall. I clench my gut, reach for my pocket mace.

Kristian lunges. The brass doors are almost shut. I will them to shut. They must shut!

His right hand breaks through, long fingers gripping the edges. The safety mechanism triggers and they open. Kristian leaps, arms thrust out. I hoist my mace, and he brings an elbow over his face.

I fire.

Nothing comes out.

The trigger—it won't budge. I've not armed it. I clicked it from off to on to off to on again so many times, it wasn't armed at the bar!

"Stupid little boy," Kristian spits, grabbing my wrist like a blood pressure cuff. He thrusts the back of my hand against the wall. Pain live-wires up my arm as he slams it into metal. Over and over and over again.

I kick outward but connect with nothing. Again, he thrusts my hand into dented brass sheeting. I scream in his ear.

"Fuuuccckkk!" he screams back, blond bangs cascading down his face. Veins in his forehead swollen and fleshy. Ice eyes rushing like roiling seas.

With a free hand, he grabs a fistful of my hair, and fire zigzags over my scalp. My vision blurs. He jerks, and my chin points to the ceiling, where a tiny security cam blinks. His eyes follow mine, and he laughs when he sees we're being recorded. "You know just how I like it."

He covers my mouth, pushes me into the wall. Bolts of neon heat shoot up my shoulders. The unarmed mace hangs loose from my fingers, and he snatches it.

I grit. "Stop—"

"Not quite scissors." He reaches in his back pocket where he trades my pepper spray for something else. "But it still hurts when it goes in."

A switchblade. He holds me at arm's length, tilts his head, and just how fucked I am sinks in. Tears film my eyes. "You can't—"

"Glad I ordered extra towels," he says as my pulse hammers in my throat. "'Cause I'm going to make a big mess of you."

"Please, Kristian!" I sob, backing up. He follows like the sweeping hands of a clock.

"Save some tears for later, baby."

When he reaches to reopen the doors, I fall into the call panel. My spine smashes floor buttons to a chorus of ding ding dings. We lock eyes.

"That was a mistake," Kristian hisses as the elevator drops.

Holding the knife close in the folds of his shirt, he steers me into a corner. He nods to the flashing recorder above. "Kiss me for the camera."

"No—"

His shoves his liquor lips to mine. Hot breath, one hand on my back, the other gripping my hair like a leash. The elevator abruptly stops. He pulls back long enough to whisper, "Be a good boy, okay?"

Over his shoulders, the doors fold open to an empty hall. Room numbers blur as I gasp for breath. They're all three hundred and something. Third floor. A fistful of my shirt knots, and I'm held in place while the doors close.

Sweat pours and we slip against each other for a second time. I reach for the call buttons. *L* for Lobby is too far. I can only hit the emergency stop, but if we stop, I'm dead.

"Behave or I will slit you open right here." He squeezes my hand and guides it to the needle tip of his blade. "Leave some of you on every floor. What do you think, huh?"

My spine must've struck 2, because we're stopping again.

"People come to hotels to cheat." His stubbled chin rakes my cheek as he grips my collar, muzzles my mouth with his. "So canoodle with me, my love."

Please let somebody be waiting for the elevator.

Something wet finds its way inside my ear. Kristian's tongue pushes deeper like a Q-tip. His stitches tickle.

Somebody be there!

We stop, a bell chimes, and the doors open. A man just over Kristian's shoulder! Tall and surprised and please help me! I start to turn, to scream, but freeze when the knife teases my belly.

"Ooh, honey, not so rough," Kristian teases, moving my hand to his own ass. "A little busy in here. Maybe you catch the next one."

The stranger must've agreed because the doors shut. And we're still alone.

"See, lover?" Kristian runs his finger up my throat.

Consciousness starts to slip. Time's running the fuck out. If we go back up, I won't ever come down. I've just got to stay unstabbed for one more floor. Now or never. I throw my knee into Kristian's gut, and his grip falters. I hurl myself at the call panel and punch *L*.

As it lights, Kristian springs. He squeezes my throat, brings the knife to my sternum. He starts to push it in. "I said—"

Ding!

We break eye contact. Doors part like theater curtains. A total scene change, and the show reopens to the ornate, sweeping space from earlier. Chatter and casual guffawing. Roller suitcases. Bellhops and coffee and piano jazz.

I tear free of his grip, stumble across the threshold. Kristian follows for a flash but thinks better of it. I slip on the floor and fall onto all fours. I catch looks from blurry, abstract faces.

I turn back to Kristian. His eyes dance around the lobby, drinking in the same worried faces. He takes two steps back. To the rear of the elevator, where he pockets his knife.

As the doors close, our eyes meet again. Mine, wide and white. His, deep and angry.

35

NATHAN

Oliver doesn't reply to my texts.

    Where are you, husband? What are you doing? Or who? Speaking of, my next text is to Tom.

Be there in 15-20.

He replies in a typical Tom-like flurry of bullet points:

Same.

Met someone.

Blue collar as fuck and fuckable as fuck.

Will tell you all about it.

Bet you won't.

I hang my lanyard around my neck. Photo ID and my CAC card.

The Common Access Card is required for everything from parking lot entry to automated dispensing of meds via Pyxis machine. Swipe your CAC card, then your fingerprint, and the Pyxis pulls your credentials. Scan your prescription and the drawer storing whatever drug unlocks. Dr. Nathan Klein is an authorized user across all Defense Department hospital systems.

I breathe deeply. The relief I should feel in the wake of Tilly's recovery is lost to a pounding pulse and a rage that's frighteningly silent.

Sea-green scrubs, white coat and no one at the National Cancer Institute campus in Frederick will question my presence here. I lied to Oliver about working today, but it's too late now. Besides, Tilly's safe. Oliver will retrieve her from the neighbor's, and I'll have to trust him alone with her for just a little longer.

I step into an elevator and send it up a floor to inpatient cancer care.

This campus was once a hub for American biowarfare. Enormous vats that cooked up anthrax by the steel drum full. It's ironic for two reasons: One, because poison is still very much used here in the form of chemo-therapeutics. And two, I've also come for a weapon—though one far more subtle than sarin gas. The elevator doors slide open, and I take to the hall with deliberate purpose.

Government hospitals are decentralized by campus. If I order meds from a Pyxis machine in Frederick, it will be recorded only in Frederick. Walter Reed will know nothing of it and barring a pattern of unusual drug dispensing—which I certainly have not created—this one impending order won't trigger suspicion.

When I pass a mobile supplies station, I pluck a sealed fifty-milliliter syringe and a trio of twenty-eight-gauge capped needles. Into my pocket they go, and I spot a Pyxis setup in a nook ahead. I also catch the eye of a scrub nurse who's clearly gay and who clearly smiles to let me know he likes what he sees. I return the gesture before slipping into the alcove and activating the same touchscreen I use every day in DC.

I'm committed to obtaining the weapon, but I've yet to commit to doing anything with it.

I swipe my CAC, then my finger, and follow the prompts to scan the prescription I'd written last night.

Whatever the hell's gotten into me is irrelevant because I won't actu-ally use it. I'll simply feel better knowing it's an option. Mother's moving forward and making good on her threat. Couriering the paperwork and I suppose the next step is to simply evict us. Oliver won't stop, can't stop lying to me. Even Tom's betrayed me. Tom, who's been talking to *my* husband. Exchanging explicit photos with *my* husband. Maybe fucking *my* husband.

I confirm my medication order and wait for that familiar click as the correct drawer unlocks. Sweat pearling on my brow, a slow tremor crawling up my arm. I would never take this exit. I just need to see the off-ramp. Vaguely, hazily, somewhere in the distance while I navigate all the lies. Pull my crushed body from under the devastating weight of all the betrayals.

Mother's.

Tom's.

My husband's.

Fentanyl citrate. Fifty micrograms per injection, but the PCA pump syringe in my hand contains fifty milliliters. Patient-controlled analgesia attached to an IV drip. I need to be careful with this. Hide it somewhere safer than a stupid duct vent full of cigarettes. Once an addict, always an addict, and I can't let Oliver find my off-ramp. He'd see the drug's name and wouldn't think twice about dumping this shit into his veins. Sure as hell wouldn't consider dosing.

Fifty milliliters contains 2.5 milligrams. As far as off-ramps go, this provides plenty of certainty.

Because as far as milligrams go, the lethal dose is only two.

36

OLIVER

I lose time.

A fugue-like state of detachment takes hold. A post-traumatic response meant to keep me from feeling anything.

I'd caught a waiting cab, but the ride home was a streaming abstract painting. Sharp angles and bold acid reds and yellows. Maybe I didn't pay the cabbie. As I stumble down the sidewalk toward the house, reality bleeds through. Slowly at first. A drip-drop of the present forming puddles and pools until enough of a picture takes shape for my consciousness to tether itself.

I rub my ear, finger the folds where his tongue wormed its way in. Kristian tried to kill me. A second time, and the bones in my hand throb where they struck the wall. My head pounds and burns from that fistful of hair, Kristian's attempt to scalp me.

Tilly was never there because Tilly was safe the whole damn time. Thank god for that. I scroll for Nathan's texts. My screen is a spiderweb of fractured glass. It must've shattered at some point in the elevator. More desperate messages from him wait.

Where are you?!

I need to see her!

His next text provided the Good Samaritan's phone number and address, three streets over from us. Another demands a photo the second she's in my arms. Proof of life.

I fumble with my keys and leave the front door ajar. The act of shutting it is overwhelming. Do I need to call Detective Henning immediately? Of course I do. Kristian's credit card—or whoever's card he used to book the room—could lead Detective Henning and her partner straight to the fucking psychopath.

Kristian had probably shoved his GoPro on a hotel-room shelf to capture the whole thing. Exactly like Haus. Is he part of some, like, international gay snuff film ring? Seems as implausible as a gay mafia, but my mind can't stop spinning. How did he come to DC? How did our paths cross inside Haus?

Seven-twenty-one. He gave the room number to the bartender, and it's all Detective Henning will need. Then she'll have to tell Nathan everything.

I note the vacant space above the mantel in Nathan's library. If I never saw those oily, glaring Klein eyes again, I'd be thrilled. It's just bizarre of Nathan to suddenly want them gone too. In the powder room, sink water runs ice-cold over my face.

My hand pulses; what if Kristian broke it? It's not bruised, so whatever wounds I have are hidden for now. A cherry rash circles my throat, but my first injuries cover for my second.

My thoughts roll and roil and wash like sea waves. Breaking against one another in sprays of rain, changing directions, riptides and currents swirling this way and that. When they draw back from shore, something's left behind in their wake. A sense I've been here before. A detached and defeated state disaster leaves. When I've lost. When apathy takes hold because I've failed.

When Detective Henning tells him the truth, Nathan will cry. He will scream at me. Flecks of spittle will strike my face, and my heart will rupture. I will know a sadness far worse than before, because *before,* I hadn't yet learned how good things could be. For people like Nathan and the people he loves. And at the very bottom of that very deep and very dark sadness, I will find some motel that I will never leave. I will book a room that will be soiled and reek of piss and whiskey and be absolutely perfect for the conclusion of my just-as-soiled life. I will log on to MeetLockr and Grindr and Casual Encounters and all the rest, and I will replace *Oliver P* with *Needs Oxy Now,* and I will pay with whatever depravity I'm asked for, and while I submit to the fetishes of strangers, I will pray that this time, this time Nathan does come across my profile and is vindicated because, after all, he deserves at least that.

That I can give him.

I stare into my own wild eyes in the sleek glass of a gilded sink mirror they've got no business in. But I have been here before.

TYRE, IN

The bottles in my bag rattled with each step across the cracked Indiana sidewalk. Early morning, and the fresh sun's rays did little to warm, given the season. But it didn't matter because scalding hot or frigid and cold, I couldn't feel anything. Certainly not pain.

It'd only been two days since the door to my and Hector's apartment shut a final time, but I'd stayed high—low?—ever since. I thought sleeping in my old music teacher's shed was clever. She'd never locked it, but I wasn't the only thing drawn to the heat it kept. My exposed flesh was a feast for fire ants deep in the wood mulch.

Up early, and I'd walked some dozen or so bleak blocks on the hunt for somewhere else. Passed through the downtown drag lined with diners and payday loan sharks. Walked beneath a faded mural painted on the brick of the old Chevy factory. A rosy woman steered a '60s Corvette with one hand and waved her sun hat with the other. Above her, in swooping ribbons of red, white, and blue: FLOOR THE GAS TO TYRE! AMERICA'S NEXT DETROIT!™

A promise long discarded by coast dwellers in their gilded fortresses of the San Francisco Peninsula and the island of Manhattan. A possum-pissed receptacle for those who bungled their shot at the American Dream. Now they only shoot meth and oxy and, speak of the devil, the barred windows of a pharmacy catch my eye.

The pad of scripts in the front pocket of my bag. Still had plenty of pills to make it a few days. Maybe a week, depending on how shitty things got. Who was I kidding? Things stood to get much shittier.

I unzipped my duffel, reached inside, and took whatever pills my fingers found first. Then I waited for them to dull the world's sharpening edges. A renewed warmth to blanket my insides. For the sense of normal and the courage to come. It'd stoke what I needed to stand, to sling my bag over my shoulder, and to walk inside Wellington Family Compounding Pharmacy.

A bell wire tripped, and the man at the front register greeted me with a passing smile. Passing because it started wide but vanished when he sized me up. Haggard, numb, armpits that reeked like wet onion. At least I'd changed my pee jeans. Hector would've found my gift by now.

Fluorescent lighting was never forgiving, but it'd never been this brutal either. A display of hand mirrors threw ten unrecognizable reflections my way. A hollow person who'd come to the end of his rope. Nowhere to go. Black soil crammed beneath nails shorn short, legs chewed up by ants.

I thought about swinging through the restroom. Washing up to invite less scrutiny from behind the pharmacy counter.

Instead, I beelined for school supplies and tore a fat black pen from its packaging. Oliver Park had come to fill a script for OxyContin. I was stupid, but not stupid enough to go crazy. Know the laws you break, as Hector would say. I wrote for a thirty-day supply since anything more would be flagged as ill-gotten.

You can do this. I steeled myself with a deep breath as if I had a choice. *You have to do this.*

"Hi there," said the on-duty pharmacist. A redhead in mauve lipstick. Overweight but Tyre skinny. Busty leopard print popped beneath the white of her lab coat and she smelled like a pink Starburst.

"Hey." I slid the paper across the counter, but steady hands were a struggle. "Just need to fill this."

When she took it cautiously, as though it were something dangerous—as though I were dangerous—I should've cut and run. She eyed the note. She eyed me. Then the note once more.

"One moment, please." She gave a smile to match her warm drawl. "If you'll wait right over there." She pointed to a nook of folding chairs. Next to the blood pressure machine for self-diagnosing the heart disease you know you've got because look at where you are. What town you call home.

"Yes, ma'am." I shuffled to a seat. She'd seemed nervous. Suspicious when she gleaned the script. My hands still quaked, and she must've seen that too. What doctor writes in Sharpie?

Five minutes passed.

Should I get up? Just get up and go?

Ten minutes.

No. I don't give up. At least not when it comes to shit that I very much should give up on.

Fifteen.

Besides, she'd smiled when she asked me to wait. People don't grin at criminals. They scowl. They scowl, and they call the police—

"Stand up for me, son." An unseen voice spiked my pulse. A boot-camp kind of deep. I spun, and my heart caught fire. I flinched. My body wanted to break for it before my brain chimed in.

"Stand. Up," the officer repeated. "I'm not fuckin' around with you, boy."

Two thick fingers beckoned. As I stumbled to my feet, he took my arm. His grip wrapped the whole of my biceps. The heat of shame flushed my chest, my cheeks, the tips of my ears.

Shame and panic. Black leather holster. The sleek black gun inside it. Black radio. Shiny black baton catching the pharmacy's fluorescent bulbs in bendy waves.

Black, black, black. Even his dark-blue uniform held whispers of slick black.

"You're a dumb little shit, you know that?"

I never saw the handcuffs, because my wrists were pulled tight behind my back by the cop reading me my rights.

37

WASHINGTON, DC

The doorbell on stately number 403 on Twenty-eighth chimes like a music box through an unseen home. The facade of stone and stained glass is far larger than Nathan's.

Footsteps, a tumbling latch, and a front door of swirling iron parts.

"Hello there." An older woman with cropped silver hair smiles. "I'm Barbara, and you must be the dog owner. Come in."

The floor is marble or something like it, and her heels clack as she gestures me into a foyer that smells like fresh-squeezed lemon and cash. She reminds me of Nathan's mother, Kathy. Women who wear their wealth on Valentino sleeves and speak in vaguely British accents. Mannerisms that say they might be New World, but they're closer to the Old one than you are.

"Oliver." I take her limp wrist delicately. "And thank you so much. I can't tell you how worried we were."

It's only now I note the concern behind Barbara's eyes as she reads me. I'd washed up and changed clothes at the house, but she's still unsettled.

"I hate to be impolite," she starts, "but do you mind showing me your ID?" I pause. I've not fully processed her request when she speaks again. "It's just that I know the address on the dog tag. I was close with the family there. Before the property passed to a charitable organization."

"The Klein Foundation," I interrupt, grinding my teeth. "And yep. That's my house."

"You don't sound at all like who I spoke with on the telephone." Her lips purse into a tight smile. "I owe it to the owner to be certain."

Despite the fact it makes no fucking sense, she's quite pleased with her vigilance. How would I know to ring her doorbell to steal someone else's dog? Mere seconds have passed, and Barbara already looks at me as Kathy Klein does: disdainfully. I'm a tragedy, which is out of my control, but how cruel of me to make needless victims of others by simply existing in their lives.

"Dog fighting," Barbara says as if this will help. "It's all over the news."

"Sure." My ears burn as I reach in my pocket. A new license hasn't arrived, but the DMV issued a temporary printout. I unfold it, and her eyes move line to line with unearned suspicion.

Yes, Barbara. The garbage at your door lives in a heritage townhome owned by something called a Klein fucking Family Foundation. You, he, and said foundation are all equally shocked.

"Lovely." She pinches the paper like a dirty diaper. "Well, I'm so happy you've found her." She punctuates her words with unnerving syrup. If she knows my house, what else could she know? Just how vigilant is Barbara?

"Lucinda." Silver chandelier earrings throw the day's last sunlight in my face as she calls over her shoulder. "Bring the dog, would you? The owner is here." She pivots. "What's its name again, dear?"

I thought this bitch had read the tag. "Tilly."

"Yes, of course. Tilly. Bring Tilly here," she calls out again, but Barbara's still wary. "Poor thing simply showed up on our back porch. The damned garden gate won't stay shut, but I suppose that's a blessing for little Tilly."

A second set of footsteps, and a uniformed woman—presumably Lucinda—rounds a corner. Tilly is nestled in her arms; her bobbed tail wags wildly.

My heart erupts, warmth blooms. I can't help myself and reach. Lucinda flinches as I take Tilly into my hands. Her warm tongue lapping my face. Sour breath I've never been happier to smell.

When I look back up, Lucinda's vanished and I start to tell Barbara about the reward.

"That won't be necessary," she says, bothered I'd mention something as crass as money.

"Okay, well, thank you so much again." I set Tilly down on slippery marble and fasten her leash. "Really. This means the world to us."

As I make my way to the sidewalk, the iron door shuts with a chorus of latches.

Barbara's done something Kathy Klein must only dream of: she's locked me out.

•   •

Back home, the sweet noises of normalcy return. Nails clicking and jowls panting, Tilly bounces from room to room, taking stock. She's finding her mooring again. Reassuring familiarity puts an eager spring in her step.

But it's not normal. She's still in danger. So is Nathan. So am I. This life is on loan to me. A bill I cannot pay is coming due any day now, and then there will be nothing to save me from myself.

Walking downstairs one slow step at a time, I'm directionless. Perhaps I'm headed to the drawing room to lie down. Not to sleep, of course. That's impossible. But to collapse on my back. To fixate on a coffered ceiling until the courage to call Detective Henning comes.

In the foyer, I first notice the French doors to the library ajar. Nathan's never careless when it comes to protecting his sanctuary. Maybe he forgot after making space for new art?

Moreover, his briefcase sits on top of his desk. Leaving it at home's not unusual. The bespoke bag is something he carries only on suit-and-tie days. If he's on call, it's a tattered book bag, scrubs, and sneakers. I part the doors enough to take a single transgressive step inside.

It's not like I've been told not to come in here, that I'm not allowed. That would be silly. Tom had wandered in thoughtlessly, but I've always *felt* like this room's off-limits.

Just as strange as pulling down family portraits and not shutting doors that always stay shut, Nathan's bag has also been left open. A latch with a three-digit spin lock hangs uselessly by the handle. And even stranger? The devilish little thing that peeks from within. Had I been anyone else I know—literally *anyone* else save Hector—I'd have simply walked right by it. But I'm not anyone else. I'm Oliver Park. Administrative assistant. Addict.

Nathan's prescription pad. A distinctive *Rx* leers behind a folded newspaper page from *Vibe,* the city paper Nathan consumes like sugary candy. I hesitate, one foot in the library, one foot still safely outside.

If it were a siren, its call couldn't be any louder. I make tight fists, bring my feet together in the cool darkness of Nathan's sanctum, and stand perfectly still.

I've coexisted with Nathan's prescription pads for five entire years. To say dark thoughts, dangerous thoughts, haven't spawned is a lie. I've steeped in them, but not long enough to count as anything but fleeting. To the contrary, my ability to cohabitate with a blank prescription pad is proof of my growth. Empirical evidence of a past that's long gone.

But I can't ignore the new call. Haus, my mistake, Kristian, everything after. The flooded bathroom, Tom, Tilly—everything is my fault. Frightening longings stir from deep slumber. Faustian little worms called to the surface by a hard rain.

The notion that my past will stay buried is a farce. I'm my own worst enemy. This is an undeniable fact, and I can't escape from myself any more than I can crawl out of my own skin. Tyre or Georgetown. Piece-of-shit one-bedroom or legacy townhome. Hector or Nathan, it doesn't make a difference. One controlled me with his hands, the other with his words, but the fact remains: I require control.

And running away doesn't make a fucking difference because I follow me wherever I go.

That same teeming knot of hornets gathers in my throat, and even my ears sweat. I step deeper into the library.

Stop, I tell myself. *Stop it.*

Another step. Nathan's Tom Ford cologne lingers in the air.

Stop it.

Then another.

You can still stop. You can still turn around. A window is rapidly closing, yes, but even a crack will let the light in. A fucking open window, Oliver. *Stop!*

Perhaps I'm only reaching for the newspaper page. See, I reason, I want to read *Vibe.* My logic is as fragile as these crinkling black-and-white pages. At the top, *Vibe* splashes in bold font. *Classifieds* beneath that. An eclectic barrel of ads: landscaping equipment for sale, substitute teachers needed, escorts of all flavors available for all tastes.

My sweaty palms pull ink from the pages, and I trade them for some-thing else.

My finger grazes its cream-colored front page. Nathan's pen has left an impression behind. A ghost of the last script he wrote. Tracing the lettering, I can't make out the dosage, but the drug he ordered is quite legible: fentanyl.

The relationship a surgeon like Nathan has with that specific drug is distinct from one a person like me might forge. It isn't just another tool in my toolbox for pain management or anesthesia. Fentanyl is dark magic. A tiny Hobbit's ring that taunts and calls and—without exception—destroys.

Hundreds of times more potent than morphine and everywhere lately. News, docs, podcasts, and AM radio. Illicit stocks have flooded US markets. Diluting fentanyl vials precisely isn't always in an addict's wheelhouse. The overdoses, the deaths, have swept the nation west to east. We're poisoning ourselves at breakneck pace.

But I opt for a slower method. I hold my breath and a ballpoint pen. When I exhale, blue ink has written a single word: *Percocet*.

• •

I'm not a different person this time. I'm the same today as I was back in Tyre. When I stood in the waiting area of Wellington Family Com-pounding Pharmacy and a cop called me *a dumb little shit* while snap-ping handcuffs shut. But to anyone who is not Nathan's parents or Neighbor Barbara, I *look* like a different person and that's what counts.

My heart again thrums like a hummingbird's. My sweaty fingers won't touch the script until they absolutely must. Folded in two, it waits in the pocket of a pair of cotton trousers. My linen crew top is airy and pastel and harmless. Smart boys in head-to-toe Club Monaco don't crib pills.

A technician at the drop-off counter shrugs a smile. I'm committed now. And rehearsed.

"Can I help you?" Braces cross her top teeth. A bit late in life for them. She's not old by any means, but her mouthful of metal takes the edge off. My confidence grows as I size up my new opponent.

"Filling a prescription." I'm deliberately flippant. No need to say what for. I'm a patient—not an addict—so I don't care what treatment the good doctor decided on.

She takes the script and reads it back like a McDonald's cashier. Let's review my Big Mac order because the last thing she needs is someone with a pickle allergy throwing them back in her face.

"Penicillin. Five hundred milligrams every twelve hours for five days." Her tone's decidedly *over it,* and I've buried the ask in a list. "And Percocet, two-point-five milligrams and three-twenty-five acetaminophen every six hours as needed. Got questions about these?"

"Not really."

"Give me twenty minutes." Like that, she vanishes between towering shelves. Not even ten minutes pass and a rattling paper bag summons me to the pickup counter. She notes my temporary driver's license information in a controlled substances log—I've been prescribed a narcotic, after all.

When she slides the bag my way, I thank her. If she replies, I don't hear it.

Hyperfocus is another survival skill I've honed. Peripheral thoughts are painful at times like this. I fixate on the immediate future and bury the cost for it. As a dependent on Dr. Nathan Klein's top-shelf insurance, I pay only ten bucks. My chest knots as I take the sidewalk faster and faster.

Sometimes the price tag on betrayal is deceptively small.

38

NATHAN

Tilly's home. Safe. Sound. Alive.

But I still have business to take care of.

"Your destination is ahead on the right." GPS makes a pleasant announcement, though there's nothing pleasant about it. "You have arrived at Thirty-Nine Dahlia Street. Frederick, Maryland."

It took everything not to confront Oliver—funny how little I mind conflict when I'm not the one with something to hide. I'd left him alone. Determined not to explore the sudden reappearance of MeetLockr or the X-rated photo of himself.

Or the ones of Tom—whose Audi is already parked street side.

When I challenge Tom, will he tell the truth? Not in the face of hard evidence—the nudes waiting patiently on my phone, but before. Would he be honest if I simply asked him to be?

Did you fuck my husband, Tom?

My car locks with a chirp-chirp. I realize the fentanyl is still in my white coat, and a tiny hint of something indulgent whispers.

He'd answer truthfully with that at his jugular.

The street with its darling storefronts. Quaint and cute and exactly like the last time I visited this studio. Number Thirty-Nine is a narrow brick front with tall windows. The hanging sign is turned to OPEN, and a bell rings when I walk through the door.

"Nathan!" Tom makes his way from the back. More flowing than walking. Tight jeans. Gucci loafers. And an acid-yellow button-down spackled with tiny blue flowers.

He pulls me into a tight hug. My palm finds his spine, and I imagine

Oliver's fingers counting its ridges as the two of them lie in bed. Like he used to count mine.

Tom gives his take on the gallery: "This space is gorgeous."

"Always my first stop for art. I need a new piece for the library anyway." I grin. "So, who's the guy?"

"Please." He skips the question. "We'll get to that. Art first!"

"See the nudes?"

"Oh my god yes." He twirls, taking my hand and leading me to a far wall.

"Figured you'd have a thing for them." My double entendre slips his radar. Narcissist.

"Guilty," he says, and I can't help but agree.

The entire back wall is covered in naked people—as I knew it would be. Men and women. Vivid colors and black-and-whites. Close-ups. Full bodies. From the overtly sensual to the deeply uncomfortable.

"Easy to see why you love it here," he says, eyes dancing from piece to piece. Dick to dick.

"I'm captivated by the human form," I say when his attention returns. "Actually, humans in general."

"They're fabulous." Tom might find them a bit overwhelming but they are undeniably good. "And figures, Dr. Surgeon."

"It's not the anatomy of them," I add. "It's the soul. People are complicated." A gallery worker heads our way. A pair of hot-pink pumps, and I think her name's Amina. "These capture an emotional complexity you don't see in the OR."

"Uh. Sure." Tom knots his brow. "You okay? You sound kind of off."

"Dr. Klein." Maybe-Amina greets me with a sharp smile and two flutes of freshly poured prosecco. "Lovely to see you again."

"Can't keep me out."

"Art's addictive." She adjusts cat's-eye glasses. "Are you looking again?"

"I am." Tom takes a prosecco, and I follow suit. No hospital shift, so alcohol's no problem. I lied to Oliver, and really, indulging is the only way I can get through this. We touch glasses, and bubbles tickle my throat like alcoholic pop rocks. "But I've mostly come for my friend here. Tom Vogt, this is—"

"Amina Khan. It's a pleasure."

"All mine." Tom beams.

We trace her steps, heels clicking on polished pine, craning our necks at pieces along the way. When we pass one that's more jarring than the others, I pull Tom to a stop and ask Amina, "What's this?"

On canvas, a frail woman contorts her limbs unnaturally, holds her body up with the palm of one hand and the heel of her opposite foot. Her head is a blur of movement as though she's shaking it side to side. Violently.

"Ah, a little grotesque, that one," Amina starts. "It's called *Janus*."

"The Greek god of duality," Tom says. A fitting name for the piece. The shaking motion gives the photo two heads.

"Very good. The model's a contortionist," she says. "She's done Cirque du Soleil."

"Breathtaking," I add.

"It's clearly speaking to you," Amina says. "I'll leave you both alone with it for a few minutes."

As she makes for the back office, I turn to Tom. "I think it's a little trite to define a human by any one thing. But you'd be surprised how much of a person you can capture with two."

"Duplicity. And please, I wouldn't be at all surprised."

"Maybe you wouldn't."

"So?" Tom tilts his head, perhaps sensing a challenge. "What two things define me?"

"Idyllic and . . ." I tap my chin, but my thoughts return to the syringe in my pocket. "Impish."

"Impish?" Tom squares his shoulders. "Like a prancing demon or some shit?"

"No, no." I laugh, though my words are nothing if not serious. "More Faustian. Devilish."

"Devilishly good-looking." He smirks, then narrows his eyes to pretty little slits. "And yourself?"

"You tell me."

"A bit knowing." He sighs. "And yet still naïve."

Naïve? Is he now challenging me? "Old, you mean. Old and dumb."

"Not at all."

"Then what are you saying?" I take a second gulp, much larger than the first. "Knowing and naïve?"

"That you've lived . . . a certain kind of happy living"—he tilts his own drink back—"but you've got a different life ahead of you. You're not anywhere near the end of your book, and the next chapters are going to surprise you. You've done the domestic bliss, the dog, the beautiful boy—"

"Husband."

"Right." He nods. "But there's another you too. A version I think you'll meet soon. And I want you to understand that he's also happy. Just as much so."

Another me. My cheeks warm as my mind wanders to scorpions. The malignant presence of feverish nightmares. Something inside me. Something *other* persisting deep down. Tom's not so blind—he sees the scorpion.

But what does he mean by *a different life ahead*? If I didn't know better, I'd say he was preparing me for something. Cushioning what he plans to say next. "And naïve?"

Tom's smile falls. His lips go flat as a sidewalk. "Look, Nathan. I'm glad you called because the truth is . . ."

Is this it? A wholly unexpected and unprompted confession?

". . . if you hadn't, I was going to ask to meet."

I've been sleeping with Oliver. I'm so sorry.

"There's something I need to tell you"—his gaze wanders over my shoulder, searching for the presence of nearby ears—"about Oliver."

I clench my jaw, and the swollen vein in his neck is growing more and more alluring.

"This isn't going to be easy to hear. It sure as hell isn't easy to say."

I'm sorry, and I deserve to die.

"I . . ." Go on, Tom. Go on and say it. Fall on the sword. Take the responsibility we both know Oliver's incapable of. Man. The. Fuck. Up. But the conversation veers: "The senator had a thing earlier today. A fundraiser. He's shit with names, so I whisper who's who as he greets donors. Anyway, that's not the point."

What is the point, Tom?

"The venue, it was at The Jefferson."

Where are you going?

"And"—he bites his bottom lip—"Oliver was there."

"Oliver wasn't at The Jefferson."

His teeth have drawn a tiny pearl of blood. "He was with someone else."

Sunlight pours into the studio, but the whole space darkens. Sweeping canvases, photos, they all melt like candle wax.

"They were at the bar—"

"So?" My voice hitches. Fog rolls over the pink coils of my brain, and my throat tightens.

"Blond guy. Tall. Looked like a fuckboy if I've ever seen one."

"How do you know he wasn't a friend?" Another gulp, and I wipe my lips with the back of my hand. The prosecco's gone, and no question, hard liquor's up next because we both know Oliver has exactly zero friends that look like fuckboys.

"This guy? Straight out of central casting for, like, gay Swedish porn." Tom talks, but all I see are two rows of perfect white teeth and the blood they've drawn from his lip. He punctuates his answer with spelling bee–like repetition. "Total fuckboy."

My husband. The scorpion inside—the one that climbs my throat and skitters along the underside of my sternum and nests between my organs—stirs. It wiggles its way between lobes of a lung. Slips through with moist ease.

"They were alone at the bar. For ten minutes I watched them. Their legs were touching."

"What are you saying?" My tone climbs because the arachnid's reached my heart at last. The thumping knot of tissue and blood that beats for Oliver. Saved Oliver. Staked-a-claim-to Oliver.

My husband who's been keeping secrets. Who's strayed and who only gives a shit about himself. He's trashed everything I've worked for—everything I care about—for the tritest of payoffs. Not once did he consider my humiliation, the fire-poker heat of shame I'd suffer from having *this* conversation with Tom. Or maybe Oliver did consider just that. And maybe he decided sacrificing me was a fair price for a few seconds of orgasm.

I've given him the world and he's made me into a cuckold.

Resentment floods the wake complacency leaves. Perhaps even cruelty. The syringe is heavy in my pocket. My off-ramp.

"Nathan, listen." Tom swallows loudly, and the scorpion hoists its stinger—ready to plunge venom into its mark. "Your puppy is off his leash."

39

OLIVER

To see Nathan's face when his eyes find Tilly is to see Nathan happier than he's seemed in an awfully long time. It was nearly midnight when he finally managed to get the rest of his shift covered. No *on the way home* text because there never is.

His book bag crashes on the floor and his arms stretch wide open.

"That's my girl!" He beams. "That's my good, good girl!"

A sliver of relief breaks through my guilt-choked heart. Nathan deserves this happiness for enduring my bullshit. It's all my fault, but delivering him his dog still warms my body like a drug. I haven't phoned Detective Henning yet, and Tilly in Nathan's arms makes the delay easier.

Let him have this. Let him live this bliss before destroying everything.

My mind travels to the Percocet I've yet to touch. In a moment of half-assed accountability, I hid it behind the very same vent Nathan had already discovered. A big part of me wants to get caught because a bigger part will never do the right thing. Maybe he'll find it. When he sees how dangerously close I am to relapse, maybe he'll know what to do.

I sure as hell don't.

• •

The next morning, the French doors to the library have been closed again, but the wall above the mantel is no longer empty. There's a photograph and in it, a woman twists her body into a bizarre posture that shakes me. Her head blurs like she has two. At absolute best, it's a lateral move from the Klein family portrait.

"Janus," Nathan says from behind. He wraps his arms around my waist, and I flinch. "The Greek god of duality. Picked it out with Tom yesterday. What do you think?"

"Very sophisticated."

"Tom also has some good news." He moves beside me. Sipping coffee, he stares, satisfied, at his new decor behind the glass-paneled doors. "Said so when we hung out before my shift."

"Oh?" News from Tom is never good, but at present, it could be catastrophic. My gut tightens.

"He wants to have dinner tonight to share."

"You're not tired?"

"Tilly's back, and Tom's got a reason to celebrate. You up for it?"

Tom wants to have dinner tonight. What an asshole. His proposition, his photos, the picture he pried from me. Now he wants to share a meal with his best friend and the man his best friend loves. The man he exploited. To navigate the world with Tom's cruel efficiency requires a total lack of empathy. Kristian's not the only sociopath keeping my company these days.

I bite my lip, and Nathan reads it for stalling.

"He met some new guy he's crazy about. On MeetLockr of all places. I've never seen him fall so deep so fast. He's turned fourteen and female."

Nathan's casual sexism would irk me if it didn't come on the heels of that app. A fountain of bile climbs my throat. Is Tom implying *I'm* the new guy from MeetLockr? Secrets are your specialty, are they? You smug ass. Then a far darker thought stokes fresh panic. Maybe he's met Kristian. Maybe said meeting was engineered because this is Kristian's next move.

"I'd rather not." I grasp for an excuse. "Tilly's home. I want to stay here with her."

"Of course." Nathan kisses my cheek, drains the last of his coffee. "Funny though, right?"

"What's funny?"

"Tom. He's so jaded. Always so cynical." Nathan wipes his mouth. "The way he talks about this guy—"

"What's his name?" I interrupt. My jarring tone gives him pause.

"I'm not quite sure."

"What is his name?" The edge in my voice is razor sharp.

Nathan arches an eyebrow. "Jeffrey or Jim or . . . Jeff, I think. What does it matter?"

I exhale. I know how Kristian works. If he found Tom, if he made the connection between vapid Tom and Nathan and me, he'd want me to know. He'd use his real name. If not his real name, something that says he's closing in again.

"Just curious."

Doubt flares in Nathan's eyes. "Do you think you might know Jeff?"

I muster whatever fumes of confidence still linger and smile. "Not at all."

Marked hesitation, then: "I'm going to hop in the shower. Do me a favor, would you? While I'm at dinner, follow up with Darryl. I'd like to use my own bathroom again."

As Nathan vanishes upstairs, I shut my eyes and see only Tom and Kristian. When I open them, the floor vent down the hall suddenly holds a frightening gravity. A cosmic pull to a dark place, and one I can no longer resist.

SOUTH BEND, IN

In the eyes of an Indiana drug court, I wasn't much danger to anyone but myself. An opioid epidemic, overcrowded prisons, and white privilege—not in that order—took jail time off the table. On the lazy Susan of self-destruction Judge Raza spun daily, I fell somewhere between *could clean up* and *might still OD and save tax dollars*.

Detox and court-ordered recovery in an outpatient program run at a regional psych clinic in South Bend. An offshoot from the main trauma center but still part of the hospital.

I showed up every morning at six o'clock sharp. Being late meant needing a damn good excuse for a waiting cop. Failing to show up altogether? Judge Raza had made the consequences of that brutally clear.

"You strike me as queer," he'd mocked. "Doesn't matter what you are, 'cause you'll strike everyone at County just the same. Best case, son? Somebody likes your asshole enough to keep it from everybody else."

I was punctual. Sitting pretty in the waiting room with the other addicts. We weren't the worst of them. I mean, I hadn't escalated to the needle, and I clung to that fact like a fucked-up honor badge. Funny what you take pride in at the barrel's bottom.

"Park," a nurse beckoned. "Oliver Park." I followed her into the next room over and blew into a Breathalyzer.

"Perfect," she'd say each time the screen read zero. Like it was praise for an aced exam or something. Don't fuck up, behave like a minimally functioning member of society, and you get an A. That's where the state set my bar. Then she'd herd me into the shrink's office like a German shepherd.

"So, Oliver. What happened?" Dr. Purvis asked during our first session. Dr. Regina Purvis looked and dressed like a Barbie doll, but empathy in her voice crowded out any expected disdain. Part of the Barbie facade, I guessed. A charade to disarm the trash in and out of her office all day.

"I got into pain pills."

"How?"

I shrugged. "My relationship, I guess."

"She started first, then? Got you into them?"

"He did," I corrected, then braced myself. Other than Blaire, I could count on one hand the people I'd come out to. I'd even driven thirty miles to an interstate triple-X warehouse for a DVD called *Satyrs of Summer*. After the profound mistake of leaving it in the same player Dad recorded Notre Dame games in, I kept Hector secret.

"Where are you staying now?" Dr. Purvis skirted right past my gayness, and that was the moment she became my ally. When she couldn't care less about the fucking pronoun that sent Dad scrambling for the belt with the biggest buckle he could find. I told Dr. Purvis everything.

"Halfway house."

"No family around?"

Her question was the perfect setup for the Story of Oliver Park. Mom's unqualified love for me. Only cancer could stop her from cleaning shit-spackled toilets at Walmart to keep our lights on. Dad's unqualified love for grain alcohol. Sometimes I could wait him out from under the kitchen table and sometimes I couldn't. How one winter, Mom stood on our porch—in front of the magpie-covered flower boxes she'd painted herself—and watched him pass out drunk in the drainage ditch by the driveway. How my welts kept her from going into the yard and pulling him to safety. Instead, she waited. Patient as death.

"Oliver, I need you to call an ambulance," she'd said that next morning on her way to gather the porch paper. "Something bad happened to Daddy." By the time she wandered into the cold—pretending for both of us that it was the first time she saw him—exposure had taken him out of our lives.

Hector too. The moment he hit me. Tried to rape me. The moment I ran. And telling Dr. Purvis felt good. So damn good. Like what a baptism must be like. A submersion in cool water followed by a cleansing retrieval. A chance to fix shit and go nowhere but up.

In fact, I'd still been high—naturally high—from Dr. Purvis's degree-decorated confessional when I first perceived that gaze. Being watched by someone who would change my life.

Every detox visit earned you a single meal ticket. The hospital's cafeteria was my next stop. Sitting down at a table by myself, two slices of cheese pizza and a diet pop, unseen eyes frosted my neck.

I turned in my seat and saw him.

Sandy brown hair, aquiline nose, and the square shoulders of a man who only ever made the right decisions. Somewhere deep in my gut, a butterfly took flight. Scrubs, stethoscope, and a wrinkled white coat. A surgical resident named Nathan Klein drank me in like the pop in my hand from a table away. Nothing but vacant chairs and unbridled possibility between us.

I grew embarrassed, but a smile—knowing and soft—crossed his face. An expression that seemed to whisper, *I know what you are,* followed closely with, *and I am too.*

His presence in the cafeteria was constant after that first, teasing moment. When he finally approached me, I lied about why I was there. But when he asked for my number, he forced my hand.

"I don't have a phone." His perfect face didn't betray how he felt about this. "I'm at a halfway house right now. Someone there stole it."

"Outpatient detox?" Nathan asked, gesturing to my pizza.

"Yeah." I broke eye contact, instead fixating on the patterned cafeteria napkins. "One week clean."

The moment I expected, when he'd stand up uncomfortably and walk away, never came. He didn't wish me luck or say I'm not quite what he's looking for. Nothing about *one week clean* suggests I've got my shit together, much less that I'm in a place for nurturing romantic possibility. Though I was uncertain this was about romance for Nathan at first either. My admission—despite the initial dishonesty—felt like an understanding. A fire of curiosity ignited. A conflagration that had me wondering what being with a real man—a right man—is like. Even if only for a fleeting instant.

"I'm actually wrapping up an overnight shift. You drive here?"

Perhaps I was looking for a fix from an altogether different drug. Perhaps we were both looking for a taste of something strange.

"I walked."

Something that feels just wrong enough—

He put his hand on the table and the tips of our fingers touched. "Would you like a ride home?"

—to remind us what living feels like.

"Yes."

• •

His Jag coupe was spanking new and flawlessly polished. When he opened the passenger door, I slipped into an envelope of hand-stitched leather and sandalwood. I'd stepped through a looking glass and the far side couldn't be more different, more intoxicating. This man sliding into the driver's seat couldn't be any less like Hector.

"What do you say we get you a phone?"

"What?"

"So I can call you."

I had no response to that.

He winked and the car cranked like slick cash. It was immediately clear that something had gotten into me. Something equal parts inexplicable and irreconcilable with the Oliver of just days ago.

Nathan shifted gears, merged onto the highway. The engine vibrated beneath me, and I worried this might be it. This man was so different from the last stranger who offered me a lift; the feel of this leather on my skin, so different. Maybe Nathan spots me for a prepaid phone or maybe he doesn't, but I didn't want this to ever end. It could've been everything and at the same time nothing at all. Either way, staying in Nathan's company beyond this moment was suddenly the most important thing.

I reached across the console with my left hand and massaged his crotch.

He said nothing, eyes on the road, knuckles white on the gearshift.

Months, fucking years of bad men and bad things and bad nights and a life so wasted I could kill myself dissolved, gave way to this moment. This nice man hardened under his slacks.

When he parked in the back lot of an AT&T, his scrubs were a full-blown tent, and I felt freer than I had any business being. Any angst or reserve or internalized self-hating bullshit gave way to something far greater: my heart was throbbing. Dopamine once more rafted through my bloodstream. I was sober as fuck and somehow still felt good.

"We're here," Nathan said.

I unbuckled and turned toward him.

"Oh my god," he whispered as I reached into his scrubs. He shifted in his seat, gave me unfettered access to himself. I took him in my mouth and tasted the salt of something new. A sudden heat grew under me, a bizarre warmth spreading from my rear to the backs of my thighs. *It can't be this good, can it? I can't be—*

He'd turned on my seat heater. A smooth move; an experienced one.

"Holy shit," he moaned, head back. "I've never done anything like this. I could lose my fucking license."

Hands. Mouth. I trembled and flushed with fever. *Nothing is free, Oliver,* and soon he can't hold back.

"F-uck," he stuttered, and came bleach down my throat.

My skull fell to the headrest. *Whatever I've just done, I'm glad I chose to do it.*

Quietness swallowed the car as I wiped my mouth with the back of my hand. He leaned in close. "Kiss me."

His tongue traveled my mouth. He didn't mind where it'd just been and seemed to enjoy the idea. I pulled away, exhaled. More silence. A brief flash of release. Like a cigarette, I'd grown stimulated and relaxed. I wanted, needed this to be the start of something larger and not the finale of something small.

He was putting himself back together—tucking his shirt, tying his scrubs, running his hand through thick hair—when I reached into my pocket and slipped a Marlboro from a fresh pack. "Does this car have one of those electric lighter things?"

He was silent for a beat while my question sank in.

"Of course not. New cars don't because smoking kills you." He said this like a joke, but my cheeks reddened. I decided I'd make a show of trashing them outside the store. A sideways smile crossed his face. "Ready to get that phone?"

"Yeah." A weight lifted as I considered the possibility that *we* might hold possibility. "If you're still sure you want to?"

"I'm sure." Nathan winked again. Then he reached into his pocket and produced a stack of napkins. Cafeteria napkins from the hospital— the pattern was plainly familiar. Did he swipe a handful of napkins on the way out?

"Sorry." He wiped a tiny drop of himself off the leather armrest. "I'm kind of a clean freak."

I laughed, but something about that bothered me. A tiny, niggling little thought soon lost in the wake of all that was Dr. Nathan Klein: If he'd never done anything like this before, couldn't possibly have expected it to happen—like he'd said moments ago—why bring napkins?

Why come prepared?

WASHINGTON, DC

"Back soon, love," Nathan says as he leaves for the night.

I nod from the drawing room and wait for the lock to click. When it does, I stiffen my spine and listen for a cranking engine. From a sliver of parted blind, Nathan's Range Rover slips from its spot to meet Tom for dinner. And his boyfriend or whatever Tom calls his new meals.

A dark part of me wished I'd gone. I can't monitor Tom's conversation in Nathan's presence from home. But a far darker part has ample reason to stay.

I make for the kitchen and the tiny screwdriver that waits in the junk drawer.

Tunnel vision draws the world dark. I move fast, propelled by a furious id—the addict that lives inside me. He deftly outpaces second thoughts with incredible ease. My ego is unsure it really will be just this one time. My superego screams FUCK.

When the bottle is in my hands, I roll over, back against the wall, and bring my knees tight to my chest. White pills call from behind translucent orange plastic. My grip is so tight, it pulses with neon heat from being slammed into elevator steel.

The inside of the bottle is painted in an appetizing powder. Terrifyingly so and saliva pools under my tongue. If the lid comes off, if I uncap it, I'm done. Game over. I'll take a handful at best, then finish them off over the course of the evening. Each dose cultivating courage for the next until there's only cosmic oblivion. A sweet nihilism and Nathan will find me passed out. Will I even wake up? It's been so long, my tolerance . . .

When focus returns, the lid's rolled across the floor. I've opened it. The bottle's open in my hands. A simple, swift motion is all that's required to feel better. Not good but better. Warm and okay enough to phone Detective Henning. To tell her what happened and tell Nathan too. Fuck if I think confessing anything sober is a possibility. Maybe the former. Certainly not the latter. The addict inside me is prosecuting an airtight case for self-harm. A talent he's—I'm—too good at.

My hand trembles. I've yet to swallow a single one but already taste their bitterness.

Flashes of Hector, of Haus, of Kristian burst like mortar rounds. I'm escalating. Flaring fireworks of Tilly, of Nathan, of Detective Henning. I'm escalating. Sparks of Barbara a few streets down. Flames from the Jefferson hotel lobby, the elevator. *I'm escalating!*

Dr. Regina Purvis: *So, Oliver. What happened?*

I'm escalating, Dr. Purvis!

Mom. In her hospice bed.

She can't lift her eyelids, much less any other part of a body that's at the end of its run. A life lived hard because that's simply the one this body was born into, and it's tired now. Gaunt and sunken and yellowed and sour. She looks dead already.

She seems asleep, but there's no way to be sure. And it doesn't matter;

waiting bottles line the same dresser she's had since she was six. Bottles and bottles and bottles of painkillers. Can she see me walk into her room? Does she know why I've come and what I'm stealing?

I snatch a single one, tuck it into my pocket. Greedily, callously, cruelly, I take a second. Then a third. *That's all,* I think. Enough. I turn but can't look at her because if she does see me, that knowledge will plague the rest of my shit-smear of an existence.

Instead, it's the uncertainty—*did she see?*—that will stalk me. Haunt me till I'm dead.

I'm escalating.

"Goddammit!" I open my eyes. Tilly yaps from the dining room. The hallway, the floor, the bottle in my hands, tablets unconsumed.

I bolt to my feet and stumble into the powder room. The lid strikes the tank like a gunshot. Before I can stop, I turn the bottle upside down, and one by one each pill plunges into toilet water.

Thud. Thump. Thud.

Before I can reach in and scoop them out, I flush. In a swirling, gurgling rush certain death is sucked into the DC sewers, and I sob.

Yes, I'm escalating.

But I don't have to anymore.

40

NATHAN

I pull into an assigned parking spot at a Motel 6 every bit as run-down as expected.

Dinner with Tom and Jeff is now behind me. The new boyfriend's so far out of Tom's league in the abs and hair and ass and smile and, shockingly, charm departments that he must have an angle. A concealed flaw that keeps him from the Dardanelles-crossing yachts of smarter, richer men but works just fine for Tom's brand of Fire Island A-gay.

If Jeff's an addict like Oliver, it sure as hell isn't alcohol. I calibrate my own drinking to match company, and he was lazy with his wine. Still, nobody like that is with somebody like Tom for free.

Jeff is bought and paid for.

Shifting the gear into park, I crank up the AC and breathe deeply, consistently, measured. I center myself and clear my mind because the game is about to change. A snap of my fingers, and the stage will tilt in a new direction. Listing like the deck of a foundering ship, and I will not drown.

Tom didn't know much, but he knew enough to put things together, didn't he? Just not quite enough to solve the whole, sprawling puzzle that is Oliver Park. Our relationship. *No, Mother, our* marriage!

But I do.

I pull a silver flask from the glove compartment. Half-emptied in the past half hour, and I finish it off in three burning, blissful gulps. Wiping my mouth, I unlock my phone and type.

Looking. Call ASAP $$$

So much weight in so few words. A text sent to a number found in the pages of a city paper, and one I'd known better than to save. My phone, clutched in my right hand like a lifeline, buzzes. A bolt of adrenaline, and a tingling works its way down my limbs. I flip it over.

Can call you now?

I chew my bottom lip, and for a cruel instant, wonder just what the hell I'm doing.

Yes. Y-E-S. One word. Three letters. Immeasurably final. I send the reply, close my eyes, let the back of my skull fall to the headrest.

And wait.

When the phone goes off again, it's the long tremors of an incoming call and my stomach plunges. I run a hand through my hair and swallow. *Unknown.*

One ring, then a second, then a third. I picture sand sinking through my fingers. If I don't close a fist around whatever's left, it's gone forever. A fourth ring. I press *answer.* Again I wait.

From my lap, a voice, muted but deep: "Hey."

I say nothing.

"Can you hear me?"

Yes, I think.

"Hello . . ."

Pause.

". . . you there?"

Something sparks in my brain, and I bring the phone to my ear. "Yeah. I can hear you."

Silence on his end, then a question: "You looking?"

"For tonight. Available?" I grind my molars. On my passenger seat—next to an unopened bottle of Maker's Mark—eyes leer from the ad in *Vibe*'s classifieds. *Metro Men: Gay Escorts.*

"Could be." His accent tastes like cake icing. Powdered sugar and sex. "Cash?"

"Enough to need four ATM transactions. That clear your calendar?"

"You wanting something weird, then?" My heart drums against my chest. How did Oliver answer this on MeetLockr? Or to Tom?

"Only discretion," I say, but would my husband have answered differently? Oliver who can't be bothered to talk to me, to say what he wants and when he wants it. But again, Oliver only ever seems to know what he doesn't want. Me.

Heavy breaths whistle as static and he says, "I'm free."

"Eleven thirty?" I try to cover my cracking voice. It catches at the confluence of impending pain and pleasure. A scalpel just before it sinks into skin.

"Where?"

"Takoma Park."

"Specifically?"

"Motel Six." Through my windshield, neon lettering blurs as a blue door comes into focus. *Room 12* lit by headlights. "I'll text you the address and room."

"No monkey business, right?"

"What?"

"Need to be careful. You understand."

"Yeah." I cough into my fist. "No monkey business."

"Text me where. See you soon."

"See you."

When he clicks off, I catch myself in the rearview mirror.

I haven't slept. How could I when my mind has done nothing but cyclone at blinding velocity? Exploring every possible outcome, hypothetical situations that would unfold after I've pulled the trigger. Another decision. Another point of no return, crossed.

My face holds a pallor that rivals Oliver's. Cheeks sunken, panic present in the darkness encircling my eyes. Simple polo, pair of jeans, but I remove my watch and lock the heavy timepiece in the console while David Bowie puts out fires with gasoline on the radio. My phone's back on the dash, motel address already typed out as a text.

I need only to send it. Eyes to the mirror for one last glimpse of myself *before*. I've come mostly undone, but not all the way. There's still enough of me remaining to shoulder the coming fallout. I have no choice. I must break my own rules. My fixation on fidelity is destroying my marriage. I'll meet an escort with an ice-cold Scandi accent, and then I'll fix everything. Save everything.

Again.

The outcome warrants the pain. Oliver's suffering will pale in comparison to what he stands to lose in an alternate future. One where I do not follow through.

Phone back in hand, and it's now or never.

The pain, sure, a scorpion whispers. *But don't discount the pleasure.*

With a single tap, my text rockets into the ether, and I will never be the same.

41

OLIVER

It's very late when Nathan returns from dinner with Tom and company. He's haggard. Unkempt and looking exactly how I feel and how I never see him. From where I sit in the kitchen, startling is an understatement.

He says nothing, slowly walking my way. My pulse starts to climb, but when he holds me, it quiets. Notes of liquor and tobacco cling to his polo. They must've gone for drinks after.

"I love you, Oliver," Nathan whispers. But his warm breath is sweet like whiskey Skittles, and I don't flinch. This time, I don't mind that he uses my name, because he's not using it *against* me. It's not been weaponized. "I love you more than you can possibly know."

"I love you too." I smile and his lips linger on my cheek. As he walks down the hall, I note the time: half past midnight.

I'd lost track of the hour after falling into this seat. After flushing every pill I'd stolen in Nathan's name. Here I sat, a petrified extension of a hand-carved chair, sinking teeth into my next—and perhaps final—confrontation.

What to tell him. How to tell him.

My mind traveled any number of twisty paths into unknowable darkness. From coming right out with it like a mercy killing—a knife into his heart, threads of cherry syrup thoughtlessly flared across our life together—to an unfolding revelation. A gentle edging to the cliffside. A couching of the mind in pleasantries and strategic reminders of love and lives inextricably linked. Then the push, and we both go over. Maybe he lives, but the slow dissolution of my charade lends a few more moments to be happy—because I certainly don't survive the fall.

I trace Nathan's footsteps to our bedroom. My mask comes off tonight. Or at least begins to slip when I start to tell the truth. Set the stage, move pieces into place. Commit to crossing a gasoline-soaked bridge I'll set aflame behind me.

Nathan's pajama bottoms are silk and hang low at his hips. His bare chest exposed as if he knows what's coming and hopes my knife finds its mark. *Haven't I endured enough, Oliver? Bring my suffering to a quick end.*

In the bathroom, I draw in breath and splash my face.

"Confront," I whisper to the man clenching his jaw in the mirror. The man I hate with unbridled fervor. *You're no fucking martyr.* I dry my cheeks. When I return the embroidered hand towel to its place, a string tied round my heart tightens. Embroidered in threaded gold: *NK & OP.*

"How about we get out of here," Nathan says from the bedroom.

"Huh?" I round the corner to find him on the bed, legs crossed, glasses resting on his navel. "Get out of where?"

"Here." His eyes lift. "What do you think about heading out of town?"

"Kimberly likes more notice before I—"

"I already talked to her," he says. "She's fine with you taking the week."

A jarring question, but not because the ask is strange. It's that he took the liberty of asking my boss and Kimberly took the liberty of answering. My life decisions do not require my input and—Jesus. I rub my brow and try to reset. This is a nice thing, Oliver. No more a cabal than a surprise birthday party requires.

"Want to go?"

It's also a surprise that contrasts violently with the hurricane inside my skull. I'm contemplating the Category 5 destruction of our relationship, and he's talking about vacation?

"Oliver?"

"Yeah," I say blankly. "Yes, but why? I mean, where?"

"We'll drive down to South Carolina." If the chop in my voice unsettles him, he ignores it. "Take a breather. Gain some space. Recoup what we've lost."

The *lost* in his last sentence ices my neck. He could mean a million different things. He could mean the sanctity of our burgled home. He could mean the pain of Tilly's absence. He could mean—

"They never summer there. It'd be me and you."

By *they,* Nathan means Victor and Kathy. By *it,* he means their sprawling beach "house" south of Charleston. A lone estate on an island they wholly own themselves. I avoid Bald Island whenever possible because said invitations always include Nathan's parents. That place is second only to their East Side co-op in misery—the *Gossip Girl* world where Nathan cut his teeth. Among people who use *summer* as a verb.

"What do you think?" Nathan prods. "Tom and Jeff might come down too. Just for a night. I invited them over dinner."

"Sure," I whisper before clearing my throat. I spin my wedding band off my finger and into my palm. Seems everyone got the invite before me. My fist closes around the ring's coolness.

"We'll pack first thing." In the dresser mirror, Nathan's peculiar face grows eager. "Leave before lunch."

"Sounds like a plan, Nat."

When I crawl beneath the duvet, my brain's numb. Lobotomized from turning too fast and in far too many directions. Going to his parents' is quite the turn of events, but perhaps it's a good thing. Kristian will be physically, geographically separated from me. The ones that matter most, the ones I stand to lose, will both be safe.

With us gone, Kristian can break as many windows, ransack as many drawers as he wants. He can piss and shit all over our things, smear feces on the walls like a fucking zoo primate, and it won't matter because things don't matter. Unlike people and pets, things are replaceable.

It also buys time. I will tell Nathan, confess all of it, carefully, diligently, but now is no longer the right moment. Or even tomorrow or the next day. I'll call Detective Henning from Bald Island, tell her about Kristian and the Jefferson hotel, the credit card he must've used, his room number, and where he's allegedly from. When I do, I'll be out of her reach too. Not truly out of reach; no one is ever that, but the timetable has lengthened. It suddenly works in my favor, if only slightly.

Victor and Kathy Klein have bought me time.

Nathan's bought me time.

Like oxygen. Tiny amounts, but enough to gasp.

To interrupt an asphyxia drawing to an inevitable end.

42

NATHAN

There's no sleeping. Not tonight.

When I returned home, when I walked through my own door, I was a different man than when I'd last passed through it. The other version of myself Tom is confident exists and Oliver hasn't met, and I know is quite possibly the *only* version of myself. It might be a little trite to define a human being by any one thing, but I'm grasping for a second. Anything other than what I crave most: control.

Now I've broken my own rules. Ones that won't rebuild easily—if at all.

Oliver sleeps, though it doesn't look restful. A leg juts from under the duvet, and moonlight traces shadows on his calf. He lies on his side, head on one pillow, arms cradling a second. I draw the covers back and watch goose bumps crawl his thighs. Barely-there briefs contour an ass that just won't let go of me. A far cry from his old baggy boxers and tight like all the others I buy him.

I slip my own underwear off. Somewhere deep in my gut, an appetite's been stoked. I imagine this is what they all feel after crossing that line—Father included. The first indiscretion making the second that much easier. And so on and so forth. Oliver's felt it. Maybe after so long, so much that my own husband has withheld—physically, romantically, truthfully—I've simply been reminded what living feels like. Now we're all insatiable, huh?

I lie next to Oliver, big-spoon-style, and reach into his briefs. I take him in my hand. When he starts to stiffen, I whisper in his ear.

"Nat?" He stirs. "You awake?"

"Fuck me."

He doesn't hear me at first: "What?"

I say it again: "Fuck. Me."

He rolls over, wipes his eyes, and after a passing moment, sees I'm naked and ready. He's awake now. Enough.

A pause as he gathers his thoughts, runs a palm over his face. "You wanna—"

"Fuck." I draw in breath. "Me."

"Okay," comes his throaty reply. He pulls his briefs to his knees because he knows I'm not asking. If nothing else, I've instilled in him an ear for tones. Oliver knows when I give him a choice, and when I do not. This will happen because I've never needed it more. He starts to climb on top, to rest his groin between my legs, but I stop him.

"Not like that."

I flip on all fours, hands and knees. Arch my back. We're both feral now, and we'll fuck that way.

"Sure." A drawer opens, lube uncaps.

I hold my breath and wait for it.

My eyes fix on the tufted headboard. I don't want to see Oliver's face because whether he knows it or not, this isn't sex. I'm masturbating with his body. Nothing more.

When my husband enters me, it'll be Kristian's hip bones pressing into my ass.

43

OLIVER

Morning breaks and when sunlight finds my face, I can't help feeling good.

Aside from Nathan's demand to be topped in the middle of the night, I've mostly slept. No frowned-upon sleeping pills or night terrors. If I'm being honest, the sex probably helped.

That and a light mind and a clean conscience.

No, that can't be it. I've yet to admit to anything. My mind can't possibly be lighter because intending to come clean doesn't unburden the heart. No. I slept because we're leaving today—shortly after lunch. For Nathan's parents' place on the Carolina coast. We're leaving, and it's instilled that all-too-familiar pleasure of getting away with something.

"We gotta get up, sleepyhead," Nathan whispers while tracing circles on my hip bone. His eyes say he's replaying the fuck I'd given in to. After he came, he'd gone for a long shower. He'd found it primal and hot like something had gotten into him. Dinner with Tom and Jeff?

"I'm up." Last night's spent condom lies on the floor beside my socks, and I roll over to pull them on. When the toilet flushes, I gather my strength and stand. As we pass in the hallway, he presses his lips to mine. Tilly's trailing, bobbed tail whirling fast enough to send her rear airborne.

Nathan's sudden affection is different.

I rest my phone on the toilet tank and lift the lid. As I do, it flames to life with blue light and a buzz. I have a message.

From MeetLockr.

A sharp pain springs in my groin. Kristian. It could only be him.

Christ, did I really forget to delete the app again after our *second* encounter? And is being slammed into an elevator wall called an encounter? Kissed. Choked. Nearly knifed. I'm never back in control for more than an hour before it all buckles under the weight of a tiny, buzzing iPhone.

I swipe it open. The message is a surprise because there's no profile pic. Just the generic placeholder with MeetLockr's logo.

No name either. Who is Anonymous and what does he want?

Hi Oliver.

Cold fear climbs my spine, and a second message confirms the worst.

It's Kristian.

Like the pills before it, dropping my phone in toilet water strikes me as a good idea.

He must've deleted his profile. Cut one head off and the hydra spawns another. I'd done the same. Countless men have done the same countless times.

A one-night stand lingers too long, and a hookup becomes the scaffolding of a relationship. MeetLockr profiles come down. Only to be reborn from the ashes of anonymous sex once the scaffolding collapses amid infidelity or undisclosed addictions or fetishes or wives or bad taste.

A third message chimes.

Let's make a deal.

This isn't a game show. This isn't a fucking game where Kristian sets rules only to flippantly change them. I follow Nathan's rules because I choose to. They're the right ones to follow and—in a vast departure from Kristian's—increase my life expectancy. I don't abide by your rules, Kristian. Not anymore.

My tensed jaw, my grinding molars, my knotted brow—they all relax with the reminder that yes, Oliver, this is a game. This is, has always been, always will be a game. Until one of us is dead.

I answer: **?**

The single question mark is all I can muster. The lid falls shut, and I take a defeated seat on pricey porcelain. His reply is instant.

Tell him.

Kristian gives a moment for his demand to sink serrated teeth into my heart. The truth is, I don't need any such moment, and my throat squeezes. What he's saying is clear as daylight in a mind as dark as mine.

Tell Nathan what you've done.

Behind my busted screen, Kristian's words scream with all the inevitability in the world.

Tell him & I'll leave you alone forever.

44

Nathan takes us down I-95. Hands fixed at ten and two because he follows rules too. Each and every one from the non-negotiable to the trite or banal. Crated in the back, Tilly whimpers while I steep in the passenger seat.

Why would Kristian give a goddamn if Nathan knows? Why smoke me out just for the hell of it? It's another mindfuck. He knows I'd never deliberately meet up again, so this is the next best thing. A new way to needle, to tug loose threads of my psyche until he catches me alone on a street at night. Or until I'm washing my hands in some rest-stop sink only to find his eyes staring in the mirror when I look up. From behind, and the last thing I ever see.

Tell Nathan what you've done.

I didn't reply to that. My singular question mark was all the confirmation he needed.

Fuck him. Fuck Kristian.

Hours later, we've passed south through Charleston proper and close in on Bald Island. Air rushing through my open window grows salty. Still hot—maybe even hotter than DC—but the ocean breeze is comforting.

Washington is a city with all kinds of baggage. It stifles the air there and its absence makes breathing easier. We exit the interstate, travel pastel towns of bungalows and palmetto trees, and onto an empty stretch of asphalt crossing inlet marsh. All saw grass and stalking herons and drifting crab traps.

"God, I needed this." Nathan offers a smile as we turn onto Nags Road. A gravel causeway that unspools across a jetty to Bald Island. So long and so narrow it barely holds space for a single car. In the rearview mirror, dust is whisked away by sea winds. Ahead, the island and the house loom large. Kathy and Victor might not be here, but my heart rate still climbs as if they were.

"Looks like the roofers finished," Nathan says. "Last year's hurricane wrecked the shingles. Speaking of, is Darryl getting the bathroom done?"

"Shit. I forgot to call him." I slip Nathan's black iPhone from the console and catch a glimpse of that damn app—lime-green Wealth Wallet—as I scroll for our contractor. "I'm sorry."

Nathan says nothing, but Darryl answers with "Hello." And before I get a word in: "Reckoned you guys got caught up in something bad. Cops asked me about my crew." I jolt when he says this. Of course Detective Henning questioned him, but what did Darryl learn from her? I try to muffle the call with wind from the window. Nathan doesn't know the man who broke into our house had already been inside it. Darryl's a loose end now.

"To be honest, it got me worried," he goes on. "Lots of folks need jobs, but not many pay a fair wage and don't ask questions. I don't run a charity but I'm protective of my vulnerable workers. When cops poke around, bills go unpaid and kids don't eat."

"No need to worry. Everything's fine now." I swallow. "We appreciate your patience until it got sorted."

"Worry? Got what sorted?" Nathan asks, clearly listening.

I shift uneasily in my seat and ignore him. "I'm actually calling because we're gone for the week. Think you could get the work finished while we're out?"

"Tell him I left a new key in the mailbox," Nathan says, which I do.

"Roger that. Where you boys off to, anyway?" Useless small talk, but anything's better than discussing police interest in Darryl's crew mere feet from Nathan's canine ears.

"Charleston area. Nathan's parents have a place." I regret my answer the second I've given it.

"Used to go crabbin' with a buddy just off Folly Beach. Great food down there."

"Nothing beats it," I say, voice catching. Detective Henning questioned him, but I don't know that he fired Kristian because of it. Either way, Darryl's loose-end status has turned life-threatening. And if Kristian somehow gleans where we are because I've just stupidly told his maybe-still boss? What happens next is as predictable as any slasher film bloodbath of an ending.

"Well, take it easy and enjoy yourselves. I'll have that bathroom looking better than you left it." I hang up as the gravel jetty bleeds into the Kleins' sandstone pavement. Nathan whistles happily as if he hadn't been diligently eavesdropping.

Enormous palm trees line the long driveway, and the cabin draws dark under their shade. Hundreds of fronds—as wide as I am tall—snap in the wind like flags.

"I'm happy to be here." Nathan pulls up to the front. "It's always been a good place for perspective. To connect."

I don't question what he means.

We brake before the pillared facade of an imposing Bahamian-Colonial mansion. Pink stucco, broad shutters, and an Ernest Hemingway vibe. If Hemingway helped tank financial markets in 2008 at no expense to himself thanks to stock buybacks and "charitable" wealth sheltering.

When I step out into salt air, the sun cooks the ground and the water, but outdoor ceiling fans cool the double wraparound porch. They spin lazily all year long because who gives a shit about electric bills?

"Grab our bags?" Nathan asks, unlatching Tilly's crate from the back seat.

Gulls cry overhead as I roll our luggage up to the front door. I tell myself they're welcoming me, but the shrill pitch is anything but welcoming. Crowning the house like a tower is a single third-story room, itself encircled by a widow's walk: Kathy Klein's sewing room.

I may have escaped, bought more time, a blithe week of sea and sun before it all comes violently crashing down, but from here on out? Everything I touch, everything my eyes find is a stark reminder of one thing: how different Nathan and I are and, barring a miracle, how doomed.

So much of him is out of reach. I can't grasp his past with any real depth. The same must also be true of me for him. Just not in a way that's so—I glance up at the house a second time—desperate.

Nathan's already unlocked the front door, Tilly trailing him, and I drag luggage into a soaring foyer of elegant decor and a rain forest of lush house plants. A lot here could steal my breath, but I lose it from something else entirely.

Lavender. The air swims in the purple cleaner. I couldn't be farther from Haus, but I'm suddenly back. No sunlit windows or white linen drapes tumbling two stories to polished parquet. No, everything darkens. Dims to a low red hue—like a darkroom for developing photographs. Purring AC fails, and a sticky heat sprouts. Steam billows in through unseen vents. I start to tremble.

"Hey?" Nathan crosses the dining room. Its muraled egrets are suddenly lost in a lavender-soaked sauna. "You okay?"

My chest tightens.

"Oliver?"

His words break Haus's spell, and I swallow. Again, invisible piano wire wrapped around my throat loosens. "Yeah. Yes. I'm okay."

"I'm gonna turn on the pool heater." Nathan's eyes are narrowed and suspicious. Once more, he's unsure just what the hell's wrong with me. "The switch is in the wine room. Want me to grab a bottle for you while I'm there?"

I nod, but the reek of lavender cleaner still perfumes everything. I chew over the practicality of recleaning the whole place. Scrubbing *that* Haus away from *this* house.

"Maybe a malbec?" Nathan didn't register my nod because he repeats himself. "Oliver, what do you want?"

The question snaps its finger—loud and sharp and asked of me over and over and over again. He means what bottle of wine, but Detective Henning meant something else entirely when she put it to me. As did Kristian.

What do you want, Oliver? I never answered because I thought I couldn't. But after the drive down with Nathan—being alone with him and away from all the bullshit and the pain and the panic—it finally dawns on me.

I do, in fact, want something. And I know what that something is. The answer is the only thing in my life worth protecting. Worth lying to shield. Worth viciously hoarding and risking my life for. It's why I've suffered so much, why I've been reckless in my efforts to contain the damage, why I frustrate Detective Henning and why I'm still terrorized by Kristian and why I can't go back to drugs or to Tyre or to anywhere that Nathan is not.

The answer is simple, and I say it out loud: "I want you."

Nathan hesitates, gives a confused laugh. "I want you too?"

"I mean, I want us to do it." By my side, I spin my ring with my thumb. "For real."

"Do what?"

"Nat," I say. Our eyes meet and he starts to smile. "I want to get married."

45

In the evening, I roll over alone to an empty bottle of malbec by the bed. A sleek table clock says it's half past eight. I throw on a tee and cotton shorts and follow the smell of dinner down a winding staircase.

"I'm yours," I'd told Nathan suddenly. "I should've said this years ago, and I'm sorry for that, but what I want more than anything is to marry you."

"You are mine." He took both my hands in his.

"So," I said, a childlike awkwardness taking hold. "That's a yes?"

"Emphatically."

Then we'd kissed and drank and made love and lain in silence under the canopy of his parents' bed. For the first time in what had been a very long time, no one existed but us. No friends or parents or dangerous people. Me and Nathan felt possible again.

I meander out to the back deck to find him grilling swordfish. A whiskey glaze, though much of the whiskey found its way to his glass.

"Smells amazing, Nat."

"Glad you like it." He kisses me and, turning back to the grill, asks, "What do you think about moving?"

"For real?" I take a seat at the patio table. "Like, live somewhere else?"

"Washington's not doing it for me anymore." He shrugs, and as his words sink in, something close to hope flutters in my chest. "The upkeep on the house is endless. It's way too big for two people. It just feels like the right time for a new beginning."

"A perfect time." I strain to temper my glee. A euphoric surge bordering on mania.

"What if we found a small cottage somewhere? Like on a mountain or a lake or"—he sips from his tumbler—"a beach like this?"

"It would be perfect." My heart swells at the thought of leaving everything behind. Same as it did when he pitched escaping Indiana. With all the hurt I've brought Nathan, it's not hard to figure out why DC's suddenly "not doing it" for him.

"I can work anywhere." He gestures to the ocean. "This could be us every day."

Nathan returns to cooking and, on the cusp of liberation, I find the courage to check my phone. No messages. But also no service. I'm not catching the Kleins' Wi-Fi yet, but the signal is never strong here.

At my back, waves break on the shoreline, rhythmic like a heartbeat.

"I'm gonna walk to the water," I say, standing. Nathan nods. Maybe he smiles, but the flames over his shoulder draw his face dark. Everything suddenly feels like a lucid dream, but I know better than to pinch myself.

The path to the ocean's edge is winding. Planked steps and landings and more steps until the final stretch crosses dunes to the beach. Flower beds line both sides. Pineapple lilies and marigolds and dahlias; even at dusk, they knit a dazzling quilt. Where the steps vanish into sand stands a steel mast. Tethered flags snap in the wind—one for New York, another for South Carolina. And an enormous rippling red, white, and blue.

The sand's cooled, and it massages my feet as I make for the waves. Tiny shards, splinters of shells, needle my heels, the in-betweens of my toes. My situation has changed. Freedom, the chance to start fresh, is within reach, and with it: oxygen.

I was suffocating mere hours ago. My face blueing and my heart starting to seize. *Barring a miracle,* I'd scoffed as we pulled up to the house. But, miraculously, Nathan's found a way to save me again. Deep in my subconscious, I must've known he'd solve everything. I just needed to buy him the time to save me. Which I've done, and now the idea of walking straight out into the Atlantic is laughable.

Low waves mask hungry riptides and no question, I'd have considered the release that simply strolling into them promised. I'd never look back because nothing and no one behind me would care. I'd be far from the first person to do it.

But now in the wake of violence and sadness and calamity, I've survived. Painkillers were mere inches from my mouth, and I still flushed
them. Nathan was mere seconds from gone, and I still have him. We
survived because we were meant to, and we're stronger than ever for it.

I have my whole world to lose again, and I stop in ankle-deep water.

Then my phone vibrates in my fist.

A stray signal carried by salt winds like a modern message in a bottle.

A message from MeetLockr.

A searing reminder I'm not free yet. And the ocean is as deep as it is
patient.

Lots of reminders, in fact. All from Kristian's account. Sent over the
course of the day. Every hour or so. Only now do they come through
and fear scales my spine like a spider.

Tell Nathan.

Tell Nathan.

Tell Nathan.

Tell Nathan.

Tell Nathan.

Tell Nathan.

Tell Nathan.

46

Tom and Jeff get in today," Nathan says cheerily over breakfast. His fork pierces a poached egg and its insides spill out. Impending Tom Vogt and his *boyfriend* sour my appetite. It's not a short drive, and I'd hoped Tom would cancel. He's never flaky when he should be.

"When?"

"Sometime before lunch." He snaps his bacon in two. "A whole boozy beach day. Figure we'll head into Charleston tonight. Maybe hit up Spin." *Spin*. One of the few gay bars within thirty miles. Spin, Trance, Dance, Duck, Hide, Sit, Squat, Shit, they're all the same.

"Sure." I tip a pitcher of orange juice. I wanted more time alone with Nathan. More quiet meals and languid sunbathing and soaking in a happiness that came wholly as a surprise. Or maybe I'm being selfish. The universe gifts me an undeserved second (third?) chance, and I still find something to bitch about.

"You'll like Jeff. A lot, I think. He's funny. Not in the cynical way Tom is. A good foil for the unending sarcasm." Nathan pauses as if weighing his next words carefully. "Attractive too. Really attractive. I think Tom's actually smitten."

As Nathan carries on, paranoia gathers like bad weather. Or the steam that blooms and wisps and swirls within jungle-humid Haus. Something about the way Nathan says Jeff is attractive. Really attractive. That's how anyone with eyeballs and minimal brain function would describe Kristian. He's attractive, but the word alone doesn't quite capture the flaxen-haired, ocean-eyed Adonis. He's *really* attractive.

You're avalanching, Oliver. You're almost free.

"I'm so relaxed just thinking about a move." Nathan stretches, changing the subject. "You'll think I'm crazy, but I called my director this morning. Told him a family emergency came up and I couldn't give notice."

"You resigned?"

"Sure did." He reaches across the table for my hand. "Asked Darryl to give the spare key to my Realtor. We won't go back for more than a day or two at most."

"This is fast," I stutter, and hope he doesn't hear it as a complaint. As great as *a day or two at most* is, I'd take even sooner.

"It is, but"—he touches my wedding band—"I never realized how asphyxiating DC is until now."

"Me too." His word choice is interesting, but I couldn't agree more. "It's like I can breathe again."

"I can't wait to see Tom's face." The shine in Nathan's own hints at how close our future is. "When we tell him we're getting married."

"I'll let you have the honor, then."

We finish breakfast in silence, but afterward I struggle to stifle panic. Rationality isn't my strong suit—sure as hell not for the past few weeks—and I note the time at every opportunity. A countdown till whenever *sometime before lunch* is. When vapid Tom and Jeff—really attractive Jeff—travel the jetty to the Klein mansion.

The minutes practically crawl by on their bellies, and keeping my phone from Nathan's sight is all I can manage. The messages roll in each time my service bars spike. *Tell Nathan,* Kristian demands. *Tell Nathan.* Two words. Over and over and over again.

I still need to call Detective Henning. When I say we're moving in a matter of *days,* there'll be no need to share the truth with my now fiancé. I'll fly back after Kristian's arrested. To ID him or testify or whatever but for now, a phone call to Detective Henning should settle it. When Tom and Jeff arrive, I may not have the chance. Or be alone at all, for that matter. That's how overbearing Tom's narcissism is. His ego swallows whatever space it occupies—even in a house as sprawling as this one.

Seated on the edge of the bed, I stare at the sea through a sweeping bay window and steel myself. *Call her. Call Detective Henning and tell her about The Jefferson.*

The *Jeff*erson. Something snaps like a firecracker. Where I met Kristian, and now a man named Jeff is on his way here. I'd been certain Kristian would tip me off, because if I don't know, it's no fun for him. My chest sinks and heat snakes up my back. He may have done just that.

Call Detective Henning now! Before it's too goddamn late!

But when I swipe for her number, Nathan opens the bedroom door.

Too goddamn late is now.

47

NATHAN

Our eyes meet, and my agenda is obvious.

"Let's have sex," I say. "Before they get here."

I'm pitching a tent in my swim trunks. There's a transgressive thrill in the shamelessness of it, but I'm a new person—an *Other Me,* as Tom says.

Other Me will live in Other City and marry Other Oliver who finds this Me desirable. Who appreciates the power of marriage. The legal codification of Other Us. The claim we'll stake in a right that's been withheld for so long. Detective Henning's going to fall hard when I kick that *spousal privilege* soapbox out from under her.

I draw closer, part Oliver's knees with my leg. My groin's mere inches from his mouth, when something in his eyes tells me to brace for disappointment.

"I'm not feeling it right now, Nat." He exhales. "Maybe tomorrow?"

A silence unspools and I dial down my expectations: "Okay. That's okay. We can still fool around."

Really attractive. It was how I'd spoken about Jeff earlier. I knew it was a mistake the instant I said it. If it bothered Oliver, my timing must be suspicious. He could think I'm blowing steam before the man gets here. Get it all out with the fiancé I'm permitted to fuck so I'm not prowling the house in heat when Jeff is half-naked in swim trunks all afternoon. If that is what he thinks, he's not entirely wrong.

"I'm sorry." Oliver's tone is both genuinely apologetic and sharp.

"Fine." I take a step back, cheeks suddenly hot. Thrilling, transgressive shamelessness becomes shameful shamelessness. I'd contrived a sexual heat—standing so close, dick hard—and now I can't help feeling foolish for it. I tuck my hard-on into the waistline of my trunks and head for the bathroom. The rejection that flushed my face is an emotion I'm all too familiar with.

Old Oliver made Old Me feel it all the time.

• •

It's easy enough to guess what I intend to do as I lock the door behind me.

Regardless, I wait three deliberate minutes. Then flip a faucet on, make for the water closet on the far side of a sunken tub, and shut this second, inner door.

My heart pumps like an animal on the verge of springing. My palms are wet. My fingers tremble while I uncoil the headphones from my pocket.

Waking Oliver in the middle of the night, and the weight of him inside me. Dinner with Tom and Jeff. I undressed Jeff and redressed him and tore his clothes and spread his legs and bent him over and slapped his ass and spit in his mouth and fucked him mercilessly. And that was just before aperitifs.

He told me where he was from, what he did, how he met Tom, and in my head, I took him from behind and choked him. Like Oliver had been.

Then there's the stranger. The one that costs so much. The degradation, the filth, the rawness of him, the unfettered power. The price for stripping the humanity from the act. What happened in that piece-of-shit room in that piece-of-shit Motel 6 can never happen again. It's an utter impossibility and could not be more so.

But I can still have him, to a degree. A tiny piece for replaying over and over and over, and maybe it will lose the sheen of novelty—certainly it will—but not yet. In fact, not for quite some time. The deeper the transgression, the more durable the high.

Even Oliver knows that.

I open an encrypted storage app on my phone, find the file, and tee up a clip. The one the escort shared with me. When it begins to play, I grip myself and stroke. Furiously.

"Devin. Twenty-two."

"I'm straight. I have a girlfriend."

"Nope. Never done anything like this before."

"I'm nervous."

"Okay. Sure."

"You got my cash? Just gotta jack off, right?"

48

OLIVER

"They're here!" Nathan shouts, and my heart thrums.

I slip on a pair of swim trunks and take the stairs like a gallows march. In the kitchen, four champagne flutes wait on a granite counter. Nathan's slicing peaches and muddling mint for the liquor he's been watching the clock for.

He's made two cocktails before the doorbell chimes. It cuts through the vaulted space like a guillotine, and I will the mint leaves to turn into hemlock.

Tilly yelps from under the table and bolts toward the sound.

Don't be foolish. Don't be stupid. Don't be paranoid. Kristian is very much not here. He cannot be here. Ten million Jeffs crawl the planet. None of them are a malicious abbreviation for Jefferson.

"Finish these for me?" Nathan asks, but he's running to the front door before I can answer. I'm left alone with only noises to scrutinize.

You're okay, I tell myself. You're seconds away from total relief. You'll simply meet a new person, that's all. Then you'll endure Tom. You'll pack your bags. And you'll flee far away with your husband, your legal husband, having proven yourself over pills, over cheating, and out of Kristian's grasp.

Wheels on roller bags and greetings unfold in the foyer. My knuckles whiten on the back of a stool. I brace myself, knees bent so they don't buckle.

"Oh my god! What a fucking mansion!" Tom's shrill tenor. "Why is this the first time I'm seeing it?"

It suddenly occurs to me that I haven't seen Tom since his messages, his photos. That head-to-toe nude with his lips cracked in a wicked smile. My flaccid dick sent in return. And now we'll share company. His and *someone* else's. Before I can swallow all that, Nathan's voice interrupts: "Come on in. Let me grab your bags. Oliver? Oliver, give us a hand!"

Terror ties a ball gag around my skull.

"Jeff!" Nathan shouts. The man I've yet to hear despite being aware of him all along.

"Hello!" Jeff replies, and I clench my jaw, shut my eyes. Is there an accent? Is Jeff's voice the one that uncoiled from deep within Haus's steam and whispered in my ear?

What are you looking for?

But whatever words Jeff might've offered are drowned out by Tom's shrieking. Tom's fucking incessant shrieking. Footsteps. Louder and louder and closing in.

"Drinks are ready!" Nathan's as giddy as a six-year-old on Christmas morning, but my knees lock. The whole room rolls and sways like the ocean behind me. My chest catches fire because I've stopped breathing.

They round the corner. First Nathan, a wide smile plastered across his face. Then Tom, mouth agape in perpetual conversation. Then Jeff. He peeks from between Nathan and Tom's shoulders.

"Oliver!" Tom waves for a hug. He steps aside and Jeff's face finally comes into view.

And Jeff isn't a Jeff at all.

But he's not Kristian because Kristian's not from Tyre, Indiana.

49

I'm stunned. A sandblaster, cranked to high, turns on me. My resolve, my steadiness disintegrates beneath the torrent.

"I'm Jeff." Hector extends his hand. He does this forcefully, and despite my being puddled on the kitchen floor, it reminds me of me. Of how I introduced myself to Detective Henning the second time we met, Nathan by my side.

"Jeff," I echo, hardly above a whisper. Reflex has my hand take his. When they meet, clasping each other for the sake of charade, electricity arcs through us. From me to him or him to me, I can't be certain. But there's energy. A relentless energy fueled by history and heartbreak. Pain and danger and unanswered questions.

Both our palms are moist like we're afraid, but Hector's firm grip says he's less so.

"Oliver?" Nathan asks. His tone indicates he's been saying my name and I've only heard him now. "You mind cleaning up in here while I show them their room?"

Yeah, I say.

"Oliver?"

"Yeah," I repeat, this time aloud.

"This way, girls." Nathan gestures to Tom and Hector. Or Jeff, rather. They maroon me in the kitchen, and I turn to the pitcher of pink froth. Another hyena's cackle from Tom rattles my daze. *Think, Oliver. Think!*

Why is Hector here? Chance, coincidence? He encountered Tom on MeetLockr—it's an encounter, not a meeting. Tom only encounters.

That makes zero sense. Hector's home—his alleged home—is hundreds of miles away. What did Detective Henning say about coincidences? No, Hector's here for me. It's why he's pretending to be someone named Jeff. A lie that's thin as a tissue, but keeping his cover isn't the point.

His parting words just days ago, spat through clenched teeth while his grip nearly snapped my arm: *Maybe I'll see you again before that flight.*

Hector has no qualms about fake identities when it serves him. He's proven that time and again. Fake prescriptions, fake Facebook, and for whatever reason, it serves him now. He's nearer than he's been in years. So close, I almost smell the staleness of his winter coat again.

"Let's toast!" Nathan reenters the kitchen, Tom and Hector in tow. The three of them each raise a glass. I hesitate, follow suit.

"To fresh starts," says Nathan.

"Fresh starts," Tom and Hector cheer. Hector's eyes meet mine as we touch glasses. He mouths *thank you.*

Thank you for what!? For not harpooning his ridiculous fraud right from the get-go? What I should've done! I should've called him out before he set a single foot inside the Kleins' home.

But now I can't, and the room tilts. The walls stretch like long sheets of gauze. I can't call Hector out because the moment's already slipped. If I do it now, my initial hesitation will invite far more than questions from Nathan.

The back of my neck tingles. What would he say if he knew who Jeff was? He'd be furious—and what would he do to Hector? Or Hector to him? There's an unstoppable force and an immovable object for the record books. A collision so violent it's astronomical.

And what about Tom? I push that thought right in front of an imaginary train. Who cares about Tom; he's brought Hector on himself.

I won't tell, Tom had taunted, and my arms gooseflesh.

A thousand questions swirl, each splintering into thousands more. They number in the millions before my mind sharpens. My gaze fell to Hector's left hand. Loose at his hip where his thumb hooks his denim belt loop, and any doubts about his intentions vanish. When he notices what I've seen, he grins at me in a way Kristian might.

Years ago, I'd shoved soiled jeans into a fridge, and never looked back. Hector is wearing those same jeans now.

• •

We gather on the back patio to finish the pitcher. Nathan's bursting chattiness belies a strong buzz. I'm silent, but my mind spirals. Desperately searching out fixes while my knuckles grip a drink I've barely sipped.

Likewise, *Jeff* is also careful. He responds to Tom or Nathan only when asked. His answers are precise, but he makes a good show of it. Like cruelty, charm comes easy for him.

This is the same place where, just a short time ago, Nathan cast hope my way. A lifeline that Hector somehow buried a hook in. I'd bit hard, and by the time the shock waned, he'd already started to reel. Steel deep in my flesh, and the line's getting tauter. Not much slack is left.

I have to get Hector alone. I have to question him and pray Nathan's presence keeps me safe. As fucked-up as it is, I ask myself how Kristian would do it. How he'd separate someone from the herd. When I do isolate Hector, I'll have to roll the dice on how far he'll take things.

He hasn't consumed a drop of liquor since the toast. Hector never *doesn't* consume alcohol when it's available. He's not sober; I know he's still using. So what is he planning and why, for the first time in his shit-eating life, does he want to stay lucid?

"Oh my god," Tom squeals as Nathan shares the big news. For some reason, he keeps the lid on our move. "This is amazing!"

"Congratulations," Hector says. His tone is off, but I'm the only one who reads it as a sneer.

When we finally make it to the ocean, Nathan's drinking goes airborne. Unbroken imbibing through cycles of sunning and wading. At one point, throwing Tilly's tennis ball down the beach takes more coordination than he can muster.

I should put food in front of him—chips, salsa, something. Nathan's taken vacation as license to get wasted, and as expected, the attractiveness of Jeff enthralls him. The more he drinks, the longer he lingers on Hector's body.

The thought of Hector and Nathan together—doing anything—shoots bile up my throat. My past and my present mixing. I separated them for a reason, to compartmentalize and control. I feared how a violent confrontation might unfold, but Nathan obviously fantasizing about Hector is almost unbearable.

Almost. An opportunity emerges, and I seize it.

"There a good place to smoke?" Hector asks Nathan as they towel off. Sand sticks to their knees and shins, dusts happy trails.

"Porch is fine." Nathan gives no indication Hector's request to smoke—something he abhors—is one bit bothersome. "Grab a coffee cup for the butts."

Just like that, Hector nods and makes his way back.

"You guys good on drinks?" I don't miss a beat. Our second pitcher has been a watery cupful for the past half hour, and I've held it close as a card to play. Alcohol is always a royal flush over any hand of Nathan's.

"Bring some beers from the fridge," he says. "Maybe move a case from the garage to the kitchen?"

"No problem. You good, Tom?"

"Beyond good," Tom oozes behind vintage aviators. Polarized lenses render his eyes unreadable. They've been covered all afternoon, making it impossible to avoid being consumed by them.

Hector's some six or seven yards ahead on the steps to the house. I trail him, unnoticed.

When he reaches the deck, I hang back, let him disappear into the kitchen. I count to ten, resume my climb, and my timing is perfect. When he returns—soft pack of Parliaments in one hand, mug in the other—our eyes meet.

He flinches. His mask slips, just for a second, because he's trapped.

I get to the point: "What the fuck are you doing here?"

His chest swells as he takes in a deep breath, steadies himself.

"I'm here with Tom." He slips a single white cigarette from his pack. Despite my anger and confusion, the crispness of unsmoked paper tugs. "Tom, who was so fixated on name-checking his own social media handles—the accounts that brag on his behalf—he never bothered to notice Jeff's lack of online presence."

"I bet Hector has one, though. You've got thirty seconds till I grab my phone and out your ass."

"Good luck with that." He gestures with his own phone. "Signal's pretty shitty out here."

"You don't think the Kleins have Wi-Fi?"

"You don't think the modem was the first thing I looked for?" He draws closer, props his elbows on the banister behind me. Our shoulders brush. Skin on skin. "Folks always put it somewhere central. Like the parlor or salon or whatever these people call a living room."

"New job in pharmaceutical sales," I mock, "sure sounds a lot like stealing home modems."

"I didn't touch it." He waves the mug, smiles. "Just got a little sloppy with my water."

Shit. The answer to how far Hector's willing to go? Very.

"Want one?" He puts a second smoke on the railing, where I leave it untouched. Pop of flame from his lighter and he sucks. "You used to smoke. Quite a bit. Guess Oliver Klein quit."

He blows in my face, and I turn to the beach. Nathan and Tom are half-naked blurs on bright towels, and Hector's capable of much worse than soaking a modem.

"Nathan doesn't strike me as the type that likes smoking." He pulls another long drag. "What is he, like, a doctor, right? Doesn't look like he'd put up with it."

This last sentence, the way Hector says *put up with it,* sharpens my ire into something pointy.

I stab: "Tell me what you want."

"You've made a good go of it, Oliver." Why does he keep saying my name? "Look at this place. Your life. Your boyfriend or husband or whatever. The ring on your finger?" His eyes fall to my hand, and I hide it in my pocket.

"You know nothing about me."

"I know about us." He steps away from the railing, turns to face me. "I know you're gonna lie. Gonna tell me you found something better. But I could smell boredom the second I walked through the door. Stinks like stagnant water, and guess what?" He sucks another drag. "You reek."

"Want some real talk, Hector?" I ask. "Want to compare yourself— who steals petty shit to pay for whatever the hell you put in your veins these days—to Nathan? Look around, asshole. You don't stack up."

"Oh, I've looked around," he scoffs. "You're a sugar baby, Oliver. And that sexist joker?" He points at Nathan with the cherry of his cigarette. "He treats you like the pool boy 'cause you let him. 'Be a doll and bring towels.' 'Serve us girls drinks, babe.' 'Don't be clumsy with the glasses.' Tell me, Oliver. When you break something expensive, does he dock your pay or just fuck you harder?"

Hector takes a step closer, and my pulse spikes. I make tight fists. The pitcher I'd brought sits on the patio table. Empty and glass and I could leap for the handle.

"You didn't stumble on some new idea." Hector's tone veers. "I've been with men like Nathan. For the same reason as you. To survive. The houseboy bit might not be abuse, but we both know he's got a dog collar around your neck. We both know the nasty shit rich guys get off on, and all the Viagra they pop to do it."

"Funny thing is I don't." I grind my molars. "Because Nathan isn't some dentist in Tyre I bang for painkillers."

"Look." Hector flicks his still-smoldering cigarette over the rail. "Lie to me, but not to yourself. You know Nathan's always watching, always tracking, never letting an opportunity to humiliate and denigrate and shit on you pass him by. Nathan knows the second you wise up is the second you leave. And you can leave, Oliver. I did."

Somewhere behind my eyes, I feel tears coming. I bite into my cheek to stop them.

"We're the same, and I can help you. Get you out and bring you home. You may not remember what it's like to be a man's equal, but I promise you will. A man who loves—"

"A man like you?" Tears break, and my voice catches. "That right? A man who tried to—"

"I get why you ran." His eyes chase mine wherever they go. An ocean to one side, a mansion to the other, and nothing to see save Hector. "I know what I did, and I'm sorry. Said so over and over in my voicemails—"

"I deleted them. Never listened to a single one. I'm happy now, Hector. I'm getting married."

"To that asshat?"

"You tried to *rape* me."

"I said." He tightens his jaw. "I know."

"I didn't care how sorry you were then, and I don't care now. I left you and drugs and Tyre fucking Indiana because I wanted to. It was *my* choice. I know what *I* want. And right now"—my whole body shivers—"I want you out!"

"You don't get it." Heat flushes Hector's cheeks and his dark eyes burn. "I came all the way from Tyre fucking Indiana, as you say. I'm not leaving. Not without you."

There's a new venom in his voice, and fear blooms. Standing here on this deck, clenching my fragile shot at happiness between his sharp teeth, Hector is breaking me. He's breaking me because he knows how. I fight against tears but can't stop them from falling fast and heavy.

I grab the pitcher, stutter, "I'm not afraid of you."

"What did I just say about lying to yourself?"

"I'm going inside." I wipe my eyes, my lips. "I'm getting my phone. I'm telling Tom who you are. I'm telling Nathan." I start to turn, and Hector's hand falls on my shoulder, his grip tight. Same as when he struck my face.

"The fuck you are." My heart thumps louder, harder.

Ice sloshes as I raise the container high. "I will break this over your head."

His grasp loosens, and I jerk my shoulder from it, half expecting him to lunge. He's got nothing to lose now, and it might take more than smashing glass on his skull to stop him.

Instead, he smiles. A sick sort of smile like bad milk. "You want me gone?"

"Jesus. Did you hear anything I just said?"

"Pay me."

"What?"

"You hear anything I just said?" he parrots, then: "Pay. Me."

"You can't be serious."

But the smile fades and a new coldness says he's deadly so. "This was always going down two ways. Only ever two."

The cold climbs my shoulders.

"You either come back with me or you don't. But no matter which"—he tips his stubbled chin to the beach—"you're cleaning out a couple of Dr. Klein's accounts, you follow?"

I scoff. The proposition's ridiculous enough to pull me back from the edge.

"I need cash. You got cash. Fifty thousand bucks, and Jeff dumps Tom over dinner tonight."

"No."

"Jeff is a needy lover." Again, Hector careens. He unlocks his phone, and where this is headed is anyone's guess. "Paranoid and prone to checking iPhones. Texts, calls, *camera rolls*." He turns his screen, and the image hits like a sledgehammer. "Your face might not be in frame, but I'd recognize you anywhere. Bet Nathan would too."

"Hector—"

"Cash, Oliver. I'm not fucking around."

I swallow painfully. Hector may have nothing to lose—and that may make him dangerous—but it also makes two of us now. "Go fuck yourself."

As hard as it is, I turn my back to him and head for the kitchen door. The pitcher in my hand keeps him from following. As I reach for the handle, I think I see Hector reflected in the glass there.

Pointing a finger gun at the back of my head.

•   •

I burst into the master bedroom, where my phone's been charging all afternoon. I yank it from the wall and unlock my home screen. Shit—no service bars. Hector's rendered Wi-Fi moot but a signal still comes every now and again. After all, Kristian's threats keep rolling in like the goddamn tide. If I'm going to out Hector—sink his credibility before Nathan sees my dick on his phone—I've got to move. Now.

I pad down the hallway, arm extended like a makeshift cell tower. The world's shortest antenna, and when I reach the staircase, a bar finally appears.

My pulse ramps up. Social media first. Surely, this pro at Facebook fraud will have one. If not, I'll find him. No one's unfindable. If nothing else, I've learned that the fucking hard way.

Before I can open the browser, the phone vibrates in my hand. Two text messages. Both from the same Washington number: *Rachel Henning, Det Sgt, MPDC.*

Call me asap.

We found him.

A surge of adrenaline. Questions burst like fireworks. I've told her nothing about meeting him or Tilly or his room at The Jefferson. My hands tremble; no amount of day drinking can steady them. She says she found Kristian. I'm now alone. Hector's brooding on the deck. Nathan and Tom are on the beach, and I have service. Fresh from a shakedown, but I have to know what the hell she means.

Crackling and popping and static-tinged, but the call goes through.

"Henning here."

"What do you mean *you found him*? As in, you know where he is? Or did you catch him? Is Kristian arrested?" Questions. Confessions. Everything erupts uncontrollably. "I should've told you earlier, but I saw him. At the Jefferson hotel to get our dog back. He booked a room. Seven-twenty-one. Now he's texting me again. I should've called sooner, but I'm terrified and—"

"Oliver," Detective Henning cuts me off. "Slow down. It's okay."

I take in a gulp of air, listen for footsteps downstairs in case Hector—or anyone—came inside.

"Kristian can't hurt you. That's why I called."

"So he is in jail?"

"You don't understand." Detective Henning sharpens her voice. "He's dead."

My heart blows wide open. Dumping panic and questions and fear like jet fuel.

"Kristian's dead," she repeats, breaking up in a waning signal. "His name is Olav Eriksen. He's Norwegian. Stateside on an overstayed tourist visa. He is, *was,* an escort for hire. Four months in New York, then three in the DC area."

A thick knot scales my throat. I finally choke out: "How did he die?"

"Overdose."

"Drugs?"

"The medical examiner's report isn't done, but it looks like he shot up bad dope. Thought you needed to hear it. Stopped by your place a few times but couldn't catch you. I need you to come back in. Make an official ID to close out your file."

As what Detective Henning says sinks its teeth in, a deeply uncomfortable question comes to mind. "What time did Kristian—Olav—die? What day?"

Crinkling pages flip on her end. "Coroner put the time of death two days ago. Late. Between ten thirty and midnight. Why?"

The detective's voice dwindles as the phone falls from my fingers. I don't need to hear any more. She can't help me.

"Why do you—wait," she squeaks from the floor. "When was your last text from him?"

She can't save me because Kristian's messaged all day today, all day yesterday, all from MeetLockr. I bring my hands to my throat and squeeze.

"Oliver? You there?"

If Kristian's dead, who have I been talking to?

V. Terminal Respiration

Cardiac arrest. Clinical death.

collapse at the top of the stairs. The railing keeps me from tumbling. All the way to the bottom where my neck snaps and I die.

And someone gets what they've wanted all along.

Kristian is dead. But Kristian is also messaging me, and not from a fucking autopsy table.

My mind surges in thousands of directions. It's explosive and primal. Dictated only by instinct. Identify my enemy. I must identify my enemy. How the hell do I do that?

The MeetLockr account. Someone's been talking to me in Kristian's name. The ramifications of this bleed through. Congeal as hard, unforgiving facts.

Kristian hadn't deleted and reinstalled MeetLockr, but the messages picked right up where he'd left off. After Detective Henning said he took a hotshot.

Someone else knows. And now Hector shows up, coincidentally, to cut the internet and extort me. What would Detective Henning say about that?

Kristian, what he's done to me, what I've done—someone knows it all, and I'm naked again like I was in Haus. Shamed. Splayed open for all to see everything inside. A scalpel has sliced my belly wide open to the air and sepsis is just around the corner. My dignity is abandoned on wet tile. Wrapped in my black briefs and flippantly discarded.

Geotagging! MeetLockr's users depend on it. I open the app, scroll for my most recent message from Kristian, and tap for the distance.

200 meters away.

Kristian is dead. Someone knows everything, and that someone is one of only three human beings within a two-hundred-meter radius.

Hector. Tom. Nathan.

Electricity snaps up my spine, and I look over my shoulder. I creep down the stairs, but a plush Persian runner muffles my steps. I came inside to grab beers, so I should make for the kitchen.

The back door opens. Laughter. The damp slapping of rubber flip-flops against slick tile. Glass on granite. I freeze.

"Oliver?" Nathan slurs. "Hey? Where'd you go?"

"Upstairs," I call back, voice cracking like a choirboy's. "Had to make a call."

"We're going out tonight," he shouts.

"Spin," Tom adds. "Party's just getting started." A boisterous shuffling as the gaggle of gays collapse on couches to check phones and catch missed messages. A breather before louder music and harder drinking.

I reopen MeetLockr. Scrolling frantically, I head back upstairs.

The main staircase winds around a vaulted, two-story living room before splashing into the foyer. Halfway up, a landing opens to the space below. An arched cutout in the wall displays an enormous vase. A blue-and-white porcelain of ponds, lotus flowers, and koi. I kneel behind it, peer over the ledge and into the living room.

I find the anonymous profile—dead Kristian's profile—and text a single character. The only thing I've ever messaged this person:

?

I tap *reply*, hold my breath, and brace myself.

• •

On one camelback love seat sit Tom and Hector. Tom's hand rests on Hector's upper thigh, nearly on his groin. Tom crosses his ankles on the coffee table of sculpted sandstone. On the opposing one sits Nathan. Fresh Corona Light in hand, liquor-fevered cheeks.

Tom has Hector, Nathan has me. But no one gives any hint they've received a new message. My heart beats in my throat. No one betrays himself by startling.

Nathan closes his eyes and his head falls back into a cushion. I duck, worried he's seen me. Then check the read receipt on my text.

Message send failure. Fuck.

Fingers trembling, I retry:

???

Message send failure.

I press *send* again. Again. Again.

Failure. Failure. Failure.

Why did Hector have to fry the goddamn Wi-Fi!? The question's rhetorical, but that doesn't stop my fear from answering.

Because, it whispers, *Hector knows exactly what he's doing.*

• •

I button my shirt before Kathy's full-length mirror and watch Nathan towel off from a shower. My hands shake as I search for a way to slam the brakes on tonight. To bring everything to a screeching, screaming stop so I can figure it out. But there are no brakes. No way to halt any of it. No escape.

Whatever *it* is.

Arms wrap around my chest and I clench my gut.

I'm thankful Nathan's as drunk as he is. Sober eyes would read me for panicked and undone, but the only sober eyes in this house are my own. Now I'm forced to go out. Play charades at Spin while Cher asks a teeming dance floor if we believe in life after love. Share a table with whichever of these men is coming for me in ways I can't begin to imagine.

Kristian seduced me. Kristian attacked me. Kristian stalked and hunted and tried to finish what he started. That was all real. His lips and his hands in the steamy darkness of Haus. The electric touch of his leg at The Jefferson while he spun tales of abuse and scissors.

And he's dead. And it's not over. No matter how hard Hector argues his own case while prosecuting Nathan, the facts are simple: he's a user, a criminal, and he's made his demands plain. He even saved my soiled jeans for the occasion.

Behind me, an intoxicated Nathan struggles with his own pant leg after crating Tilly. I'm struck by another reality: Hector could be right. Words cut deep when they're true, and Hector's practically scraped bone. How much daylight is there between him and Nathan, really? Threats.

Manipulation. Gaslighting. One uses his fist and the other his lips, but the effect's the same: complete control.

And now Kristian is dead. Which means something far worse—someone far more dangerous and patient—has been watching the whole goddamn time.

Who?

51

NATHAN

Too drunk for dinner and too early for Spin puts us in a holding pattern of freezer pizza and pregaming. I place another empty bottle on the coffee table as Tom stands.

"If you're going to the fridge, grab me a new beer?"

"You got it," Tom says.

From my phone, I crank the volume on the sound system. Seated next to me, Oliver seems to wince. The Wi-Fi hasn't worked all night, but Bluetooth still connects my playlist. A "Blue Monday" remix pulses and pounds so hard the house palms shake.

"So how many does it take to make an orgy?" Jeff winks from the opposite love seat.

"Huh?" I laugh.

"Tom says, like, six guys." He pauses, knowingly. "But I think four's the magic number."

"Anything more than two should count, right?"

"How about you?" Jeff eyes Oliver. "What do you say?"

Oliver says nothing. He smiles snidely and nurses the same beer he's had for the past hour. More fixated on his phone than ever, but just as dodgy about hiding his screen—which he's somehow managed to crack.

"You're no fun," I tell my now fiancé.

"You're wasted."

"It's six!" Tom calls from the kitchen, barely able to carry all the shit in his arms. A pile of shot glasses clink on the coffee table as they tumble from Tom's hands. A couple of beers and an unopened bottle of Patrón follow. "Four is literally just a foursome."

"Is tequila a great idea, Tom?" Oliver's disapproval is starting to grate.

"We're celebrating." Tom pulls the cork out with his teeth. He pours and downs his shot. Jeff follows suit—as do I—and Oliver sits uncomfortably. Liquor untouched.

"You wanna celebrate?" Jeff asks, wiping his mouth. Out of his pocket comes a baggie of pills. A dazzling array of rainbow colors I'm not sober enough to recognize.

"What's all in there?"

"A party." Jeff shrugs and takes two.

"Anything this small has *got* to be dangerous." Tom pinches a pink pill in his fingers before tossing it back. "Maybe we're not making it out tonight."

"Or maybe the club gets better," I say, chasing down a white tab with beer. Oliver, on the other hand, doesn't even flinch. A baggie of pills should have him salivating, but it seems to do nothing. Fuck him. I find Jeff's eyes. And also, fuck him. I give him a grin but my vision's starting to split.

"I'm obviously planning the bachelor party," Tom starts. "It's gonna be major. Like party-plane-to-Fiji major."

I laugh, gesture to the substance abuser's wet dream before us. "This isn't it?"

"Where's the hooker? The free pass before you're legit?"

"The *four*some," Jeff adds with a slick smile. "Oliver will give his boy permission, won't you, Oliver?"

I can't tell if Jeff's joking or not. The truth's probably somewhere in the middle, but whatever pill I popped is kicking in, and I like where this is going. A slow tingle crawls my scalp.

"No need." I take Oliver by the shoulder, pinch. "We're actually in an open relationship now. Did you know that, Tom?"

Oliver makes a stupid face, and Tom says, "What?"

"Don't sweat it. Oliver forgot to let me know too. But, yeah, we're apparently wide open." I finish my beer. I'm not sure if my words are meant to entice or accuse. Again, likely somewhere in the middle. "Oliver fucked around, so then I fucked around."

"Nat, stop." Oliver slides closer. "You're getting sloppy."

An eerie euphoria sweeps my spine, and tiny flames dance in everyone's eyes.

"So, ya know, Tom." I snap my fingers to the beat of electric music. "Feel free to send more dick pics to my fiancé 'cause it's totally fine now."

Drunk, drugged, and high on his vapid gay life, Tom still freezes. His posture, iconic like Joan Crawford of Arc when he finally speaks: "I don't know what you're talking—"

"I *love* the bachelor party idea," I interrupt. Jeff shifts uncomfortably. "What do you think, Tom? Wanna swap tonight?"

Jeff shoots Oliver a glance, who shakes his head as if to say *no*. But his no could mean *no, do not engage with Nathan sexually* or *no, do not engage with Nathan violently because he's intoxicated and unpredictable*. But I don't know lots of things, right? And if I didn't know different, it's almost like these two know each other from somewhere.

"Hey, Jeff, you top, bottom, or vers—"

"Chill the fuck out, Nathan. Take this." Tom slides a tablet my way. Chill? Anger erupts, and I swipe it onto the rug with shot glasses and empty bottles.

"Jesus, dude!" Jeff stands like he's looking for a fight. For wasting his score or perhaps something else. "Oliver's right. You're sloppy."

I scoff. "Don't get pissed at me because Tom can't keep his dick off other guys' phones."

"Baby," Tom starts. "It was before we got serious—"

"I don't give a shit who you sleep with," Jeff spits before pivoting back to me. I gird myself. "But Nathan over here can't be shocked. I'd step out on his controlling ass too. Prick."

"Nat, don't." Oliver takes a fistful of my sleeve, but I toss my phone on the coffee table and tear free of his grasp.

"This is my goddamn house." I rise to meet Jeff's glower. "Who do you think you are?"

I reach for the asshole's collar, but he ducks. When Jeff pulls back a fist, Oliver leaps between us, screams, "Hector!"

Silence as what he just said is absorbed by the room.

He's stopped midsentence. Tom knots his brow. They both look at me. The music couldn't be any louder and I hear none of it. There's only my heart, thumping hard like a war drum.

Maybe it's the booze or the pills slipping through my blood-brain barrier with unsettling ease, but a sinkhole opens in my chest. I've stumbled on a fresh lie. Sunk both feet into a heaping, steaming pile of a lie—one I did not see coming. The sadness is as inescapable as the rage.

"So." I brush spit from my lip. "*That's* who you are."

Oliver takes a step closer. "Enough—"

"Don't!" I thrust my hand out, and he jolts.

"Nat"—Oliver's voice catches on tears—"please."

"I'll deal with you next." I zero in on Jeff. "After this motherfucker's finished."

"Can everyone please reset," Tom cries. I break an empty bottle on the stone table. A popping crack like a gunshot, and there are no more resets. No more chances. No more bullshit.

"This is Hector, is it?" I bite into the side of my cheek. Hot blood and pain keeping my double vision in check. "Hector, your tweaker rapist."

"Put the glass down!" Again, Oliver grabs my arm but this time I shove him. Way too hard and he stumbles into a back wall.

"Listen to your sugar baby, Doc." Jeff, or Hector, rather, puckers his lips. "Before you get hurt."

I tighten my grip on the broken bottleneck. My body's on fire. Oliver, Tom, the whole room, it all darkens. Narrows to a tunnel that holds room for Hector only. Not for the first time, I wonder if I'm willing to kill a man. Before I can answer that, the front door bursts open, and a new voice screams a question of her own.

"What the hell is going on here?" Mother growls.

52

OLIVER

M y spine digs into the wall, my chest heaves.

"Mother?" Nathan's dumbfounded. As am I. As are Tom and Hector. As are Kathy and Victor, who stand just beyond the foyer. What happens next is anyone's guess. "What are you doing—"

"I asked you a question!" Kathy interrupts. Black leather pumps clicking on hardwood as she draws closer. Rosewater perfume precedes her, and the breeze sends gooseflesh down my neck.

"Son." Victor's affected basso. Straight out of central casting for *Master of the Universe,* the older, grayer, richer Nathan starts appraising things. "What are you doing with that bottle?"

Hector takes the opportunity to distance himself from said bottle but asks a very stupid question while doing so: "The fuck are you two?"

The room sinks into silence for a painful beat. Carefully, I reach into my pocket because time's running out.

Kathy narrows her eyes at Hector like a predator. The hunger in them almost looks like giddiness. I grip my phone tight. Once again, Hector unwittingly helps because he can't keep his mouth shut. He's volunteered himself as the first receptacle into which this horrible woman will pour her rage.

Her scowl is firmly tethered to Hector, but it's to Victor she speaks: "Call the police. Tell them we have a trespasser or three." She hesitates, grins. "If I'm not mistaken, there may even be a gun."

"You're right, Katherine," Victor adds cheerily as he dials. "There almost certainly is a firearm on one of them."

Shit. Victor's ordering up *homicide by cop* like it's a goddamn Uber.

Then again, the Wi-Fi modem sits useless behind an ornate planter.

Hector might still be helping. Back against the wall, I could slide my way into the kitchen. A butler's pantry connects it to the dining room. The front door goes nowhere helpful, but I can make it to the stairs if I run. Maybe lock myself in a room. I'm faster than Old Man Victor or Kathy, who—for reasons unknown but fortunate—is wearing heels.

"Why are you here?" Nathan asks, still clinging to his makeshift weapon.

"You were a no-show at the deed signing," Kathy says. "The lawyers went to demand you vacate my property—and found you already had."

Deed signing? What is Kathy talking about?

"Then you had us followed?"

"Oh please," she sneers. "The house alarm here was disabled. I saw the notification on my way to barre class." Like mother, like son, she tosses her own phone faceup on the coffee table. Open to what I assume is a smart home app.

"So, it's even worse. You came all the way down here to personally pull the trigger."

"To save you from yourself." Her gaze flits to broken glass, and maybe the woman's got a point. "To offer a last chance before it's too late."

"Spare me."

"I will if you'll allow it." Kathy pauses for a cruel head count. "The police can arrest three people or four. Your choice."

"Jesus Christ, Mother."

"Excuse me, Mr. and Mrs. Klein?" Tom breaks his silence. He must've checked Kathy's math, and irons out his voice. "I'm not actually involved in, like, whatever this is. I work for Senator—"

"I'm curious, Nathan," she cuts in. Tom is completely invisible. Unlike the pill bag where her phone landed. "Who brought those party favors? You think Oliver can float you both when a judge revokes your medical license?"

"You're insane."

"Leave the psychoanalysis to me, son."

Nathan's rattled, Hector's flummoxed, Tom is again silent on a couch, and the Kleins are busy weaponizing civil services. I could run, but if I do, everyone here has a reason to chase me. The outcome of being caught, however, varies widely among them.

Running won't cut it, and now Victor paces the room, growing agitated. Revealing he has no service defangs his threat, so he stays quiet. Kathy, on the other hand, has nothing but time.

"Booted from one home, so you simply move to another? Bring your playthings along too." She reads the room and each man in it for filth. "All of them."

Nathan's urge to leave DC, to move as fast as possible, suddenly feels calculated. His reasons are still uncertain, but romantic impulse is evidently not one of them. In my pocket, I turn my phone over. Victor can't catch a signal, but MeetLockr is my last and only shot.

Unless the Kleins brought their own gun to plant, no one's *legitimately* armed. At least until cops burst in and spray bullets wherever screaming Kathy points. Hector may have something in his luggage, but every Klein stands in his way. My mace is in some evidence locker with the rest of dead Kristian's shit. Tom can't help me. Hell, Tom would probably choose Hector over me because that's just a very Tom thing to do.

I'm deep in a nest of spiders. Maybe they all turn on one another, but the fact remains: I'm the only one here without eight legs and a venom sac.

Stunningly unself-aware, Hector says, "You people are all fucked up."

Then Victor's words set my pulse on fire: "Call's going through now, Katherine."

Service! If he's got it, I might.

Eyes down in my pocket, I unlock my phone. A full signal. I scroll for MeetLockr. It's a slow load but no doubt about it, it's opening.

"Hang up the phone, man." Hector starts to panic.

When he looks like he might leap, Nathan raises his bottle. "Don't move!"

Tension swallows the room. Humid like a bathhouse and ripe with Kathy's rosewater perfume and everyone else's fear. I find my unsent message from earlier: the question mark I'd hurled at the anonymous account and hit *re-send*.

Message sent.

Sent, but not received.

I scour the room. Their faces. Nathan stands by the hearth now, his fist on the mantel to keep steady. Expressionless Tom hasn't budged. Restless Hector rubs his arms like he's enraged or withdrawing or both.

But one of them knows everything. One of them tortures me in Kristian's stead.

"I need to get out of here." Tom.

"Hello, yes, this is an emergency." Victor.

"No one is going anywhere." Kathy.

"Take the jetty over. Nags Road." Victor again.

"Oliver." Nathan.

"I said hang the fuck up!" Hector.

Unraveling Hector whose eyes search for escape. When they land on me, invisible needles tap-dance on my shoulders. He had as much opportunity to find me on MeetLockr as Tom. When I set a trap for Kristian, Hector could've seen it.

He's gone to lengths, both great and criminal, to have his demands met. He's come for me and he's come for cash, and not necessarily in that order. He stalked me. Threatened me. Called himself Jeff. Impersonated Blaire. Check your phone, Hector. Check your phone and answer the most important question of all. Are you impersonating Kristian?

"Home invaders. That's correct." Victor.

"You can't keep me here." Hector.

"Watch me." Nathan.

"Good, Nathan." Kathy.

"I'm sorry for the photos." Tom.

My message still reads *sent*. Not received. Not opened. Not read.

"Very good. Thank you." Victor ends the most cordial 911 call of all time, and for the smallest slice of an instant, no one says anything. An uneasy quiet descends.

Then something buzzes.

A phone vibrating against sandstone. The rattling reaches my ears with all the ferocity of a screeching freight train.

My message reads *received*. Then a second later, *read*.

Trembling, I look up from my pocket and out into the room. What I see is that freight train, just before it strikes me. Before it smears pieces of myself across mile after mile after mile of iron track.

Because Kathy Klein has reached for her phone on the coffee table.

And read the message I've sent her.

53

"You."

It's all I can say at first. A tiny scratch of a whisper, but every pair of eyeballs on this island swivels my way. Invisible hands push from behind. Off the wall, and toward my enemy. I take slow steps to the one person who knows everything and yet did nothing to help.

"Excuse me?" Kathy arches her brow, but that sharp face is as venomous as ever.

She did *do* something, though, didn't she? Something cruel and pitiless. She impersonated Kristian. The man who tried to kill me. This bitch exploited my fear. Forced the choice of losing my life or losing my partner. Used it against me so flippantly, the therapist in her would have to agree it's maniacal.

"Oliver?" Nathan's voice dwindles to white noise.

Two hundred meters away, MeetLockr said. Turns out five people, not three, fell within that radius.

How she knew about the app is beside the point. Folders disguised as calculators, budgeting and smart home apps, GoPros for snuff films, good old-fashioned nanny cams hidden in the Georgetown house before her son and his trashy lover took the keys. The ways she might've tracked and surveilled me are as deep and wide as her hate.

How do we survive?

That's the question my mom was forced to answer every day. Pragmatism is leaving your husband drunk in a ditch because the next time he tears into your son might be the last. But Kathy's ruthlessness? The punishment she exacts for the crime of loving Nathan while poor? She can wrap herself in knots of pearls and rosewater perfume, but she'll never stop stinking.

She's no better than Mom. None of the Kleins are.

"I'm about sick of this shit," says Hector.

"Same, Jeff." Tom coughs. "Or Hector or, what is your name even?"

As chances of leaving this island unscathed shrink, I grow bolder. Even if I could stop the catharsis, I wouldn't. I've run too long, panicked too long, hurt way too goddamn long—and now the truth comes out.

Even if the only ears to hear it all belong to spiders.

"Kristian." I clench my teeth so hard they might shatter. "You knew him. Or, at least, knew of him."

"Nathan." Kathy's tone is as smooth as cold glass. "What the hell is he—"

"Or Olav, I guess. But maybe that's not news to you either. Tell me, did the opportunity for blackmail fall into your lap? Or have you known from the start?" My hands ball into fists. Tight and bloodless. "When he tried to strangle me to death."

"Strangle?" Nathan's voice deepens. "Is this about your mugging?"

"Either way"—I shake my head—"you get what you want, huh, Kathy?"

"What exactly is it that I want?"

I laugh. Uncontrolled, it flies from my lips. The irony of answering that question on behalf of Kathy Klein is delicious. I point my chin at Nathan. "I can think of something."

"Who is Kristian," Nathan demands, "and Olav?"

I recall Detective Henning's revelation this afternoon. "Funny thing, *Mother*."

"I can assure you," Victor interjects, "there's nothing funny about any of this."

"Before he moved to Washington?" I disregard both him and Nathan as easily as Kathy ignored Tom. "He lived in your neck of the woods. What were the chances—I asked myself over and over and over—a homicidal maker of snuff films pulls up the next stool in a bathhouse?"

"How many of those pills did you take, Oliver?" Kathy tightens her jaw.

"The coincidences, the timing, the whole thing felt, I don't know, engineered. It smacked of design. Maybe you met him in New York. Maybe you sent him down here to choke me."

"I knew you were still a junkie," she spits.

"Is that what you meant, Mother?" Nathan asks. "What you said in the car? About scaring Oliver into making the right decision?"

"Nathan, stop being silly."

He goes on, "'I hoped it would scare him.' Those were your words before you kicked us out and followed us down here. Did you pay to have my husband mugged!?"

"He's not your husband! For the last time, that man is *not* a Klein! And I have no idea what you're—"

"Stop being silly, Kathy," I mock. Nothing to hide now, and I shove my phone in her face. Where the whole rotten thing's spelled out and probably backed up on some cloud in Silicon Valley. "MeetLockr. You just opened my message."

"Meet who?"

"Show Nathan your phone, Mommy!" I point to the sleek device. Held tight in her grip, its casing tap-tap-tapped with the manicured nail of her index finger. She hesitates and—green eyes tight because she knows it's game over—glances down.

I follow her gaze to the screen in her right hand, and something's not right.

Something's not right, and something else stabs in my chest.

"For Christ's sake," Kathy snaps.

That lime-green logo is plain as day, and the stabbing comes harder, faster.

"You really are high as a kite, aren't you?"

Plunging in and out and in and out, I might vomit out my own heart.

"This isn't my phone."

Kathy Klein's black iPhone wasn't the only one tossed on the coffee table tonight. Like Mother, like son, and tears gather.

"It's Nathan's."

54

NATHAN

When do you call time of death on a marriage?
A hard question for others perhaps, but lucky me, mine's been timestamped.

9:24 p.m.

The moment Oliver's MeetLockr message was opened.

Even from across the room, his white eyes shriek in silence. That look is as old as time. The instant Brutus's blade slips into Caesar's spleen—but just before a hundred more sink into his back. As poisonous as a kiss on the cheek from Judas Iscariot. Betrayal always looks at its betrayer that way. I would know; it's how I've looked at him for so long.

My marriage was over the moment I hired an escort to scare him from straying.

My marriage was over the moment Kristian broke his leash. Fucked with my home and my dog and almost killed the man I love.

My marriage was over when I lured that monster to a Motel 6 in Takoma Park. When I served him a whiskey-sedative sour and shot him full of fentanyl.

You're not married, Mother likes to say.

But we were going to be.

Now, at 9:24 p.m., my marriage is over before it ever started.

55

OLIVER

Our eyes meet, and a moment passes between us that cannot be measured in time. Only in increments of lies and betrayal and destruction.

Me, trapped and trembling in a spiderweb of unimaginable scope. Him, stolid by the fireplace. Somewhere between gutted and glowering. The intoxication drains from his face, and he stiffens his spine.

"Oliver," he says.

An inflection point. Nothing will ever be the same. The instant when the intricate costume you've woven for yourself unspools and suddenly, you're naked. Only the truth remains. Except you've told so many lies and been so duplicitous in so many directions that even as the reckoning burns through, the truth isn't what's left behind, is it?

Because for someone like you, there is no such thing.

"We need to talk." Nathan's voice is operating-room cool. Even-keeled and controlled. "Let's go somewhere."

"You'll do no such thing," Kathy says, but Nathan's eyes track mine as he crosses the living room. His hands ball into fists, and I wonder how they'll feel crashing into my face, how many pummels it would take to kill me.

"Babe," he says. "Let's just talk."

My mouth opens, but nothing comes out. Words are sloppy, slippery things I can't seem to string together. Panic turns my bones to rubber.

As Nathan approaches, the tiny hairs on my arms rise as though electrified. A buildup of static charge before lightning strikes. I slowly slip from one flip-flop, then the other.

At last, Hector leaps over the coffee table, and Nathan's gaze breaks. "Don't move!" Victor shouts as Hector shoves past him.

"Out of my way, asshole!" No more broken bottle and he bolts for the front door. Someone screams. Maybe Kathy or Tom or both.

He throws the door open with a bang and sprints into the darkness. *Now, Oliver!* I spring for the stairs.

Nathan lunges. His fingers brush the back of my shirt as I round the corner into the foyer. Stumbling, I grab the railing and catapult my weight up the steps.

I scramble. Behind me, his steps are heavy and fast.

"Nathan!" Kathy cries as I dash by the landing archway.

In the upstairs hall, doorways whirl by. I don't know this house. Not well enough. Ahead, another set of stairs looms, and instinct decides. Phone in hand, I take them two, three at a time. Again, hoisting myself up by an iron railing.

A single door lies ahead. I fling it open and spin to catch a blur of Nathan closing in. The knob is keylock, but the key has been left in place. I slam the door, twist the key until it clicks.

The door shudders as Nathan catches his weight on it. The brass knob jiggles and whines. On the other side, sounds of panting, heaving. The light beneath the door breaks in two places where he stands. The knob shakes again. He's trying to get in.

"Oliver!"

Movement ceases, and we share a silence. All the lies, all the deceit vanish, and we both know it. Only the truth between us. The hostile truth laid naked and bare.

Thoughts register, arrange themselves logically. Nathan knows about Kristian. Nathan must know he tried to kill me, followed me, terrorized me. Nathan must know and still, Nathan messaged me *as* Kristian.

Tell him! Tell him! Tell him!

"Open the door." Nathan tries to mold his tone into something reasonable.

If Nathan knows Kristian, he also knows about Haus. After Google gave me the address, I cleared the history, the cookies, the caches, but it's abundantly clear he knows everything.

The door creaks. Nathan must be pressing his ear against it. I step backward, glance left and right, behind. The room is small. Four walls.

Three with windows. One with a glass door to the widow's walk. The ocean, the marshes, the driveway, and the jetty. Darkened and distant, they all spin.

"Oliver," he whispers. "Please."

A large sewing table stands to my right. Spools of fabrics and threads and ribbons and strings cross it every which way. Scissors and pincushions. An antique sewing machine—a pricey Singer.

"Open up." Nathan hardens his voice. "Now."

The knob turns and stutters again. I'm back to zero signal bars, but I predial 911. Maybe Victor's call was a bluff or maybe he really fed the operator life-endangering lies, but regardless, I need help. Urgently.

"Mother did this, you know. All of it. To break us up and take the house back. You see how far she'll go now."

I open my mouth to speak, but only silence escapes.

"I tried to keep it quiet because I was scared it'd trigger you. I should've been forthright about the move, but"—he hesitates—"you should've told me about Hector too. Neither of us has been honest."

Confront. Fear pulls my heart up my throat, and I try to swallow. *Confront, dammit!*

"Why?" I stutter. Unsure he's heard me, I step closer. "Why did you do this?"

"You mean why did Mother do all this?" Nathan's holding up the buckling facade. I picture him, hands on his knees, knuckles bloodless, as bricks crack and crumble around his aching back.

"Why did you message me as"—Kristian's name won't come to my lips—"as *him*?"

"What's gotten into you?" He becomes condescending. He's perfectly willing to pick up the charade where we'd left it. Ignore the smoldering wreckage that's us.

"You know exactly what's gotten into me!"

"Open the fucking door!" Nathan bangs so hard, the whole thing might come off its hinges.

My voice raises to match his. "Tell me!"

"Don't be stupid. You don't know what you're accusing me of. I protect you." There's a tremor to his words that sounds like a veneer cracking. "You cheated. You fucking cheated."

"Give me the truth!"

"The truth? The truth is you cheated, and you lied. You lied. Over and over again. You are a liar, Oliver!"

The accusation crackles and sparks with the heat of a branding iron. Searing my skin because he's right. Another jolt of the door. The brass hinges creak. Their strength is unknowable.

"MeetLockr." Nathan won't stop. "A fucking bathhouse?"

So he did know. All of it. I'm so damn stupid to think he wouldn't. After finding Wealth Wallet? Seeing the lengths he went to for information? Then there's the report. He forced me to file a police report he knew was fake. To teach me a lesson? Teach me some sadistic lesson!?

"Answer me!" His scream strikes like a crack of lightning. Flickering, splintering, scorching. It sets another thought on fire: an escort. When Detective Henning called, she said Kristian—Olav—worked as an escort. Minutes ago, Nathan accused Kathy of paying to have me mugged.

I lower my head, narrow my eyes. An impossibility shifts its shape, coalesces into quite the opposite. Nathan's and Kathy's agendas couldn't be more different, but the horrifying fact is, my attack serves both.

When I rifled through Nathan's briefcase, his pad wasn't all I found. *Vibe,* the city paper. Not the whole paper but specific pages. The classifieds. Ads for equipment and services. Teachers needed. Escorts.

"Did you"—the insides of my cheeks stick to my teeth—"*hire* him?"

On the door's far side, movement stops. Nathan's thinking carefully. Plotting a next move like he'd plan a surgery. Cutting delicately because nothing is sharper than a scalpel's edge. I won't lie still, and it all might unravel into a hatchet job.

"You needed it, Oliver. You were close to relapse." Notes of anguish replace contempt. "We worked so hard to keep you sober. This is *our* journey, don't you remember? The both of us."

Blood falls from my face, pools at my feet. Spots, purple and fleeting, form before my eyes. The ground grows unsteady, churns into a rolling boil.

Nathan hesitates, tries again, his voice softer. "He was supposed to startle you. Just frighten you a little. Scare you from risking everything again. From leaving me."

The chattering in my teeth spreads, and my entire body shivers. "You hired Kristian to scare me?" I wrap my hand around my throat. Still bruised. Still sore.

"I did it because I love you. You needed me, and it wasn't meant to go that far. How was I supposed to know he was a psychopath?" Nathan's voice escalates. He's convincing himself, making excuses for both of us.

My shock evolves into sharp anger. "Because he took your fucking money to strangle me!"

"I know." Nathan's voice plunges to a whisper as though the Kleins or Tom or both were coming upstairs after us. "I'm sorry. But I fixed it. I made a mistake. I misjudged."

"A mistake!?"

"I fixed it, okay? Kristian took it too far. Way too far. Tilly went missing. I fixed it."

His prescription pad, and the impression his pen left. The ghost of the last drug he wrote for. Detective Henning said Kristian took bad dope, and nothing makes dope more bad than fentanyl.

Nathan's sudden eagerness, his abrupt decision to leave town. To *skip* town. He returned home late the night he suggested we leave to *recoup what we've lost.* He returned from dinner with Tom and Hector haggard and disheveled. He looked like he . . .

I cough. "You killed him that night?"

"I fixed it." He's stuck on a loop. "I fixed my mistake."

Nathan hired an escort to scare me, and when it spiraled out of control, he killed him. Took a life as easily as Kristian had. The man I live with and love is a killer.

My silence tears at Nathan. He's coming apart. His voice rattles. No longer measured or controlled. It's a pressure-plummeting, artery-nicking catastrophe. "Let me in, Oliver. Open the door."

I press *call.* No service, but I try 911 anyway. A vain attempt, but one that represents a trigger pulled. I'm in far more danger now.

Low voices on the other side remind me I'm not alone in this house with Nathan. I tell myself this means things can only escalate so far—but I don't know that's true.

"We'll be down soon," Nathan calls out, before hissing at me. "Unlock the fucking door."

I press *call* again. And again.

I'm trapped. Even if the call connects, how long will it take to get my story across? How long before the police get here? Nathan's island is nothing but a bigger version of Kristian's elevator.

"Look, Nathan," someone says. I think it's Tom. "We can talk all this shit out, okay?" He must've mustered some courage because his voice is getting louder.

"You're damn right we can." Nathan's tone holds an edge, one I've not encountered. An edge so sharp and so poisonous, I wonder if anyone's lived to remember hearing it.

"I'm not losing my career over pills." Tom's close. Bodies move. Nathan's. Maybe Tom's. "Or a dick pic for that matter!"

"Actually, Tom." Nathan's shoes scuff on the hardwood. "You sure as shit are."

"Jesus! What are you—!" Tom's voice breaks. Something weighty strikes the door, thuds against the polished steps. Tumbles heavily down the staircase.

Silence.

"Now look what you've done," Nathan says coldly. "You got Tom hurt. Open the door before you hurt someone else."

A boundary is shattered. Nathan's lost it. He's out of control.

"Why do you hurt people, Oliver?"

I call 911 again. No connection.

"You hurt me. You ruined my family. After I gave it all up for you, but that wasn't good enough, was it? Because that's how selfish you are. You just take and take and take. You're a black hole of neediness and you never stop taking."

A bang nearly rips the door off its hinges, and I leap backward.

"Guess I'm the fool for believing you. When you said you'd changed."

Another bang.

"People don't change, do they? Really, I shouldn't be surprised you'd take so much."

And another.

"I mean, you stole your mom's painkillers while she was dying of cancer!"

Bang!

Everything inside my head collides wildly. I pace, searching, scouring the room, but for what, I don't know.

"Open the goddamn door! I'm not fucking asking again!" Nathan pounds it with his fists. The doorknob turns violently, shakes and shudders. A sharp pop. Splinters fly as the bottom hinge tears from the wall. He's kicking down the door!

Pop! Pop!

Destroying the first hinge makes the second all the easier. The small of my back bumps against the sewing table.

Pop!

The door rips free and drops inward. Nathan rushes over it like a breaking wave. Full-body press. Eyes aflame.

My vision blurs, everything whirls as I swoop, duck.

He grabs hold of me. Vise-like grip on my arms. I raise a fist, and he catches it. I kick out and find only air. His hands latch on to my neck, his weight falls as a wall of cement. My chin rests in the webbed groove between his thumb and index finger. My throat burns as fingers close around it again.

No out. Nathan won't give me one this time. Not like he did in Indiana. No more patience. No more holding my hand, walking me through withdrawals and cravings. Dropping me off at NA meetings and interviews.

My windpipe buckles. No more. Over. Done.

Shadow swallows everything. Light vanishes in the wake of sticky fog. Steam. Condensation runs down the walls, down my face. I'm in Kristian's rented room. The Cheshire Cat, off in the distance. For a flash, a gaping wound opens across Nathan's cheek. Jagged like the teeth of a metal key. Black, inky blood pours from it.

Nathan's red eyes bulge. He shakes, and the vein cutting down his forehead swells. So fat it might burst.

"I love you," he sobs through his teeth.

I move my mouth. Writhe like a skewered worm. Try to take in air. Speak. Anything.

"I always will." Our eyes are close, and tears gather in Nathan's. "Know that, okay?"

The tips of our noses touch. One hand crushing my throat, Nathan's other arm wraps behind my head in an awkward choke hold. He presses his cheek to mine, cries in my ear.

"I'm so sorry." His breath is warm, and his words stuttering and honest.

Pressure builds in my skull. My brain winds down. My vision is tun-
neled and blurred. My only support is my palms, flush on the sewing
table. His body shakes with mine.

On the table behind me, my index finger brushes a metal loop. I hook
it with my pinky.

Crying, he sucks in breath.

Nathan squeezes tighter. He tilts my head up and down for *yes*. It's all
the absolution he needs to finish it. I start to close my eyes when something moves behind him.

His lips quiver, about to speak the last words I'll ever hear.

"Stop, Nathan!" Kathy screams in the doorway.

His eyes dart over his shoulder. Only for a second. A slice of time in
which his grip lessens before his brain says tighten up.

I drag the metal, take hold of its handle with a balled fist. A pair of
sewing shears, Kathy Klein's sewing shears. Like a knife, I thrust in a
sweeping blow.

Nathan doesn't see the blades. They enter his throat from the side.
Plunging deep. Past skin, through sinew and muscle till they strike bone.

His mouth hangs open in silence, but his eyes howl. His hold softens,
and the dam breaks. Air floods my lungs. They expand in stuttering
heaves, ballooning back to life.

I've struck something inside Nathan—something important. A geyser
of blood, hot and syrupy, erupts where the blade vanishes in his neck.
He gurgles as if to speak, but his mouth is stuffed with soggy cotton.
His tongue is limp.

As I grab my throat, Nathan collapses to the floor. Falls on his knees
and tips over sideways. Blood still welling from his neck, he's dropped
like a curtain, unveiling Kathy.

"Oh my god!" She crawls to him, hands and knees deep in the gathering pool.

Victor emerges behind her. "Nathan!"

I bring the back of my hand to my mouth. Wipe saliva dangling like
a spider's silk thread. My chest is still on fire as Victor scrambles to his
wife's side.

"What have you done?" he shrieks. Our eyes meet, and for a second,
he tenses as if to lunge. To tear the shears out of Nathan and push them
into me. But he doesn't.

Because now he can't.

Through the window at my back, pulsing lights from the jetty. They paint the room—the walls, the floor, wailing Kathy, who straddles her son and pulls her hair—in sinister strobes of red and blue. He'd called the police. The response to his exaggerated report, now wholly appropriate.

"We can save him!" Kathy.

"My son! What the hell have you done to my son!?" Victor.

Nathan's motionless on the ground. I can't look at him. I turn a half circle, steady myself on the edge of the sewing table. Vomit works its way up my throat. Chin down, I raise my eyes.

On the darkened jetty, the line of emergency lights snakes its way to the house. Sirens scream. Brakes squeal. Steel doors open and shut. Voices shout.

"You killed him!"

Above, a quilt of twinkling stars covers the sky. An eerie beauty I appreciate for a cosmic second before my neck begins to throb and the questions come, fast and furious.

"You killed Nathan!"

What will the police do?

"You killed my son!"

Who will they do it to?

56

The uniformed officers enter first, hands close to the guns on their hips. Then paramedics. They hoist Tom onto a stretcher. Blood drips from his left ear. His temple struck something, maybe the railing, when Nathan threw him down a flight of stairs.

I've been separated from Kathy and Victor. I only notice Kathy's cream blouse when it's soaked with blood through and through.

By the time the plainclothes cops arrive, the investigators in unmarked cars, I sit on the same love seat from earlier. The house crawls with people snapping photographs and making notes and barking on phones. To my left, gloved hands unplug and bag the fried Wi-Fi modem.

"Can you tell me your name?"

A paramedic clicks a pocket light.

"Do you know where you are?"

It's bright in my eyes.

"What's today's date?"

He pulls the light from my face as Nathan's brought downstairs. A bag's been zipped over him. His vacant eyes mercifully covered. It takes four uniforms to keep Kathy from charging the gurney that carries him out.

"I'm going with him," she screams. "He can't go alone!"

I say nothing. I don't intend to either. At least not yet. People speak to me—and to the Kleins—but it's hard to keep up. Snippets about shock or injuries. Keeping us all apart must be important because it comes up often. I lose time.

"Are you able to stand?"

I give a nod, push myself up.

"I can take him down in mine," an unseen voice says.

"Nah," another replies. "She's takin' him in hers."

At that, my focus sharpens in time to see someone I know walk through the Kleins' front door. Behind her, yellow police tape snaps in the wind. Her face is wreathed in flashing red and blue.

Detective Rachel Henning's eyes hold something close to sadness.

• •

A blanket, thin and scratchy, wraps my shoulders. I sit in a cramped room. Maybe it's an office. Something about giving a statement. A hard voice snaps me to the present.

"Detective Henning," it starts. "You got everything you need in here?"

"I do," she says, setting her badge on the red folder beside her. "Thanks for your hospitality, Lieutenant."

The door shuts. My arm trembles as I reach for a bottled water.

"You're safe now, Oliver."

"I'm not." The plastic crinkles and shakes as I sip. An unanswered question surfaces. "How did you know?"

"When you called me back." She fishes in the pocket of her blazer. "You said Kristian had been texting you, but I have his phone. There's nothing outgoing to your number. There is other stuff we need to talk about."

"But how did you know I was here?"

"Nathan's private Instagram." She spins her phone around, open to an account I've never seen. "He posted a photo the night before and tagged it *Carolina Low Country*. It didn't take a warrant to find a Klein address in South Carolina."

The filtered black-and-white is of a man sleeping. The malbec on his nightstand is empty. I know his rest is peaceful because he'd just proposed. Other captions include *#InstaLove*, *#HeSaidYes,* and *#LoveIsLove*. No surprise who posted the very first reply, the content of which is cruelly funny.

@Kath_Klein: ?

I also know the photo of me was surreptitious, and I shiver. "Didn't know he had Instagram."

"I don't think you know a lot of things." Detective Henning pockets her phone. "About Nathan."

"You're right."

"I've been gunning for a warrant for his devices, but hunches don't cut it. Not before you called me back."

"That's why you played along the whole time." I could almost laugh. Almost. "You didn't keep Nathan in the dark to spare me."

"I did not, but I need to fill in the gaps." Detective Henning goes on to ask the exact question Dr. Regina Purvis had five years ago. "What happened, Oliver?"

"I killed Nathan. I killed him"—I draw in a stuttering breath—"because he was going to kill me."

"Are you aware Nathan and Olav had been in contact before your assault in Haus?"

I tip my chin for *yes* but ask how they knew my plans that night.

"Child-monitoring software on your laptop relayed Haus's address," she says. "Nathan flipped it to Olav. As for the *when,* your phone shares its location with Nathan's."

"Also like a child." A heaviness settles over my shoulders.

"Toxicology measured a fatal concentration of fentanyl metabolites in Olav's bloodstream. Cell towers confirm the devices of both men were at the same location when Olav died."

If police haven't already, they'll review everything Nathan prescribed. They'll find the drug Olav was killed with. They'll also find my forgery, and I swallow.

"Text messages show they met twice," Detective Henning goes on. "Once at a café in Columbia Heights an hour after Nathan withdrew five thousand in cash."

"Same price he offered for Tilly," I say numbly.

She's quiet for a moment, then: "Second meeting was at a Motel 6 that Olav never left."

"How long?" I ask. "Between Nathan first reaching out to an escort and Haus?"

"Few weeks," she says. "Which might explain how Olav got work with your contractor so fast. He simply had more time than we thought. To watch your routines. Who's in and out of the house. Garbage bins with junked bills out in the alley."

"Me flooding the bathroom was a lucky break." And Darryl's heart for vulnerable laborers, but I keep this to myself. Undocumented folks are far more likely to fall prey to the Olavs of the world rather than *be* him.

"Circling back to tonight." Detective Henning changes tracks. "The parents, Victor and Katherine. Each gave separate and strongly consistent accounts."

What would Kathy and Victor have said? I run through the events of only hours ago. Doing so feels cold, clinical. But detachment—and the apathy that comes with it—are self-defense mechanisms.

Self-defense. Kathy would've stepped over Tom at the bottom of the second-floor stairs. Perhaps heard Nathan shove him. She'd have seen the blood dripping from his ear. The broken door. Nathan strangling me. The fear in my eyes. She would've witnessed all this transpire before I plunged sewing shears into her son's neck.

"I acted in self-defense," I say. This is what happened and exactly what Kathy saw, but it's certainly not the story either she or Victor gave police. "Not that it matters. It's my word against theirs."

"In the early stages, you're correct."

Another realization. This, this is rock bottom. Not after Kristian and the elevator. Not after forging a script stolen from Nathan. Real rock bottom holds a body count of two. Three if Tom doesn't make it. Four if I count myself.

"I'm a murderer, then." Premeditated, of course. My motive depends on how inspired Kathy was when she crafted her statement. The woman makes an art of vengeance.

"Their account of what happened on that island?" Detective Henning opens a folder. "I don't believe it."

She fans pages across the tabletop like a poker hand covered in blue cursive. Vaguely familiar because Kathy Klein's overwrought handwriting is on dozens of our holiday cards. Only ever addressed to a single person that sure as hell wasn't me.

"I appreciate you don't think I'm capable of whatever they said." A fresh cold climbs my back. "I'm sure everyone else will."

Detective Henning reaches for my hand.

"They're saying this was an accident."

57

TYRE, IN

When something bad has teeth in your heart, you can either tear free or die.

And there's no pain worse than deciding to live. Ripping your thumping, beating self out from clamped jaws—that kind of hurt doesn't stop with scar tissue. Maybe it dulls as decades pass, like folks say, but the pieces of flesh you leave behind never grow back.

One vice at a time, I tell myself as I flick a spent cigarette into a pothole puddle.

NA's just wrapped up and the only chapter in Tyre meets inside my old high school's gym. Not my favorite place, but it's harder to repeat mistakes when you keep bad memories close.

For the same reason, I carry a certain empty pill bottle around like a talisman. I grip it tight in my pocket and start the long walk home. A morning rain shower has the air smelling leafy and good. Blackbirds bicker in tree branches, and I watch my step on the same busted sidewalks I've traveled most of my life.

There is one memory I won't cross paths with here. The drugs in Hector's luggage and a slew of felony priors landed him in South Carolina's penal system. He'd barely made it past that jetty before running into a convoy of inbound police courtesy of Nathan's father.

Speaking of police. My phone buzzes and the incoming name ramps up my pulse: *Rachel Henning, Det Sgt, MPDC.*

"Henning here. You busy?"

"No," I answer. "Just headed home from a meeting."

"Glad to hear you're going again." When someone like me says *meeting,* we never mean in a boardroom. "Your case officially closed today. Thought you'd like to know. This never relieves people like they think, but take some time with it. You've got my number if you have any—"

"The video," I interrupt. "What about *that* investigation?"

"As I understand it, FBI's had trouble ID'ing other victims. Leads can still turn up—but the reality is, violence often goes unresolved. I suspect Olav chose men with that in mind. Guys no one would miss."

"I'm only different because he didn't choose me." My hair catches in a breeze. "Nathan did."

She's quiet for a second or two, then: "Look, I've got to jump on another call. Reach out if you need me, okay?"

"I will."

"You sound good, Oliver. Stick with the meetings." Before hanging up, she quips: "Only thing as dangerous as drugs to an addict is a million bucks."

A hell of a point given Nathan's will. I was sole beneficiary, which the Kleins shockingly did not contest. Quite the opposite: I was awarded a Career Development Grant from the Klein Family Foundation. When the award letter arrived, it contained a nondisclosure agreement—and a prepaid return envelope—in exchange for my fifty-grand "grant." The price of keeping Nathan out of the papers. No statements, no media. Should New York or Washington tabloids call, no comment.

I turn onto a meandering street pushing at the edge of town. In more than one yard, cars sit—unmoved for years and decaying like rust-belt fossils on the ryegrass.

Grief isn't the right word for how I feel about Nathan, his death, and my hand in it. Of course, when folks ask, I use the word *grief.* But Nathan's face isn't what my mind conjures. I grieve the idea of Nathan. Of our home and the veneer of normalcy. I grieve a loss that's not real, and therefore unable to be lost.

When I think of Nathan, I think about prescribing myself painkillers under his name. I think about hiding those pills. I think about holding the bottle in my trembling hands, and I think about those horrifying seconds before I swallowed one after another after another.

And then I think about how I didn't.

I come to the start of a gravel driveway. It crosses a drainage ditch and ends at a small Cracker Jack box of a house. Baby blue with white shutters. Two flower boxes—each decorated with Mom's hand-painted magpies. Tilly's eager barking starts long before I make it to the front porch.

I also think about how in that excruciating moment—with an urge so deep in my bones it brought me to tears—I did the right thing. And I think about how maybe, just maybe, that means I can do the right thing a second time.

I slip my house key in the dead bolt but stop short of unlocking it. Instead, I pull my plastic talisman from my pocket and read its label for the thousandth time. Before opening my own front door to my own home where my own mistake-riddled life starts its next chapter, I think about when I turned this very bottle upside down—and the tiny slice of something good inside me that did it.

The truth is supposed to set you free, but sometimes it's not the truth that saves you.

Prescribed by Dr. Nathan Klein.

It's the lies.

ACKNOWLEDGMENTS

Though we likely haven't met—and perhaps never will—I hold an undeniable truth about you, Reader, deep in my heart: You belong in books.

Characters who look like you, live like you, and love like you belong in books. Our experiences, our communities, our lives with all their richness and depth and soul are the very things stories are made of—and I owe a profound debt of gratitude to those who read *this* story and told *this* queer writer in no uncertain terms, *You belong in books*.

My heart is full of love and gratitude for my editor, Rob Bloom. You saw something in this story before I did. And because of your skill, patience, and endless encouragement, I now see it, too. You've gifted me with an experience beyond words and dreams.

Doubleday feels like family, and I can't quite capture how grateful I am to have been warmly welcomed. I'm humbled by the immeasurable talent given so generously by Jillian Briglia, Tricia Cave, Todd Doughty, Chris Dufault, John Fontana, Kathleen Fridella, Michael Goldsmith, Tyler Goodson, Nora Grubb, Bill Thomas, and Lauren Weber. You each gave life to this book and changed mine because of it.

I'm forever indebted to my friend and literary agent, Chris Bucci. Your advocacy is relentless and inspiring, and your belief in me sustains my own. I live my dream because you empower me to. Likewise, I remain grateful to my book-to-film agent, Katrina Escudero. I'd be lost without your guidance and support.

To my critique partners Amina Akhtar, Lise Brassard, Kelly J. Ford, and Sarah L. Johnson: Thank you for always pushing me to push my boundaries. A great deal of thanks is owed to Adrienne Kerr. The moment I read your kind note was the moment I decided this story had a shot. To the community of writers and friends who give selflessly and stay ready to celebrate with fiery abandon, thank you. Cristina Alger, Ed Aymar, Sam Bailey, Renee Bennett, Chris Bohjalian, Paul Campbell, Matt Coleman, Shawn Cosby, Craig DiLouie, John Fram, Kellye Garrett, Stephanie Gayle, Dee Hahn, Robyn Harding, Wendy Heard, Penny Jones, Chris Marrs, Kimmery Martin, Hannah Mary McKinnon, North Morgan, Emily Ross, C. J. Tudor, Eddy Boudel Tan, and John Vercher—thank you for sharing advance praise and for bringing so much joy to my life.

I'm thankful for my parents, Mark Vernon and Mary Stokes, who nurtured a mind able to challenge barriers and ignore limits. For my cousins, Kristen Holt and Misty Stathos, who love me no matter who I love. For surgeon extraordinaire and friend, Anuradha Bhama, who lent her knowledge to the plot—any creative medical liberties or mistakes are entirely mine.

Above all else, my deepest well of gratitude is reserved for the love of my life, Barry Hwo. We did it, Barry. And this book is ours for the rest of our lives.

So perhaps, Reader, you and I have never met, but we both belong in books—and perhaps that's where we might meet after all.